KLLRS

"Good, solid, fast-paced adventure fiction from a guy
who knows how to write it."
—**Stephen Coonts**, *NY Times* best-selling author

"An engaging action-packed tale. The story line is
fast paced but also contains deep characterizations . . .
thriller fans will appreciate this entertaining tale."
—Reviewer **Harriet Klausner**

"Our enjoyment of *KLLRS* derives
from good writing."
—**Rob Neufeld**, *Asheville Citizen-Times*

DIAMONDBACK

"A beautifully written high octane thriller."
—**Ridley Pearson**, *NY Times* best-selling author

"An exciting suspense thriller with
a touch of romance."
—Reviewer **Harriet Klausner**

"A combustible mystery with twists galore."
—*Romantic Times*

GUNS

"Enjoyed it very much. Fast. Engaging.
A fine debut."—**Lee Child**
NY Times best-selling author

"Absolutely first rate. Outstanding read."
—Publisher **Helen Rosburg**

"Bowie did the homework to distinguish his *History-of-Violence*-style plot."
—**Publishers Weekly**

"A fine debut novel from a gifted writer."
—**Ken Gruebel**, New Bern *Sun Journal*

"Bowie, an instrument-rated pilot, breathes life into smart, cocksure Sam Bass, a man with a mysterious past."
—***Plane and Pilot* magazine**

"Bowie truly has a great plot."
—**Tammy Adams** at Novelspot

"Bowie is a skilled writer. I wouldn't have guessed this was his first novel."
—**Clayton Bye**, *gottawritenetwork.com*

"*GUNS* is an admirable debut. A good read."
—**Ken Wilkins**, "Book Beat"

GUNS won honorable mention at the London Book Festival

KLLRS

by
Phil Bowie

This book is for Naomi, for her unflagging support, encouragement, and infectious good cheer.

Thanks to all those kind souls who have helped along the way, like top-gun author Stephen Coonts, who kindly endorsed this one.

Copyright 2008 by Phil Bowie

Published in paperback by Medallion Press, Inc. 2008

Published by Proud Eagle Publishing 2015, New Bern NC

ONE

Razor Teague spent his last day on earth privately celebrating.

He was assistant sergeant-at-arms for the South Atlanta chapter of the Satan's Ghosts Motorcycle Club, doing frequent errand chores mostly, and had found himself in a unique position to take advantage of a recent pill transaction.

Six weeks ago club president Snake Conroy had told him to deliver a thousand tabs of ecstasy, packaged in twenty plastic vials of fifty each and contained in a cheap canvas briefcase, to a buyer in an Atlanta suburb, and to pick up the payment of ten thousand dollars and bring it back to the clubhouse.

At six two and two hundred twelve pounds, with long hair and the scarred face of a seasoned street fighter, Razor stood out anywhere and was well known to the law.

He knew that riding his chopper with its straight pipes to the meet in a quiet neighborhood would make him as conspicuous as a bear at a country club picnic, so he chose to leave his leather jacket with its identifying club patches—his colors—and his bike at home that night and instead drive his wife's unobtrusive gray Nissan. Before leaving the house he knelt by the couch in front of the TV, picked up his four-year-old daughter in her frilly pink pajamas, kissed her cheek, and carried her to bed. She giggled and brushed at her face where his beard tickled her. Razor's wife, Dori, knew he was leaving on Satan's Ghosts business, and so knew better than to say anything remotely irritating as he went out the door.

Razor spent thirty minutes making sure he was not followed. When he arrived at the street where the buyer lived, there were frantic blue and white lights flashing. Five cars were pulled to the curb midway along the street. Two city cruisers and three unmarked rides. *The big blue gang. Always coming down on some poor dude like a freakin' army.*

He tugged his ball cap lower to shadow his face, and idled over the speed bumps and past the buyer's two-story house, which was set on a nicely-landscaped lot. He stopped briefly at the end of the street and looked back through the Nissan's rear window in time to see two men hustling a third, who was obviously cuffed, down the walk to one of the cruisers.

He'd just missed being nailed in a bust while packing serious felony drug weight.

During the drive home to trade the Nissan for his bike and his colors, the glimmer of an idea shone even brighter than his relief and he grinned.

Maybe he could tell Snake he'd left the Nissan in the driveway of a house that was being built on the corner and had walked to the buyer's place carrying the pills in the briefcase. The contact had let him in, but then they'd seen the law coming and he'd had to take off. Out the back way. Couldn't risk getting caught with the pills so he'd ditched the briefcase.

Could say he'd been wearing driving gloves and had even wiped the vials and the briefcase handle before the meet so the ecstasy could not be traced back to him or the club, and the buyer sure had to be smart enough to keep his mouth shut about any kind of dealing with the Ghosts. The unhealthy consequences of ratting on the club were well known. *Hey, sorry, Snakeman, but that's just the way it goes down sometimes, you know what I'm sayin'?*

Suppose the cops let out what, exactly, they'd confiscated at the buyer's house and this batch of pills didn't get mentioned in that news? Okay, then, the cops could be holding stuff back from the news guys like they do a lot, couldn't they? Hell, maybe the arresting officers even split up part of the guy's supply for themselves. Been known to happen.

Before he went back to the clubhouse he would have time to stash the pills somewhere and go over the story, trying to pick it apart like he knew Snake would. Look it over from every angle and improve it. Snake wouldn't mess with him too much. Dori's aunt was married to Snake's old man, after all. He knew Snake did not like him but, hell, the man was *family*, wasn't he? Anyway it was a small deal compared to many the Ghosts made routinely, and this stock of pills had been confiscated from a punk street gang member, so it wasn't like it had cost the club anything. True, he knew that some of the others were not too happy with him already because of a few stupid dust-ups over next to nothing, but he intended to patch things up by doing selected favors. Buying beers all around.

The briefcase lay on the passenger seat.

I can pull this off, he told himself.

The pills were good stuff. Each a true ninety-milligram dose of MDMA. Pink, with a little heart molded into one side. They'd bring up to thirty retail each anywhere. He knew a tough chick over in Macon who'd pay him ten, maybe even fifteen a pill wholesale, and would probably take them all. He'd pocket ten or fifteen grand.

Worth the risk

Now, six weeks later, the empty briefcase having been burned with the trash, he had what was left of the cash stowed in his garage tool box, spread out under two rubber drawer liner mats loaded with heavy tools, where not even Dori would turn it up. Snake had seemed darkly suspicious and Razor had been badly worried for a while but now he was beginning to relax. If Snake had found out about the pill rip-off he would most likely have acted with heavy force by now.

So he was secretly celebrating his success tonight. Having a few drafts with Vern and Benny, a break from his job as a stock chaser in a sprawling tire warehouse on the outskirts of Atlanta. They were propped on their forearms at the familiar padded bar in the dim badly-misnamed Spotless Café a quarter mile from the warehouse on this Wednesday. It was a usual mid-week thing. Dori knew that, but she had already called him twice on the cell, trying to give him grief about not coming right on home after work because they were supposed to go shopping at the superstore for groceries and kid clothes like she claimed he'd promised.

Right after entering the bar he'd decided it was a good night to do a little Exing himself and had popped one of the dozen pink pills he'd shorted his buyer. It took an hour to hit him, but then it was like the kiss of a freakin' angel. All worries and the tiredness from the day's work peeled away. He felt intensely alive and supremely confident. The lights reflected in the bar mirror looked like a carnival. He held up his beer glass and studied the bubbles, which were appearing out of nothing and rising in perfect little trains of expanding globes to join the whole gang in the frothy orgy of the thick head. Seated next to him, his good buddy Vern, who could drive a fork lift around the warehouse like a freakin' NASCAR jockey, said, "You going to drink that beer or just watch it get warm?"

That was funny. That you could *watch* anything get warm. That you could *hear* bubbles in your beer. That you could *feel* so much all at once. The air currents stirred up by the ceiling fans. The slick coolness of this tall glass on the tips of your fingers. The fabric brushing against the skin all over your body. His cell went off again and he held it to his chest just to feel the vibrations. Dori again. He didn't answer it and after a while the vibrations stopped. *I'm really rollin' here. This is great E. Probably sold it too damn cheap.*

Sometime later Vern and Benny went on home and Razor started thinking about Cindy. All blonde and warm and easily wet. She'd probably be home because it was her day off. Maybe she'd be taking a shower right now. She liked to take long showers. He hadn't seen her in a week. He could give her a pill and they could get into feeling a whole lot of ace stuff together. He finished his beer and went out into the humid night. He pulled on the minimal clamshell half-helmet with a big bloody skull airbrushed on it.

They called it a novelty lid. It did not offer much protection, but hugged his head and looked great. He'd bought a DOT approval sticker from a guy to put on it so he wouldn't get ticketed for an illegal helmet. He cranked his chopped Harley Fat Boy and just listened to the slash-cut straight pipes rumbling for a while. Then he clanked it into first gear and swung out onto the road, marveling at the sweep of his headlight and thinking, *easy, now, slick. Stick to the limits.*

A black Ford pickup pulled out of a supermarket parking lot across the street and followed the chopper. The driver soon realized Razor was not headed home. *Probably to the other chick's place, then. Even better.* There would be next to no traffic on that road, and there were half a dozen good places along it. He slid the rear window aside and told the two men riding in the truck bed to be ready in about five miles.

Razor's mind was only partially on his riding. Cindy was filling his head with hot rubbery softness and throaty giggles and musky sex. He'd met her two months back. She was a waitress in a steakhouse where some of the Ghosts frequently ate in groups of two or three or half a dozen, never with any of their family members. She was already dating a biker with whom she had even discussed marriage, but she liked Razor's muscle-rippled tattoos and the boyish grin creasing his scarred face, and on a deliciously breathless little impulse one night she had jotted her cell number on his receipt.

The pickup driver kept a watch on his rearview mirror. The frenzied evening rush was well past and the mid-weeknight traffic was sparse. He drew closer to the chopper, hanging a hundred feet back with his low beams on. Razor was sticking to the posted limit, which probably meant he had at least a light-to-medium buzz on. *Better and better.*

Razor used his left hand to pull the snaps loose on his western work shirt and the tails fluttered out behind him, the thick night air pressing on his chest like a big clean pillow. Or like Cindy with her twin pillows. Maybe he should stop and pick up a six-pack. Bag it and tie it to the sissy bar.

They were on a long straight stretch of narrow two-lane country road. The limit was fifty-five. The pickup driver looked as far ahead and behind as he could see. Only one pair of headlights two miles or more back. He thought, *Okay. Right about here, then.* He picked up speed and flicked the high beams on, edging closer to the chopper.

Razor squinted against the glare from his mirrors. *There's always some dumb-ass thinks it's his road.*

The tailgating drew the response the pickup driver wanted. Razor rolled on power and the chopper darted away. Sixty-five. Seventy. Then Razor saw the broad curve ahead and stopped accelerating. The pickup driver swung out and fed the five-liter V-8 more gas, passing the chopper and swinging back into the right lane just before the curve. He stayed fifty feet ahead of the chopper. Matching its speed. Coming out of the curve he saw no lights ahead in either lane, so he eased off to close the gap another ten feet and shouted, "DO IT."

They had practiced this on a remote back road until the pickup driver had been satisfied. Now the two men rose up out of the bed and, wearing work gloves against splinters, they each gripped an end of a fresh eight-foot, six-by-six landscape timber from which the building supply store bar code had been removed, swinging it up over the tailgate smoothly, and dropping it squarely into the path of the chopper.

Razor had no time to take in what was happening, and never even went for the brakes. There were shadows shifting in the truck bed in front of him, two ghostly faces in his headlight wash, and a long shadow coming at him crossways, bouncing on the road. He thought, *what the f—*

He was jarred to the spine by the tremendous impact. The narrow front wheel actually banged over the obstacle but the chopper stumbled and reared up when the frame and fat rear tire smashed into the rolling timber. The grips were torn from his hands. He was flying and bouncing straight toward shadowy trees, aware of the bike cart-wheeling beside him, the headlight beam doing a crazy dance, some part of his confused and panicking brain wondering at the extreme sensations, and then the night went blank.

The pickup driver stopped and backed up, keeping his wheels on the pavement, shouting, "MAKE IT FAST."

One man leaped out of the truck with a flashlight and ran back thirty feet, staying in the road so he would leave no footprints. He only needed a quick look. The leaking thin half helmet had split like an egg shell. He sprinted and clambered over the tailgate and the truck sped away.

They stopped at a Burger King, choosing a slot well away from the doors and other cars. All three men got out. The driver thumbed in a number on his cell, which had a digital scrambler piggybacked to it and plugged into its earphone jack. When it was answered he said, "It's Steve. Just wanted to say everything's okay here." It was not the man's name, but rather a code name that stood for the Gamma Team leader, who was reporting job completion. Had there been any complications, he would have said so in further code. Although the electronic scrambler defeated all but the most sophisticated levels of call monitoring, the voice code served as added security should there ever be an eavesdropper or a planted bug near the caller.

"That's good to hear. Why don't you go to your next location, then? I'll be in touch." The voice two hundred and fifty miles away was calm and deep. Reassuring.

Pleased?

The Gamma Team leader ended the call and told the other two men to go get large coffees and loaded burgers. He said, "We'll be on the road for seven hours. We can eat while we're moving."

An official report would later conclude that the subject in the fatal accident, after several hours of imbibing at the Spotless Café, had banked through the curve at excessive speed on his motorcycle and had come up on the timber with insufficient time to apply effective braking or to take any evasive action. The timber had most likely fallen from a poorly-loaded truck. The damage to it, apart from what the motorcycle had caused, was consistent with that theory.

On the night of the mishap, in her fuzzy peripheral consciousness, Cindy caught part of the brief item about the biker, whose identity was being withheld pending notification of kin, on the late local news while she was mixing yet another drink for the man who was stretched out on her green leather sectional, and who, like Cindy, was naked as a snake. She absolutely *loved* the python tattoo that coiled around his torso.

The Satan's Ghosts were well represented at the funeral.

A week later, two members in their colors showed up to talk with Dori. Razor had been storing some things for the club, they said. She let them in and kept her daughter out of the way while they made a careful search, not messing the place up too much. They took Razor's colors, his stainless Colt .357 Magnum, the money they found in the toolbox in his garage, two cartons of spare Harley parts, and, as a souvenir, his antique straight razor.

Dori voiced no objections.

They thanked her and left.

***

Going up against a well-funded defense team, Detroit District Attorney Crawford Battersea had managed, with evangelical zeal, to send three Satan's Ghosts to prison for a total of forty years on rape, assault with intent, and drug trafficking charges. In front of the TV cameras on the courthouse steps, the charismatic new DA had raised a fist and vowed to bring down yet more righteous wrath on the heads of gang members of all persuasions, and in particular the Satan's Ghosts. He said, "The Ghosts would have you believe they're merely freedom loving individualists who only want to live life as a harmless perpetual party. I tell you they are dangerous common criminals who blatantly defy every law of a civilized society. Their vicious behavior should not and will not be tolerated within this district."

Crawford had shared with several associates his detailed plan to work in cooperation with federal prosecutors and go after the entire local chapter of the Ghosts under the Violent Crime in Aid of Racketeering Activity—or VICAR—law, intending to prove the Ghosts constituted a lucrative criminal enterprise, thus exposing any member to easier individual prosecution.

Crawford and his wife Linda were childless after six years of marriage, but that was the singular disappointment in their lives together. And there was always adoption to consider. On a particular summer Thursday, Crawford called Linda at her busy interior decorating company and said, "If you're free this weekend I think we should use most of it exploring what you started last night. We could drive up to the cottage and spend the night out on the boat. We'd just need a cooler of sandwich stuff and a couple bottles of that nutty wine you like. Clothing would be entirely optional."

She said, "I could debate you on just who instigated what last night, sir, but let me see what I can do to rearrange things. One of our big clients is requesting a preliminary meeting this weekend about his new condo complex. Maybe I can delegate that. You oppressive indolent public officials have no idea what it takes to run a small business."

"Not my arena. The federal, state, county, and city small business badgering and excessive taxation departments are in charge of all that. I only want to oppress the bad guys. I have other clever plans for you."

"I hope they include making me the next governor's wife. Why don't you get busy on that and let me go back to running this asylum?"

A favorite getaway for them was a rustic cottage on an acre of Saginaw Bay shore near the Huron National Forest. The place was a legacy from his parents. Their three-decades-old restored cruiser *Linda Bee* waited patiently for them in her covered boathouse behind the cottage. They had refurbished the inboard thirty-footer entirely themselves in spare hours stolen here and there over the past two years— sanding and painting the exterior, scrubbing and oiling the teak trim, redoing the whole interior in a bold scheme Linda had designed. The boat was still slow and difficult to handle in some docking situations with its single fixed propeller and undersized rudder, but it was comfortably roomy, and they had made it uniquely theirs.

The boathouse was open to the bay waters at the rear, so it was easy for the two men in the noiseless canoe to approach from the bay near midnight under a half moon and tie up inside. *Linda Bee* was chained and padlocked to a heavy dock beam but they had no interest in stealing her. Both men wore thin rubber surgical gloves, which were ninety-nine percent sure to prove unnecessary, but they were rigorously trained to be cautious. Access to the engine compartment was easy through the cockpit floor hatch. They had studied the plans of the old boat, so now worked efficiently without speaking. The first item was the electric blower, routinely used by the boat operator prior to engine start to purge the bilge of any gas fumes. One man used a thumb to push his thick glasses back up into position on his nose bridge, and repositioned the blower intake hose so it would suck air only from an outside vent and not from the lowest area of the bilge, where any relatively heavy gasoline fumes would settle. Now the blower would run reassuringly when switched on up at the steering console, but would no longer do its job.

The other man tapped into the wiring harness while the first man held a small flashlight for him. He borrowed power from the bilge blower circuit to operate a simple device that consisted of a switch, a clip, and a hundred-watt light bulb. He positioned the device on a screwed-in cup hook where it would not be seen by anyone lifting the hatch. He then bared two ignition circuit wires and twisted on lengths of new wire that dangled down into the bilge. The exposed lower ends of the new wires were held by a clothespin so they were just touching. He loosened the hose clamp screws on both ends of the fuel line. Not enough so it leaked, but just enough so gas would spurt out into the bilge if a strong force wrenched the line free of its fittings. When he was done, the other man checked over the setup and nodded approval. They replaced the hatch cover and paddled away.

One quarter cup of gasoline, vaporized in a confined space of thirty-five cubic feet, has the explosive potential of a stick of dynamite.

Earlier in their motel bathroom, following instructions their director had given them, one of the men had drilled a hole in the light bulb's base, poured in two thirds of a cup of gasoline using a small funnel, and sealed it with epoxy. When the boat's operator turned on the blower, the electrical tap would trigger the switch, releasing the clip holding the bulb, which would fall twenty inches onto a steel engine mount and certainly shatter. The sound of it would be masked by the relatively loud blower noise. The operator would likely run the now useless blower for at least two minutes, more than time enough for the fumes to saturate the bilge.

Turning the ignition key would cause strong sparking between the bared wires. The setup could wait like that indefinitely—patiently—but it was only two weeks, in fact, before Crawford and Linda Battersea arrived at the cottage in mid-afternoon on a Saturday. The brassy sky was decorated with fair-weather cumulus clouds, dappling the bay with shadows like fanciful islands. A clean breeze was dancing along the water, brushing up riffles in random patches, and where the sun shone through, the water glinted like millions of high-watt fireflies.

In an hour they had the *Linda Bee* provisioned for their overnight trip.

Crawford removed the padlocked chain and singled up the dock lines. He lifted the cockpit hatch to check the bilge for water. Sniffed for fumes and detected none. He checked the engine oil with the dipstick and closed the hatch. Linda ducked into the small galley to mix their customary departure drinks—generous margaritas on the rocks—and Crawford inserted a Jimmy Buffet CD into the portable player. She discovered the single rose he'd secretly placed in the coffee mug that bore her name, centered on the small galley fold-down table. She touched a sweet velvety petal of it and went forward to change.

Outside in the cockpit, Crawford studied a folded chart. Out of prudent habit he toggled the switch for the bilge blower. He frowned. The blower did not sound right. It seemed louder than he recalled. Concentrating on the sound, he thought of lifting the hatch again to check it, but Linda emerged smiling with their drinks. He accepted his with a contented nod. They touched their dewy glasses and sipped.

He shook his head, once again amazed at his incredible good fortune to have courted and won such a bright and beautiful creature. He said, "You are spectacular in that bikini."

She said, "Thanks for my little present. It's exquisite. But don't get frisky for a while yet, sir. I'm famished and I can't wait to fall on those shrimp wraps in the cooler as soon as we anchor somewhere. Then we might think about other appetites."

He checked his watch. Three minutes. Time enough. He toggled the blower off.

They were smiling and looking into each other's eyes when he said, "Well let's go have an adventure," and twisted the ignition key.

The blast from the boathouse crushed the rear windows into the cottage, despite the temporary blocking effect of the boathouse walls. Within fifteen seconds, what remained of the fiberglass hull was burning furiously, sending up a toxic black smear into the pristine summer sky. It took a neighbor, using binoculars from half a mile away, another thirty seconds to determine what had happened and to fumble for his phone. By the time the first screaming pumper arrived twelve minutes after that, the boathouse had completely collapsed in a welter of sparks, adding fuel to the inferno, and much of the *Linda Bee* and her contents had shattered, melted to black mush, or flashed into searing vapors in the intense heat. Despite strong streams from three trucks, she continued burning down to the waterline and sank.

In their Detroit extended-stay motel, one of the two men turned down the volume on the regional nightly news and the other pushed his thick glasses back up on his nose and used his cell with its piggybacked scrambler to call the director. He said, "Hello. This is Freddie. Just wanted to let you know both of us are fine." It was again not the man's real name, which was Ferko. It was a report from the Alpha Team leader saying the job had been carried out but two had died, and the word "fine" indicated the collateral death had been the female.

The sonorous voice six hundred miles to the south said, "That is good news. As expected." Since the couple had been virtually inseparable in their off time, the double fatality had been anticipated. It was of no particular consequence to any of them. They exchanged a few more pleasantries, during which the Alpha team was ordered to return to home base for instructions concerning a new assignment.

There would be an investigation, but the exact cause of the explosion and fire would not be determined. It had, after all, been an old vessel and this was a typical accident that happened at least a few times across the country every boating season.

The director sat at his neat desk for a time after the conversation with the Alpha Team leader, his elbows on the polished walnut and his long fingers steepled. The research and experiments were going well. The data were accumulating nicely. New tentative conclusions were emerging from the cerebral darkness.

The three-man Delta Team's next assignment concerned a younger subject. A twenty-eight-year-old male. Reportedly intelligent, fit, strong-willed, and defiant. A waste to simply eliminate him when, as a research subject, he could likely broaden and richen the data base.

The director checked his watch and used his scrambler-equipped phone to dial the Delta Team leader, who answered in three rings. Good. That was down from this particular leader's usual four or five rings.

A timed four seconds elapsed before he told the team leader, "You answered. I was about to reconsider and call another group about a new opportunity." *Perhaps this one can be persuaded to answer routinely after a single ring?*

The team leader said, "We're on schedule. We plan to complete the project early next month. Is there some kind of problem with the target?"

He laughed. But not in any nice way. He said, "The word target is not in our dictionary, now, is it?"

"Sorry. I'll, uh, be sure to keep that in mind."

All the teams had a memorized coded chatter language devoid of any possible trigger words that might attract attention from a covert listener. Straying from the protocol was not to be tolerated. Straying in any way from the director's strict rules would be dealt with harshly.

He let the silence and tension build on the connection for a timed five seconds before telling the team leader, "Why don't you bring your newest young friend here for a visit some evening? I would like to meet him. And I might have a new project to discuss."

Delta Team was to cancel the hit, then, and instead was to make the subject disappear quietly and bring him to the compound.

Whatever was to happen after that would not be their concern.

The director said goodbye.

Delta Team began going over several potential disappearance options for the new subject, which the director had previously outlined for them in their original training.

TWO

The cocoon-shaped tent was tiny, designed for two reclining persons with scant extra room. They were facing each other, their heads each supported on a propped fist. His free hand was resting on her warm bare hip. She was tracing ticklish patterns on his chest with a slender finger. Moonlight filtering through the tent fabric was highlighting her long midnight hair. By unspoken consent they were prolonging these silvered moments, though he was almost painfully hard now and tense with the want of her.

Kitty Birdsong whispered, "This feeling. What an incredible gift."

Her features were in shadow but John Hardin knew every contour and plane and cleft of her. Part Cherokee, hers was an exotic beauty darkly flavored with a hint of the primitive. He moved his head closer, brushing her lips with his. Drinking in her breath. She moaned and drifted her hand lower, caressing his taut belly.

He could wait no longer and drew her to him.

The cool breeze increased, sweeping up the mountain and cresting the ridge like a massive wave, fluttering the tent. The trees sighed and whickered above them.

John had pitched their minimal tent on a musky carpet of leaves in a far private corner of the Big Meadows Campground, midway along Virginia's Skyline Drive.

They had left their homes in Maggie Valley, North Carolina, before dawn that day and had ridden their motorcycles north on I-81, immersed in the glittering flow studded with growling, buffeting eighteen-wheelers. Up through the cities of Roanoke and Harrisonburg, four hundred miles to Front Royal where the Skyline Drive begins at the northern entrance to the Shenandoah National Park, sixty miles west of Washington, DC.

Meandering back south along the ridgeline, they had encountered only an occasional vehicle, enjoying the relaxed pace after so many miles on the hot rushing Interstate, soaking in the often simultaneous views of the Shenandoah Valley to their right and the Piedmont plains spreading away to the horizon on their left. Stopping frequently at overlooks. Touching each other like giddy teenagers.

At Big Meadows late in the day they had set up camp and walked through the high cool woods as the sun swung down beyond the Shenandoah. They'd eaten pink-hearted steaks and sweet potatoes in the rustic old lodge. Before going back to their tent they'd sat on a half-log bench holding hands on the darkened wide back porch and along with a dozen other tourists had listened to a good classical guitarist in the humid night, uncountable stars floating above and the lights of Stanley village strewn at random along the valley like a handful of fallen ones.

Songbirds woke them at first light. They dressed and walked to the showers and lingered over a big breakfast in the lodge by a window overlooking the awakening valley a quarter mile below.

Back at their site she glanced around through the trees. Reached up to hug him, combing his mass of black hair back with her fingers. She looked into his gray eyes. The wary, feral, intelligent eyes of a wolf, she had often thought.

She said, "Let's not roll up the tent just yet."

Later, they toweled the last of the morning dew from their bike saddles and packed their saddlebags. John used bungee cords to secure the rolled tent and ground cover to his luggage rack. They pulled on their helmets and she took the lead on her candy-apple-red Honda VTX 1300 and he fell into formation behind on his black Harley Road King. Not long after getting back on the Drive, heading south in a broad sweeping bend, there was a lush meadow on their left bordered by a split rail fence. Furtive movement caught their attention ahead on the right. Four doe deer broke from the trees, trotted across the road, and easily cleared the rail fence one after another, their white tails flip-flashing. Kitty raised her gloved left hand, forefinger and thumb circled to make the sign of approval.

They rode the smooth Skyline at a comfortable forty-five. Both of them sated, content, and free, the pipes rumbling, their bikes drifting through the turns without conscious guidance.

A hundred miles south of Front Royal the Skyline Drive became the Blue Ridge Parkway, which would climb to elevations well over a mile and run on through the sky for another four hundred and sixty-nine sinuous miles yet, all the way to the Cherokee reservation in the heart of the Great Smokies.

Kitty signaled for a turn into an overlook cut out of the woods on the right, revealing a vertiginous panorama of the Shenandoah Valley. There was a low stone boundary wall running beneath a permanently wind-bent tree. They took off their helmets and gloves and sat side by side on the wall in the shade, legs crossed, and munched on tart squirting apples they'd bought at a roadside stand the day before, taking turns using a salt shaker. Contemplating the hazy view of rolling farm fields and forest with a line of unreal bluish mountains strung out beyond.

John pitched his apple core into the woods as a treat for a possum or some other creature and said, "I know things are tight right now with the business. Why don't you think about moving in with me? For a while anyway. Hattie and Hank wouldn't mind. You could rent out your place."

Kitty was struggling to get her small business established at the base of Medicine Ridge Mountain, a new tourist attraction similar to the long-popular Grandfather Mountain, with riding and hiking trails, a museum, wildlife areas, and faraway views. She had quit her job at the casino in Cherokee to set up a consignment outlet for artists, potters, weavers, and all other mountain crafters, especially Native Americans, in a leased building. The whole Medicine Ridge complex itself was only slowly earning a profitable share of the Smokies visitor traffic. This trip was a stolen three-day getaway for her. She'd left her single employee, an older Cherokee woman, in charge.

"Thanks, but no. As much as I'd like to wake up in a tangle with you every morning, you don't really have the space. I might rent out my other bedroom, though, if I can find some woman I could get along with. Money's tight, okay, but I'll make it. The bank and the other creditors will just have to bear with me. I'll go back to work at the casino over the winter. I hear they'll be hiring."

"Never doubted you'll make it. You Injuns can be tenacious. Not to say hard-headed."

"Some of us, anyway. It's the only reason there's a reservation in these mountains at all. Otherwise Andrew Jackson and his cronies would have robbed it all from us when he had his goon army prod the tribes to Oklahoma in the middle of winter."

"I wouldn't have voted for the guy."

"Lord knows there've been plenty more like him in Washington before and since. But that earns you a kiss as soon as the elderly couple over there leaves. Look at them. Still holding hands."

"Yes. Where do you want to spend the night, by the way?"

"Is *that* all you're going to have on your mind this whole trip?"

Studying the faint smile lines accenting her eyes, he said, "Probably."

She touched a finger to his nose and said, "Well, okay."

He took over the lead when they swung back out onto the Parkway and she rode in a staggered position three seconds back.

They stopped for a cheeseburger lunch just off
the Parkway at a jumbled general store that had two
booths in the back and then he waited in a porch
rocking chair, his scuffed ropers crossed at the ankles
and up on the porch rail, while she poked through the
clutter of widely varied items and bought a small jar
of mountain honey and a faded discounted country
cookbook. When they decided to top off their tanks
at the single stand of pumps an older man with a
bright yellow Beemer convertible, plaid shorts, and a
beret said, "Nice bikes you have there. Always
wanted a Harley myself. Never had the time for it, I
guess."

It was a frequent observation from such men.
John smiled and nodded.

Stopping again at mid-afternoon, they went for
a forest walk on a stretch of trail that paralleled the
Parkway, and later, when the shadows lengthened,
consulted a map and noted a campground symbol
near a dot called Tyro not far ahead. They found the
correct back road turnoff and, in second and third
gears, snaked precipitously down off the ridge, their
pipes popping and crackling, into a deep forested
ravine that carried a hurrying boulder-strewn brook,
and came on the Crabtree Falls Campground, where
they paid the modest tent fee and set up in a cool
glade close by the stream away from the other few
campers.

John started a fragrant hickory fire in a grated
pit provided at their site and they ate canned soup,
crackers, and peaches with hot green tea, not talking
much. John sensed Kitty was distracted and restless.
Probably thinking about her fledgling business and
feeling slightly guilty for having left it. Musing, she

fed cracker bits to a young female calico cat, which then curled up outside their tent for most of the night.

As stolen time always does, the last day passed too quickly. They lingered by the stream a while. Packed up and found a country cafe for breakfast, and a trail off the Parkway for walking, but by afternoon a front was pushing in, scudding clouds threatening rain. At times the road penetrated swirling surreal cloud bases, the high mountain conifers that clung to the dripping cliffs emerging from the mists like dark fantasy creatures, and the overlooks revealing only mysterious gray voids.

They rode the rest of the way to the town of Cherokee, then east up over Soco Gap to Maggie Valley. They ate supper at Country Vittles, kissed lingeringly outside in a soft rain, and split up, she to her modest house on Big Pines Trail and he lashing the Harley up the steep dripping mountain flank to the log home he was slowly restoring on Eaglenest Ridge overlooking the valley. There was just room enough in the crowded garage out back to accommodate the Harley.

Hank was in the kitchen doing dishes. He said, "Have a good trip, son?"

John hung his damp denim jacket on a chair and used a hand towel to wipe the rain from his face and neck. "That's got to be one of the top ten roads in the country. No overhead wires or billboards. No trash. No crazy commuters primed to draw and fire. No freighters trying to blow you into a ditch. Great views. Where's your girl?"

"Turned in early with a new paperback by that Lee Child guy she likes. She worked in the yard and garden half the day. How's *your* gal? When you goin' to do right by her?"

"Not sure she'd have me full time."

"Only way to know that is ask, seems to me. You know she's got our vote."

He shared his home with octogenarians Hank and Hattie Gaskill, who had found and nursed him after a near-fatal run-in with some enemies on the remote Outer Banks Island of Ocracoke four hundred and fifty miles east at the other end of the state. The old people had briefly been fugitives from a rest home at the time. John had later returned the favor by permanently springing them from the depressing home and taking them in. They had seemed to shed years and acquire new spirit over the good times since.

It was a practical arrangement. Hattie cooked nutritiously and economically and tended a small but productive vegetable garden, and Hank did chores and brought in some extra money playing his fiddle with a country band to supplement his Social Security check. Hattie was confused and mentally erratic at times and thought John was her son, Roy, who had vanished at sea aboard a trawler over the Grand Banks in a savage storm, a tragedy she had never been able to assimilate. Hank and John maintained that fiction for her. She thought he'd had to change his name and appearance because of secret government work he'd hinted at doing occasionally.

He had, in fact, taken a false name and altered his appearance, but not for that reason.

The three were closer than many families John had known.

After John had changed into dry jeans and shirt, he sat at the kitchen table with Hank, savoring chicory coffee and generous slices of Hattie's strawberry-rhubarb pie.

The wiry wrinkled old man said, "Got one for ya. What was the name of Zorro's horse?"

"That's easy. Tornado, in English. *Toronado* in Spanish. Can you name three men who played Zorro?"

"Let's see. Doug Fairbanks, 'course. Tyrone Power. Then there was that guy with the tan."

"I'd forgot about Power. The tanner was George Hamilton. He did two Zorro comedies, I think."

"Yeah. I liked that guy who's really Spanish. In the last couple movies. What's his name?"

"Antonio Banderas."

"Dang. Don't know how you keep so much Western stuff upstairs. You sure got some memory, son. Speakin' of such, just remembered you got some calls while you and Kitty was gone. I took the messages. A lady wants some aerial pictures shot of her business, and a builder wants you to take him and his wife up just as soon as you're able so they can look over some land. Wrote all that on your desk pad. Then you got two calls from some guy. Somebody wouldn't leave his name."

"He leave a number?"

"Nope. Asked him mor'n once, but he didn't pay no attention. Seemed kinda strange. Give him your cell number. Said he had it but you wasn't answerin'."

"We didn't have our cells on. Part of what she wanted to get away from. Me, too. If it's important he'll try again."

THREE

John ate an early blueberry flapjack breakfast that Hattie had made, dipping each bite in a warm buttery nectar of her own creation. He kissed the frail old woman on her weathered cheek, and said, "Nobody can cook better, Flutter. You and Hank could bottle that syrup and get rich."

She smiled, brushed an errant wisp of hair behind her ear with a blue-veined hand, and said, "You be careful up there, Roy. I don't know what's the worst worry, that iron machine you ride or that little one-motor plane."

Hank volunteered to do the dishes, saying, "But it's dang sure your turn tonight, son."

John rode the Harley down the steep hill in first gear, the engine compression doing most of the braking, and pulled out onto Highway 19, heading east for Asheville, organizing the day in his thoughts.

Mist still hung magically in the cool valley, wreathing the surrounding mountains, but against the depthless blue overhead there were only scattered icy wisps about five miles up, suffused by the sunrise and promising a fine day.

With his high-wing single-engine Cessna 182, he gave sightseeing rides, took aerial photos, and flew occasional charters for a living. To supplement that income he did occasional small house repair and remodeling jobs. Most months there was even a little money left over for the savings account.

Sharing the highway with only a few early commuters, he made it to the Asheville Airport in well under an hour. He used his plastic card-pass in the automatic reader slot to get through the new chain link security gate, and parked the Harley pointed out on the gravel beside his rented open T hangar.

He loosed the tie-down ropes, clipped the tow bar to the nose wheel bosses, and pulled the Cessna out onto the taxiway. Mounted the digital camera in the belly and made sure it would shoot using the remote cable. Did a fast but thorough walk-around, fired up the 230-horse Continental O-470, and called the tower for taxi clearance, making a last inventory check of the Nikon gear on the passenger seat.

Lined up at the end of the eight-thousand-foot runway awaiting takeoff clearance, the idling prop a fluttering gray disc, he began to feel alive once again as he never quite felt while chained to the earth. When the tower gave him the okay he fed in the power and the plane responded strongly, sprinting down the runway and breaking free with only a gentle tug on the yoke. The pavement fell away and he climbed into a brilliant morning, leveling off two thousand feet above the mostly forested mountain terrain.

Within minutes a southerly heading took him over the sprawling agricultural center in Fletcher. They wanted new aerials to show recent additions to their complex of buildings, livestock pens, and parking areas. He circled and shot a series of obliques through the open window, guiding the plane at times with just his feet on the rudder pedals, then he set up several level runs for straight-down shots with the camera firing through the port cut in the belly. They'd use one of those shots to work up a new brochure site plan for convention attendees.

When he was satisfied he'd covered the complex thoroughly, he meandered farther south to overfly Hendersonville and Brevard, taking photos purely on speculation for possible sale. New motels, hotels, and restaurants were the best prospects, but almost any prosperous business might well buy. Later, he would mail out a package to each place he'd photographed, including proof prints that were ink-stamped to prevent simple scanning, a brief cover letter, and a price sheet listing different-sized enlargements with a choice of frames. It had turned out to be a significant portion of his business.

At mid-morning he landed at Asheville and taxied to the back side of the farthest T hanger row.

A man was seated astride John's Harley, hands resting on the grips, watching him taxi up and shut down.

John left his headset hanging on the yoke and walked over to stand by the Harley, hands on his hips.

The man aimed his mirrored sunglasses up at him and said, "Always wanted to try one of these things. It's got to be fun. As long as you don't get run over by some drunk or distracted idiot. Given the high number of those out there on our byways, though, I'd think that would be a sooner-or-later thing. I was waiting at the FBO and heard you radio in from ten miles out. Figured I'd meet you here. Told the guy at the desk I'm a client of yours and he let me walk right in. We need to talk. Don't put the plane in the hangar yet."

He was fit, lean, in his late thirties. A workout build. Brown hair, freshly buzz cut. Jeans and a tight black T-shirt. When John had known him he'd been with the Bureau of Alcohol, Tobacco, and Firearms, or BATF.

John said, "Nolan Rader. Vancouver."

"You're not so easy to recognize. The plastics people did a good job on your face. Subtle. But effective. And of course you're a bit older. I hope everything's good in your world. Kitty Birdsong is attractive. Pretty tough and smart, too. With her own business. The Gaskills are well I hear. I'd like to meet them all sometime."

"What do you want?"

"I know what you did."

John said nothing.

Rader crossed his arms and inclined his head. Said, "At least I know most of it. I know for sure you've killed once. And from what I've pieced together, I've come to believe twice more. But proof of only the one killing is good enough to put you down, right? And that I have abundantly. In the form of recorded eyewitness testimony just to start with. You do remember Buster, don't you?"

John studied him. Could not see his eyes behind the mirrored glasses, but his posture was confident, his voice measured. It did not feel like a bluff.

Rader said, "Do you think I'm bluffing? You want some specifics? Buster said you shot the man three times up close on that island. Forty-five caliber ACP rounds. Did a lot of damage."

That could have come from the forensics report. By itself it meant little.

"Need more?   You and Buster split up a briefcase full of money. Your end was three hundred thousand, he told me. Looks like you used half of that to set up a trust fund for the kid."

The only way he could have found out about the money was from Buster. That he also knew about the trust fund and Kitty and the Gaskills meant he'd done a thorough job of investigating.

John said, "What is it you want?"

Rader nodded at the Cessna. "What do you say we take an airplane ride? Just for two hours at the outside. A great day for it. If you need to top off the fuel we can stop by the FBO first."

When they were airborne, Rader said over the headset intercom, "Okay, just head northwest.   On into Tennessee."

"Where are we going?"

"I'll get to that."   He scanned around the rumpled horizon. Inspected the instrument panel with interest. Checked the glove compartment. Felt in the kick panel pocket and came up with a sectional chart, which he unfolded and then refolded to show only westernmost North Carolina and half of Tennessee. Smoothed it out on his knees and placed his index finger on their current position just west of Asheville.

Gazing ahead, he said, "Not that I blame you. The man needed killing, in my opinion. So did the other three. But there are customary legal ways to get that done. First, at that level, you spend about a million on an investigation. To avoid future lawsuits and legal technicalities, you arrest the perp carefully, if he hasn't wised up and moved to South America.

You run it through the court swamp for a year or two while the lawyers bleed the perp and his family dry and wring the maximum publicity out of it. He appeals up the chain for more years. Until his victims are dim history. And finally, about a decade or two after the crime, they might actually stretch him out in a small green metal room and slide an OD into a vein." He shook his head and grinned. "Except there was that one rich guy who won on appeal because he hated needles. His legal team got him reduced to life with possible after twenty. Did you catch that one? Can you believe it? He claimed the needle was cruel and unusual. This after he'd taken a claw hammer to his wife. You want to come right about five degrees, Sam."

His first Witness Security identity had been Sam Bass, after an old-time Texas outlaw. His second WITSEC identity—the one he was using now—constructed by the U.S. Marshals, was after John Wesley Hardin, reputed to have been one of the fastest gun fighters in the Old West.

John said, "When I tried to reach you they told me you'd been taken off the case. Overzealous, they said."

Rader shrugged. "Politics. Gears inside of gears. Sensitive connections. Certain government factions didn't want a series of covert arms deals to see daylight. While you were flying for that gun dealer, you must have witnessed or heard enough to know your government has sometimes armed an unsavory bunch somewhere in the world if they would only promise to shoot up another bunch we liked even less. But all that doesn't matter now. You didn't have any brothers or sisters, did you?"

"No."

Rader turned his face away to look out the passenger window. The plane bumped through a patch of mild turbulence over the Pisgah National Forest and John adjusted the trim wheel. They flew on without speaking, the minutes uncomfortably elongating, droning farther northwest out of North Carolina and into Tennessee.

Beyond the Smokies, the town of Newport lay amid foothills at the convergence of several highways including Interstate 40.

Rader moved his finger over The Newport dot and said, "I have a kid brother. Clinton. Twenty-eight this year. We were never that close. Mostly because of the age difference, I guess. Seemed like he was always underfoot. He did well in school. Hardly needed to study. Good baseball player right from T ball on through Little League and high school. Played shortstop or first mostly. I think he might have gone into the big leagues if he'd wanted it. He was that kind of good. But he was looking at a nice life, anyway. Making good money as a top motorcycle mechanic for a dealership. Harleys and custom builds. Did extra work on the side and had earned himself a rep for it. Could have parlayed it into his own business. I don't know what happened. He started running with the darksiders. Joined a small outlaw motorcycle club called the Longriders. Some club members, maybe even including Clint, apparently got involved in a few deals that drew attention from federal law. I tried talking to him but he wouldn't listen."

"Where is he now?"

Rader did not speak for several more minutes. Studied the sectional chart. Said, "No, Sam, I don't blame you for what you did. In fact, I have to admire you for it. I don't know many men who could have pulled it off. And I know there was no legal option. But I want you to listen to me. And believe."

He took off the sunglasses and stared at John with a riveting intensity. "I tracked Buster alone. On my own. He died not long after of a bad heart. But I've got him recorded on digital video from his hospital bed. He talked to me because I promised to help his wife launder some dirty money he had hidden. And now I've got the story on you, including all the bits and pieces. Motive, opportunity, premeditation, and an eyewitness account of the deed. A jury will buy it in under thirty minutes. It's on a disc, locked away, to be opened only in the event of my death. I could trade what I have on you now for good-sized federal favors, and go after what I want that way, even if it would take longer. You and I are the only people who know it all.

"I never meant to use any of this, really. I chased it down because I was plain curious and because certain aspects of your story touched on a particular South American arms deal I thought you might know about. I only wanted to find out enough to pressure some information out of you if I had to. Then I turned up Buster and everything fell into place. Nobody else cared. But my circumstances have changed, and now I will not hesitate to use what I have against you. Whether or not I do is up to you. Do you believe me?"

John said nothing. He scanned the horizon for traffic. A hollowness creeping through his belly. *You always knew a day like this could come.*

Rader said, "Yes. I think you do." He put the sunglasses back on and was quiet for several minutes as the ancient forested hills moved past below like a slow green ocean. Then in a calm voice he said, "The club Clint belonged to, the Charlotte Longriders, got loosely hooked up with a major outlaw motorcycle gang. The Satan's Ghosts. They have chapters worldwide. Their own damn constitution. Some nine thousand members. In this country and Canada. Australia and Europe. There are even two chapters in Russia. A few members have been busted and sent up on various charges. Drugs, of course, especially crystal meth. Stolen motorcycles. Assaults. An arson case in Australia. A murder in Montreal. They can afford the best legal protection, so most charges have never stuck. The SG leadership has always maintained there might be a few rogues in their ranks, yes, but on the whole they're great, patriotic fellows. Just a little rowdy sometimes. Knights on chrome steeds.

"Gaining membership is a long involved process. They have ferret-smart private investigators on retainer to vet every man they invite in, and you do have to be invited. A man starts out as a hang-around for a few months, running errands for the club, doing chores. Passing out beers and polishing choppers. Then he becomes an official prospect who's allowed to wear the top and bottom arc-shaped patches, or rockers, on the back of his jacket. His colors. The top rocker says Satan's Ghosts in flaming old English, and the bottom says the chapter. Finally, after proving himself worthy in some way, he earns the center symbol, a skull with snake's eyes. Then he's a full-patch member for life. On his initiation night he also gets the letters SG tattooed on his scrotum in front of the whole chapter. In a rare case, with an extraordinary excuse, some guy is let out of the club alive, but only after they confiscate his colors and tattoo a black X over the SG. Again, in front of the whole chapter. We don't know much more about what goes on inside because the few live ex-members, understandably, have never had much more to say, even under heavy prosecution pressure.

"Clint made full patch in the Longriders. They wanted him around because he's so good at keeping their choppers running. Because of me and what I do, though, they've probably never entirely trusted him. The Longriders are what they call an affiliated club. The SG have a few such puppet clubs they use. Sometimes the puppet club members become full patches with the SG."

John said, "What happened to Clint?"

"You want to come right another five degrees. Cross over that lake. What is it here? Yeah, Douglas Lake. Fly toward the upper right of it. Beyond that there's Cherokee Lake, and then Norris Lake. All three are strung out over miles, running northeast to southwest. If we kept to this heading we'd go over Cumberland Gap where the borders of Tennessee, Virginia, and Kentucky meet. We won't go that far."

Rader took off the sunglasses and rubbed his eyes with his thumb and forefinger. Put the glasses back on and looked toward the horizon. Adjusted the headset mike. "Clint disappeared. There was an investigation that lasted about two weeks seriously, but it dead-ended, the few rabbit trails ran out, and nobody is much interested in it now. Oh yeah, the files will stay open indefinitely. Officially, just in case anybody like me presses. Nobody is saying so, but the feeling is, because of a few weak indications they turned up—some unexplained cash he had stashed, and some rumors on the street—that Clint got into it on his own, after all, knowing the risks. Probably got twisted up in a drug deal that went south, got taken out by a particular group of Colombians the Longriders and the Ghosts have been warring with, and they'll never find his body. Tough, but it happens, is what they're thinking. I can feel it. Unless there's a solid chunk of new evidence that gets uncovered by pure dumb luck, they're not ever going to do anything more about it."

"You don't think that's what happened?"

"There are things in this life you know. Somehow. You've heard those stories about, say, a wife waking up in the middle of the night sensing her husband is in trouble or dying somewhere, could be halfway around the world, and it turns out to be true. You just *know*, sometimes. I think the rumors about Clint might have been planted, or at least purposely distorted. No, he's still alive. I can sense it."

"Maybe the law was getting too close or some drug people threatened him and he went into hiding."

"No. That would not be like him. He's cocky. Confident. He's not afraid of anything. All the circumstances are wrong. He took almost nothing with him. No vehicle, no clothes, no money, at least not from his bank accounts. Just him and his chopper. One day last month, three weeks ago now, he was showing up everywhere he was supposed to be and that night he rode out, headed for the Longriders clubhouse. On the way, he vanished. The Satan's Ghosts are suspected in two other east coast disappearances over the past three years. So I think they took him. But I don't think they've killed him."

"That doesn't make sense. Why would they just be holding him?"

"I don't know for sure. But I have suspicions. To get information out of him, maybe."

Rader was studying the terrain in a small arc ahead now. Narrow Cherokee Lake, more than thirty miles long, crossed beneath them in a silver-gold shimmer as the sun caught it. John estimated they were some sixty miles from Asheville.

Rader said, "Are you set up to take pictures?"

"Yes. There's a camera in the belly and I can shoot through my window."

"Get ready to do that."

John reached into the back seat and got the Nikon, turned it on, and rested it in his lap.

Rader said, "Over that way. You see the road that takes a big bend? It's highway eleven. Runs from Bristol, Tennessee, down in a ninety-mile southward curve and back up to Middleboro, Kentucky. We want a place by the Clinch River, about in the middle of that area bordered by the bend. There it is. On the top of that low hill. Lose a few hundred feet but don't go any lower. Stay about a thousand feet above it. Don't circle it. Just make one pass and shoot what you can."

The place was a walled compound, six major flat-roofed buildings, connected by covered walkways, including a large single-story main house built in the shape of a square around a landscaped interior courtyard with a large impossibly-blue pool. The compound was set in the center of maybe thirty acres of grass dotted with a few trees. A single winding narrow country road ran up to within a half-mile of the compound from the southwest and continued on north. The Clinch River meandered past the base of the hill. There were no other clearings within fifteen miles or more in any direction. Anybody approaching on the narrow road from either direction would be visible a long way.

John said, "It looks like a fortress."

"It is."

John opened his window and let it swing up under the wing, held floating in place by the hurricane slipstream. He drifted the plane to the right a few degrees, adjusted the trim minutely to arrest a slight nose down pitch, flew with just his feet on the rudder pedals, and shot a series of frames with the hand-held camera, pausing only to trigger the belly camera half a dozen times with the remote cable. Several people were in and around the pool. Three vehicles were parked near the house. The plane's shadow flitted and rippled across the compound.

From chairs at a slate-topped poolside table, two men looked up, shaded their eyes with their palms, and tracked the small plane.

John closed the window, flew on straight for six miles, and put the Cessna in a gentle bank to the southwest, following sprawling Norris Lake toward Oak Ridge. He kept the shallow bank in and soon they swung lazily over Knoxville, its arteries alive with swarming flows of multicolored metallic blood, feverishly competing for the available oxygen and exhaling gasses into the haze. Twenty-first century urban respiration. The relatively clean Great Smoky Mountains National Park lay ahead.

Rader said, "What do you know about World War Two?"

John shrugged. "Some fifty million people died because of a few psychopathic dictators."

"That's as good a summary as I've heard. But those dictators—Hitler, Stalin, Mussolini, Hirohito—were only as strong as their power structures. Hitler ruled mostly by spreading fear, of course. He had his SS death's head killers out in the open and his trench-coated Gestapo working in the shadows, down in the cellars where nobody could hear the screams. A lot of people just disappeared. Nobody trusted anybody. Parents couldn't even trust their children. And it almost worked. It *did* work to put most of Europe under his thumb.

"Six years ago the Satan's Ghosts set up their own group of enforcers. Called the Wraiths. The man in charge is Kurt Ganz, with a K. His handle is Brain. Promoted up from the SG official chief sergeant-at-arms. Has a doctorate in criminal psychology from Berkeley. FBI people say he's pulled together an unknown number of men. An elite cadre. They think he's been training them himself. For exactly what, nobody really knows. We do suspect he's not only in charge of enforcement, but also of intelligence, and of smuggling operations for the SG s around the world. He's turning into some kind of shadowy outlaw biker legend. Feared even by the worst evil-doers in the rival clubs. That was his compound you just shot."

"You think he's behind the disappearance of your brother?"

"If anybody in the SG knows anything about Clint, it would be this guy. And what you're going to do for me, Sam, is get close enough to him to find out."

FOUR

"I understand about your brother. But what you want is impossible," John said. They had flown back to Asheville, hardly talking, John letting Rader's demand sink in. They were still in the plane. He had swung it around in front of the T hangar and shut it down. The gyro was whining down its rpm scale and the air-cooled engine was ticking away its heat.

John said, "You told me gaining membership is a long process and you have to be invited in. Say they are holding your brother, which is highly improbable if you use any logic on it, and say I could work my way in. It would certainly take me far too long to do him any good. And I'm not even their type. I don't know anything about that life. Don't look the part. Couldn't begin to fit in. Why not use a federal undercover agent? Somebody with a lot of tattoos and some training. There was an agent who made it into one of the gangs a while back. I remember a book about it. Use somebody like that."

"Agents have gone undercover with a few of the big outlaw clubs, like the Hells Angels and the Mongols, yes. But an operation like that can take months or years. There's no time here. And you *are* uniquely qualified. You ride a bike so you do have something in common with these guys. You've at least got an excuse to pull into one of their watering holes, and you know enough about riding to talk it up. You live relatively close to Brain's compound. Much more important, you fly *this* thing, and I understand if you take the passenger seats out you can haul a decent load."

"What does that mean?"

"A lucrative business for the SG is running Afghan cocaine north and bringing in B.C. Bud and Quebec Gold. Potent Canadian weed, cheap there, but wholesaling at two to five grand a pound in the States, and it's in big demand. One study turned up thirty percent of our high school seniors having at least tried weed at some time. The growers have refined and cloned plants so the yield is a dozen times more potent than the usual hippie stuff was back a generation or so. People here can't get enough of it. The Mounties in British Columbia estimate the pot trade at more than seven billion a year in their province alone. The way they do it in Quebec, they haul supplies up into the bush with snowmobiles in the winter, then go back to plant on the bogs in the spring. Natural irrigation. They only have to sneak back once more to harvest it.

"Cooking up crystal meth is a big hobby up there, too. There are way fewer nosy people in Canada, and there's a lot more empty country to set up smelly labs in. Then there are people making the designer drugs like ecstasy. It goes for up to fifty bucks a pill here now. Canada is the new Columbia, and it's much closer, with five thousand, five hundred miles of border that's real hard to patrol. The longest common border in the world."

"Are you saying I could offer to smuggle for the Satan's Ghosts?"

"I looked up the stats on this plane. You could comfortably haul five hundred pounds. A wholesale payload of two-point-five million in ganja. More in coke or meth or ecstasy. And you can bring it in across the boonies any time of night. Vehicles have to stick to the checkpoints, and they've really been cracking down there with sniffers, more random cargo searches, the latest electronic gizmos. Seizing stuff by the multi-ton. A lot has been moved in private sailboats across the lakes and along the Atlantic coast over the past few years but the Mounties are wise to that and they're choking it off. Air is by far the fastest and easiest. Instantly makes you a valuable guy to know, don't you think?"

"No. I don't think so. For the kind of money that's probably involved, pilots must be lining up."

"Not that many, especially people who have their own planes. With your own bird there's no rental paperwork. You and your tail number aren't on any government watch lists, and you can go any time you choose without filing flight plans."

"There must be a lot of border surveillance targeting air traffic. Satellites. Blackhawk helicopters. Ground radar."

"Ah, but that's where you're going to look like Superman. Because you're going to tell them you've got an inside contact on the Joint Border Task Force. Gives you exclusive access to satellite coverage, air patrol schedules, low-level corridors under the line-of-sight radars."

"Why should they believe me? Have you *got* access to that stuff?"

"Leave all that to me   I'll teach you enough about it so you'll be able to convince them. If they should send you on a test run, which they well might, I'll tell you where and when to fly. No sweat. But the biggest convincer will be the arrogant money you're going to demand. One hundred thousand a trip. You've got to pay off your inside guy, after all, and you'll be worth it to them if delivery is virtually guaranteed. They'll love you."

"How would this get me inside enough to find out anything you need to know?"

"We do have crumbs of intelligence from here and there, and the word is Brain runs a tight operation. Holds it in his fist. He vets his major players personally. Most likely right there in his compound, where he can sweep regularly for bugs. Once you're inside, you should be able to pick up some kind of lead. I'll clue you in on what to look for. Anything at all might help. Descriptions of whoever you see hanging around. The interior layout of the place. What security do you see? What kind of computer setup have they got? Talk it up some if you get the chance. Draw Brain or some of his underlings out. To some extent, you'll have to play it the way it goes down."

"How would I even approach these people?"

"I've got that covered, too. Most of the SG stick to socializing at their clubhouses, with one notable regular exception I know of. There's a particular joint in Charlotte. The SG chapter president—who also happens to be one of the top men in the whole organization—goes there most Friday nights to hear the house band. His brother plays lead guitar for them. You'll approach him there. This Friday. Four days from now. Ride your Harley. It's a biker joint. Say you heard a rumor about their Canada trade from a fellow pilot. There actually was a pilot who flew out of Raleigh, supposedly for the SG. Hit a mountain in low clouds one night recently over Montana in a Beech Duke, hauling a big load. I'll give you enough about him so they'll believe he talked to you. We'll meet Friday morning."

"You're asking me to risk everything to try this."

Rader aimed the mirrored sunglasses at him and said, "I'm not asking. I have that interesting disc about you, remember? So you're damned sure going to lose everything if you don't do this."

FIVE

Brain was an imposing figure. At forty-seven, he was a slim six-four, with a shaven head and arresting yellowish eyes set deeply in a seamed face. He consciously controlled his body language, tone, dress, and vocabulary to project power and command respect. His inner sanctum was a large timber-beamed sky-lighted room with a gleaming hardwood floor. The walls held various styles of abstract art, from the most subtle to the startlingly garish. Softly-lighted recessed niches held selected items from his extensive collections behind glass. Instruments of persuasion from the dark ages. Implements made of wood and iron from the Inquisition. Military uniforms and accouterments.

He was seated erect behind his polished desk in a starched white shirt and a plain burgundy tie, his sleeves rolled neatly twice, studying the two men seated in straight chairs in front of him. Alpha Team was Brain's best and most trusted, his first pair to be recruited from the ranks of the Ghosts. Ferko, the leader, was nearsighted and wore thick glasses, and his team mate had mild diabetes, but those were their only weaknesses. They were loyal. Intelligent. Capable of timely sophisticated improvisation if ever the necessity arose. Both were in their mid-thirties with strong builds, yet they were nondescript.

And absolutely ruthless.

They wore no rings. Only simple watches. Conservative, unremarkable clothes. Any tattoos that had been visible while wearing short-sleeved shirts had been erased. Each man did have a relatively recent, ornate tattoo, however. On the left chest over the nipple, near the heart. A fierce, one-inch-tall, two-inch-long fiery dragon. For those few who knew, the code number 1228 could be found within the intricate design. It was a contraction of a longer composite number, 11121218, from which every other digit, or a total of four number ones, had been deleted. That original composite number stood for the eleventh letter of the alphabet, followed by the twelfth letter repeated, and lastly the eighteenth letter.

KLLR.

It was the unique mark of Brain's specially-trained cadre, bestowed only after a first successful assignment. Warriors in every elite military force on earth had always proudly worn some distinctive badge of honor—a sacred feather, a beret, a sleeve band, a uniform pin, a ceremonial dagger, a discreet tattoo. The Satan's Ghosts, of course, wore their hard-earned colors for all to see. The dragon was the secret permanent honor badge of the elite Satan's Wraiths, and every blooded member, including Brain, bore it.

Brain allowed himself a thin smile and said, "The boat assignment was accomplished well."

It was high praise. The team leader, his eyes masked behind glare on his glasses reflecting from one of the skylights, nodded soberly. There was a sheen of perspiration on his forehead, and he seemed unusually nervous. Brain was mildly curious and asked if the man was feeling well.

Ferko said, "A touch of stomach flu, I think."

Brain said, "I have another important assignment I am entrusting to you. It is sensitive because the subject is fairly prominent, although that in itself is nothing unusual for you. The subject and his wife will embark on a cruise ship from Tampa in three months. It is to be a revisiting of their honeymoon cruise of thirty years ago, you see. Under false but sufficiently secure identities, you will be joining some two thousand passengers. On the third night of the cruise, which includes a long passage far from land, the wife will be mildly, untraceably, sedated. Explainable as alcohol overindulgence. And her husband, the subject, will then simply disappear at sea. There is precedent, albeit rare."

Ferko said, "On-board security? Deck video monitors?"

"The subject has a suite reserved at the stern, opening onto a balcony with screening partitions on both sides. There are no decks or security monitors at the stern."

"Should be simple, then."

"So it would seem. You will need good apparent alibis, in order to avoid more than cursory subsequent questioning, and you will observe full forensic precautions throughout, of course. I will also formulate a contingency plan, as usual. We have a detailed layout of the entire vessel. Begin by studying that and the cruise itinerary, including shore excursion options, especially in the central American ports, where tourists have been known to prove vulnerable, in the event the disappearance at sea cannot be arranged for whatever reason. Also study your false identities. We will meet to discuss both primary and contingency plans in detail later. I am receptive to suggestions and refinements. If your performance is exemplary, there will be a twenty-percent bonus for each of you. There is some time, so I might have a few small general chores for you between now and then."

This assignment, like several others recently, lay outside the knowledge of the Satan's Ghosts leadership. As he had privately planned from the outset, his elite organization was now increasingly in demand from other elements, including organized crime, political influences, and the wealthy and powerful, who valued competence, efficiency, and, above all, discretion. Every assignment was arranged through security cutout contacts and—with only an occasional, intentionally-dramatic exception in order to make a particular point to survivors—was carried out to appear accidental or natural. The proceeds, accumulating nicely in offshore numbered accounts, were commensurate.

Brain dismissed the team and pushed a button on his intercom. He said, "Monroe, bring in subject eight."

Monroe, a deceptively-slight former professional kick boxer who'd had one too many concussions and several too many bones broken in the ring and who now obeyed Brain with slavish devotion, ushered in a man whose wrists were bound in front with plastic zip ties and whose ankles were hobbled down to a shuffle with a ten-inch stainless steel chain. The man wore a blue jump suit over only a pair of boxer briefs. Lightweight slip-on shoes with ankle socks. Longish brown hair. Untrimmed mustache and goatee. Arm tattoos but not full sleeves. His green eyes were defiantly angry. For three weeks the man had been kept in what was not much more than a windowless box cell, and only yesterday moved to more comfortable quarters. He had been examined by a Wraith who had once been an EMT, and fed a balanced diet with adequate calories. Brain had not had the time recently to devote to any new subjects and did not want any unnecessary physical health issues to skew his research, at least initially. The man had seen only the former EMT and Monroe, who had brought him meals and several bland books to read, but had not talked at all. He had been under continual video observation on miniature hidden equipment. His futile attempts to talk with the ex-EMT and Monroe had all been recorded.

Monroe now seated him in a straight chair facing the desk and took another chair close behind him.

Brain opened the desk's top drawer and removed a file folder, which he centered on the polished desk and took some seconds to review, though he knew the contents well. It was part of the ritual that would help establish his dominance.

The man said, "Why am I here?"

Brain ignored the question. Continued paging neatly through the file.

The man said, "I asked you why I'm being held here. What do you want?"

In a reasonable tone, Monroe said, "Just be quiet."

Brain closed the file and looked up. Said, in a low steady voice that made the man cock his head and lean slightly forward to listen closely, "You are Clinton Alexander Rader. Twenty-eight. Single. Above average school record. With a reputation as an excellent mechanic. Well paid. A member of what society likes to call an outlaw motorcycle gang. You know why you are here. What you do not know is that you have been chosen to participate in my private research. I believe you will prove a worthy subject, you see."

"What? Your research?"

Brain raised his voice. "You will not speak unless I ask you a direct question or grant you permission. Violate that rule in my presence from now on and Monroe will inflict sufficient pain to persuade your compliance thereafter. Monroe is particularly skilled. Do you understand? You may answer."

Rader said nothing. Squinted his green eyes and glared in contained rage.

Brain said, "Very well, then. I hold a doctorate in psychology. My current research involves the study of stress induced by an admittedly extreme variation of conflict. Everyone experiences minor approach-avoidance conflicts routinely. For example, a person is scheduled to fly to Hawaii for a vacation, but has a deep-seated fear of air travel. The person desires all the pleasures and excitement of the destination, but dreads having to board an aircraft. Thus a conflict arises that must be resolved. As the day of the flight draws nearer, the pleasurable anticipation heightens while the fear deepens. The conflict intensifies. The person has limited options.

Cancel the trip. Or, consciously or otherwise, resort to some combination of defense mechanisms in order to proceed through the ordeal of the flight. Such mechanisms could include, for example, a series of alcohol doses prior to and during the flight.

"There have been interesting studies involving much more intense and unusual conflicts. I'm thinking of Fenz and Epstein, for one. They used oral and written apperception testing, verified by lie-detecting polygraph, to determine how sport parachutists are affected by, and how they cope with, approach-avoidance. Few actions and decisions in ordinary living are as severely, immediately consequential as those faced by sport jumpers. If you do not pull the ripcord, though it is a simple act, the certain consequence is death. The researchers I mentioned proved apprehension is handled in interesting ways. One subject chose to spread, and thus dilute, the fear stress over several tasks—packing the parachute and rechecking the body harness with meticulous care, refastening the helmet several times, retying his boots, silently rehearsing the approaching jump sequence repeatedly. All quite beneficial mechanisms. Another subject denied all fear so effectively that she froze in the doorway of the aircraft when she suddenly realized what was about to occur. One man actually fell asleep in the aircraft during ascent.

"The researchers also found major differences between novices and experts. With the novices, respiration and heart rates increased throughout the sequence until exiting the aircraft. The expert parachutists also exhibited similar apprehension levels, but earlier—sometimes days earlier—with diminishing respiration and heart rates as the time to jump approached, suggesting a learned, refined ability to cope.

"My research differs in one most significant aspect. The powerfully desirable attraction, you see, is continued life. And the approaching event is your most certain death." He allowed a thin smile.

Clint Rader said, "Do some research with a mirror, because you're crazy."

Monroe reacted with practiced precision and speed, holding Rader's head steady with the splayed fingers of one hand, grasping the left earlobe with thumb and forefinger of the other hand and ripping upward, detaching a third of the ear from the skull.

Clint screamed, and Monroe immediately pressed a large folded handkerchief over the wound to limit the blood flow. He would have the chore of cleaning up later.

Clint breathed with sharp groaning gasps as the pain radiated through him like flashes of internal lightning timed to his rapid heartbeat.

Brain waited calmly, his long bony fingers laced on the immaculate desk, until the subject's groans subsided. He said, "The damage is appropriately significant because you apparently did not hear my first rule. Monroe will see to repairing the ear and you will remember never to speak uninvited in my presence. Your execution is scheduled for midnight on the thirtieth day, beginning with tomorrow. We will consider method options in one of our research sessions. If you are cooperative, perhaps the final pain can be minimized. Perhaps there is even a way out. Please take him to his room and give him a meal, Monroe."

After they had left, Brain leaned back in his chair and looked up at one of the skylights, which was framing a bloody rag of high cloud. Like a window to a soul.

Yes, this one will be interesting.

He would bend the man to his will and reap a psychological harvest from him in the process. He had already planted seeds of darkest fear and thus severe stress, and just a hint of hope, in the fertile furrows of the subject's brain.

Ultimately, however, there would be no way out for him.

SIX

John had spent the day—running on scant recent food and only fitful nightmarish sleep the night before—flying two photo jobs and then, for something to do, cleaning up the airplane and organizing the wooden lock box he'd built and bolted to the back hangar wall a year ago to contain oil, tools, and supplies. He had reached no conclusions and formed no plans while he'd worked, his mind skittering and banging from this ill-formed thought to that like a caged wild creature.

Driving his white Jeep Wrangler back into Maggie Valley, he spotted a black Harley chopper with high ape hanger handlebars parked nose out at the Salty Dog, and he slid the Wrangler in beside it.

Brandon Doyle was hunched at the bar, looking idly up at a surfing show on one of the silent back-bar TVs and nursing the last inch of a draft. A muscular blond, he was dressed in holed jeans, scuffed harness boots, and a black tank top that said "Bad To The Boner" across his broad back in white block lettering. The sleeveless shirt displayed a number of his more colorful tattoos. His hair was long and disheveled and a pair of slim dark-lensed sunglasses rested atop his head. John took a stool next to him and ordered two drafts from the girl polishing glasses.

Without taking his eyes from a bikini-clad surfer racing down the glossy flank of a monster wave only feet in front of the reaching, foaming curl, Doyle said, "Kit know you go out to party like this? Hittin' on guys like me?"

"Let's take our beers to a booth in the back and I'll spring for burger plates. I need to pick your brain. Which shouldn't take long, considering the limited capacity."

The booth creaked when Doyle lowered himself into it. He looked across the table at John and one eyebrow dropped in a frown. He said, "You got somethin' chewin' on you gunslinger?"

"What do you know about the outlaw biker gangs?"

"Why're you asking?"

"Say I'm curious."

Doyle shrugged. "Well I guess the Hells Angels was one of the earliest ones. Started up after World War Two with some ex-military guys in California. There was a bomber group had that name in the war. A fighter bunch, too, I think. Anyway, these guys rode right out there on the edges, did things their way, had some run-ins with the law. Got tagged as outlaws. Marlon Brando and Lee Marvin did a movie. Somebody said ninety-nine percent of bikers weren't outlaws, so the rest was the one percenters. The outlaws liked that. You'll see one percent patches here and there today. A lot of other clubs came along. The Bandidos. The Outlaws. The Mongols. Those are some of the big ones. Then you got a bunch of smaller ones, like the Lobos and the

Rock Machine up in Canada. I think the Lobos did
go over to the Angels a while back, though. A few of
the small clubs get swallowed up by the bigger ones,
sooner or later. Sometimes it gets down to either that
or get hurt. You got one percenter outlaw clubs all
over the damn world now. Europe. Australia.
Russia."

"Did you ever belong to one?"

Doyle studied the much-scarred, pocket-knifed
tabletop, rotating his sweating beer glass so it made a
swirled damp spot in the worn wood. He said, "For a
time I ran with a pack. Not one you likely ever heard
of. Most of our guys wound up gettin' patched over
into the Pagans. Not me. Always been a loner, I
guess. And I never held with wearin' all that Nazi
crap—iron crosses, swastikas, old-style German
helmets. My old man fought in World War Two. If
these assholes had any idea what that stuff stands
for—"

"Why do people join?"

"It's like with those World War Two boys.
They fought together. Some got broken up bad.
Some died. But they were all in it together. They had
to look out for each other to make it through. And so
they got tight. Like brothers. They call the outlaw
clubs the brotherhoods today. I'll tell you this, you
ride with a pack of a dozen or two, all with their
colors on for everybody to see, all the bikes roarin'
together like thunder, people tend to get out of the
way. You *feel* the power, you know? Feel like you
belong. The thing is, these guys in the clubs are
supposed to be livin' free, right? Nobody tellin' *them*
what or how to do. But you take a look at 'em,

they've got a list of their *own* rules you got to follow. So I say where's the big difference?"

The waitress brought their food. Doyle attacked his loaded plate with enthusiasm. John still had no appetite but made himself eat some of it anyway. After they finished, John ordered two more drafts and said, "What do you know about a club called the Satan's Ghosts?"

Doyle belched, took a long pull on his beer, and squinted. "You anywhere near ready to tell me what this is all about?"

"Can't. And I'd just as soon you don't tell anybody we talked about anything more than the weather and Harleys today."

"How's that RK runnin', by the way?" Doyle had steered John to the bike, which had been owned and well maintained by a friend. "And what does Kit think of you on a Harley? Her with that Jap bike."

"Nothing's fallen off the Road King yet. She can beat me on that VTX, it turns out, even though I've got more displacement. She says her candy-red paint is just faster than my black and not to get too torn up about it."

"That might have somethin' to do with the way you ride. I could give you a couple lessons. For a fee."

"The Satan's Ghosts?"

Doyle looked into his beer. Shrugged. Took a deep breath. "Okay. Three important words you got to know. Real. Bad. Asses. They're a big club. Big as the Angels I hear, and spread out all over the place. Powerful. Into stuff." Doyle looked steadily into his eyes. "Tell you what, gunslinger, these boys, now, you *damned* sure don't want to fool with. My advice is you stay about one whole county away from any of 'em."

"Into what kind of stuff. Drugs?"

"Sure. The usual money-makers. Meth. Coke. Oxy. Smoke. Pills in about as many colors as M and Ms. Rumor is they got a good trade goin' with the Canadian boys. And there's a fairy tale around sounds to me like they just put it out there to scare away the competition."

"What fairy tale?"

"There's supposed to be this mean dude from Hell works for the Ghosts, takes care of any problems that come up. Quick. Clean. Permanent. Supposed to have a trained bunch behind him like some kind of Ninjas or fuckin' Nazis. Some say he's set up over in Tennessee. Others say in the Georgia woods or either out West someplace. Probably all just propaganda. There've been a couple things *do* make you think, though. Word is, when the Ghosts don't just want somebody disappeared real quiet, when they want to make a point, they do things ugly as it ever gets."

"What does that mean?"

"Well, the story about a year ago was, this guy from a Latino street gang down in Jax fronted a dude that belonged to the Ghosts in a bust-up bar one night. The Latino wound up shooting the Ghost in the gut and backin' out of the place with a half dozen buddies, all with their guns out. When the cops came, nobody'd seen anything. The Ghost made it but he was really messed up inside. They found the Latino guy three weeks later out on the edge of the Okeefenokee. Somebody'd cut his head off with a chainsaw. Not another scratch on him. What does that tell you?"

SEVEN

Clint Rader was in pain. Monroe had held him down on the bed while the former EMT had injected a local anesthetic and worked on the ear for twenty minutes, cleansing it, deftly inserting stitches, and bandaging it. They had left him with four aspirin to take when the anesthetic wore off, and despite his anger he had drifted into shallow sleep for a few hours, waking just before dawn with the whole side of his head throbbing. His hands were unbound but he still wore the hobbling, demeaning chain on his ankles. Still in the blue jumpsuit, now stained black and stiff over the shoulder and down the sleeve, he got up, switched on the recessed overhead light, and despite the pain, began making yet one more methodical inspection of the room.

It was twelve by twelve, with a narrow bed along one wall. The bed had a thin mattress. A pillow, a fitted sheet, a cover sheet, and a blanket. The frame was bolted angle iron. Like the table, it was screwed to the vinyl-covered floor with steel angle brackets. He'd discovered that one of the bed legs had two of its four bolts just loose enough to turn slightly with his fingers. There was a connecting bathroom with a combination metal toilet and sink. A metal shelf was screwed to the wall. It held only a toothbrush and toothpaste, a cheap plastic hairbrush, a bar of coarse soap, a washcloth, and a thin bath-sized towel. A metal wall mirror, screwed in place. There was a plain metal shower stall with no curtain. There was no door on the bathroom. Conditioned air issued from a small screwed-down floor vent in the main room and there was another vent for return air. There was a recessed ceiling fixture in the main room and another in the bathroom. He had a wall switch to control the main fixture, but the light stayed on in the bathroom. A single tinted window—probably to keep anyone from seeing in—which was two feet square and could not be opened, was covered on the outside with heavy steel mesh. It looked out on dense woods three hundred feet away across a meadow. The door was substantial metal.

The walls and ceiling were covered in some kind of white pebbled plastic or fiberglass sheeting, probably bonded on. He began thumping the walls with the side of his fist, chest-high, every foot or so all around the room. They were uniformly solid, so either the plastic was thick or the studs behind it were set closer together than normal. He thumped along the two interior walls harder and every few feet put his good ear close to the cool plastic to listen.

Something.

A thump on the other side of the wall above the bed.

He thumped three times slowly.

Three answering thumps.

He shouted HELLO.

Listened.

Nothing. He shouted again twice, but sensed it was not getting through. He thumped twice.

Two answering thumps.

Another prisoner, then. Maybe they could work out a way to talk. A hundred years ago it could have been Morse Code, but hardly anybody knew it today. He knew some of the Morse letters, though, from his Boy Scout days. And there was a knock code prisoners used in the joints. One of the members of the club had showed it to him. He tried to remember it. The alphabet was arranged in a square of twenty-five boxes, five letters across and five down, with no K because the C was used instead. Each box had two corresponding numbers. The letter F, say, was the first letter across in the second row down, so it was one knock followed by two knocks. But both prisoners had to know the grid. He had nothing to write with. No way to get a note to the other prisoner, anyway.

But he did have toothpaste and coarse toilet paper in the bathroom. He could maybe use the end of the toothbrush, dipped in toothpaste, to block out the grid, then let it dry, fold it, and keep it hidden. Or he'd heard about writing with urine. Once dry it was not readily visible. Heated, the letters would appear. Maybe there would be a chance to pass a note to the prisoner next door.

There were more thumps on the other side of the wall. He ignored them. Without a code it was useless, and might call unwanted attention.

Trying to talk with another prisoner was a few notches down on the list, anyway. First on the list had to be some way to escape.

There was not much time. Just thirty days from today.

The yellow-eyed bald freak had said, "Perhaps there is a way out."

Had he meant that? Did he want information in exchange? Or money? Did he want something done? What?

He knew his brother would be looking for him. But that was a long shot at best, because Nolan had nowhere to start, at least as far as he could see. He'd been riding the chopper to the clubhouse just after dark. A plain burgundy car had come up behind him with a blue light flashing. He'd pulled over. Two guys got out and came up on him fast. One on each side. Something was wrong with the setup. He decided to let the clutch out and get gone in a hurry but the one on the right clamped a hand over the kill switch and the bike went dead. They were good. No hesitation. No wasted moves. The one on the left stuck a needle in his arm and everything went slow and fuzzy. There was a plain van with a ramp. For the bike. He was hustled into the back of the burgundy car. Then the whole thing skidded away into dizzy darkness.

He woke up later slumped in the back seat, the car running through the night. One driving, the other in the back beside him. The plain van nowhere in sight. His wrists and ankles were bound with heavy cable ties and there was a gag tied around his head. They stopped once on a deserted back road to let him relieve himself in the woods, but they did not talk at all. It had been a long ride to where he was now being held.

As far as anybody knew, he'd just disappeared. To track somebody you need a place to start, and neither brother Nolan nor anybody else he knew had any such place. *So don't count on that. You'll have to find a way out yourself. Think.*

He did have potential weapons. The loose bed leg might be unbolted and used as a club. The plastic toothbrush handle could be shaved down to a point on a sharp edge of the bed frame. Or the hairbrush handle. One of the sheets could be torn up and lengths of it braided and then wrapped around his hands to form a noose for strangling. He could not kick with the hobble chain on, but could still use his knees some and his fists and his teeth. Monroe was lightning fast though, and obviously a trained, tough fighter. Could he take the man? With a good enough plan, maybe there was an outside chance. But his instincts told him to wait. Sniff out the situation better.

What were the research sessions the freak was talking about?

Something else. He now felt watched. If this was some kind of crazy project the freak had going and he was the subject, it followed they might have bugged this room. Maybe for both sound and video. He studied the recessed lights and the ceiling moldings, looking for any small holes.

There.

Not a hole, exactly, but an irregularity in a corner of the black frame around the ceiling fixture.

So figure on it.

If so, then they'd probably already seen him banging on the walls. And if he wanted to make a weapon he'd have to work quietly with the main room light off. At about three in the morning when any watching or listening would be least likely. Maybe he could stand on the toilet and stuff the pillowcase around the recessed light frame in the bathroom ceiling, using his fingernails, to cut that light down, too.

Weak gray daylight was coming in the widow. He turned off the overhead light and stretched out on the bed, carefully resting his good ear on the pillow. Closed his eyes and thought of Rita.

Flashing brown eyes, a quick, innocently-sexy smile, and dusky skin like satin.

He had met her brother, Trey, first. Dark-skinned like her and friendly, but not too bright. Wanted his HD's forks raked and the engine muscled up. They did some drinking together. Then Trey introduced Rita to him. He began falling for her within thirty seconds, like it was meant to be, and it only got deeper until it possessed him entirely. They dated, but she kept a distance between them, gently deflecting his advances. She wanted time to finish college and sort out her feelings. Trey talked him into joining the Longriders. His brother Nolan had tried to steer him away from the outlaw bikers, but he'd joined anyway, mostly because he knew he could make extra money working on their bikes on the side, which might help him set up a good life with Rita.

But Trey was into something. Clint figured it was dealing drugs. And probably on something, too. Speed or ecstasy. Rita seemed not to know. Or she didn't want to know. Trey was the only immediate family she had left. He was her protector and her best friend.

Then one night she called him on his cell. Crying. Not making much sense, but asking him to come to her. He rode his Harley too fast all the way to the address on a back road outside the city. He made it inside fifteen minutes. She was waiting for him in the driveway in Trey's pickup.

He slid in beside her and said, "What is it Rita?"

She wiped at her eyes with the backs of her wrists, took a shuddering breath, and said, "We were supposed to be going shopping. He . . . he . . . he said he just had to stop here for a few minutes first. For a little business. He went inside. Then I heard two shots. I ran in. It's horrible. Trey's still in there, but I couldn't call the police or anybody, because he . . . . So I called you. I'm sorry. I didn't know what else to do. I tried to help him but he's . . . he won't move. He must have shot one of them. I didn't even know he had a gun. Then I think one of them hit him with a piece of pipe or something. And Trey must have shot that one too and then he fell down and now he won't move. He may be . . . oh God, Clint, he may be . . ."

Clint looked around. There were no other houses close. Patches of thick woods and dark fields. Only a few distant lights. He said, "Okay, Rita. We'll go up to the house now. But we need to be fast. Can you do that?"

He told her to stay on the porch just outside the door and tell him if anybody was coming along the road.

The living room was bloody. One man was sprawled on a couch, a small black hole in his forehead, the wall behind an abstract red fireworks explosion. Hand inside his vest near the butt of a partially concealed belt-holstered gun. Another man, still clutching a metal baton, was crumpled on his side in a red puddle. Both men wore patched vests. He could see the back of the one on the floor. Satan's Ghosts in flaming letters.

Trey sat slumped against the wall, head on his shoulder, very still, blood on the side of his head.

Moving quickly, he knelt by Trey and felt for a pulse. Yes. And it was strong enough. He went into the bathroom, careful not to touch anything or step in any of the blood, got a wet towel, came back and knelt by Trey, wiped his face, then bound it around his head. Slapped his cheek and talked loudly to him. In a few seconds he stirred, opened his eyes, and squinted at Clint.

Clint said, "Get up, Trey. You have to get up." Clint managed to help him onto his feet, propped against the wall.

Trey said, "They wouldn't give me the money. Bastards. Didn't mean to shoot. Only wanted my money. Tater was gonna pull his piece. I know for damn sure he was."

Supporting as much of Trey's weight as he could, Clint helped him out the door and over to the pickup. Rita swung open the passenger door and they got him inside and got the door closed.

Still no traffic on the road.

Clint told her, "I think he's going to be okay. Get him out of here. Take him home and get him into bed. Call the neighbor guy over to help you move him, but only if you absolutely have to. Just say he got drunk and fell but he'll be fine. Put some ice on his head. Wash his hands good. Gather up all the clothes he's wearing and his boots and wrap it all in a sheet or a big plastic bag. I'll get rid of it later. Now go. Drive at the limits."

"But what are you going to do?"

"I need to go back inside for a few minutes. I'll call you later, or I'll stop by to see how he's doing. Just don't tell anybody anything. I'll fix it, Rita. You go."

He went back inside, wiped the door knobs and anything else he could see that Rita or Trey or he himself might have touched. Used another wet towel and swabbed the wall where Trey's head had rested, and the floor in that area, wiped the baton where it had contacted Trey's head, but left it in the dead man's hand, wrapped the gun that Trey had used, a compact automatic, in the wet towel and took it with him.

He stopped in the doorway and looked around, trying to think. It was the best he could do. He would ditch the gun and the towel miles away. Get rid of his own boots and clothes later.

Headlights were coming outside. He ducked inside the doorway and flicked off the light. A car went by very fast on the road. The driver had to be concentrating on the road ahead. Good.

Using the towel over his fingers, he locked and closed the door. Stuffed the bundle in a saddlebag, and rode off into the night.

He was going too fast, he knew, but could not slow himself. He wanted to get miles away where he could stop and think.

A mile down the road he blew past a black SUV going the other way. The passenger swiveled his head to track the motorcycle, and said, "Hey, ain't that Clint? Yeah, I'm sure it's Clint. That mechanic with the Longriders. Forget his last name. What the hell is *he* doin' on this road? Ridin' with his hair on fire."

The Satan's Ghost driver said, "Yeah. That was him. Rader. Damn good mechanic. Maybe he knows Tater, I guess. Could even be he's doin' a little dealing with the boys. We'll ask Tater when we get there.

EIGHT

John rose out of a shallow fitful sleep and dressed in worn jean shorts and a T-shirt. In the kitchen, Hank had a cup of strong coffee waiting for him at the knotty pine table and asked if he wanted sausage with his eggs. Hattie was still asleep.

He sat across from the old man and said, "Nothing for me. I'm trying to shed a couple pounds."

"Wrong way to go about it, son. You quit eatin', your body thinks it's maybe about to starve, so it just starts storin' up where it can. You get heavier. Way to do it is keep on eatin' but just not so much, and lay back on the sugar, which I know is purely hard to do with Hattie's good cookin'. Another way is keep on eatin' like always and let your worries grind you down. Is somethin' a bother to you here lately? Gettin' along with Kitty okay?"

"It's nothing. Just a few business problems." To distract the old man, he said, "I've got one for you. A gang of six rides into a Texas town to do a robbery, but it's a setup, and a bunch of bounty hunters have laid an ambush. Sam Peckinpah directed. Bill Holden is an aging outlaw named Pike. His sidekick is Ernie Borgnine. Edmond O'Brien's in

it, and Ben Johnson. It's more than just another
shoot-up. Has a lot to do with loyalty, but it's about
betrayal, too.   And it shows innocent kids being
corrupted by violence. It got top reviews."

"Always liked Holden. And Ben Johnson. That
man was a real cowboy. I remember the story. Pretty
bloody.   Good, though.   It was *The Wild Bunch*.
What got your thinkin' onto that one?"

John looked at his cup and shook his head.

"You'll pick up the boy today?"

"Yes. He asked to go see his great-grandfather.
Why don't you fix what you want? I'll make an egg
sandwich and take it with me."

There were thunderstorms in the forecast but he
put the top down on the Jeep anyway, because he
knew the boy would like it. He drove the Wrangler
down the steep hill into the valley, the sun a low
bruise in a colorless humid haze that threatened to
suffocate the mountains.

He followed highway 19 and 276 through
Waynesville.   Near Sylva he took a narrow road
through rolling farmland for several miles, turned
uphill into a gravel driveway, and stopped by a white
clapboarded farmhouse set among tall pines in a
meadow brushed with patches of wildflowers. The
flowers could offer little cheer today in the breezeless
haze.

A middle-aged heavyset Cherokee woman
answered the screen door smiling and waving him
inside. She was Lisa Crow, Valerie's aunt. Her
much older husband had died recently of a bad heart
and she was raising Valerie's son, Joshua, now nine,
by herself. She worked part-time in a convenience
store to supplement the benefits left behind by her

husband. John helped by buying clothes and school supplies for the boy.

She said, "He's upstairs changing after he got soppy wet in the creek this morning. Trying to catch rainbow trout bare-handed or something. I've got a loaf of honey raisin bread made for you to take to the old man. Don't leave without it, you hear?"

"Lisa, you spoil everybody you know with your baking. Even Hattie is impressed."

"It's no wonder you've got Kitty Birdsong so dizzy, with that smile and the smooth talk. You go right on up. And tell him to wear those new sneakers you bought him, please."

He rapped a knuckle on the bedroom door twice and said, "Curly?"

The boy said, "Come on in. I'm almost ready."

Joshua Lightfoot—dark and almost too thin, the curly hair from his Caucasian side getting long, his Cherokee features a heart-tugging memory of her—was seated on his bed in fresh shorts with no shirt, using a muddied white towel, trying to dry his tattered dripping sneakers. He flashed a smile that loosed a whole flood of Valerie memories. There was a grainy off-color photo on the night stand. The three of them, sandy and smiling and squinting against the sun glare on the beach, their feet chopped off by the passing volunteer picture-taker, the much smaller boy standing in front of his mother with two fingers in his mouth. Lighter-skinned because his father—killed one night on an icy mountain road—had been white. Himself with his arm around her, his hand on her waist. They had been living an idyllic life on the Outer Banks island of Ocracoke, he running a shoestring air charter business and doing home repair jobs, she waitressing and doting on the boy. Teaching and shaping and strengthening him. Until an old enemy had discovered he was there and had sent the hit team. And she had died. Instead of him.

Just because she had known him.

He cleared his throat, slid his flattened hands into his back pockets, and moved around the room. There was a neat collection of *Star Wars* figures on the dresser top. On the worn desk there were several volumes held upright by bookends made of quartz clusters. Harry Potter and Lemony Snicket tales. *Huckleberry Finn.* Valerie's old leather-bound Bible. A red-and-white felt NC State pennant was thumb-tacked to the wall alongside a feathered dream catcher. A child's short version of a Cherokee blowgun with a lashed-on deerskin quiver of slender locust darts stood in a corner along with a scuffed aluminum baseball bat—symbols of two diverse cultures. A heap of soiled clothes was on the floor of his open closet. The boy was hard on clothes because he loved to prowl the forest. Another wall held framed certificates that Lisa had put up. School recognitions and awards in reading, math, and sports.

Hardin stood in front of the boy and said, "Why don't you let those air dry and wear your new ones?"

"I like these better."

"Well, they're your feet, so do what you choose. But I've got to say those sneakers smell like a pair of frogs hopped in there about a year ago and never made it out. You'll sound like a kissing cow when you walk across your great-grandfather's porch. And Lisa's not ever going to bake me another coconut pie if I don't do like she just told me and talk you into wearing the new ones."

Joshua laughed delightedly and said, "How do you know what a cow kiss sounds like? Did you ever kiss one?"

"I'm not telling."

"I bet you did. Okay, okay. I'll wear the new ones."

"And grab a shirt. It might rain, and without a shirt you'll get cold and sprout a million goose bumps and your great-grandfather won't even recognize you. He'll think you're Mister Pimples or Porcupine Man. You'll have to take a shower with sandpaper."

The boy giggled at the images on the way downstairs.

In the Jeep on the drive toward the reservation, the boy talked animatedly about a shelter he wanted to build high in a hickory tree on the wooded hill behind the farmhouse. "You know where we found that waterfall last time?"

"Yes. Is your deer pool still there?" Together they had diligently built a six-foot-diameter low circular wall of gathered stream rocks at the base of the small waterfall to create a larger pool because the boy wanted to make a place for the forest creatures to drink. It was a shaded glen of delicate ferns, moss-backed rocks, and primeval forest scents.

"Sure. A few rocks came loose but I fixed it. Oh, and I found some tracks right up near it. Not deer. A coon, I think. Next time I want to leave some food there. Bread and nuts."

"Did you think of a name for that place?"

The boy looked at him with a trace of shy doubt. "I thought maybe we could call it Little *Atagahi*?"

The legendary Cherokee magical lake of healing for injured forest creatures. Its violet waters could be glimpsed somewhere way back up in the forest, it was said, only by one who believed and who in the heart intended no harm to the creatures, and who first fasted ritually. Hardin said, "I think that's perfect."

"Just for you and me, okay? To have magic it should be a secret."

"Just you and me, then."

"Well, anyway, the tree is a little way up the hill from there. You can hear the waterfall all the way up to the top of it."

"Do you have a plan for this treehouse?"

"It only needs to be big enough for us. A door in the floor and a window. I can tie boards with a long rope, then climb it and pull the boards up. I can tie a sack to my belt to hold the hammer and nails and stuff. There's a roll of tar paper out in Aunt Crow's shed." He called her his aunt, as Valerie of course had, although Lisa was in fact his great-aunt. "We could ask her for some of it. For the roof and the sides. Maybe you could help me build it. You can see a long way off from up there. When we get it done you could come some Friday night and we could bring water and bread and bologna and apples and peanut butter in my backpack and spend all night up there."

"Let me think about it, Curly."

"That's what grown-ups always say when they mean no."

"I think it's a fine idea. It's just that I don't have a lot of time to spare right now." Nolan Rader's demands had shadowed his life. Had created a dulling, spreading hollow spot in his soul. He was here talking with the boy, guiding the Jeep through turns, but there was also an out-of-body sense of unreality. He felt cornered by a gathering, faceless darkness.

The boy looked at him intently, with a skeptical lift of his eyebrows, and said, "What's wrong?"

Am I all that easy to read? Is it written on my forehead?

"Nothing's wrong. A few business problems." He smiled. "After we visit your great-grandfather what do you say we eat out in Waynesville at that place you like? I'd say let's ask Lisa and Wasituna to come with us, but she's got to work, and you know he never likes to eat out. Says you can't tell what's in the restaurant food these days."

The boy brightened. "Okay. We can split a big steak. But I'll save room for apple crisp and ice cream."

They went past modest frame homes and single-wides clinging to the steep wooded hills around Cherokee. Roadside stands selling honey, baskets, dishes, and blankets. Along with Native American trinkets made for next to nothing in China.

At the heart of the reservation there was a vast parking lot with several hundred cars, many from hundreds of miles away, reflecting the hazy sun. Awaiting owners who were attempting to beat the long odds at the ranks of electronically-patient slots inside the casino's windowless fantasy. There were half a dozen charter busses in one area along with a custom burgundy bus with dark tinted windows, painted with the flamboyant white signature of a major country music star.

The boy said, "Great-grandfather says that's a very good place to throw your money away."

"Well, I know the people who built it weren't really gambling. All the machines in there are set up to be on their side. Kitty can tell you about all that sometime."

Mixed in among the ubiquitous dusty pickups on the roads, Hardin passed expensive new vehicles. Muscle cars. Big SUVs. Improbable and impractical trucks perched high on oversized buzzing fat-lugged tires. Over-chromed and loud and fuelish. American trophies for young Indians, who, at their majorities, were free to claim their relatively small shares of the steady casino profits that had been building up for them. Every Cherokee living on the reservation received an annual share. John figured that a lot of the profits were most probably distributed to a few others off the reservation to spend less conspicuously.

A mile outside the town they climbed a steep switch-backing gravel road through woods to a tilted clearing overlooking the village, where there was a cabin with a green metal roof and a fieldstone chimney on an end wall. He parked the Wrangler beside an old but well-maintained pickup and set the emergency brake. A slightly-bowed old man was seated in a bentwood rocker on the porch. Dressed in jeans and a loose bold colorful shirt. His coarse black hair, tied tightly back into a long ponytail, was streaked with gray. He waved a leathery hand and the boy smiled and waved back. The boy and Hardin went up onto the porch.

The boy hugged the old man and sat on the porch rail in front of him. Hardin placed a brown paper bag on the small table beside the rocker, nodded in greeting, and sat on the top porch step with his back to the handrail post. He said, "That's a loaf of the bread you like, from Lisa. How have you been, Wasituna?"

His smile lines wrinkled with his grin. "You can see how I am. I am wearing out. I wonder what part will pain me tomorrow. I will take no pills. Even our Cherokee doctors want you to take pills now. On the TV every ten minutes there is a pill for this or a pill for that. To help you sleep or stay awake or lose weight or love your woman. Can they show me a pill that does you no harm while it tries to do you a little good? Pills train the body to be lazy, to forget what it is supposed to be doing for itself. Pills help us overeat the wrong foods and avoid exercise and live too fast. We are also training ourselves to live in a smaller and smaller span of comfort. If it is not seventy-three degrees they complain. Soon it *must* be seventy-three degrees to live. But I should not preach about others. Each day is a treasure to me. I only regret to have wasted so many of them that were so generously given to me. I do have a richness of good memories stored away. I walk in the woods and I savor them. Well, what mischief have you been into, boy?"

Joshua told him about his plans for the tree shelter and the old man nodded approval. He said, "Go into my house. There is something for you on the table."

The boy hopped off the rail and went in, banging the screen door. He came out holding a seven-foot blowgun and a deerskin quiver of fire-hardened yellow locust darts fletched with pale thistle down. He was smiling broadly. He raised it to the sky and sighted down the bore, admiring its straightness and smoothness, and said, "Thank you, great-grandfather. It's perfect. I bet it took you a long time to make it."

"You must become good enough to compete in the games for our clan. I'm too old. My eyes lie to me and my hands sometimes refuse to be still. There's a big empty carton in my bedroom. Put it out there on the table and see if you can even hit it from over there by the trees."

Wasituna had used a red-hot steel rod to burn out the nodes in the length of river cane, then had heated the cane over coals and had bent it gently and repeatedly on his knee to make it straight. He'd patiently smoothed the bore with a dowel tipped with wet sandpaper. The fletching of the foot-long darts was an art. His blowguns were known to be among the best on the reservation.

Joshua got the carton, which had been marked with a black X, and placed it on the rustic table at one side of the front yard. He took the blowgun to the other side of the yard and began testing its weight in his hands, holding it close by the near end. The adult-sized weapon looked to be much too long for him, but he held it with confidence.

Wasituna squinted at Hardin and said in a low voice, "So what is wrong, my friend?"

Hardin ran a hand over his face, glanced at the boy to make sure he was out of hearing, and said, "There's a man named Rader who knows what I did. He has a video recording of the man I told you about who was a witness to the last killing. Rader knows I split some money with that man. Only the man and you knew that, so he's not bluffing."

"And this Rader will use the recording against you?"

"Not if I do something he wants. His brother is missing. Rader wants me to find him. I'll have to get close to some apparently very bad men who may be holding the brother. I believe the brother is almost certainly dead, but I think I'll at least have to find that out for sure to satisfy Rader."

"How will you get close to these bad men? You will pretend to be like them?"

"Yes."

The old man thought, squinting, watching the concentrating boy send a dart flying almost invisibly across the yard to glance off a corner of the carton. He said, "It will be a dangerous game. I think you must *believe* you are one of their kind or they will see into you. Can you do that?"

"I don't know. I must be really easy to read. Everybody already seems to know something is bothering me, even the boy."

"Especially the boy. You are a father to him. I think nobody knows your heart any better. Then you must *make* yourself believe in any way you can. And if they should still distrust you, then you must be a good actor."

"But how? I'm no actor."

"We are all very good actors at times, if you think about it. When we are making trades with money. When we are courting. When we are trying to be brave in front of our young. Were you not an actor when you went after those men? What makes people believe? You must think about that. Confidence. Standing tall. Looking them in the eyes and not blinking. Not talking too much. Stillness, sometimes. Drawing the attention away from yourself with your words. The gift of a smile, but you must mean it. The ways you move your hands. Sometimes, if nothing else works, then anger. Anger can mask your true heart."

The boy, rushing his attempts, had missed the carton completely with two darts. Struck the table with the next three attempts. He walked to retrieve the darts, carrying the blowgun with care and respect, and went back to the far side of the yard, his head down in concentration, to try again.

Wasituna said, "When must you do this?"

"Soon. Beginning Friday night."

"Then spend time alone. Tomorrow. Go into the woods to think. But first run far to clear your head. Prepare yourself. You are *strong* inside. You will do well. You will survive. You *must* survive." He nodded toward the boy. "For him."

Joshua frowned, planted his feet shoulder width apart, inserted a dart into the bore, inhaled deeply, and, puffing out his cheeks, sent the needle-sharp missile across the clearing in a nearly flat trajectory. It thwacked into the carton all the way up to the fletching.

About three inches from the crossing of the X.

NINE

John ran the woods trail like he was being chased. On and on. Until the pain built up and passed and he gained a second wind. He wore his moccasins and was placing his feet to make the least noise possible, the way the old man had taught him, climbing now, the steep path broken up with cracked rock ledges, and veined with slick tree roots. It was one of the trails he liked and knew well. It crossed the Blue Ridge Parkway near Big Witch Tunnel and a gravel turnout, where he'd left the Wrangler. The trail skirted the lip of a high sheer cliff for a hundred feet, but he did not slow the pace, and ran on until he came to a rocky knob where there was a thin stand of wind-stunted evergreens, their branches trembling in a freshening breeze, and an expansive view of the mountains all around. He dropped and did a hundred pushups and seventy-five sit ups, wiped the sweat out of his eyes with the back of his hand, and sat hugging his knees as his breathing and heart rate slowed. From here, if you discounted the dingy haze layer along the horizon and that jet scratch on the sky, there were no visible evidences of human habitation. Only rank on rank of ancient forested hills inhaling the sunlight. The view from right here must have been similar a million years ago.

Well, I can't kill Rader. So I'll have to try doing what he wants.

You must believe or they will see into you, Wasituna said. So how can I do that?

Smuggling. He'd thought about it. In an idle remote way, as he suspected more than a few other pilots also had. Never intending to actually do it. But still wondering. It posed a challenge, after all. How could it be done with the least risk of getting caught? If Rader could be believed, he had access to inside information that would minimize risk. So what if he had to actually do it once or twice in order to work his way close enough to find out about Rader's brother? Assuming he could even get away with it, they would pay him. Pay him very well. More for a single quick trip than he could likely earn in a very long time otherwise. But it would be money from a trade that ultimately ruins many lives. That fries brains and erodes bodies and spawns crimes. That spreads still more drugs and causes thefts and killings. Conscious or unconscious suicides. Could he take that kind of money?

How would a smuggler live with it?

He'd probably start by thinking if I don't do it somebody else will. And some of the trade isn't so bad, after all. Take good old pot. Probably a third of the people in the country have at least tried it. As for those who use stronger stuff, they went down that path by their own choice, didn't they? The amount of any substance that could be moved in a single-engine plane would be insignificant in the overall continuing trade, which certainly must run into multiple billions of dollars a year.

He did not have to spend the money on himself. He could beef up the trust fund for the boy. College was expensive these days. Kitty needed money to prop up her business until it could bring in enough to sustain it. Or give it to charity. Even to some drug rehab program.

Being human, we can rationalize doing anything. If the killing of absolute innocents, say, is too reprehensible personally—the murdering of old people and infants and the weak and the inconveniently obstructive—then we can easily conspire to do it collectively. Impersonally. Which allowed a Dresden. A Nagasaki. A Holocaust. A Trail of Tears. And numerous methodically efficient genocides in Africa and elsewhere. Never-ending conflicts waged using safe labels and euphemisms like engagements, initiatives, offensives, civilian casualties, collateral damage, enemy, troops, anti-personnel ordnance.

If you want to really dress it up to feel good, do it in the name of God or Allah.

And what are you doing right now? Holding up a list of vicious human behaviors that make drug smuggling look mild by comparison? Not so clever of you, because that's a tired old illusion worked by the self. Okay, maybe I threw a rock or two along with the rest of them, but I never struck the harlot. Okay, maybe I wore a hooded sheet a few times, but I never snugged a noose up on anybody's neck. Okay, maybe I drove the getaway car, but at least I didn't pull the trigger. Okay, maybe I flew some of the stuff in from Canada, but at least I didn't go out there on the dirty streets and sell it to kids.

But if you're going to do this, you must *believe. So stop moralizing. Rationalize all you have to. Go ahead and be one of them and forget all the rest of it. Just make sure you can find your way back to yourself if and when it's over. And do all you possibly can to keep anybody you know from getting seriously hurt along the way.*

***

Kitty had spent the day rearranging her gallery area to make room for half a dozen acrylic paintings by an unknown Cherokee artist. The realism and style rivaled that of Bev Doolittle's work. Subjects in these paintings were the people before the white invasion. Her favorite showed a couple with their baby near a campfire, with creatures cleverly hidden in the fabric of the surrounding forest.

She needed more shelving to display hand-embroidered dolls in traditional Cherokee clothing, and there was yet another carton of small bears carved from walnut. When she had first put out a call for consignment items, mountain and reservation artists and crafters had responded almost overwhelmingly with their creations. Colorful baskets, beadwork, small quail carved from buckeye wood, graceful double-necked Cherokee wedding vases, dream catchers, stick ball *anetsa* rackets, similar to lacrosse rackets, to be used for wall decorations. She took in only the finest work.

Her shop was in a rustic leased building on a back road beside the stone entrance gates to Medicine Ridge, a whole mountain designed to attract campers, hikers, horseback riders, and tourist families wanting to enjoy the far views from the highest ridges. The mountain was closed for three months each winter, so the tourist traffic would then decline, but if she could establish a wide enough reputation, one day people would come to buy from her year round, she knew. She planned a series of regular in-shop demonstrations by various artists that would gain free publicity in the doings pages of local tabloids and newspapers.

Her budget was stretched nearly to breaking, even worse than John suspected, but if she could hang on through the next winter, she should be on a path to enough profits to survive. She'd made overtures to a dozen interior decorators to persuade them to use some of the items she sold, and that was beginning to pay off. She'd been thinking about designing and bringing out a color catalog, and selling items online through a distinctive website, but that all took money, money, money.

She glanced up to see John's dusty white Wrangler pull into the gravel parking lot, and checked her watch. *Five-thirty already? Impossible.*

She smiled and met him at the door. There were no customers and her single employee was not in today, so they hugged for long moments, all her cares and accumulated stresses of the day melting away.

She hummed a long contented note and said, "I hope I make you feel like this with just a hug."

"You do. Listen, I thought you might like to go out and eat tonight. I won't be able to make the weekend thing. Got to meet with a client tomorrow night and fly early on Saturday. Sorry." The lie tasted sour. He had to tell it while he was holding her because he did not want her looking into his eyes.

"We could go get the bikes and ride over to that restaurant you like in Asheville at the Farmers Market. Shouldn't be as crowded tonight, anyway. Maybe we could rent a movie later."

They had planned a ride through the Great Smokies National Park over Newfound Gap to spend Friday night in Gatlinburg and come back Saturday morning early so she could still open the shop on time.

She pushed away enough to study his face.

He said, "You've got this place looking great. Those bears are new."

"Aren't they perfect? A very old man on the reservation carves them. From a supply of walnut he saved years ago. He's got dozens of them all over his house, but he's never tried selling any, even though he could sure use the money. Like a lot of the people you see represented here. Loaded with talent but light on confidence and business sense. Most of them are too willing to sell their things far too cheaply. The woman who makes those wedding vases told me about the man with the bears so I looked him up. I'm trying to talk him into demonstrating here."

"How are the workshops doing?"

"They draw some customers. We're out of the way, I know, but I keep thinking other places, like the Bob Timberlake Gallery over in Lexington, are out of the way, too, and they do okay."

"You'll make it work, Kitty."

"If there's a way, I will." She rearranged the bears on the shelf. Looked at him sideways. "So, what's bothering you? Hattie and I talked on the phone today, and we both think there's something you're not telling us."

"A few business headaches. Nothing serious. I'll probably be working more hours for a while though. Whatever remodeling jobs I can find. There's a chance I can get some good charter work."

She cocked her head, lifted an eyebrow, and smiled. "That's all pretty vague. But okay. Let's forget our woes for tonight. A salad at my place will be cheaper than eating out. You'll want to watch some old John Wayne thing, I suppose. I'll agree to that if you'll just rub my feet."

TEN

Monroe brought Rader in. He was taking small awkward steps because of the chain hobble. Monroe pointed at a comfortable padded leather chair on casters, with arm and head rests, across the large desk from the tall man. Clint sat, held his upper body erect, and glowered. There was a laptop on the desk, along with a small black box, coiled wires, and a slim computer microphone on a pedestal. The skylights above were black with night.

Brain said, "You have two immediate choices. You may choose not to cooperate. That would incur Monroe's disfavor. It would also mean you are of no use to me in my research and it might well persuade me to move the time of your termination closer. Alternatively, you may cooperate. That decision will gain you continued favor from Monroe. Initially, cooperation merely entails answering a series of questions truthfully. From now on in this session you may speak, but only in response to my questions. You have learned what violating that rule can mean. Respond now with a simple yes or no. Will you cooperate?"

Clint looked into the impassive yellow eyes for a long moment, then nodded his head once.

"Yes or no. Say it."

"Okay. Yes."

Monroe wrapped what looked like a blood pressure cuff around his right bicep. Pulled him forward from the chair back enough to run two bands around his chest, and clipped two small cuffs to the index and second finger tips on his left hand.

Brain said, "This is a digital polygraph. It will help me determine not only your veracity but also your stress levels in this and subsequent sessions. The program monitors your blood pressure, respiration and heart rates, and galvanic skin response. When you lie, your pressure rises, your heart and respiration rates increase, and you perspire slightly more, which increases skin conductance. We will begin now."

He drew the laptop closer, slid in a disc, and typed rapidly. Tapped individual keys as he studied the screen, its projected light making his darting eyes glow. Clint sat upright and tense, Monroe standing close behind the chair on his left.

"Is your name Clinton Alexander Rader?"

"Yes."

"Are you a mechanic?"

"Yes."

"Are your parents deceased?"

"Yes."

"Answer truthfully. Did you ever lie to either of your parents?"

"Yes."

"Are you thirty years old?"

"No."

"Are you twenty-eight years old?"

"Yes."

"Are you a homosexual?"

"No."

"Have you thought about when you might die?"

"Of course."

"Simple yes or no responses. Have you thought about *how* you might die?"

"Everybody has."

"Simple yes or no responses. I will not tell you that again."

He could feel Monroe shifting behind him, and he tightened up, trying not to flinch visibly, but no blow came.

"Are you a full member of the Longriders club?"

"Yes."

"Do you know any members of the Satan's Ghosts club?"

"Of course. Okay, yes."

Brain stared at him for long seconds. Finally turned his attention to the laptop and typed for a minute, using the fingertip mouse pad at intervals. Nodded at something on the screen, and said, "Now you may speak freely in response to my questions. I am interested in your true feelings and observations. What is your opinion of Monroe?"

"He's tough. But he's not real smart. I had a dog like him once. He does whatever you tell him. Can't think for himself anymore. He'd probably lick your feet if he thought you'd like it."

Monroe nudged the chair and Brain held a palm up at him.

Looking steadily at Brain, Clint said, "That's what I mean. I could back my dog down with just a hand motion, too."

"Do you not fear him?"

"I think of him like I would a mean dog."

"And what do you think of me?"

"I think you're smart. But I think you're crazy."

"Shall I tell you my initial impressions of you? You give every indication of courage, stubbornness, and independence, but those traits do not go deep in you, I think. We will see. You are understandably angry. Like a child, you are probing for your limits by deliberately attempting to antagonize. Trying to evade thinking about the consequences of your actions by directing anger outward. That will not be effective. You do not quite believe your impending fate. I assure you it is real. Your stress level is increasing by the hour. It will continue to do so along a predictable curve. At some point it will become too much to bear. Either you will employ some variety of defense mechanisms or you will break. It will be of some interest to determine which."

"You said there might be a way out."

"Did I? Perhaps. But the men you killed were important in a business sense. Your actions have inconvenienced and angered others who depended on them and who wield much power. That, of course, is why you are here. They would not be pleased if I were to default on my agreement with them. Still, I have a certain degree of discretion, and a measure of personal influence."

"You're a contract killer, then."

Brain smiled thinly, his eyes feral.

"This so-called research. Why are you doing it? You damned sure can't tell anybody about it. So what's the point?"

"A curious question, but I will allow it. Stress itself is a killer. One of the most efficient and yet most subtle. Silent. Stealthy. Feasting on conflict. The victim denies its presence. In fact, usually helps it do its business. It attacks the entire nervous system corrosively over time, works changes in body chemistry, erodes the will, and, ultimately, can cause the heart to stumble or the immune system to malfunction, allowing a host of its allies to invade. I want to know all its fascinating secrets, you see. Unlike so many others in my field, I do not need to publish in order to be fulfilled. Yet one day I might conduct interviews with death row inmates. What I learn here with you might help guide such a study and so indirectly see print."

"How many other subjects have you had?"

"Another curious question. You are subject eight. Without exception, they have been concerned only about themselves. Not one wanted to know about any of the others. They have behaved predictably. Beginning in denial and anger, attempting escape by various means, offering money or favors for reprieve, inevitably employing various defense mechanisms, and, near the end, begging. But I think that will be all for now. We will conduct another session in the morning. Take him back, Monroe."

Brain sat at his desk, reviewing the polygraph data and thinking, *he deflected my advance about the men he killed. Why? It would have been normal to deny having done the killings, to disclaim any knowledge of it, especially in this case because there were apparently no eyewitnesses. Or to justify it as the result of an argument that escalated to violence.*

Perhaps to claim self-defense. It was not normal to avoid the subject altogether. Perhaps this one will not be so predictable. That would be refreshing.

Back in his prison room, Clint thought, *is there really some way out? Or is he just offering a carrot to make me do head tricks?*

In any case, he had to keep the man from finding out about Trey and Rita.

Once again, he began going over the room.

Thinking.

ELEVEN

"The guy you'll have to find tonight is Pitt Tobin," Rader said.

They were in Rader's low-end furnished duplex apartment in Asheville early on Friday morning. It was a run-down area where tenants came and went by the month and nobody asked too many questions. Rader had paid for two months in advance under an assumed name.

"Tobin is supposedly first in line as successor to the SG throne. The man at the top for the last fifteen years has been Sutter Leonard, who lives on a ranch near Albuquerque now, but he's got bad kidneys and other major health problems. This Tobin will almost certainly be hanging at the usual Charlotte dive tonight. It's called Mothers. The SGs have an interest in the place. They're into legitimate businesses these days. Like bars, tattoo and piercing joints, custom motorcycle places. For the money, but also for the image. Some of the businesses where there could conceivably be a lot of cash changing hands, like this Mothers, make good money laundries. There'll be a guy named Wee Albert hanging with Tobin. He's a bodyguard with an assault record. Weighs over three hundred. There may be one or two other SGs there. And maybe his wife. Don't be too pushy. Just work your way close to Tobin however you can. Try to get him alone at the bar or something. Tell him you want to make some real money with your airplane. You heard Bobby Ostrowski bought it in a Beech Duke on a flight through the mountains one night in Montana. Bobby flew out of Raleigh. You knew him. He hinted he was making runs for the SG. You figure they could use a replacement. They're going to check you out, and your lifestyle won't square with having made big money smuggling, so just say you've never done it before, but you've got a friend you grew up with who's on the Joint Border Task Force. You two hooked up recently. Cooked up a deal. He's got all the inside info you need to make runs into Canada untouched. Okay, so you don't have any experience at it, but you won't be targeted by any law yet, either. You're clean. Tell Tobin you'll need one hundred thousand a trip. You're not particular what you carry."

"If this Tobin asks who my contact is?"

"You can't tell him, of course. Both to protect him and to preserve your value." Rader had placed a large manila envelope on the rickety dining table. He put a hand on it. "Everything you should need is in here. A photo of Clint. Photos of Tobin and his wife. Those who'll most likely be close to him. Directions to Mothers. A bio of Ostrowski. Take time to look it over and plant it in your head. If I was you I'd pull into the place after nine or so. Call me here tomorrow night and tell me how it went."

"You think the man in Tennessee will want to check me out in person?"

"It's what I've heard. That could be your chance to get a line on Clint. I don't need much, but I do need *something* to justify a warrant for a raid. And, listen to me, this is important. I want you to memorize every detail you can about the place. Look for security cameras. Dogs. Floodlights. What are the buildings made of? Concrete block or framing? Are the doors metal or wood? What are the floor layouts of the buildings? How many people are in there and what do they look like? What kinds of vehicles? As soon as you can after you leave, take a pad and write it all down. Every scrap. Don't skip over anything. Do you understand?"

"And if it comes to flying an actual run?"

"We'll talk about that if and when. For now all you have to do is find Tobin and propose your deal. Just take it a rung at a time. And don't look down."

He drove to the Asheville airport and parked the Wrangler by his hangar. He spent a while going over everything in the envelope, committing as much of it as possible to memory. The picture of Tobin was taken outdoors at night. A biker rally or a party. Tobin was central to twenty-three others in the scene, three of them women. They all held plastic cups or beer cans. The men wore their colors, grinning, gesturing with V fingers. One unsmiling man with dangerous eyes and enormous tattooed arms displayed by a ragged vest had his middle finger raised from his fist. The women were awkwardly lifting their T-shirts to expose their breasts. Rader had circled various faces with a felt tip and printed in names. Tobin was compact and shorter than the other men. He wore a leather do rag. No facial hair. He smiled at the camera with his head cocked, chin out.

Tanned, smile lines prominent. Confident. Affable. Likeable. And obviously the leader. Several of the men were resting a hand on a companion's shoulder, but nobody was touching Tobin.

John put everything away and slid the envelope under the passenger floor mat. He would hide it in his shed at the house later.

The chances of this leading him to any vital information about Clint Rader were close to zero. Yet he saw no other choice but to try.

After a limp salad in an Asheville fast food place, he spent an hour at a modest home in the town of Clyde, working up an estimate that would allow a small profit replacing a side porch for an elderly couple, friends of Hattie's from her church, and told the man he would get to it when he could within the next month.

A MapQuest printout in Rader's envelope had showed one hundred and twenty three miles to the place called Mothers in Charlotte. In late afternoon he told Hank he had to do some maintenance on the plane and not to expect him back until very late that night. Not hungry and not wanting to sit with the couple at the dinner table, having to make forced conversation, he told the old man he would stop for a quick supper on the way to the airport. Said he might even spend the night in Asheville so he could fly for a client early the next morning.

Lying more and more seriously to those most important in his life made him feel unclean and unworthy of their trust.

He left Eaglenest Ridge on the Road King at six and turned east on Highway 19.

Five miles out of town he recognized Doyle coming the other way all in black, hunched, with his gloved hands high on the raised handlebars. Doyle blasted past, his straight pipes roaring, and waved low with two fingers. John returned the gesture. In his left mirror, he saw Doyle slow and swing around to follow him. He pulled up on John's right and nodded.

At a stoplight, with the bikes idling, Doyle said loudly, "Where you off to, gunslinger?"

"Going to get something to eat."

"Hey, great. I owe you one. I'll buy."

"I'm a little cramped for time."

"No problem. I eat fast. Anyplace so long as they got beer."

"I don't think—"

But the light changed and Doyle blipped his throttle, drowning out any possible sound short of a flame-painted low rider with all its windows open, broadcasting rap from overdriven trunk speakers.

John thought, *we'll eat and then I'll get rid of him.*

Outside Asheville John swung into the lot of an Outback. They took a pub table near the bar and Doyle ordered two drafts and house special steaks, rare.

John said, "Those pipes of yours are loud enough to dent cars."

"You know what they say. Loud pipes save lives. I want 'em to hear me coming."

When the waitress brought the beer, Doyle grinned at her widely and said, "Thank you, darlin'. You're a life-savin' angel. Tell you what. I'll see if I got a place on my calendar for ya." She rolled her eyes and walked away, Doyle watching her. He said,

"Will you look at that ass? Nice rack, too." He took a long pull on his draft and sighed contentedly. "Been a long hot day, man. Framin' houses for the rich folk to buy with their pocket change is thirsty work."

John said, "I'll really have to eat and run here."

Still grinning, Doyle cocked his head and looked steadily at him. Said, "Okay, my man. Here's how it is. No secret how I feel about Kit. The lady is one of a kind for damned straight. But she sees somethin' in you. Just what that might be I sure as hell can't figure. I called her last night and we talked some. She's worried. You're actin' even stranger than your usual self, I guess. She said could I maybe keep a eye out for ya."

"I appreciate all that, Doyle, but I don't need any help."

"Then there was you wantin' to know all about the Satan's Ghosts. I got to ask myself why, you know? I mean, what, you want to join up? Chop that RK down and rake it? Be a real bad ass? That don't make any sense. So what's up with you?"

"I've got a few business problems and—"

"Bullshit. Kit said you backed outta your date for tonight. Where you goin'?"

"I have to meet a client."

"Hey, okay, then. I'll just tag along. Don't you worry. I'll stay out of the way."

"Doyle. You can't come with me."

"It was a free highway out there last I looked. You don't ride good enough to outrun me. How you gonna stop me? Cut a tire on my bike?"

"Maybe. If I have to. Look, Doyle. Try to understand. There's nothing you can do to help me. I don't need you intruding on my life right now. We'll eat and then split up, okay?"

"Intrudin'? Screw you, gunslinger. I'll just tag along. For Kit. You could *try* to cut a tire on me."

The waitress brought their meals and they ate in silence, Doyle obviously enjoying every large bite of the bloody steak.

John pushed his half-eaten steak away, shook his head, and said, "All right. I have to go down to Charlotte tonight. A biker joint. Talk to some people. That's all I can tell you."

"What's the name of the place?"

"Mothers."

"I know it. Yeah, it's damned sure a biker joint okay, owned by the Ghosts, last I heard. What, you gonna remodel their bar? Screw in mirrors so they got twice as many bare titties showin'? Put in a few pill dispensers? Spackle over the bullet holes?"

"Doyle—"

Doyle spread his palms. "Hey, okay, okay. But you listen to me. That ain't some place you tiptoe into for a cocktail, hear? By yourself you'll probly get chewed up like a chili cheeseburger in about five minutes. I'll tag along. Watch your back. You go ahead and talk to whoever you got to. Leave me out of it. But I'm comin'. Get used to it. Just wish we had like a machine gun with us. Now, you ain't gonna eat the rest of that steak, give it here. We don't want that hot li'l waitress thinkin' we wasn't happy."

They rode south and then east on 74, a sullen ruddy sun bedding itself in the thick haze behind them, through Forest City, Shelby, and Gastonia, where they stopped to refuel.

It was full dark when they pulled into the gravel parking lot at Mothers on the outskirts of Charlotte and backed their machines alongside a row of others lined up out front.

Inside, the band, like every other similar group trying to cover up a lack of talent with enough decibels to nudge the pain level, was struggling with something that might have been heavy metal laid over a boogie beat. John paid the cover charge for both of them and pointed at the bar. They found two stools and Doyle let out a piercing whistle and shouted at one of the harried bartenders for beers. The place was crowded and stank of stale beer, cigarettes, and unwashed bodies. In the back, low-hung fixtures lit up three green pool tables and a burgundy snooker table, the clacking of balls struck too hard adding to the din.

A slim woman in a G string, with breasts apparently augmented by grapefruit implants, undulated languidly atop a table ringed by raucous men. Eyes closed, her sweat-sheened body outlined by the pool table lights. Long-nailed fingers snapping to the boogie beat. Lost in her own universe. There were relatively fewer women than men in the place apart from the hustling waitresses, who wore tight white shorts and black halter tops. A dozen men in the colors of the Satan's Ghosts sat at two large round tables in one corner. A third table had chairs tipped to it, reserving the seats.

It was dim, and ceiling fans stirred the hot rank air. John surveyed what he could make out of the crowd. Raising the beer bottle to his lips but drinking little. The band finished the song and after a few seconds slid into another that sounded much the same. The table dancer never stopped or varied her primitively fluid hip-rolling motions.

Four men in SG colors walked in and headed for the corner tables. The one in the lead was Pitt Tobin, followed closely by an enormous unsmiling hulk who had to be Wee Albert, the bodyguard. All the men at the tables acknowledged Tobin and he grinned and nodded back. Tobin stopped to talk with several of the men before he and his followers sat at the reserved table. A waitress hurried over to take their orders.

Doyle leaned over and shouted in John's ear, "I hope that's not the guy you need to meet. You know who that is?"

John nodded. "Tobin."

Doyle shook his head and drained his beer.

John waited for the band to finish the set and announce a break. CD music took over, but not nearly so loudly. He motioned for Doyle to stay put and navigated through the crowd to the corner table. He put his hand flat on the table so he could bend slightly. Looked at Tobin. Wee Albert put down his beer and scowled.

Tobin gazed up at him, smiling, but his eyes were bright and hard. He wore a faded denim vest with various symbols on it, including a 1% patch. His hair was drawn back into a pony tail under a plain denim do rag. He was fully sleeved with tattoos, some of them old and muddy. What appeared to be recent thorny blood-red roses grew up both sides of his neck.

John said, "They tell me you're Pitt Tobin. I'm John Hardin. Can we talk?"

"About?"

"Possible business."

Tobin studied him. "I come here to get away from business, man. To enjoy a few beers with my friends. You, I don't think I've ever even met."

"You haven't. Five minutes, maximum. You'll find it worth your time."

"Tell you what, John. This is Albert. He'll give you one minute to get my attention. Starting now. He might count fast."

John leaned in closer and shielded his mouth with his hand so only Tobin could hear. "I'm a pilot. I can absolutely guarantee you unrestricted air access to Canada."

Tobin looked around. Took a swallow of beer. His permanent smile lines creased as he squinted at John with new interest. "I've got no idea why you think that would interest me in any way."

John looked steadily into the cold eyes. "I'm not any kind of law. Walk over to the far end of the bar with me and listen. I'll be brief."

Tobin considered. He said something in Wee Albert's ear and the big man gave John a clear warning look. Tobin said, "Albert, Spade, Dennis, why don't you guys circulate for a few minutes? See that everybody's enjoying themselves." The three men got up from the table and left.

Tobin said, "So sit. You need a beer?"

"No. Here it is. I knew a man who flew out of Raleigh. Bobby Ostrowski. I'd see him here or there at airports and we'd talk flying. A while back we went out one night for drinks and he had a few too many. He led me to believe he was associated with your organization."

"Hold up there. I don't have an organization."

Wee Albert and the man Tobin had called Spade were bracketing Doyle at the bar. Albert had a heavy arm draped across Doyle's shoulders.

"Bobby might have been associated with some of your friends, then. Not long after we talked he hit a rock cloud in the mountains near the border at night. I own a plane and could do what Bobby was doing, but much better. I have a friend on the Joint Border Task Force. We go back. He and I can guarantee no interference from the law. For that I'll need a flat one hundred thousand a flight. I'll give my friend his share. The cargo doesn't matter. My plane is small but I can load five hundred pounds. I know you'll have to check me out, but don't take too long. There are other people who could use my services. If I don't hear from you soon I'll have to talk with them." He took a business card out of his wallet and placed it on the table. "Don't call my home phone. People live with me. Call me on the cell. Then we can meet again and talk. I know you won't want to say much on a cell."

"Like I said, John. I have no interest in long-distance charters, which is I guess what you're talking about. Says on the card you do sightseeing flights, though. Maybe you could take me and my wife up to check out the mountains. I'll talk to her. She's interested, you'll probably get a call in a few days."

There was a commotion at the bar. Doyle was standing, tensed, facing Wee Albert. Their faces were inches apart. Spade sat leaning backward on his stool, one boot hooked on the stool rung, elbows on the bar, smiling broadly. A passing waitress with a loaded tray held high changed course quickly to cut around the two large men but otherwise ignored the confrontation.

John looked at Tobin.

Tobin stood up. Shook his head at Spade, who lifted a finger at Wee Albert and wagged it back and forth. Albert glanced over at Tobin and held himself in check. Doyle was focused on Albert, saying something loudly, his fists clenched.

Tobin said, "I hope you boys had a good time here tonight. Some of my friends will help you find the door now. See you get out of the lot safe. You might want to think about doing your drinking someplace else."

John walked over to Doyle and said, "I'm done here. Let's go."

Doyle stared at Wee Albert for two seconds, finished his beer, and they walked out with four men loosely following them into the lot.

Wee Albert rumbled, "Y'all take 'er easy, now, boys. Hear?"

By their machines, buckling their helmets on, John said, "What was that all about?"

"Fat ass over there didn't want to lift his arm off me."

"So what were you going to do? Take them all on?"

"I hope you had a good talk with Pitt Tobin. Some say he's only the new guy at the top of the Ghosts. You two gonna play a little golf? Or he wants an eight by ten of his house from the air?"

"Doyle. I need you to keep quiet about tonight. Nobody knows we were here. Are you okay with that?"

"Hey, I got a feelin' it's gonna be your funeral, anyway, gunslinger. How about you leave me your Road King?"

***

The next morning Pitt Tobin called the ailing SG chief, Sutter Leonard, at his plush ranch outside Albuquerque. They talked in vague terms about various business interests, legitimate and otherwise, and about an upcoming ride to Sturgis, South Dakota, an internationally-known week-long biker blowout that drew a quarter million riders to the remote Black Hills every year. Several Ghosts chapters would be represented there, and a late after-hours meet was planned for selected members in a rented room above a bar on the outskirts of Rapid City. Leonard would fly in for it.

"One more item," Tobin said. "I met this guy last night who's a pilot. Said he's got an inside contact and can guarantee no-hassle cargos between us and the maple-leaf boys."

"What was your take on him?"

"He didn't feel like law. Green to the game, but he's not stupid. Cocky, but what pilot isn't? Knew Bobby O, who apparently had a loose mouth when he had a few, by the way. Wants high fees, but with what's been going on along the border lately, he might be worth a pretty good cut."

"Okay. E-mail me what you've got through the secure IP, and I'll have him checked out. If he looks righteous I'll call my Tennessee man B."

TWELVE

John drove the Wrangler to pick up Kitty on Sunday morning. Hank and Hattie were in the back. A Yankee front had herded the stagnant summer haze to the south and had washed the mountains with cool clear air temporarily, bringing everything into sharper focus and lifting spirits. John parked in the fluttering lacy shade of a vibrantly green oak in the lot for the small fieldstone church in Maggie Valley. He and Kitty followed the old couple inside and took a pew that Hattie liked by one of the tall narrow stained glass windows set in the eastern wall.

The fifty or so souls present stood to sing "We Gather Together" and "A Shield About Me."

Reverend Boyer announced a birthday and directed attention to the names printed in the program prayer list. Elders passed the plates. The sermon was about listening. To each other. Especially to those with whom we share the miracle of love. To our young. Not merely hearing, but listening.

Boyer said, "The power behind all creation speaks to us. Sometimes loudly. In the drumming thunder. Or in the crying of a newborn baby. But more often, I think, He whispers to us. The sky is gloriously clear today. Go outside tonight. Gaze up from this spinning, floating sphere we've been allowed to borrow. You can look across half a billion miles at great Jupiter, so large the earth would fit into its whirling red spot, a perpetual storm that baffles astronomers. Without Jupiter to sweep up drifting rocks and ice, our Earth would be much more vulnerable to life-destroying damage, and might never have been capable of sustaining life at all. Turn your car radio to the AM band late tonight between stations and you might hear curious warbling whistles. That's Jupiter's vast magnetic field singing to us.

Turn on a television and tune it outside any stations. The static you'll hear is the background radiation lingering from the creation event itself. Train binoculars on the most distant specks. You'll see faint light traveling from across apparent infinity and before recorded time. Quasars wink in the cold blackness like beacons. Stars explode or swell and die, and new stars and their attendant planets form out of the dust. We ourselves contain stardust.

"We've been given an honored place in a universe filled with wonders. With vast miracles. Will you sense the power behind it all? Will you hear it?

"Then close your eyes and listen deep within your soul. Will you begin to hear the wonderful whisperings there as well?"

John felt uncomfortably out of place. Hank and Hattie sat attentively. They fitted together seamlessly. He could not imagine a couple any more natural and right. By her contented presence beside him, Kitty was silently declaring their own relationship. Her skirted thigh was just touching his, and he could detect the natural fragrance of her hair. He was proud of her. Proud to be considered hers. But he was lying to her, and would have to continue the lying. Until he could satisfy Rader's demands.

She found his hand with hers. Pressed. Sending him a simple, primitively intimate message. *I'm here for you. And I love you.* He looked down at the satin smoothness of her finely-sculpted fingers and wrist. His hand was rough, callused from working on houses.

It seemed to profane hers.

The tall window was filtering the white life-giving light from our burning star into its hidden symphony of colors.

Whisperings.

They went to Country Vittles for a home-style meat and potatoes meal. People greeted them, and an old banjo picker stopped by their table to remind Hank their country combo had a gig to play on the coming weekend.

As he was paying the check up front, Kitty took his arm, smiled nicely, and said, "After you drive Hank and Hattie home, make sure that Harley hasn't leaked all its oil overnight, then come to my place. We're going to take a ride to somewhere we can talk."

***

With Kitty leading on her red Honda they took Highway 441 out of Cherokee, climbing up through the heavily forested Great Smoky Mountains National Park to Newfound Gap. She took the turnoff there, which led them still higher for several miles to a parking lot with only a dozen scattered vehicles.

A steep half-mile walking trail wound from there to a fifty-foot-high observation tower—a large disc set atop a single concrete column at the summit of Clingman's Dome. At over 6,600 feet it was second in stature only to Mount Mitchell, which is the highest peak east of the Mississippi. The Appalachian Trail crossed here on its twenty-one-hundred mile trek between Maine and Georgia.

The trunks of dead spruces and firs disfigured the flanks of the peak, victims of disease and poisonously polluted air. Other obviously dying conifers struggled to live on for just one more year.

They stood apart from the few sightseers, at the metal rail of the tower, looking off to the west. Ordinarily, haze limited the visibility to an average of twenty miles, but in today's unusual brassy brilliance, the vista expanded to perhaps a hundred miles. Formed by unimaginable up-thrusting forces on a tectonic scale, these were among the oldest mountains on the planet. They stretched unevenly away in wave upon softly-furred wave, from close shades of green to far violet-tinged blues.

A cool wind was flowing steadily across the peak.

Kitty touched his forearm and said, "John, hear me out before you say anything, okay?" She looked out over the mountains, her elbows on the rail. "I used to come here a lot. This is a good place for me, because I seem to gain perspective and clarity up here, like you probably do from your plane."

He nodded.

"Also, half this mountain lies in Tennessee and half lies in North Carolina. That's a little like me. Part white, part red Injun. Half in your life and half out. I told you once that I'd been burned in a relationship. I never told you how. I suspected he had a stubborn mean streak, but it took a while to really show. He began by making occasional put-down comments, the way they do constantly on all the TV sitcoms, you know? Jokingly. Except it's never really funny. That's why they have to use a recorded laugh track on most of those shows.

"He would apologize later. So you tolerate it once. You figure he just wasn't quite himself that day. Stressed or something. Then you tolerate it slightly more the next time. You try to be more considerate, more generous, more careful of what you say and do. It becomes a pattern. It begins to grind you down. Crusts your soul. You look into a mirror and wonder just how much truth there must be to the comments. The little judgments. I don't know how I let it go on for as long as I did. Then one night he drank too much at a party we went to. Back at his house he got . . . physically abusive. That was it for me."

"I'm sorry, Kitty."

"So was he. I broke his damned arm."

John smiled, "Doesn't surprise me."

"Anyway, when you and I met, I'd retreated. Waaaaay on back. I was doing a heck of a job proving I didn't need a man. Then there you were from out of nowhere, filling my belly with butterflies all bumping into each other, and my brain with flowers. There were times just thinking of you gave me a physical ache from the wanting. That hasn't gotten any better. If we don't fit together, I don't know who on this world does. Look at Hank and Hattie. I want us to grow old together like that."

"Kitty. I feel the same way."

"I know you're a private man. You hold things inside. You're independent. So, Lord knows, am I. That's okay. Just part of who you are. I admire that. But what makes you think you can get away with hiding your feelings from *me*? The sermon this morning was about listening. I hear you, John Hardin. What I'm hearing is you have a big trouble weighing you down. So big it can only be your health or maybe something black hunting you from out of your past."

"It's not my health."

"I want to help you carry it if I can. Solve it. *Fight* it. I don't want it to wedge us apart."

"It's . . . I have to do something, Kitty. There's nothing you can do to help. I don't know how long it will be, and I don't know where it will take me. I've started lying to you about it, and that sickens me. So I'm cutting that out right now. But I can't tell you more. Try to trust that I'll handle it. If I can, that will be the end of it. Absolutely. We'll be able to go on from there."

She looked far away, squinting against the intense light, her eyes dark, her long hair making glossy little whiplashes in the wind.

"Kitty?"

She straightened up from leaning on the rail and turned to face him. "Go and do this thing, then. But carry the idea of us with you. Let it help you be stronger. You know you have my heart. I'm pretty hopeless about that."

They held each other in the clean sunlight and the cool wind.

THIRTEEN

Brain's library was extensive. Several ranks of floor-to-ceiling shelves and a bank of filing cabinets at the back of the private display room that contained all the items in his collections. There were volumes on many aspects of psychology and psychiatry, some of them valuable first editions. He had a neat stack of books and research papers about stress on the reading table and was going through them methodically. Gleaning tidbits he had perhaps overlooked or forgotten. Making notes on a white legal pad.

Three of the selected volumes were by Seyle, a former professor at McGill University, the first researcher to have used the term "stress" in a psychological sense, in 1936. Seyle had noticed that different illnesses often produced what seemed to be precisely the same symptoms in people. He had subjected laboratory animals to different stimuli such as infections, trauma, nervous strain, excessive heat and cold—the only common feature being that all the stimuli placed the animals under stress. He noted identical responses in the animals, with subsequent correlation to human subjects.

He divided those responses into three stages. First was alarm, with high central nervous system arousal. An increase in metabolism. Probable loss of appetite. Before very long there could be frequent headaches, and ulcers. But the high state of arousal was not sustainable. The second stage was a more sustainable stiff resistance, with more moderate physiological and behavioral responses. Eventually the resistance, after steadily sapping psychological energy, would inevitably decline into the third stage of exhaustion, with probable maladjustment, withdrawal, failure in a significant way to adapt to the stressful stimuli.

In some cases, failure took the form of suicide.

Stress inducers could be broadly categorized into some combination of frustration, conflict, and pressure. As with other instinctual behaviors designed into the human creature to be beneficial, stress could arouse and ready the body to escape from, or at least to deal with, a perceived threat. It could motivate a person to achieve well in personal life, business, or athletics. But, allowed to persist at elevated intensity, it could also turn on its host and inflict a slow inexorable death. It was this lethal aspect of stress that so intrigued Brain.

There was a wealth of data derived from the terrors and horrors of war. What in World War One had been called shell shock or battle fatigue or war neurosis had since been better defined to become Post-traumatic Stress Disorder, or PTSD. In *Achilles in Vietnam*, Jonathan Shay had proposed that Homer had been aware of PTSD when he wrote the *Iliad*. Among some 400,000 deserters from the armies of the Civil War there must certainly have been large numbers of PTSD cases who had witnessed many thousands of their brethren scythed to death in repeated point-blank, ranked confrontations on a succession of open battlefields. Fifty-one thousand cut down—wasted—at Gettysburg alone.

Brain scanned a World War Two Army report on Combat Exhaustion., which concluded, "Each moment of combat imposes a strain so great that men will break down in direct relation to the intensity and duration of their exposure." Many thousands had.

And it was no wonder the diagnosed cases of PTSD were even higher in Vietnam, where fear and uncertainty and frustration because of incompetent direction had been ceaseless. In World War Two, objectives on all sides were clear. Men in all the forces at least died with honor. In Vietnam, where objectives were never clearly defined, commanders sent men out as essentially expendable decoys to draw out an unseen enemy, and in so doing the soldiers were subjected to a spectrum of atrocities. PTSD silently killed many in a variety of ways long after the war ended.

He had chosen a somewhat different path to explore in the current research. He had established the usual controlled environment for Rader, with a limited but tempting choice of potential weapons from which the subject might choose to attempt escape—a goal in which the subject could invest hope, however limited. Only to meet with failure, of course, but the measure of the peaking hope prior to an attempt, and the depth of the depression following failure, would be interesting. He could also hold out hope in other more subtle ways that would enrich the interview sessions. That hope, of course, would also ultimately prove to be futile.

There had been an initial crude attempt at communication between the two subjects currently being held. That communication might be temporarily enabled. Only to be withdrawn. A view through the single window of the outside world had been provided so the yearning to live would remain strong. The view could be blocked, to elicit cooperation or simply to gauge the effect at a judicious moment. He could vary the quality and quantity of the food, decrease or elevate the test cell temperature, take away control of the room lighting and vary its intensity at will.

Employed at critical junctures, all of those tools would illuminate the research, as usual. But he was making a significant departure from the study with Rader. Exploring a new direction. By sharing his procedures, simplified for ready comprehension, of course, and explaining selected steps in the process with the subject himself, revealing how the subject was attempting to cope mentally, he was partially sacrificing elements such as surprise, shock, and fear of the unknown, but he was also systematically stripping this one of his defense mechanisms.

Leaving him to face the stark reality of his impending execution psychologically naked. How soon could a complete breakdown be expected in that case? Brain wanted to document that process in exquisite detail, as no one ever had before.

Monroe entered the room and said, "You have a call from Leonard. On the scrambler in your office."

Brain nodded and Monroe left. He noted the time on his watch, rose to his full height, and took two minutes to admire his wall-cased array of Third

Reich medals, then went into his office and answered the phone.

Leonard said, "You were busy? Next time, just call me back. I don't like to sit on my hands waiting on you. Take a minute to think about how much you're being paid. One item for now. I might have a man to replace Bobby O. He's got his own small bird and he checks out okay. No experience in the trade, but he's IFR, got eight thousand hours, and he can fly twins. This one claims he can cross up north with no hassle from law. Says he's connected. And he's hungry. Demanding big money, but he might be worth it. Check him out for yourself. Knock his price down if you can, but I want you to try using him. Start out with his own plane. Load him up both ways as soon as you can set it up. If it goes okay we can fix him up with a twin. We've been hit hard by the Mounties lately. We need to step up imports."

Brain pulled a clean legal pad out of his desk drawer and said, "I do not wait by the phone for your calls. I perform exceptionally valuable and unique services for you. Perhaps you should take a moment to ponder that. Give me the essentials on this pilot."

***

When his cell vibrated in his shirt pocket, John was in a grocery store, patiently pushing a cart for Hattie as she selected the items on her list.

The voice said, "We met at Mothers. You know who this is?"

It was Pitt Tobin. "Yes."

"Go to Morristown, Tennessee. Be there at ten tomorrow morning. Park someplace you can leave your ride for the rest of the day. Call the number I'll give you. You'll be picked up. You ready to copy the number?"

He gestured to Hattie for the ballpoint she was using, and wrote the number on his palm. Said, "I've got it."

"Okay. Now I don't know you and you don't know me, so you don't have any reason to contact me again."

***

He called Rader from his front porch that night after the old couple had gone to bed.

Rader said, "They're probably going to take you to the compound. Remember, we need the best idea of the layout you can manage. Room locations and sizes. How much security they've got. Number of people. What they look like. Names. Vehicles and plate numbers if you can remember them. What's said. Everything. As soon as you can after you come away from the place write it all down. Don't leave the smallest detail out. If they talk about a specific trip north, hold their feet to the fire for the money. You want cash in hundreds. If they talk a schedule, say you have to get with your man first. Try to get them talking as much as you can, but you say as little as possible. Call me as soon as you get clear and you've got everything written down. I don't care what time it is."

***

He told Hank he'd be gone all day flying, and left Maggie Valley in the Wrangler at six-thirty. It was only 75 miles to Morristown, and he made it in two hours, stopping for gas and a fast minimal breakfast. It was a city of maybe fifty thousand near

Cherokee Lake. He drove around for fifteen minutes, trying to push back a nagging sense of foreboding.

The city was prosperous and attractive, with a restored downtown. His map showed Panther Creek State Park at the southwest end of the long lake, a place he might have liked to explore under any normal circumstances. He parked among many other vehicles in the lot of the Lakeway Regional Hospital, where the Jeep would not become conspicuous even late into the night, and where other people tended to be preoccupied with their own serious problems. He walked the streets at a good pace for forty-five minutes, trying to clear his mind for whatever the day would bring, and stopped in Walters Park not far from the hospital. He took a seat on a bench under a tree near the entrance and waited. A young mother was reading a paperback on a blanket spread on the grass in the shade, her baby sleeping in a stroller. There were a few walkers. The day was heating up into the eighties.

At ten o'clock he opened his cell and punched in the number Tobin had given him. Taking the first absurdly simple but irreversible step that he knew could lead down a long dark path, he pressed the send button.

It rang once and the voice said, "Yeah. Talk to me."

"I was told to call this number. Hardin. I'm near the entrance to Walters Park."

"Stay right there. Look for a black GMC. Ten minutes. I'll pull to the curb and you get in the back."

The black SUV slid to the curb twelve minutes later and the rear door came open. He walked to it and got in. There was a man in the back. As soon as the door was closed the driver pulled away. Both men were in their late thirties. Tough and competent. The man in the back said, "I got to check you over, so just cooperate, okay?"

John was wearing jeans, a gray short-sleeved shirt, a ball cap, and his worn ropers. He lifted his arms and bent away from the seat back so the man could frisk him, paying particular attention to his pockets, his crotch, and his belt line all around. He said, "Take off your boots."

The man inspected the ropers inside and out, felt his socks, and gestured for him to put the boots back on.

John said, "Where are we going?"

"Not too far. Relax. You'll get a good lunch."

"Do you two have names?"

"Not today."

FOURTEEN

The narrow road threaded through forest for twenty miles from the last significant turnoff, with occasional glimpses of the Clinch River off to the left, before breaking out into the large clearing filled with meadow grass he'd seen from the air. The whole clearing was enclosed within a barb-wire-topped chain-link fence coated green so it was less obtrusive. The compound sat on a low hill at the center of the clearing. There were a few scattered trees.

They swung off the road onto a paved drive. Power and phone lines fed to a single pole and down inside a metal channel the length of the pole, into a green box, obviously running to the compound from there underground. There was a heavy ornate wrought-iron double-winged gate set between two stone pillars. A video camera was mounted atop the left pillar. The SUV driver stopped by a post topped by a box mounted window-high. He reached outside to slide a card into a recess in the box and the gates swung open. They rolled across a steel grating and followed the curves of the drive uphill. Motion outside caught John's eye. Two dark shapes came in fast from over a low rise and loped through the meadow grass a hundred feet out, matching the

SUV's pace. They looked like Rottweilers, and they posed a silent and deadly presence.

The drive was deeply ditched on both sides, and wound through a landscaped severe S curve that was probably intended to slow any approaching vehicle. A quarter mile up the drive, they came to another set of ornate gates set into a stuccoed masonry perimeter wall. There was a Y in the drive, and the left fork curved around to the side, a low sign by it saying SERVICE ENTRANCE. An effort had been made to soften the fortress effect of the wall with low landscaping and climbing ivy, but there were dull glints from at least one coiling strand of what looked like coated razor wire running along the top of the wall. The driver looked up at the security camera and spoke into a box mounted on a low pole just before the split of the Y.

The gates swung open, and they rolled into an oval-shaped slate-paved courtyard. A side drive led to a four-stall garage. There were three vehicles parked in line at the far side of the oval. The driver stopped behind the last one. John caught the Mississippi plate of the white Honda directly in front of them and memorized it.

The two men wore short-sleeved shirts loosely. Both had belt-line bulges under the shirts at their sides. Holstered hand guns. The front doors were made of heavy stacked beams hung on long bolted strap hinges. There was a spy hole in each door. One of the men spoke into a wall slot and a few seconds later the left door swung outward. The man who opened the door was short and wiry. Dressed in tight-fitting elastic black, he bore old facial scars and held himself like a fighter. After appraising John without expression he went back into the house.

His two escorts led him inside to a small anteroom. There was a large security keypad on one wall, much more complex than those he'd seen in private homes, with two long rows of steady green lights. About fifteen in each row.

The one who had searched him did so again, more thoroughly. The other one looked him over briefly, went out and came back with a neatly-folded stack. A plush towel, terrycloth robe, bathing suit, and leather sandals. He pointed to a door and said, "Bathroom. You and I will go in and you can change. Leave all your stuff on the shelf. I want you to step into the shower. Get wet all over and dry off. Put on the swim trunks. Then Dr. Ganz will see you out by the pool."

It was an effective way to make sure he was not concealing some kind of miniature bug, John supposed, and to go through his wallet.

Wearing the belted white robe, he followed one of the men into a large vaulted skylighted living area with grouped leather sectionals, a long padded bar, a cavernous fieldstone fireplace, oriental rugs on a gleaming hardwood floor. A man in casual dress, wearing thick glasses, was watching a big TV in one corner. The man glanced at him without interest. They went on through a dining area with a long mahogany table that would seat about thirty, and out through sliding glass doors onto a large multilevel deck that filled a huge landscaped rectangular interior courtyard. Ten sets of sliding doors were spaced out around the courtyard. There were half a dozen good sized trees, two fountains, profusions of flowers mixed in with trimmed greenery. Classical music flowed out of hidden speakers at low volume. A large kidney-shaped pool glowed an impossible blue at the center of the courtyard. There were five men seated at a small poolside table, and a thin, pale woman with long hair sat on the pool edge with her legs in the water. The woman looked at him briefly, with shallow curiosity. He could only see two of the men's faces well.

John's escort pointed at a larger corner table with a green canvas umbrella.

There was a tall man seated at the table, also dressed in a white terrycloth robe, holding himself erect, watching him impassively. When he got closer, John saw the eyes set deeply in the gaunt seamed face. Yellowish. Cold and emotionless, like those of a reptile.

The tall man said, "Mr. Hardin. I am Dr. Kurt Ganz." He pointed a long finger at a chair. "Lunch will be served soon. Would you like a drink?"

He sat and said, "No."

Ganz stared at him for fifteen seconds.

John said nothing. Letting his hands rest easy on the chair arms. The yellow eyes were penetrating. Unblinking. Motionless.

Ganz finally said, "Do you think I am a fool, Mr. Hardin?"

His heart seemed to trip over itself for several beats, but John forced a neutral expression, met the stare, and said, "A man who had this complex built, who commands these other men, who does what you do successfully, is not a fool."

"What do you believe I do?"

"I assume you run a competent smuggling operation. Because you're here. Not in jail. Or dead."

"And yet you have the temerity to demand one hundred thousand dollars for what merely amounts to a few hours of your time. Doing something at which you have no experience whatever."

"Eight thousand hours in the air is a lot of experience. In singles and twins. Exactly what you need, I'd think. Cargo is just weight to me, I don't care what it is, and with access to the right kind of information, a border is only a meaningless line on a map. If Bobby Ostrowski was flying for you when he hit a mountain, I'm guessing the cost of that lost load alone would have paid for a lot of guaranteed trips at my price."

"You're cavalier about this guarantee you offer, when the entire risk of loss would appear to be ours."

John concentrated on meeting the intensity of those feral eyes. "If this guarantee were to fall through I'd be risking a lot more, wouldn't I? How many years of my life?"

"Perhaps you would lose all of your remaining years, and in some most unpleasant manner. This source you claim to have. What position does he hold? With which branch of law enforcement? We must know more in order to gauge the quality of his information."

"No. For my source's protection and for mine. Either you want what we can offer, at our price, or you don't. If not, others will."

"You will not find another employer who can offer such steady work, prompt cash payments, security at both ends of the trips, and first-quality representation in the event of legal difficulties."

"I'll have to trust that all you're saying is true. And you'll have to trust what I'm saying."

"I propose a mutual trial, then. Within ten days. You will fly a quantity of merchandise north and exchange it for a quantity of different merchandise. What is the payload of your plane?"

"With full fuel, five hundred pounds, if the runways on both ends are at low elevations."

"For that weight we can pay fifty thousand dollars. No more. If this test is successful we might then explore a more ambitious arrangement. It is possible we can provide you with a twin-engine plane."

"No. My contact and I will need much more than that. He's taking a big risk and his information will be worth the cost."

"We could perhaps manage to pay seventy-five. Absolutely no more. In clean hundreds, immediately on completion of the flights. Explain to him that this is a test, of his information and of your competence."

"I'll have to talk with my contact."

"We require your answer right now. If you decline, we will simply rely on other resources. What is your decision?"

He had little choice if he was to keep contact. "All right. For the first trip only. A minimum of one hundred after that."

"You will take one of my men with you. An observer."

"That would reduce the payload by his weight."

"Perhaps you can reduce your fuel load and lighten the plane in other ways in order to compensate."

"I'll have to fly the border when and where my contact tells me. I'll have to talk with him."

"Yes. Then you will call your observer to confirm. He will provide numbers. Lunch will be served now. My assistant Monroe is an excellent cook. You will not be disappointed. Your observer is inside. The man with the glasses you passed a moment ago. He will join you at this table. Take some time after you eat to discuss arrangements with him. Swim for an hour, if you like. Then my men will drive you back to your vehicle. Now you will excuse me. I have matters to resolve." His face showed a trace of a smile but the eyes were cold. He stood, surveyed the courtyard, and went away into the building.

The man with the glasses came out and sat opposite him. Average height. Thinning brown hair cut short. Black jeans and a loose blue shirt. Did not offer his hand. Said, "You're John Hardin. A pilot. Mr. Ganz told me I'll be flying into Canada with you. I'll tell you where to land and I'll arrange the exchange of the loads."

"What's your name?" The glasses had darkened in the sunlight so he could not clearly see the man's eyes.

"Needham Ferko, with a K."

"Can you give me some idea where in Canada we're going?"

"New Brunswick. Within sixty miles of the border. I'm not supposed to tell you the exact location until we cross over. They'll have fuel for you where we land."

"We'll be going in from Maine, then."

"Yes."

"What do you weigh?"

"One seventy-three without clothes."

"Where do we pick up the load?"

"At a private grass strip. Not marked on any chart. On a farm within fifty miles of here. I'll give you coordinates by phone just before you take off from Asheville. We will be watching the area around the farm."

The wiry man who had met them at the front door came out onto the deck pushing a teak cart. He set out silverware and napkins, and served soup and sandwich plates and iced tea to John and Ferko, then set a table for the others. The food looked good, but he still had no appetite. The sandwiches were turkey with a sweet cranberry sauce on thick bread. John drank all the tea but ate only a quarter of the sandwich.

When Ferko had finished, John said, "How long have you been with this Ganz?"

"A few years."

"Nice place he's got here. What's the rest of it like?"

"Why?"

"Curious."

"Half a dozen buildings. All these rooms around the pool are for guests. They're real nice, like a five-star hotel. Some areas are off limits."

"How is he to work with?"

"The pay is good."

"I get the feeling he can be a hard man when he's mad."

"You don't want to cross him. And they call him Brain. So don't ever try to outsmart him. When you leave you'll find a piece of paper in your shirt pocket. Numbers where you can reach me. Check with your contact. Set it up as soon as you can and call me."

John nodded. Said, "That pool looks good. Think I'll try it."

Ferko, glancing at his plain Timex, said, "Just be ready to leave in forty minutes. You don't want to wear out your welcome." And he went back inside.

Walking to the pool, John smiled and raised a palm at the group of three men and the one pale thin woman at the other table. One of the men nodded back without smiling. The other two ignored him. The long-haired woman cocked her head and appraised him as he shed the robe and sandals. He kept smiling, memorizing facial features so he would be able to describe them well later. He wind-milled his arms to loosen up his shoulders, took four long fast strides out onto the springboard, bounced, and dove cleanly.

The same two hard men drove him back to Morristown late that afternoon. After they left him in the hospital parking lot he sat behind the wheel in the Wrangler and spent an hour with a pen and a pocket spiral pad, describing in detail everything and everyone he'd seen at the compound.

On the way back he stopped in Newport, Tennessee, at a steak house, and asked for a booth in a back corner where he could sit and think, realizing he was hungry, finding some relief from the stress

that had been building up in having got through the
initial contact with Ganz, and in actually having
something to do, regardless of what that was. At least
it gave him something to focus on. He ordered the
large house special sirloin. He devoured the meal and
lingered for a long time over coffee, reading back
over his notes and trying to sort out where to go from
here. He did not want to make the smuggling run, but
saw no real choice if he was to stay connected to
Ganz. So he began going over the trip.

Outside, he stood in the deeper shadows of a
tree skirted with landscaping bark mulch, already
feeling guilty of something, and called Rader. He
answered on the second ring, and John said, "I'm in
Tennessee. I have some details. The man wants me
to go on a trip as soon as possible."

"Where to?"

"New Brunswick."

"Meet me here at one tomorrow."

It was late when he drove up the steep incline
to Eaglenest Ridge and parked in the yard. He
thought the old couple would be in bed but Hank was
up. In his recliner, watching a movie. He thumbed
the mute when John walked in.

John forced a smile and said, "Must be a good
one to keep you up this late."

"There's one chunk of Hattie's banana bread
left that's been callin' to me. You run for the kitchen
right now, you might beat me to it."

"All yours. Ate heavy on the road."

"This here's a shooter set in Montana. An
older cowboy protects a woman and her son from an
outlaw and his sons. Charlton Heston's the good guy.
You know what it is?"

"Joan Hackett's the woman. Heston plays Will Penny, and that's the name of it. A good one. Don't let me interrupt."

Hank grinned, shook his head, and thumbed the sound back on.

***

In his rented apartment the next day Rader listened while John read the notes from his pad, then told him to go back over it all again, stopping him repeatedly to interject questions. And then a third time. Surprising himself, John remembered several additional details. Rader wanted a layout on a sheet of computer paper, and John drew it twice, refining it and labeling everything he'd seen.

John said, "He'll pay seventy-five thousand. Said the trip will be a test. I don't know what the loads are. I'm supposed to bring one of his men with me."

"You wouldn't be holding twenty-five back, would you?"

"No."

"You couldn't push the price up any more than that?"

"I tried. But I felt he was at his limit at seventy-five. I told him it would have to be a hundred after this."

Rader said, "Okay. You'll make the trip."

"So far I haven't broken any laws. If I do this there won't be any going back."

"There's no going back for you, anyway. Bring all the money here to me. I'll count it and log it in. Lock it in a safe place. That way I can explain you as a volunteer undercover informant if I have to. I'll tell them there wasn't time to go through channels. They won't like it, but it should take you off the hook. You can cross the border from northeastern Maine, anywhere between Calais and Presque Isle, any of the next four nights between five in the afternoon and five in the morning."

***

He stopped at an art and graphics supply store in Asheville and then went to the airport. Had the fuel truck come by to top off the tanks, and checked the plane over with extra care. The open T-hangar was on a back row, facing only a taxiway and woods beyond. Nobody was likely to come by on a weeknight. The hangar neighbors were all normally just occasional weekend flyers.

He unbolted the rear passenger seats, put them in one back corner of the hangar, and covered them with a tarp.

It was late in the afternoon when he swept an area of the concrete in the other back corner of the hangar clean. The Cessna's paint scheme was simple. Accent striping on the fuselage in grey and burgundy over a glossy overall off-white. The registration letters and numbers were painted on both sides of the fuselage in burgundy. He began by washing the registration areas with soap and water, scrubbing to remove any traces of wax. On the floor in the corner he unrolled two long sheets of white vinyl he'd had custom cut at the graphics supply store, each five feet long and fourteen inches high, and used strips of duct tape to hold them flat on the concrete. The glossy vinyl had a peel-off backing that exposed a layer of adhesive. It was used extensively to create displays and signage. He ran two strips of masking tape a foot apart the length of each white sheet as guide lines.

He chose a number that was easy, straight lines with no radii—N714HH—and laid it out on each sheet using two-and-a-half inch burgundy vinyl tape, cutting the ends cleanly with an Exacto knife and a steel ruler as a straight edge. He had to re-do the two fours before they looked right.

Using masking tape to hold it in place temporarily, he stretched one of the sheets over the real registration and stood back to appraise it while he rolled up the other sheet. The colors did not match precisely, but were close enough so when he actually stuck the fake numbers on later it should pass anything but a close inspection.

There was movement at the front of the hangar and he turned to see Kitty standing there with her fists on her hips. The soft sunset glow was highlighting her hair.

She said, "Nice job."

"Kitty—"

"I've been worried about you. Called your house and Hank said you'd probably be here. Thought I'd take a chance and run by. Sorry I surprised you. I walked over from the FBO. You should know I had a talk with Brandon Doyle. He didn't intend to tell me anything and it took a while, but he said you two had a nice little guy ride to Charlotte. Stopped at a bar called Mothers just for beer and pretzels. I know that place and it's a hangout for a motorcycle gang with an interesting reputation. I won't ask you what you're into because it's pretty obvious when I fit the pieces together. I hope they're paying you really well, because it will probably wind up costing you me, not to mention everything else you have."

"Kitty, I can't explain it all to you. I know what it looks like, but—"

She held up a palm. "No. No, don't bother. Just . . . don't. That's enough. It looks like we both need some distance. I don't want to hear anything from you right now. No more talk."

And she turned away.

He stepped quickly outside the hangar to go after her, his hand raised, but stopped himself. Feeling a hollow ache spreading inside him, he stood numbed, watching her walk angrily away from him.

He stayed there for long minutes after he could no longer see her.

Thinking, *better this way. She'll be out of it.*

FIFTEEN

By now Clint was so familiar with the tree line he could close his eyes and still see it. Among the hardwoods there was a grove of deep green pines rising tall from the tangled undergrowth, reminding him of a similar grove he'd spent solitary hours in as a boy, enjoying the scent of the thick bedding of needles and the sound the wind made high in the topmost sunlit branches, letting his imagination roam free, with the whole world out there ahead of him. Now it had all crushed down to this cell room and a yellow-eyed crazy man trying to peel his brain before ordering him killed.

At dusk the night before, a buck deer had ventured out into the strip of meadow grass beyond the fence to feed, only to tense at some potential threat that Clint could not see, maybe the roaming guard dogs, and bound back into the woods to disappear as though it had never been.

He spent hours at the tinted window, watching the play of light and shadow along the tree line, the clouds shepherded by the winds, and the slow wheeling sparks of starlight in the night.

It must be this way for old people, he thought. With time closing in on them, they must begin to see the world and others around them more clearly, and realize the value of every minute of life.

If he did not find some way out of this, his days and minutes were going to run out soon. He'd imagined—and discarded—a dozen plans. One thing was for sure. He would not be killed like a damned sheep. He would fight at the last with his hands and his elbows and his teeth, and he spent hours of each day doing stretches, push-ups, and sit ups, and jogging in place until his heart was racing and he was breathing deeply.

Whatever else was going to happen, they must not find out that Trey had done the killings. It was increasingly harder to avoid any hint of that in the long sessions of grilling. If they found out, they would go after Trey, and Rita might get in their way. And Ganz would kill him anyway, now, because of what he knew went on here.

The thought of Rita was a constant presence, except during the grilling sessions, when he would deliberately push her away so Ganz was less likely to zero in on his intense feelings for her. At such times the thoughts of being alone and isolated were so strong they threatened to suffocate him.

Low and off-key, he hummed Warren Zevon's *Carmelita,* which always made him think of Rita. He could lose himself daydreaming of her. The feel of the dark warm flesh sheathing her taut muscles. The flash in her eyes and the proud toss of her head when her volatile temper flared. Her knowing smile that could still make his heart race.

It was dark in the cell room now. He'd spent a long time at the window watching the sky-glow fade and a few stars emerge above the black tree line.

The wall switch no longer worked and for the past two nights the strong overhead light had kept going on and off by itself at seemingly random times. When his eyelids grew heavy and he nodded, he lay on the bed in the darkness and thumped the wall softly twice slowly, followed by a single quick knuckle rap. Then a thump and a rap. The letters G and N. *Good night*. After a few seconds he got the same quiet signal back. It wasn't much, but it was something. To know there was another prisoner here.

It had taken two nights of delivering the G and N, curled on his side facing the wall and shielding his fist beneath the blanket on the bed, before the other prisoner caught on and came back, just audibly, with the same signal, neither one of them doing any more that night. They would wait now until just before first light made a slightly-less-black rectangle of the heavily meshed and tinted window. They were developing at least part of an alphabet code.

The first signal, still in the dark of the morning, and if his overhead light was off, would be the G and two slow thumps for M. Good morning. Clint was using what he remembered of Morse Code, which he had memorized as a Boy Scout for a brief stint many years before. They had S and O, from the universal distress code of SOS—three raps, three thumps, three raps—which many people knew, especially if they'd had any experience around boats. They had an F, which was two raps, a thump, and a rap, first done on the vinyl tiled wood floor with his heel. And the C, initially coded out in darkness on the ceiling. Thump, rap, thump, rap. Seven letters in all. But only one of them a vowel. Tomorrow before dawn he might try tracing out an A shape, basically an inverted V, with regular thumps two feet apart, using a large expanse of the wall, followed by the code for it. Rap, thump. If that worked, they'd also soon have the I, then the E and the U. He couldn't remember the U code, but could make one up.

They would be able to talk some.

Maybe work together. Make a plan.

SIXTEEN

It was seventy-five miles from the Asheville airport to the coordinates of the pickup point, which Ferko had given him at the last minute over the phone. From there it was about eleven hundred statute miles to New Brunswick. Taking into account the predicted winds along the route, the whole trip one way, to roughly sixty miles beyond the central border of New Brunswick, would take nine hours, plus the time to land at the private strip and load up, and a refueling stop halfway. There was a front predicted to blow down over the whole of New England out of eastern Canada beginning in fourteen hours, bringing heavy rain, strong winds, and moderate turbulence. But if all went well he should be able to get into Canada, back out, and far enough south again to avoid the weather.

He took off just before dawn from Asheville without filing a flight plan, and flew up into a sun that broke over the horizon with the intensity of a welder's torch, so bright it made him squint behind his darkened amber sunglasses. Positioning the sun visor limited the glare and allowed him to make out strongly back-lighted hills and buildings throwing long shadows like accusing fingers toward him. He had told the old couple he'd be flying a pilot friend west to inspect an airplane the friend was considering buying, and would probably be gone two days. Hattie had insisted on packing a small cooler with lunch for two. He wore his ropers, jeans, and a long-sleeved shirt, and had stuffed his denim jacket under his seat.

As expected, the private strip was grassed and short, but the Cessna was equipped with a Horton short takeoff and landing, or STOL, kit. Transverse aluminum fins on the wings, together with flap and aileron gap seals to reduce drag and clean up the plane aerodynamically, lowered the stall speed, and resulted in somewhat shorter and slower takeoffs and landings, so this strip was no problem. There was a faded windsock on a short pole, twitching in a fitful breeze. A slow pass over the strip at fifty feet revealed no holes or soft spots, so he came back around and landed gently into the breeze on the main gear, using back pressure to hold the nose wheel out of the long grass until the plane had slowed almost to jogging speed.

He taxied to a plain low steel building and shut it down. Got out and looked around. It was deserted and quiet. He walked to the corner of the building and relieved himself. Drank half a bottle of water from the small cooler.

The vinyl fake registration number panels were rolled up behind the rear tail cone panel. He got them out and used masking tape at the top corners to hold them in place against the fuselage on both sides of the plane between the back of the wing and the tail, covering the real numbers. He lifted the panels to wet the fuselage surface with a water-detergent mixture from a two-liter soft drink bottle, reached under the panels to peel away the backing paper, adhered the panels in place with sweeps of his palms, and used a plastic squeegee to press out the water and smooth away air bubbles. The vinyl panels stuck nicely, covering his real numbers completely, and from a few feet away the fake numbers looked even better than he had hoped.

Thirty lengthy minutes later he heard a vehicle coming. A plain white Ford van pulled up near the plane. Ferko and another man got out. Neither spoke. John opened the passenger door on the Cessna and slid the front seat forward. He let them do the loading. Small bales of something wrapped tightly in heavy gray plastic and taped. The bales filled the rear of the plane to just above the lower edges of the windows. They spread a gray tarp over the load and tied it in place. The second man waved a hand and drove the van away. Ferko had a nylon overnight bag, which he wedged in behind the passenger seat. He climbed into the seat, slammed the light aluminum door hard, and fumbled for the safety belt.

John got in on the left and said, "Easy on that door. This isn't a pickup truck."

Ferko pushed his thick glasses back up on the bridge of his nose and said, "Get going. I don't want to sit anyplace longer than we have to." He was nervous and had a sour odor. His complexion was pasty white.

Making no move to start the plane, he passed a headset to Ferko. He pulled his own headset on and adjusted the mike. When Ferko had the headset figured out, John said, "Push the mike closer to your mouth. Did you weigh this load? It looks heavier than five hundred pounds."

"It's close enough. Don't worry about it."

"Have you flown in a light plane before?"

"Why?"

"It makes some people nervous. It can make some people sick. And you might want to tighten up on that belt."

"I'm not sick or nervous. Go."

The Cessna started easily and he taxied back to the far edge of the grass. Swung it into the wind and held the brakes while the engine built up to full power. Holding back pressure on the yoke to ease the weight on the nose wheel, he released the brakes and they bounded through the grass with the engine bellowing and the prop slapping the air, the tree line looming rapidly closer. Ferko had his right hand braced against the top edge of the panel and was peering intently ahead, a sheen of sweat on his forehead. John pulled the plane off and held the gear four feet above the grass in ground effect to let the airspeed climb, then purposely waited until the very last moment, much longer than was necessary, to lift them in a steep climb, the wheels clearing the tree tops by only a few feet.

Ferko closed his eyes and let out his breath. His hand was trembling slightly when he removed it from the panel top and tightened his safety belt.

"A few pounds more and we could have hit those trees," John said. "If you start feeling nauseated, I want to know right away."

Ferko wiped his forehead with his sleeve and looked out his side window. John wondered if he was going to be sick.

The morning was glowingly clear, with scattered tendrils of fog in low cool areas between the hills.   John chose a course northeastward to eventually pass over central Pennsylvania and New York State, and to skirt the congested airspace over the five-hundred-mile-long megacity formed by Washington, Baltimore, Philadelphia, New York, and Boston.   He did not want to talk with air traffic control anywhere along the route, and so was avoiding all the controlled airspace and military operations areas, or MOAs. It would add some miles and time to the flight, but the anonymity was worth it.

He kept up a continual scan for traffic. The radio was set to UNICOM, the universal channel used at most small uncontrolled airports.   He had the transponder on, set to 1200, the standard code for a VFR aircraft, so he would show up brightly on ground radars, but as just another innocent unidentified flight. They droned on a mile above the foothills of the Appalachian chain, up into western Virginia, the air smooth, the day warming.

Ferko had been quiet. He looked very nervous. Fidgeting and continually scanning out the windshield and his side window. Two hours after takeoff, he said something.   John pointed to the mike and Ferko repositioned it closer to his mouth and shouted, "I said, when are you going to stop?"

"Why?"   The man did not look good.   He shouted, "I need a bathroom. Now."

For the planned halfway fuel stop, John had chosen a small country airport north of Elmira, New York, where there was self-service fueling. He shook his head and consulted his *Flight Guide*. Found a small airport in rural West Virginia that looked good. It was only ten minutes away and not far off course.

And it had self-service pumps. He said, "Okay, but you'll have to wait."

"How *long*?"

"Under fifteen minutes."

The GPS took them to the airport with its single narrow runway. From five miles out John called them on UNICOM and a voice reported no traffic and gave the wind speed and direction. He entered the traffic pattern, landed, and taxied to the fuel pumps. Ferko grabbed his overnight bag and set off for the airport office building at a fast awkward jog.

Using the stepladder provided, John brought the tanks up to the three-quarter marks, paying with a credit card, which would leave a record, but was better than paying cash somewhere in person and risking some line man seeing the load in the plane and remembering them. And maybe noticing the faked numbers. Three-quarter tanks put him right at gross loading, figuring in Ferko's weight, his own, and the load at five hundred pounds. But the plane felt like it was over gross, so the load was probably heavier than five hundred. With this fueling he could now push on farther than the previously planned halfway stop. He consulted the sectional chart, but could find no suitable rural strip close along his route, so he decided to keep to the original plan and stop at the strip north of Elmira, anyway. If he filled the tanks there once again to the three-quarter marks, he should have a good margin to spare.

John waited in his seat. Ferko was gone for almost fifteen minutes. He came back looking much better. He had a pair of dark flip-up sunglasses hooked over his glasses. He replaced his overnight bag behind the seat, climbed in, and slammed the

door harder than before.   Pulled on the headset.
When John looked at him he cocked his head and
smiled.

John said, "That took a while."

"So?"

"You talk with anybody in there?"

"I know what I'm doing. This is wasting time.
Let's go."

The air began to cool as the day wore on and
they moved farther north. They passed over the long
corrugated hills of Pennsylvania and on into New
York State.

With one of the Finger Lakes showing in the
haze off to the northwest, John altered course slightly
eastward and landed at the planned fuel stop. He
wore his sunglasses and a ball cap and followed
Ferko into the airport office to use the rest room.

Ferko pointed at a pilot's lounge that had
sandwich and drink machines and said, "I'll get
something to eat while you gas up the plane."

John waved a hand at the woman behind the
service desk in the small office, and walked out to the
plane. Ferko had left his overnight bag in the back.
John glanced toward the airport office, got in, put the
bag on his lap and unzipped it. Used two fingers to
look inside, taking care not to disturb anything too
much. A medium weight jacket, a change of clothes,
a kit with toothbrush, toothpaste, mouthwash. A cell
phone with a similar-sized black box affixed to the
back of it with a pigtail plugged into the earphone
jack. Probably some kind of scrambler, making it too
bulky to carry in a pocket or on a belt clip. And a
worn leather case. He unzipped the case. Inside were
a hypodermic needle, a spoon, two butane lighters,

and a small plastic zip baggie containing a brownish crystalline substance. That explained why Ferko had looked so bad earlier, and so refreshed after he'd taken this bag into the restroom at the last stop. He put the leather case back, careful to position it where it had been, zipped up the overnight bag, and wedged it behind the seat.

When Ferko came out, taking thirsty pulls on a soft drink can, John was finishing up filling the tanks to the three-quarter marks. He spread a sectional map out on the elevator and motioned for Ferko to look at it. He said, "All right, where exactly do I cross the border, and where do I land over there?"

Ferko drained the drink and tossed the can into the grass behind the pumps. He did not look at the sectional. "You cross between Presque Isle and Mars Hill. When we get to the border I'll tell you where to land in New Brunswick."

"Why not tell me now?"

"I do what Dr. Ganz says. You better learn to do the same if you want to stay healthy. He probably doesn't trust you yet and didn't want you to have a chance to let the law or anybody else know about the pickup point. It would be the best place to stage a raid, to get both loads. Whatever. I don't know how he thinks and I don't really care. I just do like he says. The pay is good."

John folded the sectional so as to show only northeastern Maine and New Brunswick, and got out his handheld radio. The automated weather report had changed. The robotic synthesized voice said the front was moving faster than anticipated and would now blow through the whole area starting not long after sunset. Rainfall amounts would be heavy and there was a warning for dangerous turbulence starting at five thousand feet above sea level. The sky all along the northern horizon was already hazing and filling with thin cloud. He had planned to make one more stop at some unattended strip, preferably with a self-service pump, and wait for at least late dusk to make the crossing, but now that would be pushing the weather. Rader had said it would be safe to cross anytime tonight after five o'clock, which was about when they would reach the border if they took off right now. Fuel was going to be a close thing, but they were supposed to have a supply for him at the transfer point.

It was probably not a good idea to cross in daylight.

He thought a moment, studying the horizon. He said, as much to himself as to Ferko, "All right. We'll do it."

Before they left the small airport he made sure the transponder was off so their image on any inquisitive radar screens would be minimized.

The northernmost reaches of the Appalachians stretched ahead all the way into Canada. John flew over several ski areas, the mountain flanks veined by meandering trails. They pushed on over sprawling Moosehead Lake, and then passed just to the north of mile-high Mount Katahdin, the highest point in Maine, and the north end of the Appalachian Trail. He dropped down to less than a thousand feet above the mountains. There were patches of mild turbulence as the increasing headwind flowed down out of the cold northeast to ripple over the humps below. The sun was lowering behind them, making the plane's shadow bound and dance capriciously over the rugged wooded terrain ahead of them. The area was so desolate and thinly populated that John began to feel better. As they drew closer to the border he climbed back up again. For the crossing, he wanted to be at least a mile above Highway Eleven and US One beyond that, where his engine could not be easily heard and he would be only a dot in the sky.

Like most pilots, John often played a what-if game. *What if I blow a tire right now, just at touchdown? How will I handle that? What if I lose power on this takeoff? I'll lower the nose immediately to avoid stalling, then I'll have to land in the best possible place ahead, because there's not a prayer of turning back to the airport this low, so I'd better not let myself be tempted to try that. What if, right now while we're soaring along up here fat and happy above the wilds of Maine, the engine decides to go quiet and the prop abruptly solidifies out of its invisible powered disc? Where will I land?* For mile after mile of this wild country, there were very few places to set the plane down with some reasonable assurance of walking away uninjured. An occasional private grass airstrip was marked on the sectional. *Maybe that isolated farm right over there with a rough pasture cut out of the woods. That looks just barely possible.*

They passed over a narrow dirt road winding through the trees, but he knew there would not be enough clearance for the wings to attempt that. There were many lakes. Ditching close to a lake shore was a possibility, but this far north at any time of year the water would probably be cold enough to threaten crippling hypothermia within minutes. As a last resort, he could put it into the woods at just above a stall, trying to pass between two trees that would shear off the wings but would hopefully dissipate enough impact energy in the process to leave the cabin intact.

After dark, of course, especially without a moon, like tonight, even those risky options would be taken away. At times, faith in God and Cessna and your mechanic would have to suffice.

He was keeping the sectional open on his knee so he could recognize landmarks. Before long he passed over V-shaped Squapan Lake and Aroostook State Park, with Presque Isle a light patch off to the left. The forested mountains were somewhat lower here. He was automatically registering prominent features that would blaze a trail he could always follow on the return flight, a habit from his old training days when his instructor had made him fly a number of solo cross-countries by using landmarks and dead reckoning alone, with no help from any instruments other than the compass and directional gyro. He could still hear his instructor saying, "You should always know exactly where you are, and not just by the instruments, which can fail on you when you need them the most."

Down to the right there was one peculiar mountain. On the side of it was a large bald patch, a great up-thrust slab of rock that covered several acres, inclined like an incongruous patch on the mountain's flank. It made an excellent landmark.

The fuel gauges were showing less than one quarter, but he should have no more than eighty miles to go. It would be close. The headwind had robbed him of time and fuel. He pulled a hundred rpm off to conserve.

He said, "We're at the border now. That's US One below."

"You want a private strip twelve miles northeast of a small town called Jupiter." Ferko took a card out of his shirt pocket and passed it over. Said, "Here's the coordinates. These are new people we'll be meeting, amateurs, but it could turn into a good steady source for us."

John scrutinized the sky all around and found it empty, then made a quick estimate from the sectional. The destination looked to be only about forty miles in from the border. That was good. The whole horizon ahead now was turning very dark and the sun behind them was dimming as high cloud began to veil it. He punched the coordinates into the GPS. There were several jolts of turbulence that startled Ferko, and John could tell just by looking at the ground drifting past below that the wind was cutting even more sharply into their speed over the ground. He was also having to crab about ten degrees to hold course.

Within twenty miles they were flying through dirty wisps of cloud and the rough air was almost constant. He began a long shallow descent, scanning all around for a menacing black insect that would quickly swell into the shape of a patrol helicopter.

He saw the grass strip from six miles out and descended to about eight hundred feet above the ground. The needles on the tank gauges were bouncing off empty. The strip was aligned within twenty degrees of the wind, and three miles out he slowed to drop the flaps. He would not do an inspection pass, wanting to get it on the ground as soon as possible now,

Ferko tightened his seat belt. John glanced over to make sure he was well away from the dual controls. Passengers sometimes had a dangerous instinct to press on imaginary brakes during a final approach, inadvertently pushing on a rudder pedal and causing the plane to yaw. Ferko's eyes were wide behind his thick glasses, staring ahead at the short strip, and he was breathing fast, but he wasn't interfering with the controls on his side. To make sure, John said, "Keep your feet flat on the floor. Don't touch those pedals," but Ferko seemed not to have heard.

John drifted the Cessna in over the trees, slipped it to drop in fast, anticipating losing the headwind, keeping on low power as they descended below the tree line, and planted it, at just above a stall, gently on the grass, which dragged at the wheels and shortened the rollout. A vehicle flashed its lights ahead at an opening in the woods and he taxied there, bouncing over the grass tussocks, and shut it down.

Ferko took a deep breath and said, "You stay here for now," and got out to meet two nervous-looking younger men, probably in their mid-twenties, dressed in work clothes. They talked for a few minutes, then Ferko led them over to the plane. John got out into surprisingly cool air and looked up at the thickening clouds. To hurry the process, he helped the three men unload the Cessna and stack the bales in the back seat of a muddy black extended-cab truck. Ferko and the two men each carried a large, obviously weighty cheap brown suitcase to the plane. John tied the three case handles to the seat supports, spread the gray tarp over them, and tied it to the rear cargo hooks and the seat supports, to keep the suitcases from moving too much in the coming turbulence.

John asked one of the men, who was thin and bearded and wore a plaid flannel shirt, "What does the load weigh?"

In a heavy accent, he said, "Maybe 'bout twenty-one kilos."

Just over two hundred pounds, then, which at least solved the weight problem from here on out.

"You're supposed to have fuel for me. Avgas?"

"We could not get the aviation fuel. We have the very best car gas."

"How much?"

"Maybe 'bout eighty liters."

At just over a quart per liter, that was only twenty gallons. Not enough, and anger seethed under his skin. He had told Ferko to arrange for at least fifty gallons when he'd called to set up the takeoff time for the trip.

He said, "I need more than that. At least twice as much."

"It's a pretty good ways to get more. Forty kilometers."

John looked at the scudding clouds, noted the treetops thrashing in the breeze, and said, "Bring what you have."

He stood with one foot on the strut step and they passed a series of what looked to be three-gallon-sized cans up to him. Seven of them. He managed to pour about equal amounts into each of the two wing tanks. He took the time to catch a fuel sample in the test cup at each wing sump, looking for water. He found none, but that was no guarantee some was not still mixed in with the fuel but had not settled out yet.

He hoped there was no ethanol in it, which could damage engine seals.

He and Ferko climbed into the plane and he taxied back to the far edge of the rough, short strip. The tanks showed just over one quarter. He ran the engine up to full power, released the brakes, and they bounded over the tall grass. He hauled back on the yoke and the faithful Cessna leaped into the air. Above the tree line their ground speed slowed momentarily as the plane butted into the wind, then climbed away. John set a reciprocal course and reduced the power to conserve fuel. One good thing was the increasing quartering tailwind, adding to their ground speed. If he only had enough fuel, he could duck up into this soup and fly southwesterly on instruments until he broke out of the weather, but he would have to land for more fuel soon. He did not want to risk doing an instrument approach into a larger airport close to the border, where a fuel attendant would almost certainly notice the suspicious load in the back and might well spot the fake registration numbers on the fuselage. And he was not flying on a filed and approved instrument flight plan, anyway. That only left staying beneath the clouds and flying into Maine visually. There was a self-service strip near Saddleback Mountain, unattended this late in the day. It was the only one like it within range marked on his sectional, and there was not a published instrument approach for it. The sky was closing in so fast the cloud could soon reach all the way down to the mountaintops, leaving him in the soup with not enough fuel. Out of options. He would have to make for the unattended strip visually. And he would have to find it soon.

The setting sun was fully obscured ahead, and the whole sky was leaden and close. He leveled off a thousand feet above the ground, scud-running and bucketing along in streamers of cloud under the solid overcast. Despite the tailwind it seemed to take far too long to reach the border. It was a familiar feeling. Groping through thick cloud on an instrument approach to an unseen airport had a way of slowing time down.

Once, way back in his early student days, flying a tiny two-place Cessna One-fifty in dirty haze on a solo cross country, he had strained to make out landmarks for so long he began to convince himself the destination must be close by now, despite the actual time aloft, and had fitted landmarks into his self-deception. *That must be the water tower I'm looking for. That's the town over there. And there's what must be the bend in the river near the airport.* But there had been no airport in sight, and he had finally realized he still had twenty miles to go to the actual destination.

The fuel gauges were registering below the one-quarter marks. There was nothing but wilderness in sight.

Then, staring ahead through gathering mist, he could see sparse vehicle lights on two roads cutting across his flight path, flanking the St. John River that wound along the Canadian side of the border.

They were almost over the border, with a few widely-spaced vehicle lights inching along on US One, running parallel to the US side of the border. Only about forty miles to that unattended strip now.

He caught movement in his peripheral vision and snapped his head around to see a plane flying in formation a hundred feet off of his right wingtip.

He and Ferko both stared at it.

John recognized it as a Cessna 210, a larger and faster single-engine cousin of his own high-wing Cessna.

It was white, with red accent striping. The engine cowling bore a red maple leaf flag and the bold letters RCMP.

The Royal Canadian Mounted Police.

SEVENTEEN

John was monitoring the UNICOM frequency. It came alive with, "Cessna aircraft November Seven One Four Hotel Hotel. This is the R-C-M-P. Please acknowledge and follow us for landing."

Ferko glared at him and shouted, "What is *this*, Hardin? This is not supposed to be happening. What the hell *is this*?"

The voice demanded, "Cessna November Seven One Four Hotel Hotel. You are crossing the Canada-United States border. You are ordered to acknowledge immediately and follow us for landing."

Ferko shouted, "What are we going to do *now*?"

John turned down the radio and ignored Ferko. The Mounties would stick to him no matter where he flew now. All they had to do was radio the US border law, if they had not done so already, and a Blackhawk helicopter, equipped with excellent radar and infrared sensing, could be on him in no time. He was low on fuel. Trying to run was not an option. The ceiling was lowering and he had to descend even now to stay out of it.

He scanned the terrain all around and something off to the right and slightly behind the right wing caught his attention.

Ferko shouted louder, "God*damn* it, what are you going to *do*?"

He considered for a moment. A fragment of an account he'd read somewhere surfaced from his subconscious.

In order to establish an apparent course, he banked slightly left, the other Cessna matching him smoothly. He held to the new course for several seconds, looked all around again, trying to orient himself as well as possible and gauge distances, lowered the nose and firewalled the throttle to pick up airspeed, and hauled back on the yoke.

The plane responded with an abrupt steep climb. He caught a glimpse of the RCMP plane flashing past, overshooting, then they punched up into the overcast and were in solid dim grayness, the windshield running with moisture blown back into quick wild runnels by the prop. He immediately started a right ascending turn, fighting turbulence, keeping the power and the back pressure on, and automatically scanning the instruments now. The airspeed began to bleed off steadily as gravity fought the bellowing engine for control of the climbing plane.

Ferko was shouting, "*What? What? What?*"

The maneuver was a chandelle, used often in World War One when a biplane pilot wanted to shake a tailing fighter.

Timing would have to be just right.

As the airspeed indicator unwound to a few knots above the stall, he leveled out and reduced power. He had reversed direction. Hopefully, the RCMP plane would continue on the old course for a few minutes at least, watching for him to pop out of the overcast on something close to his original heading into the US, and they would not figure on him having doubled back. He gave it a full fifteen-second count and lowered the nose into a shallow descent. They broke out very low to the crumpled terrain, but close to where he'd wanted to be, and he racked it over into a left turn, coming around ninety degrees to fly north. The RCMP plane was not in sight. From this low he could see only darkening forest undulating away in all directions.

The flank of the mountain he'd chosen loomed ahead. He would have a crosswind on the approach, but at the last of it the mountain itself should shield him from most of the wind.

The steep bald rock slab slid into view as he half-circled around the mountain. The upper expanse of the rock was already blurred by the swirling, lowering overcast. Crabbing into the wind to hold the mountain centered, he reduced the power and set in ten degrees of flaps for some stability.

Ferko was becoming hysterical. John glanced at him briefly to make sure he was away from the controls. His eyes were white and bug-like behind the thick glasses. He screamed, "What are you doing *now*? Trying to land on that rock? Don't you see it's like a . . . like a goddamned *cliff*? It's way too steep. You're going to *kill* us. Don't try it. Turn away right now, do you *hear* me?" He scrabbled at his belt line, ripping his shirt, and came up with a compact black automatic. He brandished it and shouted, "Do you see this? Turn away right now."

John saw the gun in his peripheral vision but ignored it and concentrated ahead on the rock slab, studying it for fissures and uneven areas. There was one long deep crack slanting down across the lower left and the surface was rippled here and there. The near end of the expanse, he could see now, was broken jaggedly away from the rest of the formation, creating an undercut cliff at least two hundred feet high. Beyond the top lip of the cliff, the tilted slab looked a little better toward the right side and he adjusted his aim.

That account he'd read somewhere had told of an Alaskan bush pilot who had once landed with skis on a very steep snow-covered glacier in order to rescue two climbers. At the back of his mind he tried to recall details of that landing.

"Too late," he told Ferko. "You shoot and we both die. I'm going to land. Brace for it."

Ferko jammed his hand, which was still holding the gun, against the top of the panel, and stared ahead terrified as the up-sloping rock slab filled the windshield.

The trick was going to be matching his approach inclination precisely to the upslope of the rock, which looked to be thirty degrees or more from horizontal. He would, in effect, be landing in a slight climb, so would have to keep the power on throughout the touchdown. Too shallow an approach and they would slam into the rock face and bounce away like a toy hurled against a wall. Too steep an approach and the plane would not find purchase on the wet rock before simply stalling and tumbling away.

Best, then, to plant it firmly. Just not *too* firmly. He lowered the flaps another ten degrees and aimed for the center of the rock expanse, still holding the plane in a crab because of the strong crosswind.

There was no doubt this would be by far the most difficult landing he had ever attempted. It was next to impossible, in fact. Yet that bush pilot had managed something similar on a steep glacier, and on skis.

He began the climb so close to the rock face that Ferko was mewling something unintelligible now.

He pulled off a fraction of power, ready to retract the flaps to kill lift as soon as the wheels touched. At least the crosswind had eased, the mountain shielding the plane from it now.

It was too fast. And too shallow.

The gear hit hard and the Cessna rebounded from the rock, the stall warning horn blaring. He eased the power back a fraction and retracted the flaps and they hit hard again, but stuck, though just barely. He powered up the slope, the wings rocking, jouncing over the uneven surface, trying for the top so he would have as much downslope as possible later for a takeoff.

The speed bled off.

He could not simply stop, because the brakes, even locked up, would not likely hold the wheels from sliding and skidding back on the wet rock, so just as the Cessna lost momentum he pushed the right rudder pedal hard to swing them sideways to the slope. The plane stopped in a right-hand cant, held there precariously crossways to the incline solely by the side pressure on the tires.

That bush pilot had done a similar last-minute maneuver to hold his plane on the glacier.

He set the hand brake.

Pulled the mixture to kill the engine. Switched off the ignition. The prop solidified and the plane rocked, threatening to topple sideways. Bracing his right hand on the seat beside his thigh, he leaned left, trying to help the Cessna hold its perch. He peeled his cramping left hand from the yoke, flexed the fingers, and wiped the palm across his face. The adrenaline rush was making his hands unsteady now. He let his breathing and heart rate slow.

Ferko was leaning heavily against his door, his eyes closed, still stiff-arming the top of the instrument panel. He was trembling.

The gyroscope whined down into silence and everything became quiet and still.

After some seconds, Ferko shook his head, his eyes wide behind the glasses, and said absently, "That was not supposed to happen. The law showing up. You're supposed to be protected. By somebody inside, you said. When I tell him about this, Dr. Ganz will have us kill you."

"So you kill for him, too?"

"What?"

"Do you kill for him?"

"What are you talking about? Why did you do this? You could have killed *me*."

"Put the gun away. Unless you plan to shoot me and get out of here yourself."

Ferko looked at the gun as though he was just realizing he still held it, and awkwardly, because of his seat belt, replaced it in his concealed belt holster. He said, "You didn't answer me. Why did you land here?"

"Put yourself in that RCMP plane. What would you expect me to do? Doubling back and putting down here on this mountain would not appear to be an option, would it? I figure they'll search along a reasonable southward fan to either side of the last course I was holding when they lost sight of me, out to the limit of my possible fuel range. That's a vast area. The weather and the low altitude should have cloaked this landing from radar, and we're hidden from satellites. They'll put out an alert with the tail numbers they have. Before midnight they'll most likely figure I've landed someplace far south of here. Or crashed."

"What about your so-called protection?"

John thought, *that's a question I plan to ask Rader.*

He told Ferko, "It could have been a random, unscheduled flight. Not even associated with border patrolling. Or somebody on the ground saw us and called them. Maybe one of your friends back there turned us in to save his own neck. It doesn't matter right now. They haven't caught us yet."

As he spoke, the weak sky light faded further and grayness swirled down to envelop the plane, leaving them as isolated as if they had been on some remote dank island. The cockpit was growing colder, but Ferko had a sheen of perspiration on his forehead. His face was pasty and his eyes were nervous.

John said, "We've got a long time to wait here. This front should blow through in a few hours. With any kind of ceiling, I'll take off two hours before dawn. Gas up at a self-service field. Between now and then you're going to tell me all you know about Ganz and his operation."

Ferko squinted at him. He said, "What? Why should I tell you a goddamned thing?"

"Because you don't want the doctor to know you've got a serious drug habit. I looked in your bag."

Ferko darted a glance toward the back seat. Used a thumb to push his glasses back up on the bridge of his nose. He glared and said, "Who are you? What are you? Why do you want to know about Dr. Ganz?"

"Let's say I like to know who I'm working for. Don't worry about why. I already know a lot, so don't try to lie to me."

"What do you think you know?"

"I know he's been training his own elite group he calls the Satan's Wraiths. Like Hitler's Gestapo. You're one of them." He could tell by Ferko's startled eyes he'd hit a vein of truth, so he said, "You do his dirty work."

"How do you . . . no, that's not true."

John reached over the seats and pulled the overnight bag onto his lap. Ferko growled and made a grab for it but John pushed his trembling hand away and unzipped it. He pulled out the small leather case and shoved the overnight bag in the back. Holding the case out of Ferko's reach, he said, "This is what you want." He cracked the side window open and held the leather case outside. "I told you I know most of it. Another lie and I'll drop this out the window. Tell me the truth and you can have it."

Ferko started to go for his gun again, but stopped.

"Good thinking. Go ahead and take that gun out. Give it to me. You're not going to threaten me with it again on this flight. I'll just hold it for you."

There was such hatred in his eyes John knew the man would try for him as soon as he could. He shoved the case farther out the window and said, "Give me that gun. Now."

Ferko held out a hand and said, "NO. Don't. Don't. Okay, here." He ejected the magazine and fumbled it into a pocket. Passed the gun over. Said, "Okay, you hold it."

John took it with his free hand and slid it under his thigh. He said again, "You're one of the Wraiths."

Ferko wiped a hand over his face and nodded.

"You kill for Ganz."

Ferko was staring at the case. Shaking his head. But not saying no. He could not sit still. He pulled the seat belt away from his chest, trying to breathe more deeply. Unbuckled the belt and put a hand to his head, pressing his thumb and middle finger over his temples.

He glared at John, his eyes wild, and said, "You stupid fool. You don't know what he can do. How much power he has. He can get to anybody. Big people. Starting right now you're a walking dead man, and there won't be any place you can hide."

"Where will you hide if I tell him about your habit? You make some people just disappear. Here's the important one. If you even start to lie to me about it, I'll throw this outside. Ganz holds some people. Who is he holding right now?" It was pure bluff, but again he could tell from Ferko's eyes it had hit at least close.

Outside, a gust cleared away the mist to reveal the wet rock again. John waited.

Ferko was more agitated now. "I don't know. Okay, okay. For God's sake don't drop that. Two, I think. Men. I don't know names. Dr. Ganz talks to them. Studies them or something. I have nothing to do with that part of it. Monroe helps him with that.

He's into all that psychological stuff. He's smart, I told you."

"Is one of the men in his late twenties? Brown hair. Under six feet. Tattooed arms. Green eyes."

"Maybe."

"They're being held there at the compound?"

Ferko might have nodded. He looked sick.

"Where in the compound?"

He braced himself and opened his door, which swung out to bang against the stop mounted on the wing strut. "I've got to go to the bathroom."

"Don't get out—"

But Ferko was already climbing out, saying, "I can hold onto the wing strut. Then I need my case when I get back in. You don't give it to me I swear I will kill you, you hear me?"

The light was dim outside. Ferko gripped the seat belt strapping with his left hand until he could wrap his other arm around the strut. He fumbled at his belt buckle, swearing and sweating freely now. His pants slid down around his thighs.

Pulling on the strut was acting like a lever on the plane. The wings wobbled and John looked down out of his window to see the left wheel lift up from the rock. He opened his own door wide and leaned out to counterbalance but the wheel still hovered six inches above the rock. All that was holding them to the rock were the right tire and the nose tire. The left wheel began to rise even higher, the right wing lowering. When the wing tip lowered enough it would touch the rock and prevent a complete flip, but the nose wheel could lose its grip, and with only the right wheel holding them the plane could pivot on the wingtip and begin a slide down the rock, with John powerless to stop it, finally plunging off the cliff.

Ferko said, "*What? No . . .no . . . no.*" He stared up at the wing as it lowered slowly toward him. Realizing it was his own weight causing the imbalance, he unwrapped his arm and tried to hold the strut closer to the plane with his hands. Then he crouched and tried to transfer his grip to the right wheel fairing but the glossy painted surface was wet and his hands slipped, the nails scraping.

John had unbuckled his own seat belt, flung the case in back, and was reaching for him when he looked up at John with wild eyes, his feet skidding and his arms wind-milling. He made a frantic grab at the trailing edge of the wing, causing the plane to teeter even farther before settling back on all three wheels, then he slid away on the wet rock. He stayed upright at first, arms waving wildly, feet skidding jerkily, but his pants were hampering him and he fell heavily and rolled away down the rock, screaming with each rapid breath and scrabbling with his hands, his glasses knocked loose and skittering.

John caught a last glimpse of the wide terrified eyes.

The series of throat-ripping screams receded.

The frantic sounds abruptly changed in volume. Muffled and distant as he went over the two-hundred-foot undercut cliff at the lower end of the rock expanse. Becoming a thin continuous scream.

Echoing in the murk.

Then the inhuman sound was chopped off.

EIGHTEEN

During the night the gusty wind shifted enough to curl around the rock, buffeting the plane, rocking the wings, and there were periods of heavy rain that sounded like flung gravel pelting the aluminum. There were distant grumblings of echoing thunder. He tried to get some sleep, braced uncomfortably against his canted door with his safety belt tightened, and he must have dozed because it was after midnight when he looked at the luminous dial of his watch and realized the cabin was much colder.

To conserve battery power, he was not using the cabin lights. He reached under the seat in the enveloping darkness, pulled his denim jacket out, and put it on. Found the cooler by feel. Ate one of the sandwiches Hattie had made and drank half of his last bottle of water. Pulled up the jacket collar and tugged his ball cap tighter. Clamped his hands under his armpits, closed his eyes, and thought of the bike trip down the Blue Ridge that he and Kitty had shared so recently. Her amber eyes so full of intelligence and promise. The unique throaty timbre of her voice. Her uninhibited laughter. Their minimal two-person tent and her lithe dark body fitted against his in the humid night.

It seemed a long time ago. In another life.

He thought of her pained disappointment and disgust when she had found him making the fake numbers for the plane, and he felt a soul-deep ache of great loss.

By two in the morning the wind eased and the rain stopped, and in another hour and a half the grayness lifted to reveal rents in the overcast, letting enough starlight through so he could make out the tree line as a rough density a shade blacker than the surrounding night.

He gave it another interminable thirty minutes before switching on the cabin overhead light and studying the sectional chart briefly.

To the plane, he said, "Okay, let's get out of here, old girl."

After running through the pre-start checklist, he keyed the ignition, the prop swung around through two revolutions, the starter motor grinding at the flywheel ring gear, and the engine stuttered alive. He let it warm and the piston beats even out while he rehearsed the takeoff.

Taking a firm grip on the yoke with his left hand, he set in ten degrees of flaps for additional lift, held the brakes clamped with the toes of his boots pressing on the rudder pedals, released the hand brake, and pushed the throttle to the stop. He was rewarded with the full bellow of the powerful engine, the prop slapping the air smartly. He pulled on both the landing and taxi lights and the tree line leaped into garish focus. He eased off on the brakes and gave the yoke some back pressure, pushing right rudder to swing the plane around ninety degrees and head down the slope. The brilliant lights washed the rock face and shafted through lingering mist into the blackness down the mountain beyond the cliff, faintly lighting the forest trees far below. As soon as he was aligned he released the brakes, holding his hand firmly on the throttle as his instructor had taught him so many years ago, to prevent any chance of it slipping back and reducing engine power just as it was most needed during the takeoff. The clawing prop, with an assist from gravity, accelerated the plane quickly down the steep slope. Now he was grateful for the relatively low frictional drag of the wet rock.

He caught a fleeting glimpse of something glinting on the naked rock.

Ferko's glasses.

The engine stumbled, the prop slowing out of its smooth invisible disc to become a chattering, ineffective black blur.

The Cessna had two tanks, one in each wing, feeding fuel to the engine by gravity. He glanced down to make doubly sure the fuel control valve was in the BOTH position. There was a crossover tube between the tanks to help them feed evenly so as to maintain the lateral balance of the plane in flight, and he knew fuel from the left, upslope wing tank would have drained down into the right wing tank as the plane had sat canted sideways on the rock face, but that in itself should not have posed a problem, so long as he had either the RIGHT tank selected, or BOTH tanks. With very low fuel in the tanks it was possible that tilting the plane too far in any direction could un-port the fuel feed tube at the bottoms of the tanks, and so starve the engine, but the right tank, at least, should have sufficient fuel remaining to prevent that. Dirt or a trace of water in that Canadian auto fuel, then, probably. All of this flashed through his mind in the span of a second or two.

There was absolutely nothing he could do about it now. He was committed to taking off. Or to crashing into the trees below.

The rock was sliding back under his wheels, but too slowly. Keeping his hand on the throttle as the engine stumbled and coughed, he said tightly, "Come, on, girl. Come on. Come on."

Then the engine cleared its throat and roared back to full bellow and the rock flashed by, but he saw the ragged line of the cliff edge coming up rapidly, starkly outlined by the deep darkness of the woods below. He tested the yoke but she was not yet ready to fly, and the Cessna plunged off the cliff and dropped, the landing lights revealing a jumble of jagged rock fragments and tangled brush and trees speeding closer.

Free of the rock, the wings at last found purchase in the damp air, and he hauled back on the yoke as much as he dared, feeling for the first mild buffeting that would signal the impending stall.

He held his breath as the Cessna soared down and down to flatten out her dive just above the reaching trees.

And began to climb.

Breathing again, he banked right and lowered the nose to stay very low above the forest, on a heading that would take him to that unattended self-service strip near Saddleback Mountain.

By the time he spotted the strip at the edge of the forest, near a sleeping settlement, the fuel was so low he had stopped looking at the gauges. He floated it in over the trees and put it down on the unlighted

grass.   He taxied to the single avgas fuel pump,
hoping it would not be padlocked for the night.

It was not, and he paid by credit card and filled
both tanks to the lips. Working quickly, he stripped
off the fake numbers and stuffed the crumpled vinyl
panels under the tarp in the back.

He took off from the heavily-dewed grass into
the darkness, and banked onto a westerly course over
the Maine wilderness.

As he made the southwesterly course change
that would lead him down over the vast chain of
mountains in New Hampshire and Vermont and New
York State, first light was graying the long low cloud
streamers that were the remnants of the front.

The gun that Ferko had been carrying was a
black Glock, with the model number 27 stamped into
the slide. It was about six inches long and four inches
tall, probably designed mostly as a backup weapon.
He waited until he was over a large area of forest.
Ejected the magazine, cleared the chamber, and
disassembled the slide. He opened the side widow
and dropped the handful of parts out.

The countryside below spread out to display all
the varied evidences of man's efforts to rework and
shape the earth's surface to his own ends. Neat fields
in a variety of colors. Arteries of asphalt connecting
the collections of buildings named Greenville or
Springfield or Somethingdale and the much larger
spiked and spired cities that rose up way off on the
horizons in clusters here and there. And each of the
countless homes and buildings and crawling bug-like
vehicles represented another unique human story.
Spread out in all directions below, humanity in its
multiple thousands was going about the business of

life. The pain and despair and euphoria and hope and love and hate and striving.

For a time, at least, he could draw apart from it all and become a remote, aloof observer.

He stopped at small deserted self-service strip in Pennsylvania.   From vending machines under a shelter near the fuel pump, he bought a large bottle of water and some high-calorie junk food, and then got the cell phone out of Ferko's overnight bag, thought a moment, unplugged the piggybacked scrambler, and started calling the list of only seven numbers in the memory.   A man answered the first number with, "Yo, go ahead." He held the connection long enough so the voice said, "Yeah, dude, hello? You there? Talk to me, my man," but he did not recognize the voice, and broke the connection without speaking. Neither of the next two numbers was answered.

The next number drew, "Ferko. Where've you been? We've been waiting on your call, man. Did everything go okay?"

John said, "Not Ferko. I'm using his phone. I have the merchandise he and I went to get."

"Who is this?"

"I'll bring it to the place where I picked him up yesterday. Three hours from now." He thumbed the END button and turned it off.

Two hours and fifty minutes later, he came in three thousand feet above the strip in Alexander County, scrutinizing the landscape for five miles around the field. A plain white van was parked near the metal building, most likely the same one that had delivered the load he'd taken to Canada.

He spiraled down to land into a gusty breeze, taxied over to the van, and pulled the mixture knob to full lean, killing the engine.

The same man who had helped to load yesterday, the one who had answered the cell phone call, opened the passenger door and said, "Where the hell is Ferko?"

"Long story. I'll tell it all to Ganz later. Right now I want to get rid of what I'm carrying."

They unloaded the three heavy suitcases and closed them into the van. The man covered them with bags of fertilizer and mulch. There were rakes and shovels in side racks, coils of hose, two well-used string trimmers, and various other commercial yard maintenance gear cluttering the rear of the van. The man was dressed in dirty work clothes.

John said, "Where's my money?"

"I don't know anything about that."

"You can get in touch with the boss man in Tennessee?"

He nodded.

"Do that. Tell him I'll be there by five o'clock to get my money."

"He might not like that."

"Tell him."

***

He drove up to the outer fence gates of the compound in the Wrangler. He waved at the camera and thirty seconds later the gates swung open. The procedure was repeated at the compound wall gates, and he parked in the courtyard. The same two men who had searched him before met him at the double doors, ushered him into the anteroom, and did so again thoroughly. He was carrying Ferko's overnight bag and they went through it. One of them opened the small leather case and squinted at him with a raised eyebrow.

John said, "Put everything back like it was in that bag. I want Ganz to see it."

They made him wait for thirty minutes, then led him into the large office. Ganz was seated behind his desk, looking through a file folder. One of the men placed the overnight bag on a corner of the desk and stepped back. John sat in the chair facing the desk, noting that it was two inches lower than Ganz's chair, a subtle trick of the man's to assert dominance. The two men stood quietly flanking John's chair and a pace back. Ganz had not acknowledged him at all.

John propped his elbows on the chair arms and laced his fingers. In a low voice, he said, "Ferko is dead."

The yellow eyes flicked up to stare at him. He had a vision of turning around in tall grass to confront a stalking lion and looking into eyes like these. Ganz closed the file folder and pushed it away, the fierce eyes never leaving his, and said, "How?"

"Fell off a cliff. I had to land on an inclined granite-sided mountain in very bad weather. Before I could stop him, he got out to relieve himself, and slipped on the wet rock. There was a cliff at the lower end of the rock face. I'd say it was at least two hundred feet high, with broken rock at the bottom. He rolled over the edge. It was not a survivable fall. But he was no great loss."

The eyes became slitted and even more riveting, and color rose into the gaunt face. Ferko had been one of his best team leaders. Had carried out the

Battersea contract and five others with efficiency. "What did you say?"

John met the yellow stare and leaned forward six inches. One of the men rested a hand on his arm, but Ganz made a small motion with a long index finger and the hand was withdrawn.

John did not blink. "I said he was no great loss. Look in his overnight bag. In the small leather case."

Ganz pointed at the bag and one of the men unzipped it and began placing the items neatly on the large polished desk. When the leather case was lifted out, Ganz reached for it and opened it himself, inspected the contents, fingered the baggie of crystalline substance.

John said, "All those things will have his fingerprints on them. And there are seven numbers in the memory of his cell phone right there. I'd be willing to bet one of them was his supplier. You should tell your men to memorize all the numbers associated with your business and keep the chips wiped clean in their phones. The scrambler is a great idea, but a misplaced phone with a memory could be bad for you."

His men had, in fact, been instructed to memorize the important numbers. What angered Ganz more than losing a man was that he had not suspected anything amiss, and that Ferko's partner had made no report to him about Ferko's habit, though he must have known. That definitely called for serious consequences. He would consider arranging a session for the partner with Monroe as the disciplinarian.

John said, "But that's your business, not mine, which is only to make money doing what I can. Both loads have been delivered safely. You and I had an agreement in the amount of seventy-five thousand."

Ganz stood and tented the long fingers of both hands on the top of his desk. He stared down at John and said, "Relate for me, please, in detail, why you landed on that rock mountain, putting not only the unfortunate Mr. Ferko, but also a most valuable quantity of our goods, at risk?"

Like an aroused animal, Ganz was focused on him with implacable intensity. John sensed that this man would be able to pick up on a minute increase in his breathing or heart rate, or the slightest glistening of brow perspiration, or a flickering behind the eyes, or change in voice pitch, and know if he was lying.

He remembered Wasituna's counsel. *Anger can mask the true heart.*

It was not hard to summon the anger he needed. He raised his voice and stuck to the truths. "Ferko died of his own stupidity. He was a walking liability, and you saddled me with him. When I got to the exchange point those idiots only had twenty gallons of automotive gas for me. I needed at least twice that much aviation fuel. I couldn't fly far enough on the fuel I had and on instruments to make it to a suitable strip. So I had to fly visually, and the weather was turning to crap fast. I'm going to assume Ferko arranged that major blunder and not you. Now he's broken up at the bottom of a cliff. By the time anybody finds him, he'll just be gnawed bones. I did what you hired me for, what I had to do, and saved your goods. Now I want my money."

Ganz remained motionless, appraising him intently, for ten seconds. Then he gestured to one of the men, who left the room and came back carrying a black hard briefcase. He set it down beside John's chair. Ganz sat back down behind the desk. "Seven hundred and fifty hundreds. For two days' work." He resumed contemplating the pages in the file folder.

John stood with the briefcase and turned to go. When he reached the door, Ganz said, "Mr. Hardin."

He stopped and turned.

Without looking up, Ganz said, "You are hiding something. I will eventually find out what that is. But we will call again. Perhaps a twin-engine aircraft can be arranged for you."

John said, "Good. Any time. But it will cost you a lot more. And everybody's hiding something."

NINETEEN

"An RCMP Cessna intercepted me on my way back out, just over the border," John said. "You told me a crossing would be safe within twelve hours after five that afternoon."

They were in Nolan Rader's cheap rented apartment, seated across from each other at a rickety plastic dining table. The hard black briefcase with the money in it stood upright in one of the other chairs.

Rader shrugged and said, "I don't know. Maybe it was a last-minute unscheduled flight and they just happened to spot you. Pure coincidence, probably. Or somebody on the ground saw you and called it in. I never said chance and bad luck weren't going to be involved. It's done. You got back from it. I'll lock this money up for now. I'll assume it's really what you contracted for and it's all here." He pulled a yellow legal pad closer, flipped through his notes to a fresh page, and clicked a ballpoint. "Tell me everything about the trip. Where you landed. Who you saw. Names and descriptions. How you managed to shake that Mounties plane. Everything."

John ran through it all, from the pickup in Alexander County to the transfer in Canada and the landing on the mountain, Rader stopping him here and there to get clarification or more detail, making neat notes.

John said, "While we were stuck on that rock, I got some information out of Ferko. He was one of the Wraiths, and I think he killed for Ganz."

"Past tense?"

"He got out of the plane before I could stop him. The rock was steep and wet. He slid down it and went over a cliff."

Rader frowned. "Did you try to find him?"

"No. It wasn't survivable."

"How do you know?"

"The cliff edge was at least two hundred feet high, with broken rocks at the bottom. But from a height like that, the G force of the impact alone is lethal."

"What else did he tell you?"

"Ganz does hold some people."

Rader stared at him. "I knew it, dammit. I *knew* it. Did you ask him about Clint?"

"He didn't know any names and he wasn't definite when I gave him a description. But he did say that Ganz holds and studies people. Somebody named Monroe helps him. I think he's probably the smaller man I described earlier, the one who looks like an ex-fighter. It has something to do with psychological research, it sounded like. That would fit with my impression of Ganz. I don't think he's sane."

"Did he say these people are held at the compound?"

"When I asked him that, he didn't say they weren't. He wasn't in good shape."

"What else?"

"That was it. I delivered the Canadian load to the same man who first showed up with Ferko in that white Ford van with the plate number I just gave you. I don't know what either load was. I went to Ganz and got paid. I didn't notice anything new at the compound. But you should have enough to act now. Go get a warrant or whatever you need. Pull people together from all the enforcement alphabet groups. BATF, FBI, DEA, SWAT. Surprise Ganz and have a look. And I hope you can confiscate enough drugs somewhere in the organization to make up for what I delivered. Leave me out of it from now on. And what about that file you put together on me?"

Rader tapped the ballpoint on the pad, absently making a cluster of random dots, looking out the dirty window and thinking. "Okay, go home. Be normal for the next few days. But you're not necessarily out of it yet. Let me know if anybody from Ganz's bunch gets in touch with you. We'll talk later."

"Nothing has been normal since you showed up. But I hope you find your brother."

After John left, Rader snapped open the black case and riffled through the banded hundreds. He punched a number into his cell phone. When it was answered, he said, "Do you know who this is?"

"Yes."

Rader said, "Okay, I have the money."

***

In the dawning, John stood in his front yard, a hot cup of Hank's strong chicory coffee in his left hand. The atmosphere over the valley was clear and still. He could see the planet's very slightly curving satiny shadow on the sky along the western horizon, giving way to a liquid blue above, which brightened to a bold glow from the east as the earth rolled obediently toward its star.

Dew jeweled the grass and in the night had made delicate beadwork of a writing spider's web cast intricately between the porch rail and a boxwood bush. Songbirds were declaring themselves in the trees. Frogs and crickets chirped and buzzed in the undergrowth. It was going to be a fine day, and all nature was awakening to it.

His cell phone was in his right hand. He had twice flipped it open and thumbed her number, only to close it. She would be getting ready to leave for her shop. She liked to get there early, well before opening, to sort out paperwork, rearrange the items on display, dust and vacuum, and make phone calls.

Probably intending to ride her red Honda. She had a rusty twenty-five-year-old pickup, as well, but used it only when the weather really closed in or she needed to haul something. He could imagine her moving around in her small kitchen, making a fast but healthy breakfast and packing her lunch. Planning her day.

But he had a shadowy lingering sense that the business with Rader somehow was not over. For now, then, she was probably better off out of his life. Safer, certainly. He would have to try making repairs later.

If that was possible.

He thought, *have a good day, Kitty.*

He was unaccountably restless. Nerves strung taut. Thoughts half-formed and unfocused. He had several aerial photo jobs waiting, and an addition to a shed to build for a man, but could not concentrate on any of that. It all seemed remote and part of another life.

He opened the phone again and poked a different contact.

She answered, "Yes?"

He said, "Hello, Lisa. I thought Josh might like to work on his treehouse today, if that's okay with you."

"Well, surely it's okay. Lordy, you ought to see how that boy is when he knows you're coming. Hold on. I'll get him."

He heard her calling up the stairs, and half a minute later Josh came on with sleep in his voice. "Those things that were bothering you. In your business. Did you get them fixed?"

"Everything's a lot better now, Curly. Do you want to start on that treehouse today?"

"Really? I drew a picture of it for us. Aunt Lisa said we can use that old pile of wood in the barn. And whatever tools we want, as long as we put them back where we found them. Wait a minute. Aunt Lisa, will you help me make a lunch? Okay, we'll pack a lunch for us. I'll go out in the barn right now and get stuff ready."

"Grab some breakfast first. I'll see you in two hours."

He ate breakfast with the Gaskills and kissed the old woman on the cheek. He gathered up tools from his shed and stopped by a building supply store to load up the Wrangler.

The boy was delighted with the gift of a nylon tool pouch, held up on his slim hips over his frayed shorts by a Velcro belt. They sat at Lisa Crow's backyard picnic table and Josh spread out and smoothed the pencil drawing he'd done. It was well-proportioned and made sense. They discussed it with all the seriousness of builders preparing to erect a Hilton, then set about carrying some of the materials to the site in the woods on the hill, which took several trips.

The boy had dragged an old wooden ladder all the way up the hill from the barn and had propped it against the rough trunk of his chosen tree. They climbed it together for inspection, selected a spread of stout branches a third of the way up, and set about building a floor framework with two-by-fours. They did the measuring together but John did all of the cutting with his own sharp hand saw, and most of the nailing, letting the boy try it only when he had secure perches straddling the limbs, concentrating fiercely with perspiring furrowed brow and protruding tongue clamped between his teeth, using both hands and bending some of the nails before they were driven all the way home.

By mid-day they had a well-braced seven-by-eight-foot frame floored with scraps of sheathing plywood, with a square hole in the corner closest to the trunk that would serve as a hatchway with a hinged cover.

They sat on the edge of it side by side with their feet dangling, and shared the lunch that Lisa had packed. Peanut butter, sliced banana, and honey sandwiches on thick slices of homemade wheat bread, washed down with un-chlorinated cold water from the farm well that tasted better than any sugared soft drink. As he munched, cheeks pouched out, the boy kept looking at the platform, running a hand over the wood and peering down through the leaves, smiling and nodding. Swinging his feet. He was careful to put his refuse back into the cooler.

With dark eyes shining, he said, "It's going to be awesome. I like it."

"Maybe we can get the framing up for the walls today, but it will take another day or two after that to finish it. You'll probably want to work on it yourself, but wait until I can get back to help, okay? It's more fun doing it together."

"Okay."

They took a break to climb down and walk along a leafy path to the small stream that leaped and cavorted down the hill, making soothing, mesmerizing sounds like liquid crystal, to plunge over a mossy rock shelf into the pool they had made weeks earlier. The boy grinned and pointed and they squatted on their haunches to study two neat sets of cloven tracks in a muddy patch. At that moment John felt a strange sense of closeness to the boy's Indian heritage, which in these ancient mountains stretched across his mother's and his great-grandfather's generations and dimly back through countless others over at least ten thousand years, to the end of the last ice age. He closed his eyes and imagined the boy's mother, Valerie Lightfoot, in a slender traditional beaded dress, standing proudly a way off in the soft dappling forest shadows among her ancestors, watching her son explore the wonder of life.

He opened his eyes and resisted looking around into the forest, reluctant to disturb whatever spirits might hover there. In a low voice, he said, "I think the deer like your Little *Atagahi*. They probably think you belong to the *Anikawi* clan."

One of the seven ancient clans, the *Anikawi* had been the fleet-footed keepers of the deer, husbanding and protecting them, but also expertly hunting them, killing cleanly, not for sport, but for their much-needed flesh and skin and bones, which were put to good use and never wasted. The boy belonged, in fact, to the *Anitsiskwa* or bird clan, which probably once included the messengers who ran news to other tribes and between the *Tsalagi* villages scattered over parts of what had become eight states, just as the birds are messengers in many Cherokee legends.

The boy looked at him and said, "This is our lake. Yours and mine."

John nodded. "It could use some work. Do you want to make it a little deeper?"

They gathered more stones from up and down the stream bed and placed them carefully around the edges to deepen the pool, chinking the openings with gravel and mossy dirt, both becoming absorbed in the task. They were soon muddy to their wrists and the boy rested a moment on his crusted knees and inclined his head. "You're not like other grownups. I'm glad."

John realized his concerns had faded as he and the boy worked together on the deer pool. The water was clean and cold as it tumbled down the hill from some high spring or seep and dove into the pool, radiating ripples that caught glints of filtered sunlight. "Thanks, Curly."

The boy looked into the water that shivered the images of the stones lining the pool bottom, thinking deep thoughts. He said, "I have no mother or father, and I'm like Kitty. Not Indian and not white."

"But you're alive. That's the greatest gift any of us ever gets. A lot of young people in this world have no parents. Some of them let that poison their lives one way or another. Or use it as an excuse. I know you won't. You'll be strong. And most of the people in this country have mixed blood. You've got the chance to be the best of both. Indian and white. There's not another boy just like you on earth. You have a good heart. Your aunt and great-grandfather are proud of you. So am I."

The boy looked into the pool and nodded.

TWENTY

Nolan Rader waited in the darkness just after the last of the sunset glow had faded. He was in his Buick, parked behind a large abandoned greenhouse with half of its glass panes missing, outside Chattanooga near Chickamauga Lake. The man was late. He pushed the button on his watch to make the dial glow.

Sixteen minutes late.

He looked up to see a car coming around the derelict greenhouse, lighting the broken concrete of the lot and making the long grass growing up through the cracks send out moving shadows like bony claws. The car parked nose-to-nose with the Buick and the lights went off. Two men got out and Rader hit the button to unlock the doors. One man got in the front passenger seat and the other sat in back on the right side. The man in front held a flashlight shining downward to light the car interior dimly.

Rader nodded at the man in front and said, "Keller. I thought you were coming alone."

Keller said, "This is Engel. He's righteous. Knows all about it."

Rader twisted around to look in the back, and the man grinned and flashed a thumbs up. He looked nervous and his eyes held a strange glitter, as though he was high on something. Rader looked back at Keller. "Are you set up to do this thing? I have some information that should help us. How soon can you get the others?"

"Everything's ready, partner. I just need the front money to keep everybody happy. Where is it?"

Rader pulled out the ignition key ring and passed it to him. "It's in the trunk. Fifty thousand in hundreds. You'll get the rest when we're done."

Keller got out and went back to the trunk.

Rader tapped the fingers of his left hand on the wheel and said, "You're on the assault team, Engel?"

"Hey, you bet. Piece of cake. Piece of angel food cake, man."

Keller closed the trunk and put the briefcase in his car. Came back to sit in the Buick by Rader, smiling in the up-glow from the flashlight. He said, "That's great. All there, it looks like. You sure held up your end, man. Give you that. Little problem on my end, though."

"What is it?"

He laughed, looked back at Engel, and nodded. Stared Rader in the eyes and said, "There's no team. Just Engel here and me. That works out to twenty-five kay each, and we do thank you, man. Now we've got to go. Things to do. People to screw."

Rader was lunging for the Glock in the door pocket, but Engel already had his nine millimeter out and started shooting through the back of Rader's seat, down low, at butt level and working up, Rader's body slinging to the side. He fired nine rounds, the flashes lighting up the interior and the detonations very loud inside the Buick. The last slug bit a hole through the windshield.

Rader slumped forward to lean against the wheel and the horn blared out a long angry note. Keller grabbed him high on the shoulder and heaved him back into the corner formed by the seat and the door, to stop the horn. His hand came away slick with blood and he said, "Goddamn it. Somebody could have heard that." He wiped his hand on Rader's sleeve.

Engel said, "Okay, man, okay, let's dust on down the road."

They both got out. Keller hit the door lock button and slammed the passenger door. Engel got behind the wheel of their car. Keller opened their passenger door and took a long strip of blue sheet and a big screwdriver from the floor. Brought it back to the Buick, hurrying. Used the screwdriver to pop out the fuel fill door. Pried the neck filler flap back out of the way, stuffed the rag down into the tank to wet it and brought it out, reversed it, stuffed the other end into the filler pipe, and let half of it hang down outside the car. Lit the bottom of it with a butane lighter and ran for the car. Engel had it moving before Keller could close his door, and they squealed around the end of the greenhouse, the car leaning heavily, thumping and bouncing over a hole in the concrete and fishtailing out onto the road, a porch light coming on in a nearby shotgun house set back in a grove of trees.

Rader groaned, his whole back numb and the seat warmly wet under him, his right shoulder on fire, lights patterning at the backs of his eyes. He had not entirely trusted Keller, and so had worn his ballistic vest, which had stopped most of the slugs, though each impact had slammed him like a hammer blow, but he knew he was hit somewhere down low and also through the shoulder muscle close to his neck. His right arm did not want to work.

He groaned again and became aware of a flickering in the night. Right in front of his face. He moved his head carefully and in the outside rearview mirror saw the flames licking at the gas tank filler and it hardened up his brain enough so he scrabbled for the door handle, but could not find it.

He managed to move his upper body two inches over to the right, into a world of increasing, blinding pain, got a weak grip on the door handle, and pulled. It did nothing. He felt for the door lock button. Pushed the window button instead and it slid down. Now he could hear the whisperings of the fire licking at the paint. He found the door lock button and all the locks clicked loose. Located the door lever again and pulled. His weight sprang the door open and he fell out onto the concrete, trying to tuck in his head, but he banged it numbly, making everything go gray. He tried to push the car away with his right foot, and clawed at the concrete with his left hand, the glass panes and broken shards like fangs in the greenhouse reflecting the fire merrily.

He managed to gain an agonizing thirty feet of separation before the tank went up, bouncing the Buick off of the concrete and smashing more of the glass panes. To a startled eighteen-wheel truck driver passing by out on the road, it looked like a huge, terribly-beautiful blossom from Hell was rising up out of the overgrown dead greenhouse.

***

John swam up through pressing darkness to hear the phone ringing out in the living area. He groped for the bedside light and saw the clock reading three-twenty. He sat up and pulled on his jeans, knowing that good phone calls do not come in the small quiet hours of the night. He had set the phone ringer loud so the old couple would hear it, and Hank, looking groggy in his baggy pajamas, met him out by the desk. John beat him to the handset.

A woman's voice said, "Yes, is this Mr. John Hardin?"

"It is."

"This is Memorial Hospital in Chattanooga. We have a man named Nolan Rader in critical condition. He insists on seeing you."

"What happened?"

"We're not sure. The police are now trying to determine that. His injuries are extensive, I'm afraid. He came through surgery, but he's still in very serious condition. He's refusing any further sedation. Is it possible for you to come here?"

It was a three-hour drive at the posted limits. He could make it in half that time in the plane, but then there would be the added drive time to the Asheville airport, plus the time to find a ride from the airport to the hospital at the other end. It was early enough to avoid the morning traffic crush, and he could push it on the deserted roads. He said, "Yes. I'll be there inside three hours."

"Just ask for directions at reception. They'll be expecting you."

Hank said, "What's up?"

"A friend over in Tennessee was in an accident. He's asking for me. I'll call you later."

He dressed while Hank made coffee and two ham sandwiches for him, and he did the drive in two and a half hours.

They had Rader in one of the instrumented bays in postoperative care, in a chrome-railed bed, the covering sheet tented up away from his body, his head elevated slightly on a pillow. There were side walls on the bay for some privacy, but the front was simply screened from the wide common hallway with fabric for ready access. He was hooked to the monitors and a drip fed colorless liquid into a vein. He was extensively bandaged and his eyes were set deeply in bruised waxy flesh. His eyelids were drooping and he was obviously fighting to keep them open.

Rader looked at the nurse who had escorted John and in a low graveled voice said, "Get out."

She inspected John sternly and said, "Only for a few minutes, then. He's very weak." She checked the IV and the instruments and left, drawing the curtain closed.

John leaned close and said, "What happened?"

"Fool. I was a fool. Thought . . . mercenaries. Took it. Left me for . . . dead."

"Who took what?"

"Keller. Engle. Money."

John listened for anyone coming. "The money I left with you?" Then he understood. "You were going to pay them to do what? Raid the compound?"

He coughed weakly. "Yes."

"But why? Why not go in there with your own men?"

He closed his eyes and John thought he'd passed out, but he struggled to stay awake. "Fired. Fired me. You . . ."

He drifted away again.

He was not with the BATF, then. There had probably been no special contact in the Joint Border Task Force. He had only wanted the money to finance storming the compound.

John said, "Rader. Tell me about the men. Keller and Engel. Rader?"

Rader once more floated up out of the shadows that were trying to enfold him and his eyes became fever bright. He stared at John. "You. Get him out of there. You . . . only one now. No time. Tell me."

"Rader, I can't do anything more. I—"

"*Tell* me."

John inhaled deeply and blew it out. "Okay. I'll see what I can do."

Rader held the stare for a moment but his eyes lost their intensity and his lids drooped and closed. His breathing was very shallow.

John leaned closer and said, "Rader. The file on me. Where is it?"

The nurse rattled the curtain aside and swept in. Checked everything efficiently, saying, "I'm afraid you'll have to leave now, please, sir. He's sleeping, and rest is what he needs. You can wait out in reception if you'd like."

From the central desk on the floor he got the name of Rader's attending physician. The desk nurse picked up her phone and said, "If you'll wait here for a few minutes I think I can catch her."

Outside the postoperative area a young female doctor named Banks checked her watch and said, "I'm sorry, are you a family member?"

"A friend."

She looked at her clipboard. Flipped two pages back. "Mr. Rader's condition is guarded, verging on critical. He came through surgery to partially repair damage caused by two gunshot wounds, one bullet entering through the right kidney, grazing the spine, and lodging in the lower abdomen, the other fracturing the left collarbone and exiting. The internal damage is extensive. He was wearing a protective vest, which apparently stopped seven more bullets that impacted along his back. In addition he has second- and third-degree burns, worst on the backs of his legs. He has lost a lot of blood. One of our concerns, of course, is infection, as always with burns, but especially in his weakened condition. He's stable for the moment and everything possible is being done." She glanced at her watch again. "You'll have to excuse me now. If you'll leave your number at reception, someone will get in touch if there's any change in his condition." She gave him a distracted sympathetic smile and walked away.

Two fit, sport-coated men met him in the reception area. Both middle aged and competent-looking. One introduced himself as Grimes, an investigator for the Sheriff's department. The other was Peterson with the FBI. Both flashed their badges and Peterson said, "Mr. Hardin. Let's sit over there in the corner. We have some questions about Mr. Rader, if you don't mind."

He should have been prepared for this. He had noticed the men looking at him when he'd arrived, and had suspected they were law, but had promptly forgotten them when he'd seen Rader. There was no time to concoct an elaborate story. Something simple and close to the truth would be best. Something with no discernable cracks they could probe. He said, "Sure. I'll help any way I can, but I don't really know much about this. What happened?"

Neither man spoke. They bracketed him. Grimes gestured toward the corner, away from the few other people in the large room, and guided him with a touch on his upper arm.

They sat at a round table. Peterson stood a slim digital recorder up in front of John and said, "Let's start with your information. Full name, age, address, phones, what you do for a living." Both men were relaxed except for their eyes, which were focused intently on him.

John told them, and asked again, "Do you know what happened?"

Grimes said, "We were hoping you could help us out with that. What's your relationship to Mr. Rader?"

"A friend."

Peterson said, "You must be a close friend. His doctor only let us in with him for five minutes, and that wasn't any help. He was barely coherent. Wanted the doctor to kick us out. Wouldn't answer any questions. He insisted on seeing you, though, and even refused any further sedation until he could, although he's apparently in pretty severe pain. Can you explain why he would act that way?"

"I don't know. He wasn't making any sense, and then he fell asleep. His nurse asked me to leave."

Grimes said, "So fill us in on this friendship."

John shrugged. "One of those things. We met in Vancouver a few years back, out running in a park. I was flying one charter or another then. We hit it off. Sat on a bench and had a long conversation about politics, sports, stuff. He told me he was working with the government. Something in enforcement. We exchanged phone numbers. Promised to look each other up some day. He called recently and said he was staying in Asheville for a while. We got together for some conversation. That's about it."

Peterson said, "That doesn't explain why he was so insistent about seeing you, in his condition."

"You said it yourself. He's barely coherent. Not making sense. Maybe he doesn't have any family close by and I just came to mind. Who knows?"

Grimes said, "He was wearing a protective vest and we'd like to know why. Parked out in the country behind an abandoned greenhouse. Do you have any idea who wanted him so dead they shot him nine times in the back and then tried to incinerate him? His doctor says if a passing truck driver hadn't stopped and administered some fast first aid, he would have bled out before an ambulance got there."

"None. A robbery, maybe? Revenge for fooling with somebody's wife? You never know what goes on in people's private lives these days. And we all know there are a lot of crazies out there."

They were skeptical. Sensing something hidden beneath the surface. For fifteen minutes they asked the same questions in various forms, probing and sniffing, but John gave them no more, only repeating what he'd already told them, and finally saying, "I'm sorry, but I don't get it. Why are you grilling me about this?"

Peterson said, "Okay. Enough for now. When they put him in a regular room, we'll have a guard posted outside. In three shifts. Somebody might want to finish the job on him. We'll let them know you can see him, with some ID. We'll probably be in touch again when we learn more. If he tells you anything, or if you remember something else, even if it seems insignificant—something he said or hinted at, some impression you had—we'd appreciate you getting in touch with one of us right away."

They left their cards with him and went to the reception desk.

John found the hospital cafeteria, ordered coffee and sweet rolls, and took a newspaper to a back booth to wait and think. He needed to see Rader again for any more information he might have about Brain, and to find out where the file on himself was.

He gave it two hours, then went back to the surgery recovery wing. The desk nurse said, "I'm sorry, but your friend developed complications. They had to rush him back into surgery. If you'll have a seat over there, I'll let you know as soon as we find out anything more."

Within another hour, the nurse took a call, glanced at John, her forehead furrowed, and came over to sit beside him. She said, "The attending physician will tell you more, but I'm afraid Mr. Rader did not make it through the procedure. I'm really sorry."

Her name tag said Anne. He mouthed a few appropriate expressions of loss, thanked her sincerely, and walked out, avoiding the reception room and leaving by another exit, running out to the Jeep. He made a quick stop at a convenience store for fuel and a pair of cheap driving gloves, and pushed five and ten miles an hour over the limits to Asheville.

Circling the block where Rader had rented the apartment, he looked for anything remotely out of place. It was a shabby brooding neighborhood with several blank-eyed peeling houses that had overgrown yards and piles of trash on the sagging porches, and he saw only an elderly man walking a nervous quick-stepping mop dog.

He parked in one of the many empty curb slots within sight of the run-down duplexed apartment house, aimed in the opposite direction. Pulled on an old baseball cap. Took a flat screwdriver and a pair of vise-grips out of the small tool bag under the back seat, and slipped them into the rear pocket of his jeans, covering them with his shirt tails. He stuffed the gloves in the front of his jeans behind his belt buckle. Walking to the house, he kept his head down, looking at the sidewalk. A man in deep thought. Avoiding looking around like a prowling thief, trying to take in as much as possible in only his peripheral vision.

If anybody was in the adjacent apartment, he would have to come back later. He walked up onto the front porch, stood in front of Rader's front door, and made a show of checking his pockets twice and shaking his head. He moved to the adjacent front door and knocked, looking at his watch impatiently. It did not feel like anybody was in the neighboring apartment, but he needed to make sure. He had a story ready. The friend of his who lived next door had asked him to stop by as a favor and pick up something from the apartment, but then he'd gone and forgotten the spare key. He was just wanting the neighbor to know he wasn't trying to rob the place or anything.

He waited two minutes and knocked again. Satisfied nobody was home, he went to Rader's front door and patted his pockets some more. To anybody watching from a nearby house, he hoped he looked like the legitimate tenant who had simply lost his keys. This was not a neighborhood where people were likely to pay much attention to who their neighbors actually were. Moving briskly, again trying to look like he belonged here, he went around to the back of the house. The property had a rotting privacy fence enclosing the scrap of rear yard. Good.

The two apartment doors were side-by-side under an overhang that partially protected a common deck. There had once been a petition nailed to the back outside wall to create separate deck areas, but it was missing. He had a choice of breaking a pane of glass in the door or trying to pry it open at the doorknob lock using the screwdriver. Either would make noise, but prying could take longer. He put on the driving gloves.

There was a pile of stuff up close to the house. Two paint cans and a stiff brush. A carton with a dirty paint-spotted sheet wadded up inside. He held the folded sheet over the door to muffle the noise and used the vise-grips to strike once hard through the sheet, breaking out a pane. Ran the screwdriver around the edges to clear out pieces. Reached inside and unlocked and unchained it.

He spent twenty minutes quickly but thoroughly going through the place. A thick manila envelope under the mattress contained information Rader had put together on the Satan's Ghosts and on Brain and his compound. There were eight by ten prints of the aerial photos John had shot, marked up with black lines and arrows, and a spiral pad full of neat hand-written notes. A silver laptop was in a nylon case on the top closet shelf under a folded blanket, with three cased CDs. A plastic freezer bag holding banded packs of hundreds was duct-taped to the back of the toilet water tank. He gathered all these items up on the kitchen table.

He had found no hint of a file on himself, and had not really expected to. Rader had said, "It's locked away, to be opened only in the event of my death." So it could be with Rader's lawyer or a family member. His only hope was to somehow get his hands on it before the law did. Maybe Clint Rader could help locate it, but first he would have to be freed. If he even was being held at the compound. Still. And how much time did he have left before the probate system chewed through the routine paperwork and the damning file would come to light?

He was in the living room, lifting the sofa to check underneath it, when two car doors slammed out front. He darted to the window and with one finger pried the slatted blind apart just enough to see out. A man and a woman were coming up the walk. The woman appeared faded and tired and was wearing too much makeup. She was looking the house over and seemed to fix on the slit he was making in the blind. He froze, knowing any movement would betray him. Her eyes moved on. The man was smiling and talking fast, concentrating only on the woman. He stumbled on the top step and laughed. Fumbled to unlock the door.

If they were moving all the way back to the kitchen in the other apartment, he had only seconds to get out the back way without being seen. He ran for the rear of the apartment, pausing to strip a towel from the bar in the bathroom. He grabbed the carton from the deck and packed the items inside, covering them with the towel. Eased the door closed, took off the gloves and stuffed them in the box, and went quickly down the back steps and around the house. There were no shouts behind him.

If they were in the front of the apartment, they still might be able to see him coming around from the side of the house. He took a breath and kept his eyes straight ahead, carrying the carton casually under his arm. At an unhurried pace, he walked out to the street. Moved past the house and down the sidewalk to the Wrangler.

He put the carton on the passenger seat and drove away, resisting the clamoring urge to speed.

TWENTY-ONE

A gradual drop in temperature and a burst of harsh rapid blinking of the overhead light dragged Clint Rader up from a feverish dream of trying to run out of a shadowed swamp in thick clinging ooze.

The light stayed on, and a few minutes later the door opened. Monroe came into the room and Ganz stood in the doorway. Rader, in a fresh blue jump suit, sat up on the bed.

The tall Ganz said, "Most clever of you. To develop a knocking code. Based on Morse Code. What did you intend to do with it? It is, after all, an exercise in futility. An empty hope. But I thought you might like to actually meet your fellow subject." He gestured, and Monroe moved in to zip tie his wrists, this time behind his back, and check the security of the chain hobble. Monroe urged him up with a strong hand behind his upper arm, and pushed him toward the hallway.

They filed into the adjacent cell room, which was an identical mirror image to Rader's room.

The overhead light was blinking at about two flashes a second, giving the room an atmosphere of jerky unreality.

A man was seated naked on the bed, his shadow pulsing against the wall. His arms were zip tied in front of him and he had a chain hobble at his ankles. He was covering himself with his hands. A tight band of silver duct tape sealed his mouth. His eyes followed Ganz with hatred. He was fit, in his forties. Clean shaven but with long slightly graying hair. An area two inches square above his left nipple looked like it had been badly burned. It was raw, smeared with some kind of ointment. He focused on Clint, blinked, and frowned. Then there was recognition in his eyes. And pleading.

Clint nodded to him.

Ganz looked at the man and said, "Subject seven." He gestured at Clint and said, "Meet subject eight. Your attempt at communicating must be cut short, I'm afraid, though it might have been of some interest to watch it develop." He looked at Clint. "You see, subject seven once worked with us, but he botched an assignment badly, putting us in danger of exposure. That could not be tolerated, of course. Further, he has refused to cooperate fully in my research, so we are advancing his termination date."

There was deep fear in the man's eyes now. He stood awkwardly, and took two shuffling steps backward toward the window, still trying to cover himself.

Ganz said, "Subject seven, we have learned, has a deep-seated abhorrence of choking, the result of a near-death boyhood experience." He nodded at Monroe.

The man started shaking his head, terror blooming now behind his eyes. Monroe brought a two-foot length of thin nylon cord out of his pocket.

There were small wooden toggles at each end. He whipped it taut between his fists and the man began to tremble all over. He put his hands out in front of him to ward off Monroe, still shaking his head. Pleading now with his eyes. Monroe easily batted the hands away and, moving with efficient cat-like speed, eerily strobe-frozen in fractions of time, got behind the man, whipped the garrote over his head, crossed it behind his neck, and cut off his air. The man's face went red and his wild, now insane eyes bulged. He flailed backward with his tied hands, but Monroe held his own head tucked in so the man's frantic blows were ineffective. One of his legs was twitching, thumping the heel against the floor.

Clint stood dazed, his heart racing, his breathing rapid and shallow, unable to look away. The horror of it was made even worse by the quiet sounds in the room. Only the shuffling of the struggle and the steady whispering of the ventilation system. He became aware that Ganz was watching him and not the dying man.

The man's struggles became weaker as the seconds dragged out interminably. His fingers clawed and scratched at his throat, drawing blood, trying to dig at the cord, his chest convulsing, his face purplish red, his eyes staring into some unholy void. Clint realized he was hoping it would mercifully end.

The man finally sagged to the floor but Monroe kept the pressure on, the cord biting deeply into the swollen neck, the eyes protruding, until the hands flopped away and he was still.

Ganz inclined his head and said, "You see how simple it was. How hopeless it was for him in the end. What have you learned from this? You may answer."

Clint looked into the yellow eyes that were flashing in the strong light, tried to stand up to the intensity, but shrank away. Tried to swallow, but his throat was dry.

They took him back to his cell room.

Before he closed and dead-bolted the door, Ganz said, "Our morning session should be especially interesting. I will expect your best cooperation. You still have sixteen days left, and I know you will not want me to advance your time."

Clint Rader paced like a caged animal. Back and forth. Ceaselessly.

Far down along the blind-cornered corridors of the hours behind midnight.

TWENTY-TWO

Rita Flores looked out at him over the front door chain and through the screening of the storm door with apprehension and distrust in her eyes. Her face was drawn and there were grey smudges under her eyes.

She looked haunted.

It was an old but neat clapboarded house with a front porch and tended window boxes in a crowded row of nearly identical modest houses in Gastonia, west of Charlotte. He had found the address in Rader's extensive notes.

He smiled and said, "Hello, Rita. I'm John Hardin. I've been helping Nolan Rader. I understand you and his brother are close." Careful to use the present tense.

She darted a glance back into the house and said in a low voice, "What do you want?"

"I want to find Clint Rader."

"You are with the police?"

"No. I'm a friend. Could we talk for a few minutes?"

Some of the apprehension dissolved. Her eyes widened a fraction and studied him with new interest.

She said, "Do you have some ID?"

He dug out his wallet and showed his driver's license. "I want to find Clint Rader. Help him, if I can. And you might be able to help me do that. I'd like to ask a few questions."

He could see her make the decision. She unchained the door and he caught a glimpse of an old woman asleep in a recliner in front of a TV. Rita pushed open the screen door, closed the main door quietly, and came out. She pointed at a chain-hung swing at the end of the porch and they sat side by side. She hugged herself, her shoulders rounded over, as though cowering from a dank wind, and looked warily out at the street. Said, "What do you want to know?"

He smiled. "I understand you two plan to be married?"

She nodded. Not meeting his eyes.

"Do you mind telling me about him?"

She took a deep breath and closed her eyes. "He is a good man. Good to me. We . . . we've been trying to save up for—" But her voice caught on a sharp involuntary intake of breath, lines incised her forehead, and quick tears squeezed out from her clenched eyelids.

He started to put a hand on her shoulder. Withdrew it and waited for the moment to pass. Said, "I'm sorry, Rita."

She wiped at her eyes with her fingers, took two deep shuddering breaths, and shook her head. "No. No. It's okay. I will be all right. If you think you can find him, I want to help. Go on. Please."

"Where do you think he is?"

"I don't *know*."

"You haven't heard from him?"

"No."

But she knew something. It was in her eyes when she gave him a darting glance.

"You must have an idea, Rita. Maybe from something he said before he disappeared. Or from something that happened. The police questioned you, didn't they? What did you tell them?"

There was real fear crouching behind her eyes now. "He . . . I think he is hiding some place."

"Why, Rita?"

She looked down and shook her head.

John said, "His brother told me the police think he got mixed up in a drug deal that went wrong."

She shook her head more. "No. He did not do that. He might have known about some illegal things but he was not involved."

"What, then? Why would he be hiding?"

"I did not tell the police. I believe the men he is hiding from *think* he killed two of their own. But he did *not*."

"Are you sure of that?"

"*Yes*, I'm sure. I know. I know."

"I have to ask how you know that."

"I was . . . nearby when it happened. I called him and he came to me. He did *not* do it. I can't tell you more. So I think he is hiding. From those men. They are the Satan's Ghosts. Maybe you could go to them. Tell them he did not do it, and they won't hunt him any more, and he can come home to me. Could you? Will you do that? Please?"

"They'd want proof, Rita. Something more than your word. Can you give them proof?"

She leaned her head back and let out an agonized little wail. Chopped it off and pounded her fists on her knees, then made a visible effort to suppress whatever it was that threatened to burst out, grasping it all and gathering it in and pushing it back down into her soul out of the light. She hugged herself again and said, "Where is Clint's brother? Why isn't he here with you if he really is your friend?"

"I'm sorry to tell you this. Nolan Rader is dead. It happened near Chattanooga."

She stared at him, her body gone still but her head twitching just perceptibly with barely restrained tension.

"I went to him in the hospital yesterday. He'd been shot. I promised I'd do what I could to find out what happened to his brother. I think you know more about all this, Rita."

A chopped motorcycle rumbled into sight at the end of the street. It rolled up and stopped by the curb and a dark-skinned man dismounted, removed a black half helmet, and stared at the porch.

The effect on Rita was electric. She sprang up and went over by the door. The man combed his black hair back with his fingers and came up onto the porch fast, scowling. Looking at Rita, he inclined his head toward John and said, "Who is this guy? Why are you talking to him?"

John got up and moved closer to them. "I'm John Hardin."

Rita said, "Trey, they killed Clint's *brother* yesterday. Do you understand? They *killed* him."

"Calm down. I think you need to go in the house now. Rita? Now. Go check on Momma. I'll be right in."

Rita glanced once more at John and went inside, but she stood behind the screen door, hunched and hugging her elbows, watching him.

Trey faced John and said, "I don't know who you are or why you came here, but you got my sister all upset, so I think you better leave."

"I'm a friend. I'm trying to find out—"

"Didn't you hear what I said? Go. Don't bother us no more." And he pointed at the street.

John held his gaze for several long seconds, wondering what was going on behind those angry eyes. But it was obvious he'd get no more information here today.

He looked at the woman and said, "Sorry to disturb you, Rita. I only want to help find Clint. Will you please let me know if you see him, or if he gets in touch with you? John Hardin. I'm in the phone book. Maggie Valley."

She gave him a bleak look with her lower lip trembling, then turned and faded back into the shadowed house.

He lifted a palm at Trey and walked away down the steps.

***

An hour after sunset, he rapped two knuckles on the plain red metal door on the outskirts of Charlotte. Waited thirty seconds and rapped again, louder. Waited.

Everything about the man who answered was oversized, but there was little fat on him. He filled the doorway. Scuffed boots, black jeans, a worn black vest over a white T-shirt, a square head with thinning hair set on wide shoulders. His thick tree-root arms were sleeved with old muddy tattoos, the predominant theme being hollow-eyed skulls and flowers. He said, "This here's a private club, friend. You want a drink try the Blue Moon Saloon down on the corner."

There was a rattling burst of laughter inside. Thudding rock playing loudly somewhere in a back room through overdriven speakers.

"If this is the Longriders clubhouse, I've got the right place."

The man squinted. "And who would you be?"

"John Hardin. I'm looking for Clint Rader."

"Yeah, well he ain't here."

"He's disappeared. I want to find him. I'd like to talk with somebody who knows him well. I'm not with any kind of law. I'm a friend."

The man gazed steadily from beneath dense eyebrows. Evaluating.

A slim girl in a red halter top and white shorts that looked painted on walked unsteadily up behind the man and hugged his arm. Said, "Hey, what's up, hon? Scooter said he wants to see you about the Sunday ride."

Still gazing at Hardin, he said, "Tell Scooter I'll be back in thirty, Gina. I'm gonna go down to the Moon and have a talk with this dude."

Seated opposite each other at a sticky table in a dim booth that stank of stale beer, the man said, "So okay. Let's hear it. Then I might decide to either shake your hand or pinch your head off. Depending."

"Permanent damage either way. Can I buy a pitcher?"

"Never turn that down. But the draft here is piss. You don't want their cheeseburgers, either, 'less you got a cast-iron gut. A shot of Seven and a longneck ought to keep my good side out, though. I'm Turk. I head up the Longriders, and proud of it."

"You always go to great places like this, Turk?"

"Wouldn't be here right now it wasn't for you, dude."

"Myself, I like these places once in a while. Builds up my immune system."

"Long as you don't go so far as date'n the waitresses."

"Wouldn't want to crowd in on your action."

The man's grin was wide and genuine. "Come here some Saturday about midnight. The place is a real petting zoo. I don't like fingerprints all over my women. You know there was a famous Western gunfighter had your name. John Wesley Hardin. You a gunfighter?"

"Not against a man like you. I'd use my feet."

"How's that?"

"To run like hell."

He barked out a laugh and signaled a waitress who was wearing about a pound of fruit cocktail-hued makeup that had probably been applied with a putty knife.

After she had delivered the drinks, Turk's eyes changed, losing the smile, betraying a glimmer of intelligence, and he said, "What is it you want to know about Clint Rader?"

"What can you tell me?"

"A damned good bike wrench. Good man, too. Cocky, some would say, but keeps his head down. One of those might surprise you if you was fool enough to cross him."

"I was told the law thinks he got into a drug deal that went bad and somebody killed him."

Turk shook his head. "Yeah. That's the story. But it don't fit right with Rader. He might have a few and get a tad frisky like the rest of us, sure, but far as I ever knew, he had no truck with any of the candy."

John had a fleeting image of this man getting "a tad frisky" that resembled what a crane swinging a wrecking ball might achieve. He said, "What do you think happened to him, then?"

"Right about here I got to ask why the hell you want to know all this?"

"His brother Nolan was a friend. I was helping him look for Clint."

"Was?"

"Somebody shot him."

Turk was raising the beer and stopped halfway. Put it back on the table and looked up at a dirty neon bulb that was flickering.

John said, "Nolan Rader thought the Satan's Ghosts are behind this. I heard from somebody else these Ghosts might think Clint Rader killed two of their members. This somebody swore Rader didn't have anything to do with the killings. Wanted the Ghosts to know that."

Turk leveled a hard startled look at him. As though he had just made some major connection. He looked around, and in a lowered voice, said, "Listen to what I'm tellin' you, friend. Drop this and back it on off. Hear? You want to go on takin' up space, you back way on off right now. That's all I got to say, dude. Get on out of here now. I'll wait a bit."

TWENTY-THREE

Brain sat on the end of a white couch in the living area of his compound, wearing his customary crisp white shirt and red tie, in a soft wash of light from the recessed fixtures, squinting up into the darkness beyond a skylight, his feet up on a massive oak coffee table.

Opposite him, in a gray workout jumpsuit, Monroe sat erect and attentive in an ergonomic leather chair, his elbows on the arms and his hands folded on his taut belly so his thumb could touch the wrist pulse, counting his resting heart rate to himself. No one else was in the large room.

Brain had returned the day before from a quick trip by commercial flights to Dallas, where he had met with a cutout contact and finalized arrangements initiated months before. A large wire transfer to one of his offshore accounts had been confirmed.

He began talking again, to himself as much as to Monroe. "This will be by far the most lucrative contract we have undertaken. Because of the targets' prominence it also involves the most risk. The investigation will be intensive and unrelenting. How, then, can we thwart such an investigation from the outset? There is only a single alternative."

He looked at Monroe, who nodded unblinking and said, "A disappearance."

"Correct. A conjuror's trick. An illusion. A vanishment. Far better than any arranged apparent accident or illness that, however clever, nonetheless always leaves threads behind and thus the potential of an unfortunate unraveling. Jimmy Hoffa is an excellent example. No evidence. No loose ends. No effective investigation even possible. A media storm will rage, of course, but impotently. The targets will be venerated in endless but useless speculation. As Amelia Earhart flew into immortality in the Pacific, so our target subjects shall disappear into the infamous Bermuda Triangle."

A month previously, in anticipation of this contract, Brain had assigned a discreet investigation to a trusted private operator, who had just within the last day uncovered the impending opportunity. The target couple was even now sailing on a fifty-foot ketch in secrecy to Elbow Cay, three hundred miles off the south coast of Florida, where they planned to polish memoirs and rest in seclusion for ten days. With the couple would be their teenaged adopted daughter and a lone bodyguard. Four. Far fewer than the usual entourage, but the trip was supposedly secret. Unknown to the press and to all but a few of their most trusted business associates and friends.

The contract could be accomplished with a minimum of two teams. One pair to carry out the terminations and the disappearance of the targets in the Bahamas. The other pair to simultaneously eliminate the private operator in Birmingham. Though trusted and well paid, he was not, after all, among the cadre of Wraiths, and in the weeks and

months to come, the temptation would be strong for
him to go to the authorities with what he knew and
surmised. Better to sever that possibility at the outset,
as well.

There was one detail still to be arranged,
however. The Epsilon Team must be inserted on
Elbow Cay to carry out their instructions. Then they
must be extracted. The team could simply take a fast
boat across from Florida, but there were problems
with that, not the least of which was the round trip
range of six hundred miles through a gauntlet of
increasingly frequent Coast Guard and DEA air and
sea patrols of late. He did not want the team
members to be spotted by authorities or anyone else.
The scrutiny of all events in the region prior to the
disappearance was going to be exhaustive, and he did
not want any linkage, however tenuous, to exist with
his team. The final insertion, at least, must be by
boat, because there was no air strip on the cay. But
the team could perhaps be flown in secretly by light
plane—one that would be less conspicuous than a
business twin—to nearby Marsh Harbour, where
there was fairly frequent inter-island air traffic, and
where this flight could be made to appear
unremarkable. A small boat could be arranged. The
pilot would be told to wait in Marsh Harbour. It was
almost certainly not possible for the pilot to be
deceived so thoroughly as to pose no subsequent
threat, so he would simply have to be terminated not
long after completion of the contract. The money
involved was certainly sufficient to warrant
extraordinary measures.

The pilot Hardin had displayed ingenuity and a
calm daring on that recent flight into Canada, and

now had personal liability because he had been involved in smuggling, and so at the very least would be reluctant to cooperate with any authorities, even if he should entertain any initial suspicions about the purpose of the trip.

Brain came to a decision, nodding.

He looked at his watch, arched his back against the white couch in a stretch, yawned, and said to Monroe, "I want you to begin conditioning subject eight now. Use the light in his cell, set at the same intensity he associates with the termination of subject seven. Do this in fifteen second bursts at random over the next two hours. Vary the temperature twenty degrees once each way from the norm. Then I will conduct a late session tonight."

Subject eight was close to breaking as his stress level intensified. Symptoms of dissociation were appearing, although he had learned a number of surprisingly effective stress reducing and anxiety management practices on his own. Conscious control of his breathing. Fantasy diversions.

But stress was inexorable and ultimately unavoidable under his circumstances, and now there were resultant memory lapses. Nightmares. Periods of talking illogically to himself. Stretches of constant robotic pacing to the point of exhaustion and beyond.

The mind can only tolerate so much.

Any human's mind.

As usual, stress would triumph.

He had discovered that this particular subject harbored a deep-seated revulsion for blades. Skillfully applied, that knowledge should prove most interesting.

***

Clint lurched up in bed out of one nightmare—about neat razored slits all over his body parting like thin lips to drool blood—into another nightmare induced by the flashing overhead light. He stood and teetered through the strobing light, which was filling his head with images of the naked-strangling-twitching-dying man the freak had called subject number seven. Across the room to the bathroom sink. He ran some cold water, filled his cupped hands, and splashed his face three times, trying to ignore the goddamned light. He looked into the metal mirror at his distorted image and did not recognize the sunken-eyed creature in there.

The flashing stopped and the light stayed on.

They had taken away use of the bathroom light days ago. Now it was always off.

It was getting colder in the room.

His greatest minute-to-minute fear was losing control of his mind. There had been memory lapses like blurry gray limbos and each time he slammed back to reality from one of those he was filled with a gut-churning dread it would happen again and he would not make it back to sanity and then he might as well be dead.

He had fought the tall freak with his mind. Struggling to control his heart and breathing rates during each one of the crazy question sessions by forcing his mind to focus on simple good things. A bluebird perched on a twig. A pet border collie named Belle he'd had as a kid.

Or he would pinch his thigh to divert his mind from a question he did not want to answer, like all those questions about sharp-edged things that made something automatically cringe back into a shadowy recess deep inside him.

After he'd become aware that he was able to get snatches of sleep only when facing the door of his room, he deliberately turned his back whenever he lay on the bed now, pushing away the feeling that Monroe would steal in without sound or emotion sometime in the darkest hours and attack. It gave him some small measure of control.

He had taught himself to chop off the first despairing thought he knew could only lead him down an ever steeper path into a bottomless pit of depression. He would wrench his mind away from the diminishing time he had left by talking to himself. Going loudly through the steps necessary to rebuild the clutch on a Harley Sportster. Running down the list of tools he kept in his wheeled red steel box in the garage. Reciting multiplication tables and the graduated fractional sizes of wrenches. Silently mulling over every possible escape option, however illogical, in case he had forgotten some detail that might help save him. Plotting ways he would fight Monroe when the time came.

Avoiding all thought of Rita now because that was just way more than he could handle.

The light in the bedroom began flashing again and he pressed the heels of his hands against the images of the choking-strangling-twitching man.

An indefinite time later, when he removed his hands from covering his eyes, the light was on steadily and he realized he was kneeling by the bed.

Then it went out like a last snuffed candle, wrapping him in hopeless night.

TWENTY-FOUR

John was seated at the same worn desk Valerie had used when she had lived here with her grandfather Wasituna, growing into the woman he had so loved and ultimately had indirectly caused to die. He still missed her with an abiding visceral ache, and probably always would. Kitty Birdsong had filled the hollowness of his soul like a fresh bouquet in a tomb, but now she, too, had left him to contend with his demons. Better that she was out of it.

In an Asheville computer cafe he'd searched Nolan Rader's laptop hard drive and taken printouts and notes from what he'd found. Because he did not want to involve Hank and Hattie, he had come here to Wasituna's cabin and had gone through all of Nolan Rader's cramped hand written notes, news clippings, and printouts. There were highlighted sections of investigative reports about the suspected criminal activities of the Satan's Ghosts. Copies of arrest records. Part of a chapter from a book by some psychologist, discussing the behavior of deviant groups. There were captioned photos clipped from biker magazines, with heads circled in ballpoint. Two dozen compressed long-lens photos of individual and grouped bikers Rader had evidently taken himself.

John had several times scrutinized the aerial photos he had taken of the Tennessee compound, using a large round magnifying glass the old Indian kept for reading. In one frame the tiny white faces of two men seated by the pool looked back at him, palms shielding their eyes from the sunlight. He knew they could not possibly have noted enough detail from that distance to identify the Cessna, but there was threat beneath their attention. They were the enemy.

He now agreed with Rader's assumption that Clint might be held at the compound.

So what do I do now?

He could not approach the law, even anonymously. He still had no proof. Everything was circumstantial. A leaning shack constructed shakily from rumors and puzzle-piecing and guesses.

He was out of options and rapidly running out of time, certainly. Both for Clint Rader and for himself. If Clint was, in fact, serving as a subject in some bizarre psychological experiment, his usefulness must have a limit, and somewhere there was still evidence gathered by Nolan Rader that could put himself in a prison for life. Somebody could be looking at it, listening to it, right now. He let out a breath and started in on the pile again, searching for synapses he might have overlooked connecting two or more meager facts or suppositions.

Wasituna came to the doorway of the bedroom and said, "You need to take a break from that. Come. We will walk."

They followed a rough path into the woods up the mountain behind the cabin, Wasituna silently leading at a steady brisk pace. A pair of squirrels rippled and skittered in a mad spiral chase down a shaggy tree trunk. Birds chirp-whistled some avian gossip through treetops thrust up into a building humid breeze.

On the rocky spine of the ridge, Wasituna stopped in a small clearing to look off across the ancient furred serrations of the Qualla Boundary, this ragged crumpled scrap near the heart of what had once been the vast Cherokee Nation.

The old man said, "You still miss our Valerie."

"I do."

"Memories are a wondrous part of the great gift of life. She lives on in them. As you and I and she will live on in her son."

Neither of them said anything for a time.

Far below, a falcon launched itself from the topmost branch of a dead hardwood and expertly rode the invisible torrent flooding up out of the shaded valley, its wings glossy and perfect as they caught the sudden sunlight like blades, its acute eyes alert for furtive movement below, and Wasituna smiled and nodded. "It goes on all around us. This miracle flow we have been invited to join. Each of us in a small way for a brief time."

"Yes."

"Sometimes to see it well you have to step back. To give yourself a new view. That can also work when you are facing some big task. If you want to climb a cliff and you are standing too close, it might appear impossible. But if you step back so you can view it all, you might begin to see a way up."

"You're saying I've been picking through Rader's stuff too closely, looking for threads. Maybe missing something big."

Wasituna squinted at him.

So, standing there beside the old man on the spine of a mountain in the wash of a warm wind, he pulled back from the enveloping thorn-thicket confusion and the dark foreboding that was looming tall and wide in his mind.

And immediately spotted a crack in the cliff he might be able to exploit.

The phone in his front jeans pocket vibrated like a wickedly insistent little creature and he dug it out.

With a jovial air the voice said, "Do you know who this is?"

"Yes." It was one of the men who had driven him to the compound for the initial meeting with Ganz.

"We were pleased with the aerial work you did for us. We need a bit more of your talent, but we're right up against some business deadlines so I'm afraid everything's in a rush. Any chance you'd be free starting tomorrow?"

"I can rearrange my schedule."

"Fine. That's just fine. Why don't we meet tomorrow morning right where we did the last time? Say nineish. We'll pick you up."

"Okay. I'll see you then."

On the walk back down along the leafy path to the cabin, he surveyed that crack in the black cliff.

If the tall man in Tennessee was, in fact, conducting some kind of weird psychological study, it was very likely without the sanction of the powers in the Satan's Ghosts, because it could not possibly serve any productive purpose for them.

And what else could the yellow-eyed man be doing that his employers might not sanction?

At the least it made Ganz vulnerable, as well, and not quite so daunting.

***

After they had thoroughly searched him in the anteroom at the compound, one of the men said, "Why don't you go have a seat out by the pool? Dr. Ganz will be with you in a few minutes."

He walked through the living area and out onto the large pool patio.

A woman was standing hipshot by one of the round tables under a dogwood, smoking a cigarette and staring at the sapphire pool. Slick lipstick-red shorts, low heels, and a too-small halter top. There was a tote bag on the table. She shot him a look, one eye squinted as she exhaled a jet of smoke, and he saw a fresh bruise discoloring her jaw line. Her hair was a spiky bleached tangle with garish red tips. She brushed at it with one long-nailed hand and took another deep drag. She looked like any of the numberless nameless women who claim stretches of curb in a given city and gradually merchandise their souls until nothing is left. There were two small silver rings through her septum and anger and revulsion in her eyes.

She said, "Are you my ride? I want out of here."

"Can't help you. I'm just here on business. They drove me in."

Her eyes shifted off him and changed. She paled and swallowed.

John turned and Ganz walked up holding a small intercom to his ear, saying, "Lupo. By the pool."

Ganz pocketed the intercom and fifteen seconds later a man dressed like a groundskeeper came out onto the patio.

Ganz said, "Why is she still here? Make sure Monroe has compensated her and then take her back."

The man named Lupo beckoned her. She picked up the tote and moved quickly to follow him, eyes downcast and heels tocking on the ceramic tiles.

Ganz said, "Please sit. Would you like coffee?"

"No."

Ganz took the chair opposite him, against a backdrop of lush landscaping, and leaned back, his head inclined. He said, "I have another job for you."

"Canada again?"

"How creative are you, Mr. Hardin?"

"My creativity depends on incentive. Enough money might stimulate my imagination."

Ganz smiled thinly. "Of course. A small test then? I will propose a problem. For creating a workable solution to this problem within three minutes, and for carrying out that solution very soon, I will pay you one hundred thousand dollars. For every minute longer than three you take to propose a viable solution, I will deduct twenty thousand dollars, down to a minimum of twenty thousand, at which point I will tell you how to accomplish the task. If you agree to take this test, you must give me your word you will do whatever is necessary to complete the task, whether by your plan or by mine. Will you consent to taking the test?"

John smiled. "I won't kill anybody to get a job done."

Ganz hesitated, his eyes fixed and intense. "Of course not."

"How long is the job likely to take?"

"Perhaps three days."

"Subjective. You deciding whether or not what I might propose can be carried out."

"Granted. But the best of relationships are built on trust, are they not? A long-term relationship with me could prove most lucrative for you. And, after all, you will be the one who must make the proposal work, so I am assuming you will want it to be viable, as well. Enough evasion, Mr. Hardin. Do you agree to the test and the terms?"

John nodded.

"You must say it."

"I agree."

"The problem, then. I need to have two men with minimal luggage transported to a discreet location for an important meeting and brought back within the following day or two. The meeting is on an island in the Caribbean called Elbow Cay. Three hundred miles from the coast. There is no airport on the island, but there is one nearby in Marsh Harbour, where there is fuel available but where there unfortunately are customs personnel during daylight hours. There are strips, which are mostly private and unimproved, but far less trafficked, on other islands fairly close by. My men must not be seen by authorities at all, and they should be noticed by as few others as possible. Preferably by no one. How will you accomplish this?" He looked at his watch. "Three minutes for one hundred thousand dollars."

John looked at the dogwood, caged here with no other of its kind in the interior of this compound.

He said, "Well I know they're watching island boat and air traffic pretty closely now. No good trying to sneak over in clear conditions. So I'd say do it right out in the open. I take my back seat out so your men can lie down at critical times and not be seen from outside the plane, maybe even under a tarp. No problem picking them up unseen and then leaving Florida from any unattended strip that's well out of the way. There's no requirement to check in with Customs to leave the country. I fly to a boondocks Florida pickup strip. You have your men dropped off there ahead of me so there'll be no vehicle left while we're gone. Then I file a solo IFR flight plan by radio so I'm talking with Air Traffic Control all the way. I've flown some in the islands, and things are pretty laid back. If I'm not mistaken, Marsh Harbour has a single short runway out in the bushes. It does have maybe two customs people, in a small office at one end of the strip. Their primary job is to smile and welcome tourists and their money, so they don't look too closely at anything. I'll have to call them an hour before arrival.

"We arrive very early in the morning, maybe, so there won't be a lot of traffic at the field. No. Better if I plan it so we arrive late, near sunset, and swing the plane around at the far end of the strip, with my landing lights on, or I land short if the wind favors the other direction, so your men can slip out and hide in the brush. I taxi to the office and go through customs, apologizing for my late arrival. Tell them I'm there to look at investment cottages, maybe, or just to do some fishing. I have the tanks topped, chat with the customs people a while, and then take a taxi into town to my reserved room. Your men slip out after full dark. There's no perimeter fence, as I recall. Even if there is one it shouldn't be any real problem for your men.   They're dressed like tourists.   Long-billed fishing caps and variable-tint glasses. Even if they're seen once off the airport, nobody is likely to remember much about them. They steal a small boat and go out to Elbow Cay.

"They come back to Marsh Harbour late the next night and abandon the boat on a beach. The police, when they get around to it in a week or so, will probably think kids took it to joy ride. We reverse the procedure and take off just after dawn, because you can't take off or land at Marsh at night. I file in the air with Nassau. Call Customs at West Palm to let them know I'm coming. Notify ATC in Florida when I cross into the Atlantic Defense Identification Zone, and then do a quick stop at the same unattended strip to let your men out. But you don't have them picked up right away. They walk through the woods for a few miles to their pickup point. I fly to West Palm Beach Customs and let them take apart the plane if they want to. That's it. Time?"

"If customs wants to know why you have no rear seats?"

"I'm carrying some bulky fishing gear, a couple long rods and tackle boxes that fit better that way. And I can tell them I do cargo charters and hardly ever use the back seats, anyway. I do have a commercial endorsement, of course, to back that claim up."

"Why not have my men picked up directly on arrival back in Florida at the unattended strip?"

"You don't want anybody seeing a vehicle near there, especially while I'm on the ground. If our customs people find out I did land there on reentering the country, I can say oh that, well I thought the engine was a little rough so I stopped to check it out. They won't like it, but with no witnesses or evidence they can't do anything about it except to put me on a watch list. These questions are eating into my time. Not part of the agreement."

Ganz looked up at the sky for fifteen seconds. Assessing. Brushed some speck from his red tie. Did not consult his watch. "Quite good, though it needs refining. Better than even I would have credited you for. Sixty thousand."

"The questions were not part of it. I think the full hundred. With half in advance."

That thin non-smile again. "No. A firm sixty on completion. More than you'd make clear in two years of taking snapshots for developers. There is no product involved, so your risk is minimal. I am confident greed will prevail. It always does. I require your answer now, Mr. Hardin. Take it or leave it."

"I suppose greed is a familiar ally to you, since it fuels the whole drug trade."

The thin smile widened fractionally, but the eyes glittered. "Sixty is the offer. Yes or no."

He hesitated for several seconds and said, "All right."

Ganz nodded, smiling his cold smile.

John said, "When do I leave?"

"The day after tomorrow. Thursday. The weather forecast for Florida and the islands is favorable. Picking up my men at an out-of-the-way strip in Florida is workable. We have access to online airport information, so you and I can choose that strip before you leave today.

"Refinements.   Having my men steal a boat poses unnecessary risk. Do you have experience with small boats?"

John had handled small boats when he had lived at the ocean end of North Carolina on the slender Outer Banks. He said, "Some, yes."

"Good. We will exploit the premise of doing this apparently in the open. We will use the internet to confirm rental of a cottage we have already located near Marsh Harbour. For a long weekend. A deposit has already been sent electronically in your name. It is called Windward Reef, on Guano Road. It comes with an eighteen-foot outboard boat that is equipped for fishing, except for tackle, including a combination GPS and depth finder, and lights for night operation. You will pick up keys from a man named Albury who lives an eighth of a mile from the rental cottage and who will be expecting your arrival late on Thursday. He and his wife serve as caretakers for the cottage. You will take my men out to Elbow Cay in the boat just after dark Friday night and drop them. You will return to the island before dawn on Saturday to pick them up, and you will take off to return to Florida after dawn. The rest of your plan is acceptable."

Ganz had a man bring him a laptop and they agreed on a particular remote Florida strip. Then he stood to his full height and looked down like a raptor.

John met the feral yellow gaze and said, "You assumed I'd do it. You already had that end set up."

Ganz just smiled.

John got up and walked away, wondering, *why are you willing to pay sixty thousand dollars just to smuggle two men to a meeting?*

After John left, Ganz made a slow circuit of his office before summoning the two-man team for their final briefing. Hands clasped behind his back. Gazing at the works of art.

He had made the final decision on a further refinement to the plan that would require another two-person team. Yes, he decided, the pilot would most definitely be an unnecessary loose end. Having flown his team for this assignment, the wisest move would be to eliminate him. But how best to do that?

Perhaps a chemically-induced heart attack.

Just after Hardin returned to North Carolina following the mission.

Hopefully before the news broke all across the country.

TWENTY-FIVE

John sat in a bentwood rocker on the porch, taking in the layered dawn, his boots crossed up on the split hand rail. Bottom-lit furls a mile overhead burned against a snowy backdrop of ripped-lace cirrus strewn at five times that altitude.

Hank came out onto the porch carrying two cups of coffee that steamed in the cool air. John accepted one of them and nodded.

Hank sat beside him, his wrinkled fingers wrapped around the hot mug, looking up at the angelic sky art with a smile and an appreciative shake of the head.

The old man said, "There was one had Sharon Stone and Russell Crowe as the good folk. Gene Hackman did a great job as the bad guy, runnin' a quick-draw shootout game in his town. Place called Redemption. Gunfighters squarin' off. See who's faster. For money. One dyin' each time. Somebody had to go against Hackman himself in the end. You remember that one?"

"Sorry, Hank. I wasn't paying attention. Run that by again."

"It was *The Quick and the Dead*. Dangerous game. You into somethin' dangerous, son? Some kinda game could get you killed? You go, you show up, at all hours. Stay away days. Act like you're hidin' some big secrets. Don't eat right. Don't sleep much. Look like you're luggin' a hundred pounds of bad around. I got to make up stories when people call wantin' your work. Hattie and Kitty been talkin' some. Thing is, you got friends here. Not fair-weather friends, neither, by damn. I don't believe you can ever accuse us we wasn't there to lend a hand best we could, you needed one."

"You and Hattie saved my life. I'll never forget that. But this is something I have to do alone. You can't help. And you're better off not knowing about it. I'll get through it." *Or I won't. And if that's the way it goes, at least you won't get hurt.*

"You been studyin' up on maps. Goin' on a trip?"

"For a few days."

"This is part of it?"

John nodded. "It is. I'll be leaving tomorrow morning."

"Then we'll all appreciate if you'll try to keep your skin on."

An hour later, while he was going through papers from his fire safe and making notes, the desk phone rang.

The boy said, "I thought we could work on the treehouse some today, if you have time."

"Can't do it Curly. Business."

"Tomorrow then? Just for a little while? I can't on Friday because I have to do chores. Maybe we could do it Saturday morning."

"I'm sorry. I'll have to call you when I can get back over there. I need you to promise you won't work on it yourself meanwhile, okay?"

"You're afraid I'll get hurt. I can climb any tree on that mountain."

"I know it. Like a raccoon. But you don't need to be thinking about the work and hanging on up there in squirrel country at the same time. I'm sure your Aunt Crow will agree. Promise?"

"Okay, but you have to promise we'll finish it pretty soon."

"If there's any way I can. Listen, I have to go away for a few days. I'll call you when I get back. I want you to know…"

After several seconds, the boy said, "What?"

"Nothing, Curly. Maybe we can camp out at Little *Atagahi* some weekend."

"Yeah. Are you flying somewhere?"

"Yes."

"Don't you be thinking of too many things at the same time, either."

That afternoon he went to an office in Asheville and talked across a polished conference table with a white-haired lawyer named McCoy, who scrawled notes on a yellow legal pad.

The lawyer said, "You have no living kin, then?"

"No. I want everything to go to five people. That includes the contents of a safe deposit box. I just filled out a form at my bank that allows access to the box by Hank Gaskill and Kitty Birdsong. They'll be co-executors."

It was no fortune, but Joshua Lightfoot was to have the bulk of all he had, with portions to the old couple, Wasituna, and Kitty. A new insurance policy would pay off the house, and the Gaskills would have use of it for their lifetimes, after which it would pass to the boy. Hank and Kitty would have control of the boy's portion until he reached his majority.

While he waited, McCoy drew up the will. John signed it, and a secretary and two paralegals witnessed and notarized it. He wrote out a check.

Offering his hand, McCoy said, "I've been around long enough to know when a man's looking over his shoulder at something gaining on him. If what we did here today gives you some peace, that's good, and I'll make sure everything goes according to your wishes. Including that safe deposit box. My hand on it. Old fashioned, I know, but my father and his father before him did business that way all their lives, and earned ironclad reputations around here. Can't let them down, can I? Y'all take care now, Mr. Hardin."

He stopped at a large sporting goods store to buy a number of items including three inflatable life jackets, a snug fitting pair of reef walkers, and, with recommendations from a clerk with a fringe of salt-and-pepper hair and the weathered face of an outdoorsman, two salt-water fishing rods in different sizes and a tackle box that contained a colorful array of lures, sinkers, swivels, rolls of monofilament line, and a stainless multi-tool containing pliers, wire cutter, saw, scissors, screwdrivers, a can opener—all in an ingenious fold up handle less than six inches long. He looked over a display of binoculars and almost bought an image-stabilized pair to replace his old ones, but something called a Midnight Monocular caught his attention.

The clerk said, "That's a great little gadget for night fishing or spotting deer or varmints. Works in low light on an electronic ambient light enhancer or you can switch on the infrared beam and see in full darkness out to two hundred fifty feet. Waterproof. It even floats. Uses a three-volt lithium battery."

"What's the magnification?"

"One to one, but you can screw on an accessory lens that will boost it to a three-ex. We've even got thirty-five millimeter camera adaptors. It's on sale today for just two ninety-nine. You aren't going to beat that anywhere."

John said, "I'll take it."

* * *

The next morning was overcast, the mountains dank with shifting fog that had materialized out of the night, and he drove the Wrangler through shades of gray to the airport in Asheville.

He removed the rear seats and left them in a back corner of the hangar under a tarp. With the fishing tackle, the life jackets, and a tote bag and small suitcase loaded, he used his cell phone to file an instrument flight plan with Air Traffic Control, strapped in, and taxied out to the runway, the airport beacon punching alternating green and white fuzzballs into the mist.

He waited at the taxiway hold line, the Cessna's prop flickering darkly at idle, while a 727 floated as if by magic out of the grayness and touched down ponderously on the wet pavement. The tower controller issued the standard wake turbulence caution and cleared him and he lined up and took off into the enveloping overcast. The Cessna climbed inside the cloud limbo for long minutes, seemingly motionless, the engine beating faithfully and the electronics precisely tracking position, velocity, attitude, and altitude. Then there was a bright flickering. He burst out into stunningly brilliant sunshine flooding a deep blue vault of sky brushed with a few high wisps, and he was utterly alone gliding above soft glowing whiteness spreading away to the horizon in all directions.

On a southerly heading, he climbed another fifteen hundred feet to the assigned altitude and imagined what his plane might look like to an omnipotent being checking on this particular world from the perspective of cold infinity. Merely an insectile speck momentarily suspended in the immensity. Certainly inconsequential to any of the uncountable far larger affairs playing out on this particular slow rolling sphere.

He felt a stab of loneliness. And as he often did when witnessing something beautiful, he thought of Kitty. They had fitted together so well. Until Nolan Rader had come out of his past. He missed her with an ache that reached into his soul.

The radio spattered a burst of static into his headset and ATC politely informed him he was drifting westward of his course. He acknowledged and gave the Cessna a touch of left aileron.

This flight was an unwanted diversion, although it seemed his only choice to stay within the range of the bizarre and dangerous man in Tennessee. From what information Rader had collected, and from personal impressions, he was coming to believe Ganz might be demented in a rare, insidious way, in possession of a power that could warp and wither the souls of others in his presence. Sipping from the same evil brew that Hitler and Manson and too many others had over long history. It might be possible to learn something more from the two men he was to pick up, or from the destination in the islands, something he could use to free Clint Rader, but he felt caught up in a dark current with no way to prevent it from carrying him wherever it would.

He descended through the cloud deck for an instrument approach into Charleston, breaking out of the grayness at six hundred feet and landing in murky light rain. He had them top off the tanks and got a bottle of water from a machine in the pilot's lounge. He ate a meatloaf sandwich Hattie had made for him, as he studied the detailed weather on a computer screen.

Aloft again, the cloud deck began to thin, and ahead fair weather blooms of cumulus were decorating a more tropical sky. By the time he passed to the west of Jacksonville he was flying above a scattering of lower-lying clouds casting a pleasant pattern of shadows onto the humid Florida peninsula.

He kept well to the west of I-95, and Palatka, Crescent City, and Deland moved by in slow succession below. Beyond the sprawl of Orlando that lay off to the right, lazy crossroads like Holopaw and Yeehaw Junction dotted the marshy scrub forest land under him thirty miles inland from the rushing coastal frenzy on US One and the Interstate.

He landed again at Vero Beach to top off. Ahead of schedule, he killed time doing a detailed walk around inspection of the Cessna, looking at a Google Earth view of Elbow Cay in the pilot's lounge, and studying the sectional chart of the islands, and he took off at quarter to five.

After banking inland at Stuart to take up a southwesterly course, Lake Okeechobee lay ahead along the horizon. As he drew closer it expanded to display a broad patch like a hammered bronze shield under the westering sun. He flew over a chart dot called Indiantown, where there was a nearby turf strip with a few hangars and a shed office, only attended on weekends. About ten miles beyond that, south of a settlement on the lake shore called Port Mayaca, at the end of a disused gravel road through patchy woods and brush, there was a short paved strip once used by a shoestring fixed base and flight training operation like two hundred others barely hanging on all over Florida. This one had gone bankrupt and the strip was now abandoned, though not officially closed. Circling it at eight hundred feet he saw no vehicle or person near it. On landing, he had to dodge two potholes in the rough broken pavement. He back-taxied, swung around into the wind, and shut it down as two figures carrying small duffel bags slung on their backs came out of the trees.

The obvious leader was the same man who had first driven him to the compound. Muscled, in his early forties, wearing a salesman's false smile and oversized sunglasses under a plain billed cap. He said, "Hello again. You can call me Brewer. This is Swint."

The other man carried less bulk but also looked very fit. He wore a flop-brimmed safari hat and small round red-tinted sunglasses. He was chewing gum but otherwise stood motionless.

John felt an instinctive caustic dislike for Brewer. He said, "Load up. We need to leave now."

Smiling, Brewer said, "Let's get one thing clear up front. You may be the airplane captain, but I'm the four-star Air Force general. Understand that and we'll get along." He motioned Swint toward the plane and followed him. They loaded their small duffel bags and Swint got in the back, seated on the floor with his knees drawn up and his back against the rear bulkhead. He hugged his knees and chewed his gum, self-contained with his own thoughts. Brewer climbed into the passenger seat, pulled on a headset like he'd done it before, and buckled up.

Aloft on an easterly heading, John called ATC and filed a flight plan, reporting Indiantown as the departure field and Marsh Harbour as the destination. One soul aboard. He asked for and was granted a cruising altitude of seventy-five-hundred feet.

He also radioed Customs in Marsh Harbour, to give them the minimum one-hour notice of his arrival they required.

Leaving the country was not the hard part. Getting back in cleanly could well prove to be.

The Florida coastline stretched away straight to the horizon on the north and south under scattered low cloud puffs, the main arteries thick with streams of sun-sparked multicolored vehicles, toy buildings crowded up close all along the narrow strip of surf-licked sand that drew a constant attendance of humanity.

Over the headset, Brewer said, "They look like ants at a big puddle of ant killer."

The sky and the ocean were clear ahead. A cloudy greenish tint close in along the beach line gave way to the clean cobalt blue of the Gulf Stream, flecked with whitecaps and the random feathers of boat wakes. Florida receded behind them under the lowering sun until there was no land in sight in any direction. Below there was only the impossibly blue sea with the occasional bright white shape of a boat trolling for billfish or wahoo or coruscating dorado, rocking over the swells, its outriggers splayed to separate the dragged foot-long bait fishes with the big hooks sewn inside and make them dart and plunge along as though still alive.

Brewer pushed the headset microphone closer to his mouth and said, "What would happen if a piston blew through a cylinder wall right now?"

"You'd miss your meeting."

That cold non-smile again. "I mean it. What would you do?"

"Tell you to put on one of the inflatable jackets from under the seats. Tell you to take off a shoe and wedge your door open with it. I'd get off a mayday with a position. Try to ditch within sight of a boat. Hope the sharks come up out of the shadows for you two first."

Brewer nodded lazily, his smile fixed, his eyes unreadable behind the sunglasses. He said, "Every pilot I've ever known has been a cocky smartass."

"Next time charter a boat."

Brewer started to say something, but touched the tip of his tongue to his upper lip and looked down through the passenger side window.

After a few minutes he said, "You ever see sharks from up here?"

"Not at this altitude, but down lower, yes. Sometimes they look green. Or black if they're deeper. In these waters there's about every known kind of man eater."

John could see the corner of Brewer's eye twitch, and he seemed nervous at the planted thought. Not unusual. Sharks, like snakes, lanced an atavistic nerve that bled irrational fear into the souls of many people.

The Cessna droned on dutifully, apparently unaware it was boring ever deeper into the Bermuda Triangle, where many a strange occurrence had confounded logic and twisted fates.

TWENTY-SIX

Two hundred miles east from the polished glitz of West Palm Beach, across the ceaseless northward flow of the Gulf Stream, Great Abaco Island lay like the eighty-mile-long blade of a scythe atop the shallow Bahama Bank. The big island was protected somewhat from the sometimes savage Atlantic by an outlying fringe of many coral islands ranging from less than an acre to several larger ones with small populations and piratical names like Spanish Cay and Man of War Cay. From tiny Walker's Cay in the north down to Hole in the Wall in the south, the chain stretched one hundred and twenty miles. Marsh Harbour was on Great Abaco and midway in the chain. It had the smaller of two airports on the island. The other was at the resort of Treasure Cay eighteen miles to the north.

When he was twenty miles out, John pulled back the power and began descending toward Marsh Harbour. The relatively shallow waters below were so clear that even in the lowering light they took on surreal tints from the bottom sand, coral, and grasses. Patches glowed like uncut emerald. Other expanses were lit with the heartbreaking hue of sapphire. Vast amoeba-like areas were even violet.

The airport was uncontrolled, and John called from ten miles out on the universal UNICOM frequency. Three attempts drew no response, so he gave up and altered course enough to do a shallow banking orbit. There were half a dozen light planes at tie-downs, and a turboprop King Air was pulled up in front of the little combination terminal and customs building, which should be open for another half hour yet, by the east end of the strip.

The narrow five-thousand-foot pavement ran due east and west, and the stiff windsock showed a strong breeze blowing in from the sea. He told Brewer to be ready to leave the plane fast, and pointed below. "When I let you out, make for those trees to the south of the strip, and wait there. Give me an hour and a half to clear Customs and get the rental car and the cottage keys, and to let it get full dark, and then I'll pick you up on that sand track over there that runs through the woods from the main road to that little bay. You see it?"

Brewer nodded.

"Wait in the trees there by the middle of that shallow bend. If anybody else is in sight I won't stop, but I'll come back fifteen minutes later. Got that?"

"You're doing fine so far, smartass. Just make sure it stays that way."

John set up for a left downwind to runway nine. He banked onto base and final legs and the Cessna floated in over waving casuarina trees at just above a stall, with full flaps out, and he set it down firmly very short, the headwind helping to reduce the rollout.

The sun was four fingers above the horizon and bright behind them, certainly blinding anyone who might try to look their way from almost a mile off near the terminal, and he had his landing lights on to further mask what was happening. It could not have been better timed. He stopped the plane and told Brewer, "Okay. Now."

They got out fast. Swint slammed the passenger door behind him and they ran off to the side toward the trees, crouched and carrying their duffel bags. John immediately added taxiing power. He had been stopped no longer than five seconds.

He taxied up to swing around and park on the apron behind the King Air and pulled the mixture to full rich to shut down the engine. An older blonde woman in shorts and a halter top was standing outside the Customs building. She looked at the Cessna and frowned. A paunchy balding man came out of the building followed by a middle aged couple. The woman tugged at the balding man's gaudy shirtsleeve and pointed at the Cessna, still frowning. She said something to him and he gave the Cessna a puzzled look. The other couple took no notice and that man got a small portable electric tow bar out of the King Air and clipped it onto the nose wheel hubs. He began moving the sleek twin toward one of the tie-downs and the balding man standing beside the blonde shrugged and turned his attention to directing the one using the tow bar. A dented dusty taxi pulled up on the other side of the building and the blonde walked toward it, giving the Cessna one last look over her shoulder.

John got out and walked around the tail. And saw what had caught the blonde's attention. Swint had slammed the door on the passenger-side safety belt strap. A two-foot length of it dangled down below the door, swinging slightly in the wind, the chromed end glinting in the low sun. Any pilot would know that, left like it was, the belt would have clattered loudly against the Cessna's fuselage throughout the whole flight to get here. The only other explanation was exactly what had happened. Somebody had just exited the plane after landing and had closed the strap in the door. Luckily, the balding man and the blonde must be passengers in the King Air, and so probably had not realized the full implications.

John opened the passenger door and clipped the end of the passenger strap into its buckle. He took his flight briefcase and the single small suitcase out from behind the front seats and walked to the building.

Two young black men in short sleeved uniform shirts were standing behind a counter talking in the fluid island dialect. The larger one smiled and beckoned him forward and pointed at the suitcase, saying to his partner, "It's gonna be a big party, mon. Half dis island gonna be there. Gloria sure be there. Maybe that's your chance, hey?"

John put the suitcase and briefcase down in the low cut-through in the counter. He took his passport and papers out of the briefcase and handed them to the smaller man. The passport had actually been provided by WITSEC, and bore a few innocuous entries dated over ten years. There were two entries for the Bahamas.

The bigger man nodded at him, checked his watch, and laid the suitcase down on a side table. Clicking it open, he said, "Welcome to Marsh

Harbour and to the Bahamas. What brings you to our humble country today?"

John smiled. "Thought I'd do a little fishing. Eat a plate of crayfish. Drink one or two Bahama Mamas."

"So you have been with us before," the smaller man said as he looked through the passport.

"I do some charter work. Once you've been here you want to come back, you know? Never seen better beaches anywhere." That much was the truth.

While the smaller man attended to the paperwork, the bigger man used a baton to poke through the suitcase. He clicked it closed and peered into the briefcase and again checked his watch.

John paid the fees in cash. They showed no interest in wanting to search the plane. The bigger man gave him a set of rental car keys that had been left for him, and they smiled and waved him on his way.

The rental was a blue Neon with blistered rust patches. He put the suitcase and briefcase in it, then went back and used the tow bar to pull the Cessna over to one of the tie-downs. He drove away from the air strip with the fishing rods poking backward out of the rear window, the front end of the Neon protesting that it badly needed new tires or an alignment, and a feeling of relief suffusing him. He could almost believe this really was just a stolen getaway from his troubles on the mainland.

He stopped at a grocery store and paid a hundred dollars for two small paper sacks of food. He had no trouble finding the modest home with D. Albury painted on a neat yard sign. Albury, a sun-leathered man in his sixties, came to the door and gave him keys to the rental cottage called Windward Reef, which was farther along Guano road. He said, "The wife makes the best Bahama bread on the island, and I can fix you up with fresh crayfish a lot cheaper than the market in town."

John bought a loaf of the bread and thanked him.

Windward Reef had been well chosen. It was out of the way, set among casuarinas, palms, and tropical shrubs with no close neighbors. The eighteen-foot center console fishing boat sat tied at a dock on a short gut leading out to open water. John was pleased to see it had a whisper-quiet hundred-horse Honda outboard hung on the transom. He spent a few minutes emptying most of the tackle box contents into a bucket he found in the cottage, selecting other items to pack into the tackle box, and stowing the box in the center console storage cabinet of the boat beneath some life jackets. He placed a powerful flashlight from the plane's tool kit on the steering console. A laminated local navigational chart had been included in the gear for the boat, along with a flare kit, in the overhead radio cabinet. He clicked on the radio and the lights to be sure everything worked, and checked the fuel tank gauge.

In the small, well provisioned kitchen of the two-bedroom cottage, he made himself a cup of instant coffee to go with a canned meat sandwich and ate it standing out on the porch, watching the last of the sun's ruddy glow fade from the sky. The spatter of other, far more distant suns taking over for the night. The sweet Bahama bread was good.

A big slice of moon would rise later, and that, too, would be good.

There was nobody on the rutted sand track winding through the woods a half mile from the air strip. He drove all the way to the end of the track, where it ended in a clearing at the bay, slewing the little car out of the ruts at times in the soft sand to avoid the larger water-filled depressions, and turned around. On the way back out to the main road he stopped by the bend. Two shadows detached themselves from the trees and Brewer and Swint got in.

Brewer said, "You're almost twenty minutes late."

"But there aren't any police with me. Pay attention to your own details. Your partner slammed the plane door on the seat belt strap. Left it hanging out. Two people saw it. In front of the Customs building. That could have turned into a major problem."

In the glow coming through the windshield from the headlights, Brewer smiled and said, "You know, I was fed up with listening to you five minutes after we met. Let's go get the boat and do this."

"I thought you wanted to go tomorrow night."

"I've decided we go now. No need to wait. We won't be conspicuous if we make the crossing while there are still a few other boats out."

John drove to the cottage and parked the Neon close by the boat dock.

When they were aboard, he laid the navigational chart on the steering seat and lit it with the flashlight. He said, "Where do you want to be dropped on Elbow Cay?"

Brewer looked at the chart and put his finger on a hook-shaped bay a quarter of the way up from the toe of the island, which was called Tahiti Beach. The only settlement on the island, Hopetown, was strung like a necklace around a harbor marked by a stubby lighthouse near its entrance more than two miles farther north.

Brewer tapped the chart and said, "Drop us just inside this hook. Cruise by the mouth of the bay first to see if anybody is around. Three or four boats will be on mooring buoys inside the bay. There's a small dock. You can use that or just nose up to the beach near the dock. Let us off and get back here and wait. Come back to pick us up an hour before dawn. Don't be later."

The Honda started easily, and purred and burbled softly as it warmed. John slipped the dock lines and backed the boat around until it was headed out the narrow channel, reversed it with the shifter, and idled out into open water, using the flashlight to pick up the first reflective channel marker. Going by the laminated chart, he set a course for the next marker and put the boat up onto a plane, the water looking and sounding like crushed crystal in the navigation lights as the hull cleaved through it in the night. The silhouettes of the smaller out islands were humped along the horizon and flecked with sparse lights. The Hopetown lighthouse was a welcome landmark beacon, winking steadily. The boat's speed added to the humid breeze coming in from the Atlantic, and John had to reverse his billed cap so it would not be snatched away. Brewer and Swint stood behind him, holding onto the rail mounted at the seat back. A half-moon was riding low, gilding the choppy water with shifting bluish silver.

There were a few other boats with their firefly navigation lights traversing the protected water between Great Abaco and the outer islands chain.

Approaching Elbow Cay, John slowed the boat to a fast idle, inching along the shoreline, avoiding shoals marked on the chart, and picking his way from marker to marker. There was a blinking white marker off the entrance to the small harbor. He made a slow pass off of the harbor mouth and could see no activity inside, so he brought it around and idled into the hook-shaped entrance. Three boats rode at moorings. One of them was a ketch with the name *Sea Song* in script on its stern. It looked to be about fifty feet long and well kept, its fittings and teak trim glinting, an inflatable dinghy hanging on stern davits.

A strip of steep beach glowed white in the flashlight beam. He nosed up to the sand and held the bow against it with the engine in gear at low power.

Brewer said, "An hour before dawn. Be here." He and Swint went over the bow and faded into the trees behind the beach.

John backed around and guided the boat out of the little coral bay at just above an idle. He kept it slow until he was two hundred feet from the bay inlet.

There was another small boat maybe two hundred yards ahead, moving away and slightly to the left. He pulled the fishing tackle box close by his feet and powered up onto a plane at full throttle to chase after it. The Honda was still relatively quiet. Sighting back to the bay mouth, he pulled up to within a few hundred feet astern of the other boat and stayed aligned right behind it so his white light would apparently nearly merge with the other boat's white light if Brewer and Swint happened to be watching from the shore. Then he toggled all the navigations lights off and swung the boat hard left. Feeling down at his feet, he got the night monocular out of the tackle box and switched it on to gather and amplify ambient light. He would not use the more powerful infrared beam mode unless necessary, to conserve battery power.

Holding the scope to one eye, he could clearly make out the marker he wanted, bathed in a weird greenish glow, and began steering the boat toward the southern tip of the island. He was aware that sound travels remarkably well over water. At times back in Pamlico Sound off Ocracoke Island on the Outer Banks, he had heard conversational voices on sailboats carrying to him from a quarter mile or more away as he'd drifted in a rowboat. But the Honda was whisper quiet, and the sounds of the other boats out tonight would mask any he was making. The wind was also at his back, and that would help mute his sounds for anyone behind him.

He had to hurry or he would lose them. Ahead, he could see why Tahiti Beach had earned its name. A long graceful arc of sand was populated by many palms, their fronds nodding in the breeze that swept in from the open Atlantic. He moved the monocular's field of view along it and could see no other boats or people.

Powering in until the last moment, he let the boat wash up so the bow came to rest on the sand at the water's edge. He switched off the ignition and reached into the tackle box once more. Got out a small flashlight and slipped it into his back jeans pocket. He grabbed the anchor line, quickly figure-eighted it to a cleat, and jumped off onto the beach.

Carrying the anchor in one hand out to the length of its line, he sank the flukes hard into the sand, setting the anchor firmly with his feet and then, awkwardly using the monocular, set off along the shoreline at a jog. It was difficult, because while the monocular offered a clear view well ahead, gathering ample light from the partial moon and stars, it offered no peripheral clues closer in, so for that he had to rely on the scant information the other eye was supplying. He had to be careful not to trip over a fallen palm trunk or stumble into a depression. If he fell, he could break the monocular or disable himself.

But Wasituna had trained him to run over uneven terrain and through woods partially on instinct. Sensing rising or falling ground and any change in the nature of the footing, placing each footfall with extreme care, ready to shift his body instantly to compensate for a loose rock or a tripping vine or a rotting deadfall, making him run in moccasins so his feet would be more sensitive, and carrying rocks of different weights in each hand to challenge his sense of balance. At first he had bruised his soles on roots and rocks and had stumbled frequently, but he had gradually improved until he could run the trail along Eaglenest Ridge behind his home in Maggie Valley like a ghost in near darkness, and he used those honed skills now. The beach tapered and finally blended into an impenetrable thicket of brush right up to the shallow water, and he was forced to go inland around the brushy area until he found fairly clear ground again, dodging through palms and scrubby pines.

He approached the little bay and circled it to where the two men had gone into the tropical brush and trees. Moving at a fast walk now and scanning ahead with the monocular, he struck out in the direction they had taken along a sandy path.

The path forked and he was forced to choose. He knelt off to the side and used the flashlight, shielded with two fingers, to study the sand. Both forks were pocked with indistinct depressions, but there were what looked like slightly more recent ones following the main path and going off to the right. He chose that way. The path wound through a stand of pines and up and over a low rise. He kept going. After a half mile he still could see no movement or human shapes ahead and was beginning to feel like he had taken the wrong fork when he saw lights through the trees and the shape of a cottage. He moved closer, scanning ahead to both sides of the path.

And saw them.

And immediately knew something about all this was badly wrong.

He had sensed something darkly askew ever since Ganz had first laid out the details of this trip for him. Now that instinctive feeling coalesced and surfaced like the head of some evil creature risen in a still midnight pond.

They were crouched behind an island of landscaping centered on a cluster of palms and John could see what was holding them up. The cottage was a single story but long, with probably three or more bedrooms, set in a small clearing and facing the ocean. Low surf was rumbling along the shore two hundred feet beyond the cottage and the surrounding palms were clattering in the onshore breeze.

A large shaggy dog that looked like an Irish setter was standing near the back of the cottage, straining back and forth at the end of a staked leash, wagging its long brush tail, looking intently at the cluster of vegetation where Brewer and Swint were hidden, and making short head-low prances, panting happily. Out of frustration, it let out two short barks. The pair were not upwind of the dog, so it must have glimpsed or heard them.

John knew they were not aware he was a hundred feet behind them, but he *felt* as though they should know, clearly exposed as they were in the eerie green glow of the monocular's vision. Only low light was coming out through two of the cottage windows, but it flared brightly in the monocular.

One of the men lifted what looked like an oversized futuristic hand gun and took aim. *Swint*, he thought. There was a soft pop, barely audible above the sound of the surf and the vegetation rustlings stirred by the wind, and the dog pivoted to nip at its flank. It whined and twisted around frantically several times, tangling the leash and flicking up spurts of sand from its paws. Then it wobbled, its flop-eared head unsteady and its hind legs losing purchase, and crumpled into stillness.

After a wait of ten seconds, the other man, certainly Brewer, made a series of hand motions and drifted away in a crouch to circle the cottage. Swint stayed where he was, watching the back door.

Maybe some atavistic prickle deep in Swint's brain startled him, and he reacted to it by turning his head and staring back over his shoulder, straight at John.

TWENTY-SEVEN

Standing outside Mothers near Charlotte, Brandon Doyle adjusted his flame-printed do rag and said, "The last time I was here there was a guy could probably hammer a railroad spike into my forehead with his thumb. These are some really bad dudes. I don't think you want to do this, Kit."

They had parked their motorcycles at the far end of a lineup of assorted machines that were resting on their kickstands under a parking lot light, their chrome glinting like blades in the humid night. Many were radically raked choppers with skulls airbrushed into gas-tank and fender paint jobs that looked two inches deep. A few were nearly stock cruisers carrying studded saddlebags and sissy bars. Including Doyle's bike with its distinctive ape hangers, all were Harleys except for Kitty's lipstick red Honda, which made Doyle think of a merry-go-round pony come to life in a pack of hungry velociraptors.

Kitty padlocked her white helmet by its strap to a saddlebag buckle and said, "I'm going in. Are you coming?"

Holding the grimy front door open for her and letting blasts of deafening heavy rock and a smell that was a blending of stale beer and stale armpits escape into the night, he shouted, "I can't remember if my insurance is paid up."

Inside, Kitty pointed at the bar and they took two empty stools. A four-piece band was working hard. The drummer was filling the smoky haze with harsh brass and almost visible bass pulses, and the thin leader was sweating under flickering multicolored lights. To Kitty he appeared to be trying to find some way to make love to a futuristic glittering guitar and becoming more frustrated and angry by the second because he couldn't. She thought the guitar did, however, sound like it was being raped.

Doyle raised an eyebrow and she shouted, "See if they have unsweet tea. Never mind. A bottled water."

He closed his eyes and shook his head. A blonde bartender who was not quite erupting from a strained dayglow orange halter top shot a bored look at Doyle, who leaned over and hollered, "A Bud long and a bottle of water." She gave Kitty a glancing appraisal and a sardonic smile, and asked for the money from Doyle up front.

Drinks in hand, they sat with their backs to the bar. Doyle tilted his head close to hers and said loudly, "What now?"

"Is this guy Tobin here?"

Doyle gestured with the neck of his beer. "At that big corner table. The mountain beside him is Wee Albert. He'll probably be the guy who kills me. I don't know the others."

"Let's wait. The band is either going to break something soon or need a rest."

The band labored through another set and quit for an announced ten minutes, and the sounds subsided into a babble of voices punctuated by clinking glass and raucous laughter.

Kitty said, "Okay, let's go."

Doyle followed her, carrying an empty longneck and weaving through a maze of tables and hustling waitresses bearing trays aloft. She walked up to the corner table and looked down. "You're Pitt Tobin?"

All four men at the table were in the colors of the Satan's Ghosts. Tobin's blood red rose tattoos vined up onto his neck out of his leather vest and the outline of a large flaming skull showed through his chest hair. Wee Albert overflowed the chair on his right. On his left a brunette with bleached tips and a row of tiny silver rings clipped through one eyebrow and more at the corners of her nose was leaning on her elbows, her forearms under her breasts, displaying a valley of pale cleavage as she curled her tongue around the tip of the straw in her tall drink and took a sip. A single red rose was tattooed on the hill of a breast. She was looking up through heavy makeup at Kitty with amused curiosity.

Tobin adjusted his pony tail and looked at her through cold eyes, a smile creasing his features. He nodded once.

Kitty said, "Where is John Hardin?"

"Why are you asking me? I don't think I ever heard of the guy."

Doyle said, "That won't crank. I was in here with him. Saw him talking with you."

Tobin transferred his smiling gaze to Doyle, but there was no hint of smile in his eyes. Nodded again and aimed a cocked forefinger at Doyle. "Oh yeah, now I remember you. Albert here was thinking about breaking your back on the bar because you weren't being real friendly."

Wee Albert was tensed, with one meaty hand braced on the table top, his chair pushed back. Doyle was holding the empty beer bottle in plain sight and pretended to take a pull on it, ready to grab it by the neck with his other hand, thinking, *hit the big bastard across the eyes as hard as you can before he stands all the way up. Grab Kit around the waist and make for that EXIT sign. Kick over a couple chairs behind you. Run like hell for the bikes.*

Kitty said, "I know what he's doing for you. Where is he now? Mexico? Canada?"

"Whoa, back up there, darlin'. Who are you?"

"Kitty Birdsong."

"Okay. This guy Hardin, he's a pilot if I remember, isn't he? Came in here trying to sell rides. I wasn't much interested. If you're his cousin or something, though, I might take to the guy after all. Or if you've got a thing for him and he's gone and got himself lost, I guess I could ask around. How's that?"

The spiky brunette said, "Hey, and meanwhile, if you're lonely tonight, sweet cheeks, I could probably hook you up. Any special way you like it?"

Kitty said, "Honey, if the strip mall is still open you ought to go get your money back on that boob job. And you ought to think twice about whose face you decide to get in or one day somebody might recycle all the junk in yours."

One of the men snorted and said, "You got to admit that's pretty good, Pitt. A strip-mall titty job."

The brunette squinted and sat back. "Listen, lady, who do you think you are? Coming in here trying to break up the party. Do you have any idea who this guy is?"

"He's a local leader of a pack of misfits called the Satan's Ghosts. And I don't think he's going to want any trouble in here tonight if he can help it. Wouldn't look good in his resume to sic his pets on people out in the open. And I don't think he wants some of his party games exposed to daylight."

The woman glared. "You *bitch*—"

Tobin said, "Shut up, Marie." He was no longer smiling, his mouth gone white around the edges and his dark eyes glittering. "All right. I think we're done talking here. You two can sit down at a table over there and have a drink on the SG or go find someplace else in town. What's it going to be?"

Kitty leaned over, rested her knuckles on the grimy table, and stared into the holes of Tobin's eyes. She said, "Listen to me. I don't care what you and your merry band of reject boy scouts do for fun and profit, but I'm telling you if John Hardin is damaged in any way, you're going to have worse enemies than the police or other little chopper clubs with equally stupid names. I belong to a bigger gang than yours."

She straightened up and walked away.

Tobin looked at Doyle and said, "Can you tell me what in *hell* she's talking about?"

Doyle grinned. "She belongs to the Cherokee Nation. And there's somethin' else you guys might want to think about."

Wee Albert rumbled, "Yeah, what's that?"

"Back in the day, when the Indian braves took prisoners they didn't want to feed? Had no use for? I heard they gave 'em to the women."

***

Later that night, Tobin called Sutter Leonard at his ranch in New Mexico and said, "How you doing, Dude?"

"The damned medics want me to go on chemo again. How the hell you think I'm doing?"

"Sorry, man. You know I'm with you. Listen, does our man in Tennessee have something going for us right now?"

"He shouldn't. Why?"

"That new pilot Hardin? His bitch showed up at Mothers tonight. Looking for him. She thinks he's off working for us. So you're saying the only way that could be happening is if Brain's got something going on his own."

"I'll look into it."

"I never really trusted the guy. You know that. If he's doing something serious now on his own and gets taken down, we could all wind up hurting."

"I said I'll check it out."

"Okay, man. You're the boss." *But not for long.*

***

I have nothing to lose, Clint Rader thought again. *If I'm quick enough, if I don't hold anything back, if I focus everything I've got left on it, I can do it. If I've fooled them, I can do it.*

He lay curled on the bunk, facing the wall, not long after darkness had filled his window. He'd long ago assumed he was observed by at least two concealed monitors. He knew he was in bad shape. He'd felt far detached from reality at times and had more frequent and severe memory lapses now. He would pace endlessly, his thoughts diffusing and sinking away into a grey mist. He would lurch back into the world to find himself standing still in the center of the room, or staring into the metal mirror in the bathroom. At times the tentacles of fear would break through his defenses and invade his core so rapidly and pervasively it would turn his insides to jelly. But some stubborn ember in him refused to be quenched. He'd taken a shred of pride in that, and he had continued fighting off the cold, black, mind numbing terror that stalked ever closer.

Calling on what he suspected were his last reserves, he had made a plan. For three days he'd feigned a deep lethargic depression—not difficult considering he was constantly teetering on the brink of one anyway—inwardly gathering himself. He had rehearsed it in his mind, and had tried to tone himself by working his muscles against each other, clasping his hands under the blanket and pressing them together in reps of a hundred each, lacing his fingers tightly and pulling for more reps, bunching his fists alternately and incessantly on a wad of blanket, pressing his feet against the wall as he lay on his side in more reps, clenching his abdominal muscles, all without visible motion and mostly when the room was in darkness.

Repeating to himself, *I can do it.*

It could happen any minute now.

The two obvious potential weapons were the plastic toothbrush and the plastic hairbrush grip, either of which he might have sharpened to a point by scraping on an edge of the steel bed frame in the darkness or under cover of the blanket, but that would be expected, and to the eyes of the hidden monitors they would be missed from their places on the metal shelf in the bathroom. He had also rejected the idea of trying to detach one of the bed legs, and suspected that the loose bolts in that leg were just a deliberate temptation, anyway.

Slowly he had pieced together his plan. Turned it over in his mind to study it. Knowing he had nothing at all to lose by trying it.

Now, then, while he still had enough grip left on reality.

Earlier, as he lay under the blanket he had stealthily removed a sock and hidden it in the sleeve of his jumpsuit. And tonight at sunset he had gone into the bathroom, apparently just to stare into the metal mirror for long minutes and to wash his face listlessly. Bent over the sink, he had soaked the sock in cold water and smeared it with toothpaste. He had shuffled back to the bed in the hobbling ankle chain, the dripping sock concealed in his palm, and had hidden it just under the edge of the small pillow.

And he waited, with his knees drawn up, facing the wall, unmoving, his left hand cupping the sock under the pillow, trying to keep too much of the water from seeping away into the mattress.

He heard the door opening and the light came on and he waited to feel Monroe's touch on his leg to wake him. Feeding time. The touch came but he did not move. Monroe slapped his calf twice sharply.

He jerked reflexively, groping out with his right hand and bracing the palm against the wall, as though disoriented and trying to stabilize himself. At the same time he turned his head slightly to the pillow edge and squeezed the sock, filling his mouth with water and toothpaste.

He shook his head and rolled over, keeping his eyes and head down. Monroe was standing two feet away, his feet shoulder width apart. Holding a small tray.

Clint rested his elbows on his knees and held his head in his hands, trying to look utterly defeated, watching Monroe's legs through his fingers. Slid his own lower legs slightly back so his weight would be more on the balls of his feet. Waited.

Monroe moved inches closer and put a hand under his armpit to urge him to his feet.

Clint exploded up and spat the water directly into Monroe's eyes, at the same time grabbing a handful of his shirt in his left fist to hold him close in where he could not kick, and striking out with his balled right fist with everything he had at Monroe's groin and feeling his knuckles mash flesh and jar against bone. Monroe, one hand to his eyes, the tray clattering on the floor, and the other hand windmilling to maintain balance, let out a deep grunt of pain. Roaring like an animal, Clint unleashed a wild desperate flurry of punches at his head, connecting again so well he heard Monroe's teeth click and he went down. Not all the way out, but groggy and confused. Clint knelt and found the retractable keychain on his belt, yanked violently on it three times with the supercharged strength of the adrenaline reserve flooding him, until it broke away.

Earlier, he had seen which key Monroe had used to lock the leg chain and now he fumbled to unlock it. Took the keys with him.

He lunged for the open doorway. Pulled the door shut behind him. Fumbled to find the right key for the deadbolt. The third one he tried fit and locked it. Swung out into the hall. Turned the corner and tried to orient himself as he ran awkwardly on legs he now realized were even weaker than he'd thought.

There. The double service doors to the kitchen. Stopped and looked through the glass. Saw nobody. Went through and grabbed a long knife from a cluster stored in a heavy wood holder. He hated knives but it was the only weapon available. There was a door to the outside. *The dogs.* He looked out through the glass window in the door and could not see them. And there seemed to be a wall around the compound between the buildings. The dogs must be outside it, between it and the far perimeter fence, of course, or nobody would be able to move freely within the compound.

He slipped outside and ran low in the shadows along the building, toward the front of the compound, thinking, *get to a car. Break out through the gate. Or go over the wall and run for the fence. Just get to the road. Stop somebody—*

The two taser darts, capable of arcing fifty thousand volts between them, struck into his back on either side of his spine and began injecting nineteen complex pulses per second. He lost all motor functions and crumpled against the wall jerking crazily in an agony of panic, the knife twisting out of his hand as it bent in the dirt.

Brain walked up holding the boxy laser-sighted pistol device that was still firing pulses through the thirty-five-foot insulated wires connected to the embedded probes. He watched Clint twitch for a few more seconds and then shut the taser off.

He said, "Congratulations. You showed clever initiative. Monroe is not an easy man to surprise. When he recovers I'm sure he will want to spend some quality time with you and, within certain limits that will preserve the integrity of our research data, I will allow him that. He is quite skilled at inflicting maximum pain just short of causing irreparable damage. No, do not move. Two of my men are on the way. They will help you to my study. You and I have much more remaining to accomplish. We need to discuss how our sessions will proceed over the course of your dwindling days, you see. And it is time we begin considering your termination options."

Clint, his nervous system still in painful chaos, squinted his eyes tightly closed.

Squeezing out tears.

TWENTY-EIGHT

John froze.

Swint was prominently bathed in the eerie green glow displayed by the monocular and it felt as though the man must surely see him just as clearly. John had to resist the almost overpowering urge to dive for cover and instead remain still with the monocular held to his eye. He knew there were no significant lights behind to silhouette him, but there was low moonlight filtering through the trees. Was he just another indistinct shadow among all the others, or would Swint be able to discern his man-shape, make out his white face and hands if he stared long enough?

Swint scanned the darkness behind him through a wide arc several times and listened intently, but finally returned his attention to the cottage.

John took a breath and thought, *they're here to kill whoever's in that cottage. So maybe these are bad guys inside, too. Maybe drug trade rivals. But what if they're not? Do something. Right now.*

He used the monocular to search the sandy ground around him. There. He moved quickly, knelt, and picked up a coconut in its rough husk. Tested the weight of it. Heard the milk slosh inside. It would have to do. He swept the monocular's field of view over the cottage to make sure Brewer was not in sight, and moved fast up the path, carrying the monocular at his side now in one hand and the coconut in the other.

Swint had become just a crouched shadow himself and John focused on that shadow, gripping the rough husk and drawing back at the ready. His arm would be a club, with the coconut the club head.

Swint stood up and started edging toward the back door of the cottage.

John broke into a jog and was ready to swing the coconut, but again Swint, sensing something, stopped and whirled around, bringing up his right hand and aiming straight at John's chest.

Instead of swinging the coconut like a club, and still moving, he took the best aim he could in the shadows and threw it at Swint's head. It caught him a glancing blow on the shoulder and made him stagger back a step and deflected his aim, but he did not go down. John closed the last twenty feet between them and grabbed for the extended arm, and the weapon, now held slightly to one side and coming to bear on his chest again. He dropped the monocular and clamped his left hand on the weapon in Swint's right hand. Not a pistol. But whatever he had used on the dog. Felt the thing kick pneumatically and a sharp pain under his arm. Tried to wrench the thing free.

Swint lashed out with his other hand and the side of John's head bloomed into white pain. Dazed, feeling the ground lurch under him, John stabbed clumsily out at Swint's head in slow motion with his right fist and missed. They were both grunting and taking rasping breaths, trying to make no noise, John because he did not want Brewer to hear and be drawn into it, and Swint because he did not want to alert whoever was in the cottage. Swint caught him again in the same place, the blow glancing off his upraised forearm and pounding his ear numb.

But Swint was not swinging with full force or accuracy with that arm because the coconut must have damaged him. Swint let go of the weapon and used that fisted hand to send a short powerful blow into John's ribs under his heart, driving air out of him.

John was dimly aware that he was going down in the next two or three seconds if he did not do something to stop it. He dropped the weapon and raised both forearms to ward off more blows. Brought his fists together and in a last instinctive burst of lucidity drove them like a single wide ram at Swint's throat. Swint fell away and John fell with him onto his hands and knees in the sand. Tried to raise his head and make sure Swint was out of action, but could not see him. There was a roaring in his head. He saw Swint's leg drawing back. A sneaker sole in an intricate pattern came looming at him, caught him on the collarbone and he fell back and over onto his side, trying to scrabble away from more kicks. Came up hard against a rough tree trunk at the small of his back.

Fought to make the world stop lurching. Shook his head. Focused on a patch of yellow light thrown onto the sand from one of the cottage windows and willed himself not to pass out.

Gradually the roaring in his head faded and things settled down around him. Swint was on his back, one leg repeatedly kicking out at nothing, both hands to his throat, his head bobbing jerkily, his chest convulsing, then he twisted on the sand and pushed himself up into a sitting position. Went back to his neck with one hand and groped wildly with the other hand. He nodded jerkily several times, supporting himself with one palm pushing down and skidding a track into the sand, and he fell over onto his side and went limp.

John lifted his head against the dull pain and managed to sit up. Felt the side of his head and his hand came away wet. His ribs throbbed. There was a burn in his side under his arm. He explored it with two fingers. Not deep. The projectile in the hand weapon must have grazed him. Had apparently not penetrated. He pushed himself up to stand, one hand propped against the sticky pine tree.

He knew without looking closer that Swint must be dead, must have had his larynx crushed, and he suppressed a wave of nausea at the thought.

The whole fight must not have lasted more than three minutes. Brewer was still on the other side of the house. He swayed away from the tree and headed for the back door of the cottage. Got to it and thudded on it quietly with the butt of his fist.

Five seconds went by and he thumped the door again.

A fit weathered man about an inch shy of six feet, with a white crew cut and wearing a tight black T-shirt with the Olympics logo on it, with a holster on the belt of his shorts, pulled the door open. Looked at him through the screen door, frowning.

John held up both hands shoulder high and palms out and said in a low voice, "You need to watch the front. Now. One man. I think he's here to kill you. The other one is down and out of it."

Thought, but could not bring himself to say, *I just killed him*.

The man drew the pistol, a compact black automatic, and aimed it at his chest. Trained blue eyes on him and said, "Lace your fingers on top of your head. That's it. Now, slowly." Stood back three feet and motioned him inside. Pushed him up against the wall and ran a hand over him thoroughly.

John said, "You're wasting time. The one on the ground outside used some kind of dart-firing pistol on your dog. The other one's out front right now."

"Who are you?"

"John Hardin. I'm on your side."

The man locked the door deadbolt. Thought for several seconds, staring into John's eyes, and said, "Okay. Sit at that table."

John sat.

The man backed up so he could keep his eyes and the pistol trained on John, but spoke in a low calm voice to somebody in the living area beyond. "Ma'am. Sir. I need you to please take Erin and go to the back bedroom right now."

"What is it, Alden?" A woman's voice. A strong, familiar voice.

"Please hurry ma'am. Quietly. There's no lock on the bedroom door, so push the dresser close up in front of it, lock the windows, then all three of you get down flat on the floor. Wait for me."

There were rustlings and footfalls in the living area, then only the muted sound of the wind and the clattering palms outside.

There was a polite knocking on the front door.

Alden, his face betraying only an intense concentration, said, "Come here."

John got up and Alden motioned him into the living area.

A small desk against one wall, covered neatly with paperwork.   Bamboo furniture with bright cushions.   A worn rattan rug.   A laptop lit up but abandoned on the couch, ear phones connected to it. An open book on the floor by a beachy recliner, and a gaudy glass with ice and amber liquid on the side table.   A net with shells caught in it hanging on a wall.

A relaxing family in a comfortable place. Interrupted.   Probably not bad people, after all.   A family.   And an incongruous scene for sudden violence.

The knock again.   Still polite but a bit more insistent.   A hint of impatience.   John thinking, *surprising how much you can read into just a door knock. It sounds innocent.*

The door was rippled stained glass.   Birds and flowers.   Probably to catch the dawn sun and fill the room with pleasing morning colors.   Now showing the indistinct shadow of a man.   The wind was louder here, flooding through partially-opened windows out of the moonlit darkness beyond.   Making a low rising whistle.

Alden said, "Count to five. Go slow.   One thousand, two thousand.   Then answer the door.   It's not locked.   Don't think.   Just do it."

John focused on the door and began the count as Alden moved fast to the end of the room and slipped out through a set of double doors onto the porch, which John realized must run around the side and front of the cottage.

Stepping closer to the door. . . . *Four thousand. Five thousand.*

He put his hand on the knob and opened the door.

Brewer stood there with his right hand in his jacket pocket, his left hand raised to knock again. He tensed up like he'd been electrically shocked and froze, his eyes going wide.

From the side, Alden yelled GUN ON YOU. DON'T MOVE.

Brewer jerked his head to the side. Took in Alden. Stared back at John. Not assimilating.

John said, "Swint's out of it. You're alone."

Alden hollered, SHOW ME BOTH HANDS. SLOW. DO IT NOW.

Brewer focused on John, his eyes going dark and narrowing, his face contorted into a grimace of hatred. He growled, "You *bastard*—" His right hand darted out of the jacket pocket holding a small syringe and he stabbed out with it, John drawing back instinctively so the needle just missed him, and Alden shot him.

John saw the bullet pluck at Brewer's leg. He grunted and took a staggering step around to face Alden, who, moving closer with the automatic held competently in a two-handed grip, shot him in the other leg and he went down, slamming his back against a porch post, dropping the syringe and grabbing at his legs. His fingers gnarled into claws.

Keeping the automatic trained on Brewer's chest, Alden toed the syringe out of reach. Then he held the gun in one hand and searched Brewer. Came up with a telescoping baton slid behind his belt and a small revolver from an ankle holster. Two more plastic-sheathed syringes and five plastic vials were in a nylon fanny pack, along with a dozen heavy opaque zip ties bent in half to fit inside the pack. No wallet. Nothing in the pockets. Dark stains were spreading out onto the porch from the leg wounds and Brewer was grunting. Taking short breaths.

Alden held a cluster of the ties out to John, his eyes not leaving Brewer and the gun held steady for a heart shot, and said, "Use one of these on his wrists. In front of him. Not too tight."

John strapped Brewer's wrists together and Alden said, "Okay, now link three or four of them end to end and strap his left arm to the post there. I think three might do it." He scanned around into the night. "Are you sure there were only two of them?"

"Yes. I brought them here."

"What?"

Instinctively beginning to trust Alden, John said, "Long story. I'll explain later."

Alden reached inside to flick on the porch light, and bent to look at Brewer's legs. Said, "Go in and get the medical kit. First door along the hall. Bathroom. In the cabinet under the sink."

Alden used the contents of the kit to cut away the legs of Brewer's jeans to expose the wounds, shook a disinfectant onto the holes, and bound pressure bandages in place, slowing the bleeding to seepage. He said, "One is through and through. The thigh bone stopped the other slug. Stay here and watch him. I'll go put my people's minds at ease and then you and I are going to talk."

John said, "Okay."

Alden went inside and was gone for several minutes. When he came back carrying a small but bright aluminum flashlight, he said, "They'll stay in the back bedroom until we get this sorted out. Friends are on the way but won't be here for an hour. This one will keep. Let's go look at the one out back."

They walked around the cottage, Alden scanning the vegetation. He washed Swint with the flashlight beam, then went down on one knee to lay two fingers against the side of his neck. Said, "Nothing there. He's dead."

"I know. I hit him hard in the throat."

Alden went over to check the dog, shook his head, and said mostly to himself, "Also dead. Erin will be devastated." He stood up and stepped back to face John. "Okay, you brought them here. Who and what are you?"

John said, "That was a clever piece of work on the porch. What if Brewer—that's the one you shot; this one is Swint—what if Brewer had just started shooting when I opened the door?"

"Then I still would have tagged him, but not in the legs. Protecting the family has to be top priority. I didn't trust you, so I had to keep you busy, at least. And I figured whoever the guy was at the door, he'd be surprised to see somebody who wasn't me or one of the family. It would give me a little extra edge. He was surprised all right, but that was because he knew you. And you look like you've just been in a fight. But I wasn't sure you'd open the door."

"I figured he'd be startled to see me, too. And I had to do something. Because I brought them here."

Alden nodded. "So what are you? Undercover?"

"John Hardin. Not any kind of law. I flew them into Marsh Harbour past customs and brought them over here in a rental boat. Supposed to pick them up before dawn and slip them back into Florida. They work for a man named Ganz in Tennessee. I think this Ganz carries out contract killings using trained teams like these two. Something like a modern Murder, Incorporated, that the mob had going back in the Thompson submachine gun days. I'm only involved because I think he's holding the brother of a man I knew and I need to learn enough about the operation. Enough to find some way to cut the brother loose. *If* he's really still being held, and if he's being held where I think. To do that I've had to get close, and I wound up working for them. I have no idea why he sent them here. Who's in the house?"

"A family. Three people. I'm a friend and longtime bodyguard. Xavier Alden. Just call me Alden. I'm the only security they've got right now. I'm going to fix that quick. And I think I do know why these two were sent here. But let's find out for sure, shall we? Right now."

"Talk with Brewer?"

"Something like that. Bear with me."

With the help of the flashlight, Alden thoroughly searched the body. Another telescoping baton and another snub nosed revolver on one ankle. A dart-firing pistol in the sand, with spare darts and more wrist ties in a fanny pack. No ID of any kind. No rings. Only a cheap watch. When he pulled the black T-shirt up, a small tattoo over the left nipple was exposed. He said, "What's this?"

They both studied the intricate dragon.

John said, "I don't know. But Ganz is affiliated with an outlaw motorcycle gang. The Satan's Ghosts. He supposedly leads an elite cadre within the Ghosts called the Satan's Wraiths. So maybe it's some gang symbol."

"Look closer. Are those numbers? Worked into the design?"

"Could be."

"Maybe Brewer's got one, too. We'll check."

"What do you have in mind here?"

"Let's think. We never told Brewer just now that his partner was dead. You only said he was out of it, right?"

"Yes."

"So let's resurrect him."

TWENTY-NINE

Using zip ties to bind Swint's wrists together at the front, Alden said, "First thing we do is set up a little dramatic scene. How good an actor are you?"

With a pen knife, Alden cut a long length of the dog's leash, which he stuffed into his pocket. He picked up the dart weapon and, holding the end of the small flashlight in his mouth, studied it. Loaded it with one of the darts. Passed the flashlight to John, held the dart pistol in one hand, and grabbed Swint by an armpit. He said, "Help me move him."

Together, Alden indicating directions with his head, John lighting the way with the flashlight, they dragged Swint's body around the side of the cottage into the vegetation and along a path to a clearing that overlooked the ocean, surf crumbling on the reef in long white ropes under the broken moon. Alden propped the seated body up against a palm tree and used the leash loosely around the neck to hold it in place. Left the dart pistol on the sand three feet away and said, "Okay, let's go get Brewer."

Alden cut Brewer away from the porch post and they dragged him, groaning and swearing, along the same path. Alden selected another palm tree in the clearing, fifteen feet from where Swint's body was strapped up. They propped Brewer against the tree, looped zip ties around his biceps, and connected them behind the tree. His face was filled with hatred and pain in the weak moonlight.

Alden looked at Swint's body and then at Brewer, seemingly pondering. Said, "Okay, which one first?" Pointed a finger at the shadowy mass strapped against the tree. Nodded. "That one, I think. His throat's damaged, but he can still whisper."

Alden stepped over to stand in front of the still body.

Brewer twisted against his bonds to look up at John and said, "You're a dead man, smartass. *Knew* something was wrong about you. He won't stop now until he sees your severed head. Spits in your eye sockets."

"You'd better worry about your own skin."

Alden knelt on one knee in the shadows and bunched the dead man's shirt in his left fist and slapped the face hard with his right. "Wake up, killer." Used the bunched shirt to bobble the head convincingly. "I want to know who paid you guys to come down on us here." Slapped again. "YOU HEAR ME, KILLER? I want to know all of it. I might start poking holes in you with my jackknife. Take my time. All the soft places. Belly first. Upper legs. Crotch. Not enough to spill things, just so you bleed a little more out of each hole. We'll count the holes together. Let's set a goal. Can you take a hundred before you die? I'll make a bet with you. I figure you'll have told us everything you know before I get to twenty." Swint's head lolled groggily and Alden leaned in close, partially obscuring the body from Brewer's view. "What's that? LOUDER, you bastard. Who the hell is Ganz and why would he want us dead?"

Brewer looked over at Swint and growled, "Shut up. Don't tell them anything."

Alden leaned even closer. "What? Tell me that again." His head blocking the view of Swint's head, as though straining to hear. "LOUDER."

John's scalp prickled and his breath caught when he heard, or thought he heard, parts of an answering, rasping whisper mixed with the noises of the breeze, ". . . *contract . . . Tennessee . . .Ghosts . . . Marsh Harbour . . .*"

Brewer shouted, "SHUT UP, SWINT. They don't know ANYTHING. JUST SHUT UP."

Alden said, "Okay, so why the needles? TELL me." He apparently listened. Said, "Everybody? The kid too? What?"

Alden, still with his left hand clutching the bunched shirt, reached for the dart pistol, held it two inches from the dead man's chest, and fired, the pneumatic *phut* clearly punctuating the breeze. The body bucked and twitched convincingly for several seconds and finally went still. Alden let go, stood, and looked out to sea, apparently calming himself out of his rage.

Brewer was staring at Swint's body.

Alden ran a hand over his face and took a series of deep breaths.

John stepped over to him, both facing away from Brewer now, and said, loud enough for Brewer to hear, "I understand how you feel, but you didn't have to kill him so soon. He might have told us more."

Alden said loudly, "What the hell did it matter? He was pretty broken up, anyway. Wouldn't have lasted much longer. We've still got the other one."

"Okay, but just calm down, will you? Come here a minute. Listen to me." John walked out onto the narrow beach where Brewer would not be able to hear, and Alden followed.

John put a hand on Alden's shoulder, as though trying to calm him down, and spoke low. "That was pretty convincing."

"I'm pretty damned pissed. What is it you want to know?"

"Is Ganz holding a man named Clint Rader? If so, is he being held at the Tennessee compound, and where in the compound?"

"That's it?"

"Anything else he knows about the compound. Security. How many guards."

"Okay. Let's go squeeze him."

"Wait. I think he has a deep fear of sharks."

Alden nodded and gave him a tight-lipped smile in the moonlight.

They walked back and Brewer looked up at them. Hate and defiance. But cracked. Weakened by fear that crawled behind his eyes furtively in the indirect glow from the flashlight that John held low to one side so Brewer could still see them.

Brewer licked his lips, and a drop of oily sweat hung in one eyebrow. "Not saying a damned thing."

John said, "You're alone now. A long way from Ganz. Do you realize what he had you doing here? These people, this family, are known all across the country. You're supposed to be working for the Ghosts. Do the Ghosts even know anything about this? Or was it just Ganz on his own? What kind of heat would this have focused on you? I hope Ganz was going to pay you very big money for it. Or maybe he was just going to have you killed later, too. What do you think?"

Brewer looked up, but his eyes had lost a lot of the hostility, replaced by shadows of doubt. He started to say something, but then shook his head and stared at the sand.

John said, "You'll need a doctor soon. You just have to tell us what you know and we'll get you fixed up. All you've done so far is kill a dog. What can they do to you?"

Alden said, "To *hell* with *that*. Swint said they were going to do us all, even the kid. Then make us disappear." Alden reloaded the dart pistol, his movements angry. He pointed it at Brewer's right eye from a distance of two feet. "I ought to kill this one, too, right now. The same way they were going to kill us."

John held up a hand. "No, wait. He'll tell us what he knows. Then we can get him a doctor. Call in the local cops. They must have some place to hold him. Brewer, is what he just said true? You had orders to make them all disappear? Look, nobody's recording this here. We already know most of it. Just lay it out for us and we'll see you get help."

Brewer stared at his feet and shook his head. Thinking, *let the Bahamas cops take me. Get word out to Ganz, and he can send a team to break me out.*

Alden lowered the pistol and said, "Second thought, a dart would be too quick. Too easy. I say we take him out in the boat." With a motion of his head he indicated the sea behind him. "Just before dawn, when they start feeding. I've been out there on dives. The reef falls away like a cliff way down out of the light, but the water is gin clear under the surface. You can see a long way all around. One minute there'll be nothing but pretty little fishes playing along the reef and the next minute you look around and out of nowhere here they come. In the first of the daylight. Up out of that blackness."

Brewer stared up at Alden and swallowed twice. A tick twitching at his temple. Said, "You aren't going to do that."

Alden smiled. "They like to cruise along the reef wall because there's a lot to eat there. You see all kinds. Grays. Six-, eight-foot black tips. Damned big hammerheads. Once in a while a great white, like a fat torpedo with teeth, and you'd better be ready to scramble out of the water then. Cold black eyes. Sometimes a pack of them will get crazy fighting over a big meal. Rip and tear at it."

Brewer cringed and shook his head. "No—"

Alden said, "I say we put a life jacket on him so he doesn't drown. Cut his wrists loose. The blood from his legs will drift off in red threads and pink clouds. They'll lock onto that trail and follow it. They probably won't attack right away. Just circle and bump him until one of them figures out he's helpless and starts the picnic."

In feigned disgust, John said, "No, you couldn't really do that." And Brewer gave him a pleading look.

Alden said, "That's going to be up to him. If you don't have the stomach for it I have friends here who'll help me. What about it, Brewer? The cable ties. They weren't to hold us, were they? They were just to make the bodies easier to handle after you'd done us, right? Then what? You load the bodies onto the sailboat tonight or tomorrow night, motor out two or three miles. Turn on the auto steering. Point it at Africa and crack the through-hull valves. You two come back in the inflatable. Get closer to shore, deep-six the outboard, paddle in the rest of the way, cut the registration and serial numbers off the inflatable and set it adrift. That's how I'd do it. Was that the plan? Was it?"

Brewer let out a groan at the pain in his legs, his eyes clenched tight and his chin falling to rest on his chest. He was quivering with the mixture of fear and pain now.

John said, "Answer him or he's going to kill you, too. He already figures that had to be the plan. Was it? Tell him, for God's sake. We'll get help for you."

Nothing.

Then Brewer nodded. Resigned and defeated. He squinted up at John and said, "Don't know why. How much. Any of that. We were just . . . just following orders."

Alden said, "You two were a hit team. How many teams does Ganz have?"

"Don't know."

"HOW MANY?" Alden shouted.

Brewer moaned. "Okay, okay. Five teams. Twelve of us. No, eleven."

John said, "Is Monroe one of them?"

"No. Trained us."

John said, "So it's eleven plus Monroe and Ganz. Thirteen."

Brewer nodded.

Alden pulled open Brewer's shirt, popping the buttons off. The dragon was there, above the left nipple. "This is the mark of your hit crew, right? Something that makes you assholes proud. It looks like numbers worked in. Is this like the Skinhead double eights? Eighth letter of the alphabet is H. So theirs means heil Hitler. What do your numbers stand for?"

Brewer hung his head.

Alden said, "Okay. Ask him what you want to know. Then he and I are going to chat some more."

John said, "I think Ganz does some kind of psychological studies on people, is that right?"

"Don't know anything about that."

"What have you heard?"

Brewer looked up. "He'll kill me."

"We'll see you get protection. Does he do studies like that?"

"Could be."

"I need more than that."

"I think so. God, my legs—"

"Is he holding a man now?"

"Heard yes."

"Tell me about that."

"All I know."

"Would he be held in the compound?"

"Yes. Ganz most never leaves."

"Where in the compound?"

"Don't know. Could be that separate wing in back. Behind the kitchen. Through the hall. Locked. Locked hall. Supposed to be storage. But only Ganz and Monroe . . . only ones go back there. Maybe connects to the library or office. Don't know. I need a doctor."

"Soon," John said. "Compound security. Tell me about it. Are there motion detectors? Infrared sensors? Cameras?"

"All that. Won't get in."

"How many guards?"

"Changes. Mostly six of us there, maybe. Legs. My legs—"

"Including Ganz and Monroe?"

"All I know. Swear it. All I know. A doctor. Please."

Brewer was getting groggy. Lethargic. John brought the flashlight beam to bear on him and saw the blossoming stain under his legs. His face was becoming pale and tinged with a gray pallor.

John said, "Alden. Something's wrong. Look."

Alden knelt and propped Brewer's head up by the chin. The eyes tried to focus but rolled white. Brewer went slack. Alden felt for a neck pulse. Long seconds went by. He said, "Nothing. I must have nicked the femoral and it just let go. I think he's bled out. The sand soaked it up so we didn't see it sooner."

They stood and Alden considered both bodies. "Friends will be here soon. They'll help me clean this up. And I'll have more security from the States here by late morning."

"How are you going to clean it up?"

"These two are going to be shark food, after all."

"What about the gunshots? The neighbors?"

"Sound doesn't carry far across this wind. There's a lot of vegetation on both sides of us and it's noisy. People out here tend to keep to themselves. Just two shots spaced out could be put down as somebody testing a pistol, if anybody did hear them clearly. I think we're okay on that."

"Why aren't you calling in the law?"

"I'll explain later. What are you going to do?"

"I haven't thought about it. But it's good for me if you don't pull in the law."

"Come in. I'll make some calls. You can wash up some and meet the family. I'm sure they'll want to thank you."

"For bringing these two down on them?"

"For probably saving their butts. I was stupid. Complacent. We were all vulnerable because we thought nobody knew we were here. If I had opened that front door, thinking it was a neighbor or one of my friends from the big island, Brewer might have stuck me in the neck or the chest with his poison before I could have reacted. The family would have been no match for the two of them."

"Why the syringes?"

"Minimal forensic evidence. They didn't want bullet holes or blood. I think it was supposed to look like the family and I and the dog just sailed away over the horizon on a day cruise and vanished. They would have left the cottage as clean as possible. No bodies. No evidence of struggle or break in. So no crime. Just a lot of speculation in the media. The *Times* might have tried to connect some theoretical dots and might even have come close to the truth. The supermarket tabloids would have dragged out all that old Bermuda Triangle stuff, or would have held aliens responsible. Like with Jimmy Hoffa or Amelia Earhart."

They went back to the cottage, John feeling the aches from the fight now and favoring his right leg.

Alden held the front door open for him and he
stepped inside. A willowy teenaged girl with long
dark hair in disarray sat on the end of the couch in a
white terry robe, her legs curled under her, fingertips
held to her lips and her eyes wide and desolate. She
had been crying and was still sniffling. A tall thin
man in his fifties, who, from the obvious physical
resemblance, was the girl's father, stood beside the
end of the couch, one hand resting on the girl's
shoulder, looking from Alden to John with a
questioning scowl. He said, "She ran outside before I
could stop her and saw Rowdy."

"I'm sorry, girl," Alden said. "I'll wrap him up
in a blanket and take him over to the big island. He
can rest out behind old Tom's place. You know he
liked it there. Okay?"

The girl started crying quietly again, holding her
face in her hands. She tried to nod in answer.

The man patted her shoulder.

Alden said, "Leland, this is John Hardin. He
just helped eliminate a serious threat to us. We owe
him. It's apparently safe for now, but we'll need
more security."

The thin man said, as though he already knew,
"What was this threat? What were those shots?"

A woman came out of the hallway dressed in
her customary worn jeans, tucking a red western
blouse in at her waist. She was about five ten, in her
late forties, with short dark hair attractively seasoned
with silver threads. A plain face, without makeup.
With a too-large nose and startling eyes of Arctic
blue.

A face John knew well.

THIRTY

The woman glanced at Alden and John, went to the couch, and sat half turned toward the girl. Gently took the girl's hands down from her stricken face and held them.

The girl said, "I want to know what's going *on*. Why is this *happening*? Rowdy is . . . is *dead*, mother."

"I know honey. I know. And we *will* find out the why of this. What's important right now is that Alden says we're safe. I know you believe him. We need you to be as strong as I know you can be." She smiled and used her fingers to brush away the girl's tears.

The effect was immediate. The girl closed her eyes and straightened her back. Sniffled once more and nodded.

The woman's face registered concern when she looked up at John. She said, "You're hurt. I'm sorry. I hadn't realized. Erin, honey, please go get a warm washcloth, a towel, and the hydrogen peroxide. There's a bottle in the linen closet in the big bathroom."

The girl combed her long fingers through her hair, uncoiled from the couch, and went obediently.

John noticed from her fleeting glance she had her mother's eyes, and thought her lucky.

He had not moved, staring at the woman.

He said, "But you're Crystal Campion."

She smiled like sunshine breaking through overcast. "And you're John Hardin. Please sit, John. I want a look at your head. Are you hurt anywhere else?"

He said, "No, ma'am," and sat at the dining table. Erin brought the towels quickly and the woman bent to inspect the wound, tilting his head gently toward the light. Daubing with the washcloth. As she worked she said, "Erin honey, why don't you go to your room and start packing? Your dad and I need to talk with Alden and this man about what to do. But in any case we'll be leaving soon."

Alden said, "Your mom's right girl. And please don't call anybody, okay?"

The girl went down the hall to her room.

Few people in the country would not know Crystal Campion on sight. She was heiress to a vast Texas ranching and petroleum fortune and headed the charitable Campion Foundation, known for involving itself in apparently hopeless and usually dangerous causes. Rescuing bruised and dirty children from the most recent tribal genocide in central Africa. Bringing medical help to dying victims of horrifying and highly contagious diseases like Ebola. Fighting against the inexorable degradation of the planet on several fronts. Her blend of simple incisive logic and infectious good humor won converts on the talk shows. Her books made the top ten lists. Presidents and a host of lesser politicians wanted to be imaged with her.

Yet for all her wealth and status she insisted on living without any pampering, excessive luxury, entourage, or pretension, which only endeared her to the public more. She had been famously photographed on horseback in snow on one of the Native American reservations, reaching down to grasp the hand of an old woman in a shawl. And at the flap of a medical tent, her shirt stained with perspiration, in a jungle with an unpronounceable name. There was some memorable footage of her testifying before Congress, dressed plainly but possessing enough sincerity, knowledge, and straight-spined presence to back down the most seasoned and jaded of snipers working for special interests opposed to her efforts.

When she had cleaned the split and applied a square adhesive bandage, she said, "There, now. What would you like? Water? Coffee?"

"Nothing, thank you. I don't understand."

Alden had been on the porch, talking on a cell phone. He stepped inside. "Understand what?"

"Why anybody would want to harm Mrs. Campion and her family."

Leland Campion seemed to come to a decision. He gestured at the table and said, "Let's sit and think about this."

He sat across the table from John. Crystal and Alden took the other two chairs.

Leland said, "How many?"

Alden said, "Two. We're sure of that."

"Their condition?"

"Both dead. Our friends from Marsh Harbour are on the way. I think it's best if we clean it up quietly. I'll have more security tomorrow morning at the latest."

Leland propped his elbows on the table, cupped his right fist with his left hand, and studied John. Said, "You seem to trust him, Alden."

"He probably saved us all. I wasn't ready for this. Didn't think anybody outside the first circle even knew we were here. It was a discreet cruise. Nobody should have seen us leave there or arrive here. No paper trail. We're using a borrowed cabin on a small out-of-the-way island. But I should have known better."

Crystal said, "No, Alden. Not your fault. I've always insisted on minimal security."

"That's irrelevant right now, anyway," Leland said. "We need to focus on what comes next. How did you become involved in this, Mr. Hardin?"

He gave them a highly condensed version, leaving out why he had agreed to help Nolan Rader.

Leland pondered for a few seconds and said, "So apparently somebody contracted with this man Ganz, and he sent a team to kill us."

"To make us disappear," Alden said. "Any kind of straightforward killing would have drawn down too much heat from the law and the media. They wanted to plant the logical probability it was an accident. The plan was to take us all out in the sailboat, ditch it offshore and come back in the dinghy, then scuttle that."

Leland said, "I didn't think these people had anything like that kind of malicious resolve. Such evil *arrogance*. Obviously I've grossly underestimated them."

John said, "Who are they?"

Leland said. "How much do you know about, say, the Enron debacle?"

"Not much. Complex corporate thievery. Some kind of cover-up. I think a few of the executives got charged and sentenced. Probably to easy time."

"Over only a decade and a half, Enron grew to become the seventh largest company in the country, employing some twenty-one thousand people in forty countries, making all kinds of deals involving energy. Some said influencing energy policy itself in several countries. Strong political ties right up to White House level. They had a healthy public image. Shared a king-sized bed with some of the world's largest, most respected banks. Their stock was gold-plated and in demand. But it turned out they were using what are euphemistically known as aggressive accounting practices—not uncommon in corporate America, only they were being somewhat more aggressive than the norm. Creatively hiding debt and enhancing cash flow on electronic paper to pump up apparent profits, for example. Some of their individual deals tipped over from shady into outright fraud, when you strip all the glossy veneering away and call it what it was. You might imagine the company as a beautifully-wrapped Christmas present with a rat's nest inside. One of their executives finally blew the whistle and it all came down like a child's fantasy sandcastle at high tide. Unfortunately, it's not all that unusual a tale around the corporate campfire."

John was deciding he liked Leland Campion. The man seemed to be built around a core of quiet integrity that radiated from him.

Crystal Campion said, "A few of those involved at the top eventually paid a price, but thousands of Enron employees who had their pensions and the bulk of their savings wrapped in company stock, and people outside the company who were invested heavily, lost billions in the bankruptcy. Think of a couple who've worked faithfully, relentlessly hard for years, for decades, suddenly facing the loss of their home. Or a college fund gutted. People watching their retirement dreams evaporate."

Leland said, "For twelve years, I've served on the boards of several large conglomerates, and two years ago, I moved into the chairmanship of one. The name is not well known, but several of our linked companies certainly are. What I'm going to tell you now absolutely must not leave this place, do you understand?"

"Yes."

There was a low call outside. Alden said, "Our friends from the big island. I'll be outside a while. Not too far away. Be back as soon as I can. If there's any problem, call me on the cell." He got up, locked the back door and the porch doors, and went out the front, locking it behind him. The breeze had picked up, jostling the palm fronds outside and flooding through the partially-opened windows.

Crystal got up and went to the small kitchen. She said, "I'll rustle up some coffee. I think we're going to need it."

Leland focused intently on John and said, "A scandal has been brewing in my company that could make Enron's misdeeds look amateurish."

From the kitchen, Crystal said, "And it could financially cripple many thousands of folks who've invested heavily. The pension fund is almost entirely *built* on corporate stock, which Leland and I've always thought was a bad idea in the first place."

Leland spoke in a low voice, but it still betrayed his deep sense of outrage. "The chief financial officer, the senior accountant, and a small group of executives have worked a series of highly lucrative schemes so devious and so convoluted and concealed I might never have caught a whiff, but an old friend in the company came to me, and together we've unraveled much of it. We've been working to offset the damage, to effect corrections and compensations before it all comes to light, and there's a good chance we'll be able to save the company after the scandal breaks—it most certainly will break—but we need more time, and we need to control *how* it breaks. That's one of the reasons for this little getaway. To plan strategy. We must have tripped some alarm wire and alerted them. I think one or more of them decided to neutralize the threat we pose. It must have been expensive."

Crystal set a colorful mug in front of both men. "Just instant, but it's strong."

John took a sip and nodded.

She brought her own mug to the table and sat with her hands cupped around it. Said, "You know it always amazes me how these people seem to think they can get away with covering up crimes like fraud and embezzlement indefinitely. They're smart enough to concoct these elaborate schemes, but not smart enough to realize sooner or later somebody's bound to see what's going on."

"It's a sweet trap," Leland said. "All you need to be drawn into it are a few easy rationalizations.

You find yourself in a position of trust and access in a thriving company. Your own finances are a bit tight, so you decide there will be no harm done if you borrow what you need and pay it back later. Or you're just going to do this one tempting over-the-line deal and go right back to being honest. If you don't do it somebody else will. And deals like it are apparently being done in other companies all around you. So you tell yourself, just this once. But then nobody *does* seem to notice, so you borrow a little more. Or you do one more tempting deal. Then you come to realize at least some of the truth. You've gone and committed the crime. It was easy and nobody cared, and you're well down that path into cover-up mode. The old saying; in for a penny, in for a pound. It's too late to go back, so you convince yourself the only way is further down this path you've chosen, or that has seemed to choose you. Those nice rationalizations become much more sophisticated and labyrinthine at top corporate levels, but it's essentially the same core reasoning. It all becomes so self-convincing, you're dumfounded and offended when you're finally caught out."

John said, "What are you going to do now?"

"Take Alden's advice and keep what happened here quiet for the time we need. Go back. Face it. Do the best we can to mend or limit the damage done to the company, and then break the news on our own terms."

Crystal said, "We've taken on tougher challenges and won. We'll win this one, too." Leland nodded with confidence.

"I believe it," John said. "And you should be safe now. Alden's a good man."

"The finest," Crystal said. "He has an honorable Special Forces record. His wife Meg was one of my best friends all the way back to high school. We lost her to cancer. Alden retired and adopted us. He's been family for many years. And he's pulled me out of more than one scrape in the work for the foundation. So I have to believe him when he says you're largely responsible for pulling us out of this one. Thank you, John Hardin, for saving Erin and Leland and me. You'll find we can be good friends."

Crystal went to talk with Erin, and Leland set about packing, so John went outside in time to see two men, one black and the other white, carrying a tarp-wrapped body quickly toward the lagoon. They glanced his way but said nothing. Alden was kicking sand over the stain close by the palm tree where Brewer had been bound. A dark mass that was Swint's body was still tied to the other tree. Alden walked to it and cut the leash free from the neck and dragged the body closer to low vegetation. He swept the flashlight beam around on the ground, and said, "Okay, that's good enough for right now. I'll come back and do it better. My friends will get Swint here in a minute. They'll weight them both down and take them a mile or so out. I wasn't lying about the reef sharks. By morning there won't be anything left to see around here. Come on, you can help me with Rowdy." They went around to the back of the cottage. Alden found a tattered blanket in a small storage shed and together they wrapped the dog in it and carried the bundle to the shed. Alden said, "I'll take him over to the big island tomorrow after my men get here from the States."

They followed the path out to the beach. Alden turned the flashlight off and they stood looking at the moonlit surf. The breeze had gentled. It was warm and salt-humid.

John said, "Brewer was carrying a cell phone. Do you have that?"

"Yes. It's got a scrambler on it."

"I'd like to take that with me."

"It's back on the porch. Take it. What now for you?"

"I don't know. I was supposed to fly these two back to Florida early the day after tomorrow, but they decided to move tonight. I'm sure they were supposed to report in by that phone. Ganz might figure something went wrong, and allow another day or two waiting to hear from them. Then I figure he'll send out men to find out what went wrong. He's sure to want me, and I absolutely can't allow his men to get near anyone who knows me. So I'm just about out of time. I have to find a way to free Clint Rader. I have to assume he's still alive. Whatever I do, it will have to be very soon."

"Why not just go to the law?"

"I'd need some kind of convincing evidence, which I don't have. It would take too much time now, anyway, and too many people would have to be in on it. I don't know what kind of contacts Ganz has. If he gets any hint of something threatening him, I'm sure he'll have Clint killed and vanished immediately. Even remotely supposing some kind of coordinated lawful assault could be set up in time, Clint could get killed in the crossfire."

Alden considered. "John, you're a man of many layers. What aren't you telling me?"

John blew out a breath. "That's not my real name. WITSEC set up this identity. Once, I flew for a man who dealt in weapons. I saw too much. Went into the protection program. They found out where I was and came hunting. I wound up killing. Nolan Rader—this was Clint's older brother—worked for BATF then. I thought it had all died down, but not long ago Nolan started digging into the whole thing on his own. He recorded the only eyewitness to the killing. That witness died not long after. That's how Nolan pressured me into helping him. He told me it was all laid out on a CD, locked up, to be looked at after his death. Now Nolan's dead, too, shot by two men he thought were mercenaries who would help him go get his brother. But there's apparently enough on that CD he left behind to put me away for a long time at the least. Somebody might already have turned up the disc. His lawyer. A family member. I don't know. I've been half expecting to get jumped by the law any time."

"So that's a large part of why you wanted this kept quiet."

"There's . . . there's a boy who's counting on me. If I can avoid it, I don't want to get taken down."

"I'm going to set up a charter flight out for the family in the morning. With at least two escort men to help watch their backs. Stay here until we leave. Maybe I can help you think this through."

"Thanks, Alden, but no. I'll find a way. Have to."

"When are you flying back?"

"Just after dawn. As planned, only a day early. I need to clear US Customs so I don't have them after me, too. But I'm not going to count on more than forty-eight hours left after that to make a move."

He retrieved the night vision monocular, which still worked, and took the scrambled cell phone. He ran the boat back fast across the bay under a humid sky strewn with white sparks and washed with ghostly light from the indifferent chunk of moon, cutting through a light chop, slowing only to hunt for the gut near the rented cottage, and left it tied to the dock. After gathering everything he'd brought, he took a long steaming shower, made coffee and a sandwich with canned meat and the Bahamian bread, took only a single bite, and sat at the table, his thoughts threading an indistinct maze bounded by dead ends, his insides hollowing as the remaining night hours crawled by.

A half hour before dawn he left in the Neon. Wound through the deserted narrow lanes to the airstrip and left the little car unlocked with the keys under the floor mat, behind the dark customs shack. He was taking a load of his things to the plane when he saw a shadowy figure standing under the wing, and he stopped. Several possibilities crowded into his mind. A backup sent here by Ganz? A man from Bahamian law? Somebody trying to break in or steal it?

The figure turned on a flashlight and shone it on his own face.

John walked closer.

Alden said, "Figured I'd hitch a ride with you. My two friends here in Marsh Harbour are handling everything. The family will be okay."

"I don't think this is a good—"

"No arguments. I'm going. You need help. Crystal and Leland agree. Now, shouldn't you kick the tires on this kite or something? Make sure the rubber band is wound up tight? It'll be light soon."

THIRTY-ONE

He tilted his head back and looked up, hands on his hips, considering. The forest canopy was filtering the early morning sunlight into smoky shafts and the mossy hillside was soaked with night dew. The cool woods smelled musty good. Birds were chattering about the new day. A light breeze was coaxing several leaves on the tree to flutter and beckon him.

Joshua Lightfoot had promised not to work on the treehouse alone.

Okay, then.

But what would be wrong with just bringing some more boards up there and stacking them on the platform? He would not do any sawing or hammering.

So he made five trips along his path to the barn, each time running flat out downhill in his moccasins, arms out like wings for balance, ducking under the familiar reaching branches, avoiding tree roots that could make you trip and sprawl like a clown, nimbly bounding from one exposed rock to another, the blood singing in his veins.

Then lugging an armload of gray weathered boards back uphill from the old tarp-covered pile Aunt Crow had said they could use. Each time huffing and sweating by the time he reached the tree. After the last trip up he stopped under the tree to let his breathing slow. The leaves beneath the tree had been trodden into the dirt by both of them earlier as they had worked here, and the tree's roots writhed out of the ground like gnarled fingers.

The muscles in his lean arms and shoulders and legs burned under his tattered shorts and T-shirt, but it felt good. He made fists of both hands and tightened his biceps, pleased when they stood out just a bit. All summer long, he decided, he would keep running his path far up this mountain to the very top every day, carrying squeezing stones in each hand, the way John ran along his Eaglenest Ridge trail, and one day he would be just as strong. Old Wasituna would be proud.

He could only take two boards at a time up the old wooden ladder under his curled right arm, stepping up a rung, then quickly letting go with his left hand to grab the next rung up. He had brought all the boards but two up to the platform and had stacked them neatly.

These last two were longer and harder to handle. He labored up the ladder, his tongue nipped between his lips. Up near the platform, his awkward motions caused the ladder to shift and his hand slipped as he lunged for the last rung. Grabbed the edge of the platform instead, but the wood there was slick from mud he'd tracked up before. He teetered, holding his breath, trying to regain his balance as his left hand lost its purchase. He flung the boards away as he fell, the ground rushing up at him impossibly fast, and he was instinctively tucking in his head and arms when he hit.

***

Kitty was in her small kitchen, holding a mug of coffee in both hands, gazing out the gaily valanced window above the sink as the sunlight broke over the eastern ridges and began flooding into the valley. Thoughts of John were a constant dull ache now deep in her soul. Shadowing her life and disrupting her concentration daily so she could not give the attention to her foundering business that it needed. She thought, *what are you going to do, girl? He's running off down a path he chose. You can't stop him or change his mind. So leave him to it. You have your own life to live, dammit.*

Her cell phone on the kitchen table played an electronic cavalry charge. Could it be John? Every time the phone rang lately she hoped it was going to be him. Wanting to see her. Wanting to talk. She set the coffee mug on the table and flipped the phone open.

It was some woman, crying.

Kitty said, "Lisa? Is this Lisa Crow? What's wrong?"

"It's the boy. Where is John? I . . . I called his cell. What he said do in an . . . an emergency, but he didn't . . . didn't answer."

"Lisa, what's happened?"

"The boy . . . he fell. Please, Kitty. Find John. Tell him to come to the Haywood Center. Please?" And the line went dead.

She dialed John's home number and Hank sleepily told her he was off on some trip. Didn't know where or how long he'd be gone. She decided not to say anything about the boy until she could find out what exactly had happened. She slapped the phone closed and ran for the garage. Pulled the door up. Strapped on her helmet and straddled the Honda. Cranked it and squealed out of her driveway, fishtailing as she went up through the gears, thinking, *damn you, John Hardin. Where are you? Why won't you wake up and come back to us?* Out on Highway 19 she narrowly missed sideswiping a dusty black pickup that shied away from her, its horn sounding like a startled animal. She took her left hand off the grip long enough to wipe the tears out of her eyes with her fingers, and then rolled on too much power with her right hand.

***

From thirty miles off, the Florida coastline was an indistinct blue line in haze. John had called Nassau to file, and had called Customs at West Palm, as required, to advise them he was coming. In the passenger seat, Alden had a yellow legal pad on his knees. They both wore headsets, so the thrumming sound of the engine was muted. Ever since they had lifted off from Marsh Harbour he'd been questioning John and sketching, holding up the pad at intervals so John could point to a particular feature and tell him corrections. He would erase and adjust, until John finally said, "The scale is still off some, but that's pretty close."

"Brewer said they'd be holding your man in a building back from the kitchen. Would the kitchen be about here?"

"Makes sense it would be somewhere toward the back there. I only saw the front entrance, an anteroom, a large main living area, the interior courtyard, and Ganz's office. You get to his office along a hallway from the living area. It's a big room.

Thirty feet square. There were two other doors in there. One was a double set. Ornate. Closed, but I got the impression those lead to a private library, or to his master bedroom. The other door could connect to the back rooms."

"What else do you remember from the office?"

"Skylights. Everywhere. I saw that from the air, too. All over the complex. Weird art on the walls. Impressionistic. Intricate. Dark. Lighted recesses in his office walls with exhibits. Looked like iron tools, mostly. Plush furnishings. The whole setup must have cost major money."

"Describe them. The things you saw in the wall recesses."

"Pincers. Pliers. Small screw clamps or vises. Unusual shapes. Obviously very old."

"Sounds like maybe the kind of toys the churches used during the Inquisition. Torture tools. Knuckle crushers. Like that."

"Now that you say it, yes."

"This Ganz must be something else. Describe him."

"Tall. Six four. Bald. Lean, but I'd say he's strong. Yellowish eyes. Intelligent. Dangerous to underestimate him or try to fool him. He's confident. Arrogant. Sure."

Alden flipped the page and poised the pencil. "Let's think about security. Brewer said usually six men besides Ganz. So let's allow for as many as ten. He also said the place is well covered with motion sensors. Cameras. You mentioned dogs. How many did you see, and what kind."

"Two. Rottweillers, I think."

"Bad, because they can certainly be lethal. Stronger than Dobermans or shepherds. But maybe also good because, like Dobermans they generally like to attack without barking. Okay, run down for me everything else you saw."

"There's an eight-foot chain link perimeter fence around the whole property, topped with three strands of barbed wire. There's a pole near the entrance, with a green box mounted on it. I think the power and phone lines probably feed down to that box and then run inside the property underground. Remotely operated wrought-iron driveway gates between two decorative stone pillars, covered by a camera mounted on top of the left pillar. The gates are operated by a plastic card inserted into a box beside the driveway, reachable from a driver's window. The driveway is deep ditched on both sides and takes a sharp S curve, I suppose to slow down anybody approaching in a vehicle. The whole complex is walled. Stucco-covered masonry. Topped with razor wire. I saw another camera covering the wall gate. That gate's card-operated, too. Part of the wall is formed by one wall of some of the buildings themselves. The place is a fort, but it doesn't look that way on first impression. The perimeter fence, for instance. It's all that coated green wire so it blends in. Even the barbed strands. The compound sits on a low rise in the middle of maybe thirty or forty acres that's mostly grass, with a few trees and a lot of good landscaping up close all around the compound. It's been designed to look like a rich southwestern ranch or a hacienda."

"Back entrance to the inside wall?"

"Yes, hold up your sketch. Right there. A plain door. Painted. There's a tall tree outside, maybe twelve feet away. A cedar." He touched his index finger to the pad, and Alden made a note of it.

Alden fell silent, studying the pages he'd filled with neat script. Tapping the eraser end of the pencil on the pad in quick staccato.

When they were ten miles off the coast, John thumbed the push-to-talk switch mounted on the yoke and said, "Palm Beach International." He gave Whiskey Romeo's full call sign and said, "Ten east for landing."

The approach controller came back immediately with a squawk code and a request to identify. John set the four-digit code into the transponder and punched the ident button, which would make his particular dot glow brightly on the controller's screen. Three seconds later the controller reported, "Radar contact ten east," and gave him a vector to join the busy landing pattern.

Alden said, "Always in the movies, a pilot will transmit something like, 'Airport, this is *Aluminum Overcast* one two three four five,' and then say, 'I repeat, this is *Aluminum Overcast* one two three four five.' "

John said, "Or it will be, 'I say again, Airport, this is *Aluminum Overcast* one two three four five. Acknowledge, please.' Never happens in real life. You try abusing the radio like that over a busy area where the controllers don't even have time to sweat— New York, say—they'd probably scramble a fighter to shoot you down."

It was just idle conversation as both men's thoughts eddied and whorled. To lend an air of normalcy when the situation was anything but.

Approach slotted him in between two heavies and the controller asked him to "expedite," so he kept the power on most of the way down his final approach to runway three one, throttling back and dumping flaps only very close to the threshold. He taxied fast off the active runway and directly to the customs building, and shut down, the prop solidifying out of its gray disc.

After a fifteen minute wait in the office, two polite officials walked out to the plane with them and asked John to remove most of the inspection plates under the wings and fuselage and on the tail, and to remove the rear panel in the baggage area for access to the tail section. He used a screwdriver from his tool kit to do so and they peered inside each opening with strong flashlights and wands with angled mirrors on their tips. Alden helped him remove all their items from the plane and pile them on a flatbed cart. One of the agents went through everything on the cart while the other lifted the carpet and probed the kick panel pockets and all other areas that might be hiding contraband. He was very thorough.

John and Alden stood twenty feet away and watched.

In a low voice Alden said, "What have you been thinking?"

John turned his head to watch a landing Citation. "I don't know. Land somewhere close. Someplace I can rent a heavy car. I buy a briefcase with a combination lock on it. One number set just a digit off so I can roll the right combination in and snap it open fast. Inside it I have a weapon. Maybe a shotgun I can buy and cut down with a hacksaw. Drive up to the gate. Let them see me on the camera. I'm upset. Tell them I need to talk with Ganz, fast. They'll let me in. If his men insist on a search, I pull out the weapon right away. Tie or tape them up. Then go for Ganz. If you want to help, you hide in the back seat and be ready to drive. Once I get into his office I use the weapon to force Ganz to turn over Rader, if he's even still alive, and then we get out of there with the shotgun muzzle taped to the man's head. Something like that."

Alden gave him a skeptical grin and said, "Well, that would be ballsy, all right. But you'd have better odds playing the state lottery. Let me make a call." He walked another forty feet away, turned his back, and put his cell phone to his ear.

The agent poking through the cart items stood up, looking sternly at John, and called out, "Excuse me, sir. How do you explain having this item in your possession?" He was holding up the night vision monocular.

John walked closer and smiled. "Sure. I brought that over to the cays with me. Thought it might come in handy for getting back to the dock in the boat after dark, and it sure did. I've been over there before on fishing trips and it can get pretty damned black out there. All those islands and bays start looking alike."

The man was dubious. Inspected the monocular. Said, "Are you aware there are stiff penalties for taking night vision equipment out of the country?"

"Sorry. No, I was not."

"This kind of item is in heavy demand by terrorist factions. I'm sure you can understand why, sir."

"I hadn't thought of that. It certainly won't happen again."

He hefted the monocular. "I'm not going to confiscate this, but I will record your possession of it, and the serial number." He studied John with some intensity, but finally let it go.

The two inspectors finished up. He was issued a clearance form at the desk and was politely wished a pleasant trip back to North Carolina.

Alden finished using his phone and came back to the plane. After topping off and waiting for ten minutes in a lineup for takeoff clearance from the tower, John powered down the strip and pulled the Cessna up into a climb on a northward course, following the narrow fringe of beach flanking the strung-out thousands of buildings. Cottony strings of surf materialized in ancient lazy rhythm out of the benign blueness to curl in and lick at the sand, but from up here the coastline looked fragile.

It was only a matter of time for any given swath of this coast before a particular ragged gang of thunderstorms would rage out of Africa and organize themselves into a giant white pinwheel disguised like a flower from space. Up close it would be churning under its banded skirts with unstoppable fury. They'd give it some innocuous name like Hugo or Katrina or Andrew.

And it would take aim.

Only a matter of time.

John said, "I'm running out of time. And having serious second thoughts. Maybe I should turn this over to the law, after all."

Alden looked out the side window, then focused on John's profile. "And tell them what? You have no evidence. Only a wild story. They could already be hunting *you*, in fact. And you were right. The first hint this Ganz has that something is sour, he's likely to kill and dice up *whoever* he's holding. Clint Rader or anybody else. Eliminate all evidence. You just said it. There's no time left that we can count on beyond tomorrow, when you and Brewer and Swint are supposed to be coming back. There's something else. The Campions have become my family. The only one I have left. They're among the good people. This Ganz—this animal—attacked them. For that, he's going to pay. You and I can make him pay. Believe that."

John thought of Nolan Rader's feverish, desperate eyes as he lay on that hospital bed in his burn bandages. And his last appeal to find and save the kid brother.

He met Alden's level gaze and said, "Okay."

Alden nodded and squinted ahead into the haze. He said, "We need to make a stop. Set a course for Atlanta. Cobb County-McCollum Field. It's a small strip twenty miles north of the city. You can find it?"

"Yes. It'll be in my *Flight Guide*. In the kick panel pocket on your side. Why do you want to go there?"

"I want you to meet an old retired friend of mine. I called him from Palm Beach. He can help. Trust me." He got out the yellow pad and pencil. "Now how about running it down once more, only in better order. Go over it all again. Everything you can remember. Let's make sure you're not forgetting some detail that might help us. Start with a wide-angle overview of the compound and the terrain surrounding it."

He remembered the overflight he'd made with Nolan Rader pointing the way. Tried to place himself back there on that day. Wishing he had the photos he'd taken. "The clearing is a good way out in the woods, in low foothills, at least ten miles from the nearest neighbor. On a two-lane country road that does a lot of twisting. Low traffic, I'm sure. There's a narrow river. The Clinch. Runs close by the road for a ways. The compound sits up on a low rise, surrounded by acres of grass, with a few trees in clusters. The landscaping is simple but professional. Intended to tone down the fortress appearance, I think."

Alden made another plan sketch, this one in more refined detail, John telling him everything he could remember, as the day ticked on and the Cessna droned north-northwest toward the sprawl of Atlanta.

THIRTY-TWO

He was only dimly aware when Monroe entered the room followed by Ganz, who closed the door behind them. He could no longer bear to face away from the door, so he was on his side on the narrow bed, watching their legs as the two men moved to stand side by side in the center of the room.

He lifted his head and looked up a great towering distance into the yellow eyes that glowed, floating. The room seemed to swell and shrink. Tinted sunlight was slanting in through the caged window. Dust motes drifted in the bruised light.

Ganz smiled and said almost gently into the stillness, "Well, Mr. Rader. Your time has finally come."

What Ganz was saying got through to Clint and he sat up abruptly, a wave of numb dizziness stealing through him like a fog, cold fear trying to ice his gut. He licked at his dry lips with his dry tongue. He was still only half awake. Half in some feverish surreal world apart from all this. Watching it happen from a distance and still not believing it. He croaked out, "What . . . you mean? No. No. Can't be. Time left. Days yet." Trying to remember how *many* days left.

Why would he forget *that*? "Sorry, sorry, sorry. You
. . . didn't say I could speak."

"On this day you may speak at will. Monroe
and I have discussed it, you see, and we feel your
usefulness is at an end. You can no longer contribute
in any significant way to the research. Come now,
Mr. Rader. Surely some part of you is well resigned
to—even somewhat welcoming of—an end to it," the
tall figure said reasonably.

Monroe had spent a lot of time alone with him.
Time in which he had learned there were dimensions
of pain he would not have believed existed. Part of
the reason his voice was so hoarse was because at
some time during the most recent of those sessions,
he had screamed until no further sound would issue
from his throat. He had paid a terrible price for his
escape attempt.

Now Monroe reached into his pocket and
brought out a folded knife. Pressed the button and the
four-inch blade sprang free. Clint's eyes fastened on
it. Glinting in the tinted sunlight. He could see
scratches along the edge from a sharpening stone.
His fear-based hatred of knives ran deep. Ever since,
as a boy, he had slipped with a pocket knife and had
slashed a finger to the white bone.

Ganz said, "Monroe wishes the choice to be
yours. Heart or head. You and I can hope he will
strike true. You have done well enough in our
sessions together that you should not suffer unduly
now. Head or heart? Which will it be, Mr. Rader?"

The room swung and steadied and he swam
back to full consciousness, everything standing out in
crisp detail. Every sound, even the rapid suck and
blow of his own breathing, clear in his brain. And

from some deep recess in him there was a single remaining spark that fanned into a pitiful flame, but the heat of it spread through him and he thought, *no. Not like this. Not like some cringing kicked dog. I won't give them that. Goddamn them.*

He pulled his stare away from the blade and fixed it on those yellow eyes, which betrayed just a flicker of something. Surprise? He took a deep deliberate breath and stood. Weaving at first, then planting his feet wider apart, head and shoulders back, apparently ignoring Monroe. Heart thrashing in his chest. He said, "Not gonna choose . . . evil bastard." *And when I see the first twitch from either one of you, I'm going to fight. Fight you both. With my hands. My teeth. All that's in me. Until I'm dead. I love you, Rita.*

The three men stood still for several long seconds. Clint unsteady but determined not to show it.

Ganz allowed a slightly wider grin. "Perhaps there is still something to be learned in a further few sessions. So I think not today. I have decided to grant you a temporary, though indeterminate, reprieve, Mr. Rader. Put the weapon away, Monroe. Give him a meal and a further hour after that to order his thoughts. Then bring him to me."

They backed away from him, opened the door, and left. He heard the deadbolt snick into place and the room went still and quiet again. The dust motes danced in the shafting light. He stood there. Swaying.

His tongue clicked dryly in his mouth.

Felt a coolness on his cheeks.

Reached up and wiped away wetness.

THIRTY-THREE

His *Flight Guide* listed the particulars on the small Cobb County airport north of vast Atlanta, which lay off to the west in thick haze. Atlanta approach gave him vectors through their complex airspace, and when he was ten miles out he called on the UNICOM frequency for a traffic advisory and wind. There was a single paved strip, narrow but plenty long. A brisk thirty-degree crosswind was blowing for the active runway, zero nine, so he brought the Cessna down final in a crab, only correcting to line up with the dashes at the last possible moment, then dumping the flaps and cranking aileron into the wind to keep it planted. He taxied to the apron in front of the single building, swung into a tie-down spot, and pulled the mixture to full lean, killing the engine.

An affable older man behind the counter in the office greeted them and John answered yes to his question about fuel. Until this was over, he would take every opportunity to keep the tanks topped. The man took a phone call.

Inside the empty pilot's lounge, a computer was lit with colorful weather information. A large chart of the United States hung on the wall. A nail had been driven in at the airport location, and a weighted string hung from the nail, so pilots could measure distances. John's gaze went to Asheville, North Carolina, then slightly west to a dot that was Maggie Valley.

And farther west. To Tennessee. Where a man who traded in death waited.

They came back out into the office. Alden checked his watch and said, "My friend won't be here for another hour, at least."

"Is this necessary? We're burning time."

"I know. It can't be helped. Let's get something to eat while we're waiting."

"I'm not hungry."

The man behind the desk lifted a set of keys from a peg behind him and held them out. "Overheard you. We've got a courtesy car. Why don't you use it? It's an old beater of a barge, but it runs. There are half a dozen fast food joints within two miles. Probably none of them will kill you."

Accepting the keys with a smile and a nod, Alden said, "Come on. We need fuel. Energy. And we can talk some more."

They ordered loaded sandwiches in a nearly deserted Burger King and took a back-corner booth.

John became aware of his hunger and ate mechanically. Thinking. When he'd finished, he said, "Let me use your cell phone. I left mine back home for this trip."

"You don't feel naked without one?" Alden passed his over.

"No. They nail you down. Control your life just a little more every day. I have one for business and emergencies, but I don't like carrying it. You see people walking around with them permanently plugged into one of their ears and it looks like they're talking to themselves. The next step is a chip implant. They can hide the antenna up your nose."

He punched in the number from memory.

Trey answered.

He pitched his voice higher, picked up the cadence, and asked to speak to Rita Flores, please.

Trey said, "Who is this?"

"I work with Shoe Carnival Dot Com, sir. I just have a question about an online order." It was a good bet. All women in his experience loved shoes, and most Americans had by now at least experimented with shopping online for everything from books to bedroom sets.

When Rita came on he said, "It's John Hardin, Rita—"

In a strong squealing whisper she said, "Omigod. Have you found him?"

"No, Rita. I'm just calling to see if you've had any word from him. Or about him."

"No. No. I thought—"

"I'm sorry, Rita—"

But he heard, "Give me that. This is you, Hardin?" Trey was back on. "I *told* you not to bother us, you son of a bitch. *Listen* to me. You don't ever call here again. You do, I'm going to come looking for you. You *hear* me?" And the connection went dead.

It was natural for Trey to protect his sister from aggravation and emotional stress, but something was deeply wrong here. He was being too belligerent. John thought, *It's like he's trying to hide something.*

Alden raised an eyebrow.

"Just checking to see if Clint Rader has turned up, by some miracle. He hasn't."

"Listen. While you're holding my phone. It would be good to have one more man. Do you know anybody you can trust?"

"What have you got in mind? You have a plan cooking?"

"We'll go over options when you meet my friend. But whatever way it goes, another pair of hands could be useful."

"I don't want to put any more people at risk in this than seems necessary."

"For what I'm thinking, there shouldn't be any real danger to the helper."

John thought for several seconds. Flipped open the phone and poked in a number.

After the fifth ring, Brandon Doyle answered with a shouted, "Yeah. What? Go." There was a loud whispering in the background.

He brought the phone closer to his mouth. "Doyle. John. What's all the noise?"

"I'm straddlin' the ridge beam of this fancy-assed two-story house we're framin' for some dude who's got way more money than I'll ever have. It ain't real comfortable on the two big boys here, the wind's blowin' a gale, and I'm pissed off. Tell me your gonna improve my day, gunslinger."

"I've got a situation. I could use your help."

"I knew it. You got your sorry ass in a sling with the Ghosts, right? Did I *tell* you?"

"Something like that."

"When and where?"

He looked at Alden and said, "Over in eastern Tennessee. Probably tonight." And Alden nodded.

Doyle said, "Is this gonna be a party like the last one?"

"Probably."

"Well, hell, everybody's gotta die sometime."

"I'll call you in a few hours. Be careful up there."

"Yeah, *now* you give a damn."

John closed the phone and handed it back. "His name is Brandon Doyle. He's strong. Tough. Smarter than he sounds. And we can trust him."

"Can he handle a weapon if it comes to that?"

"Yes. I know he can shoot a handgun accurately. And he usually carries a gravity knife in his boot."

"Okay. So we've gone over the layout. You touched on Nolan Rader and what he uncovered on this Ganz. Tell me more about that."

John gave him a condensed version of all he knew and all he suspected, and Alden took notes on his yellow pad.

Alden said, "So we're up against an unknown number of hit teams this Ganz—this Brain—controls from his fortified complex. Like more than a few psychologists, Ganz obviously has several thousand misfiring synapses himself, which only makes him more unpredictable and dangerous. Brewer said there are usually six security. So we'll figure on that, minimum, plus Ganz himself. At least seven trained and armed, say. Against four of us. But we have several edges."

"One of those being surprise?"

"Yes. And maybe a secret weapon or two. We don't want law in on it, at least until we get Rader clear, but Ganz can't call in the cops, either. So he and his men are fortified, but they're also isolated. That's another edge. When my man gets here, we'll harden up a plan."

"Who's this friend?"

"Mitch Carlyle. He was an instructor. Special Forces. Retired. Done some mercenary work here and there. We wound up on a job in Central America together that got dicey. Works as a consultant to law now, setting up SERT and SWAT teams and timed training courses that are changeable so they stay surprising to the trainees. He's got a reputation for getting devious about that. Booby traps, obstacles, a lot of moving simulated bad guy and hostage targets that test reaction and judgment with the three usual weapons—handgun, shotgun, and submachine gun. He's very good at what he does."

"What's SERT?"

"Sheriff's Emergency Response Team. Law enforcers are the only people outside the military who love acronyms more."

John drove the rattling old courtesy car back to the airport. Mitch Carlyle showed up fifteen minutes later, driving an immaculate black GMC extended cab pickup. John was skeptical because, although Carlyle appeared to be fit, he also looked to be well into his sixties. The initial impression was of an affable, harmless middle-school football coach. He was short and stocky but carrying no excess fat. He had pure white hair clipped short so it stood up like a brush, and his clear pale blue eyes were framed with deeply incised smile lines. John could feel the man appraising him as they shook hands, and, looking into his eyes, decided this was no mild-mannered coach.

The three of them sat at a picnic table on the grass next to the airport building.

Carlyle laced his fingers on the table, looked at both of them, and said, "What's the overview?"

Alden went through it quickly and efficiently, consulting his notes, making no unnecessary comments, repeating nothing, revising nothing, looking at John several times for confirmation of some point or assumption, John nodding agreement, impressed.

Alden said, "That's it."

"You figure late tonight?"

Alden said, "Best, yes."

Carlyle looked at John. "Does Doyle have any training? Ex-military?"

"No, but I'd trust him as much as I would any man. He won't back out. Or back down."

"You told Alden he can shoot a handgun. How about you?"

"I've shot with a forty-five. The old model nineteen eleven."

"That's still a great sidearm. Reliable. Hits like a sledge. But only seven rounds. I'll show you how to handle a Beretta nine. If you have to. So, good enough. You figuring a diversion and fast assault, Alden?"

"Yes. But it would be good to improve the odds first."

John said, "There might be a way to do that."

Both men looked at him.

"We could pick a place not far from the compound. Some unattended or closed airport. Or a forest service grass strip. We need to meet Doyle somewhere, anyway. I'm thinking we've got

Brewer's scrambled cell phone, and if we're lucky the redial on it should get through to Ganz. He should be expecting some kind of report, and I don't imagine Brewer made a lot of other calls on that phone. I make up a story. Something quick but believable. I tell him everything went haywire in the islands. Swint is dead and we had to leave him. Brewer is with me but badly wounded."

Alden said, "Maybe you were hit yourself. So you're not in shape to talk long."

"I'm fading. I'm confused. I tell him where I've landed and we need help right now. And I hang up."

Carlyle said, "We can think about it more. You can practice it. Ganz will send at least two. In a vehicle."

"A vehicle that's not traceable to us," Alden said.

John added, "A vehicle that Ganz's guards will recognize when it returns with us in it. For us, it's also an expendable vehicle."

Alden said, "At least one of them will have a key card for the perimeter gate. The down side is that we'll be putting the whole place on alert. We'll lose most of our surprise." To Carlyle he said, "The dogs?"

"Complete surprise is always momentary, anyway. Your man Doyle can do the dogs. I've got what we need there."

"Did you bring everything else on the list?"

"Yes," Carlyle said, "Weapons, vests, gloves. Plastic. Restraints. Med kit. I've got TG and a few FBs for diversion, but something more unorthodox might be better." He was looking at the plane.

Alden nodded and smiled, seeming to understand Carlyle's thoughts, and said, "That devious mind at work again."

John said, "If you two are going to start talking in abbreviations and telepathy, you'll lose me."

"Sorry," Carlyle said. "Tear gas and flash-bang grenades. Not lethal, but effective. And in this case, along with everything else I've got, untraceable to us. Anybody scope the weather through tonight and tomorrow morning?"

John and Alden looked at each other.

John said, "I'll go in right now and check it on the computer."

"Alden and I'll load my gear into your bird," Carlyle said. "When you come out, let's pick a landing place in Tennessee, and then you can call your man Doyle. What does he drive?"

"Either a polished, chopped Harley or a pickup that looks like it's been rolled over in the dirt, but it runs okay."

"Tell him to drive the pickup. And while you're inside, why don't you ask them where the nearest Walmart and a Lowe's or a Home Depot are? We do need a few more things, on second thought, including energy food and water. It could be a long night."

***

It was midafternoon when they took off. Alden was again in the passenger seat, going over his notes on the yellow pad. Carlyle was in the back, propped against the fuselage, his feet stretched out, booted ankles crossed, using a felt-tipped pen to mark up a Tennessee map torn from an atlas he'd bought at Walmart on John's credit card, along with a number of other items from there and a Home Depot. Now there was just room enough for Carlyle, even with the rear fuselage panel removed to allow loading of the longer and bulkier items. On top of it all were two black heavy nylon duffle bags and two metal suitcase-sized containers he'd brought with him, presumably holding the weapons and associated gear. Clustered white plastic Walmart bags added a note of everyday normalcy.

Three friends returning from a shopping trip for hunting supplies.

The weather was gradually going down along with a falling barometer, a front sliding in from the west ahead of a low-pressure complexity. Scattered light rain showers would scout the whole of eastern Tennessee and the western Carolinas for ranks of much meaner clusters of heavy thunderstorms that would follow, but they were predicting the worst of it, at least, to hold off until the middle of the following day.

John had chosen two possible landing sites. One was marked on his aviation sectional chart as a circle enclosing a capital R. It was the symbol for a private strip, but it lay at the heart of a large forested area, and so was a good bet to be a seldom used, unattended Forest Service turf strip cut out of the woods for use by the occasional single-engine duster plane or fire spotters. It was eighteen miles by road from the compound. The other was a circle with an X through it, an abandoned airport that might still be useable. It was closer to the compound at eleven miles, but it was also within a dozen miles of a village called Rogersville, near a finger of Cherokee Lake. The more remote strip in the woods would serve them better. No line to it showed on the sectional, but many roads were not marked on the aviation sectionals, and it only made sense there would at least be a gravel road to allow access with a Forest Service truck carrying a refueling tank.

His guess later proved to be correct. The strip was completely surrounded by dense forest, with a single rutted gravel road winding to it from a secondary paved road. It was deserted, but had been mowed some time ago, though there looked to be a soft, wet area near one end. Avoiding that, he set the Cessna down gently on the long grass and back-taxied nearly to the end, swinging it around before shutting it down so they'd be ready for a fast takeoff into the predicted wind if necessary.

John called Doyle, who answered from his pickup truck, to give him directions. After he finished work for the day he would head their way in his pickup.

The three of them spent the remaining daylight hours working, with thin disposable rubber gloves on to eliminate fingerprints. They removed all the store bar coding from the materials, cut two-by-fours to lengths, and used toothed metal connectors to bang together collapsible saw horses, which they painted bright yellow with quick-dry spray cans. They applied evenly-spaced diagonal stripes of reflective tape to four ten-foot studs, Alden cutting the tape flush to the two-by-fours using a very sharp switchblade borrowed from Carlyle. They made eight sets of legs, two sets supporting a ten-foot horizontal stud. Four barriers. Carlyle stepped back and said, "What do you think?"

Alden shrugged, wiping at his chin with his blue-clad wrist. "It probably won't fool a Sheriff's deputy or a highway patrolman who looks too close."

"Agreed," Carlyle said, "but it'll be very late. Hardly anybody on these back roads, anyway. Highway bureaucrats all home in bed. So it ought to hold any curious law off at least until they can check on it through channels in the morning."

They painted six two-foot-square plywood panels red and used more reflective tape to form DETOUR on each with an appropriate arrow according to Carlyle's plan for where they were to be placed. Carlyle said, "Your man Doyle can nail four of these to trees or telephone poles near the intersections I've got marked, three hours or so before we put everything else in gear."

They nailed the other two centered on two of the striped ten-foot-long studs.

The fading day was turning shades of gray under a solidifying overcast, and the breeze was picking up, rustling through the trees like a throng of ghosts. John hoped the weather experts had got it right, and they would have the whole night ahead fairly clear to work with.

They used the last of the light to eat a meal of canned tuna and fruit, washed down with bottled water, and to inspect the area, making sure they would be leaving nothing behind. Carlyle handed a loaded compact Beretta nine millimeter in a nylon belt holster to John along with an extra magazine, and went over how to operate it, then made John simulate the use of it three times, unloading it and reloading it. Holding it in an extended, stable two-hand grip. John safetied it and threaded the holster onto his belt.

They broke down the barriers and piled the components by the plane wheels. The spray painting had left streaks on the grass. They plucked up handfuls of the worst of it and scattered it in among the trees, and kicked dirt over the rest. Then they sat in the plane, and by the harsh light of compact LED flashlights, went over the plan in detail, estimating times, assigning tasks and positions. Trying to allow for variations and contingencies. When they had gone over it all, they sat still, each wrapped in his own thoughts.

Mosquitoes had found them, and Carlyle brought out a spray can of repellant.

Then bouncing lights stabbed through the trees. Alden got out on the passenger side of the plane, standing close by the door, ready to clamber back in, and John was ready to start the Cessna, but as the lights came farther on they saw it was only one vehicle. A battered pickup that John recognized, and he said, "It's okay. That's Doyle."

John popped the landing lights on for five seconds, long enough for Doyle to spot the plane and skid to a stop on the gravel in the small clearing beside the strip.

They all met at the pickup's tailgate, and Doyle said, "Okay, my men. What's this party all about?"

John said, "This is Alden. And Mitch Carlyle. The four of us are going to rescue a man we think is being held in a compound sixteen miles from here."

"Whoa, already. Some guy you *think* is being held?"

"We're pretty sure," John said. "Here's how it is . . ."

And he laid out all of it for Doyle, who listened intently, his hands slid into his rear jeans pockets. John tried to be as concise and clear as Alden had been when he'd briefed Carlyle, leaving out irrelevancies and explaining only the situation and the plan. "We need you to nail up the detour signs. Carlyle has a marked map for you. You'll set up road barriers and take care of the dogs. Alden will drive in through the perimeter gate. You'll let him take it from there, and you'll be ready to drive out fast."

"What do you and I do for that first part? Cuttin' the odds."

Carlyle said, "You only need to drive your truck out of here. That will be a good time for you to go nail up the detour signs. It's going to take you thirty minutes at least. Wait for a call. John's the decoy, right here. When we're ready, you'll set up the detour barriers. Then take care of the dogs. Leave your truck on the shoulder. Just make sure you're out of sight of the compound. I've marked a stretch of road on the map. That's where Alden will pick you up."

Doyle shook his head. "You guys come up with this plan over a quart of Wild Turkey?"

"Do you have any suggestions to improve it?"

"Hey, it ain't *my* ass in this sling." But he was smiling.

Carlyle studied him for a few seconds, and said, "Do you want a weapon?"

Doyle reached back under his denim vest and brought out a short-barreled stainless revolver. "Three five seven." He replaced the gun and dipped a big hand to a boot top, pinching out a gravity knife. "All I need."

"Ammo?" Alden said.

"One speed load."

Carlyle said, "You don't use either the gun or the knife unless there's absolutely no other way, understand? Let Alden and me do that stuff. Both of you. Agreed?"

Doyle shrugged and nodded, and John said, "Okay."

They loaded the barriers and signs into the back of Doyle's truck and covered them with a tarp they'd bought, securing the bundle with bungee cords. Doyle had his own hammer and nails in the pickup's toolbox.

Carlyle said, "I've got some gear for all of you. Black ball caps, vests, gloves. Extra larges so they ought to fit. It's basic SWAT stuff. Keep you quiet, less visible, and your body mass, at least, protected. It might also convince them we're the real thing and make our job easier. We'll try the gear on you right away, then you can suit up just before we start. Now, let's go over the plan. A lot depends on timing. John, this wind's getting stronger. You sure you can swing your end of it?"

"If the forecast holds true."

They went over it. And over it again.

And then Carlyle made them go over it yet again.

THIRTY-FOUR

"You may speak, subject eight," Brain said. "Tell me why I should not allow Monroe to terminate our association right now." He was seated behind his polished desk, which held only a bulky wireless phone, his fingers neatly laced, his head inclined, with the thin smile Clint Rader had long since come to loath and fear. Ganz was dressed in a crisp white shirt, cuffs rolled twice, a single glinting jewel pinning the red tie back.

Clint was trying to sit up straight in the leather chair positioned squarely eight feet in front of the desk, Monroe stationed to his left and slightly behind, just out of his peripheral vision. But dimly he knew he must look as bad as he felt. Defeated and close to the end of his sanity. It was late, sometime around midnight, he thought, and he was bone weary. He swallowed, looked at the floor, and said, "I think . . . I know I have days left."

The smile vanished. "You have not one minute left, if I decide so. I've been weighing whether or not you are owed perhaps another eighteen hours in which to make your final peace. Your contributions to my data have been significant, after all. Monroe could return you to your room and provide you with pad and pen so you could put down a summation of your life. Some bits of wisdom you have acquired. Perhaps a farewell note to Rita. It might be possible to see that she gets such a message, paraphrased, of course, to eliminate any attempt to convey hidden meanings. Ah, I see that does stimulate your interest. What will it be, then? A quick and merciful end to our research, here and now? A relatively painless end? Or eighteen more hours in which to record your life synopsis, but with the possibility of a considerably more difficult ending for you, depending on Monroe's mood tomorrow? I want this to be entirely your free choice, albeit your last."

Clint stared at the heavy opaque cable tie that held his wrists crossed, but he did not see it. He saw Rita greeting him with her mischievously hinting, spontaneous smile that had the power to warm his soul and make him stand taller.

"What did you just say, subject eight?"

He summoned something from the dregs of his dignity, raised his head, and looked into the insane yellow eyes. "I said I'll take the eighteen hours."

When Monroe had escorted Rader back to his room and was himself seated in the leather chair, Ganz said, "I was wrong."

Monroe raised an eyebrow.

"Yes, I was wrong. I underestimated this one. He has resisted long beyond the norm. Fascinating. But he has now spent the last of his reserves. I'm sure of that. Still, tomorrow, there could perhaps be one final reprieve—"

There was an insistent pinging from the phone with its piggybacked scrambler. He thumbed the green pad and put it to his ear. Said, "Yes?"

The voice on the other end was just audible, and he pressed the phone tighter to his head. "What?" Irritated, he snapped loudly, "Speak into the phone."

"Is this you, Ganz?" Then, again in a barely audible voice, "It's . . . me. Hardin."

Ganz reacted quickly, pulling out a drawer and placing a contact pickup onto the phone's ear speaker, turning on the small digital recorder connected to it. He said, "Where are you?"

"Dead."

"What. Speak into the *phone*."

"Swint's dead. Had to leave him. It all went to hell . . ."

"Louder. Speak *louder*. Where are you now?"

"Brewer's hit bad. Me, too. Close. Landed close."

"What? Where? *Listen* to me. *Where*?"

"Need to talk. Now. Can all be okay. But . . . need to talk. Fast. Forest strip. Service strip. In woods. Sixteen miles. Heading two-eighty-five . . . from you . . ."

"Hardin. *Hardin*." But he was only talking to a buzzing, irritating line tone.

He slid out the main desk drawer and pried open the laptop. Turned it on and connected the tape recorder to a USB port. Clicked up the Truster software. Ran the recording into it for analysis. Glared at the graphs on the screen. High global stress level. Very high cognitive numbers, which could mean Hardin had been manipulating his voice. Indecisive between 'Exaggerating', 'Inaccurate', and 'False Statement' on the Brewer claim and again on Hardin himself. He played the recording again. Said partially to Monroe but mostly to himself. Swint is dead. Yes. Hardin is down at some strip close by. That is definite. But . . . "

Monroe said, "What?"

"He's lying. Hardin is lying about some of this. About Brewer, certainly. The sound quality was bad, so the conclusions may be tainted."

Ganz stood, slightly bent over behind the desk, his long fingers braced like giant bony spiders on the wood, staring at the phone.

Monroe waited.

Ganz said, "Get Lupo. Wake Pease. Bring both of them here. Armed. They'll have to go investigate this. And I need a map. The detailed one of the entire county. In the library."

Monroe got up to hurry out of the study and had his hand on the ornate lever when Ganz said, "No. Wait. Lupo and Pease, yes. But bring me Cruz and Waco, also. It could be a trap. We need to make allowances for that possibility. After you bring the four here, get the map and then wake the rest. Everybody to be on alert and armed. Now, quickly."

***

Carlyle said, "Not bad, John." He aimed the compact flashlight at his watch. "So, twenty minutes at absolute minimum. Say, up to sixty minutes is most likely. Providing he took the bait, and I think he has. I would have. He has no choice, really."

Alden said, "Time for you to go, Doyle."

Doyle gave them a grin and a gloved thumb up and left in the dented pickup, the tail lights bouncing away through the woods. He would nail up the detour signs and get in place to put up two barriers across the road at a fork two and a half miles north of the compound, then he would drive fast along the road past the compound and three miles farther south, to put up the other two barriers at an intersection, hoping no traffic came by in the meantime. It was a calculated risk. The hour would be well into the depths of the night when most folk, especially out here in the wilds, ought to be in bed, so the odds would be heavily on their side. Doyle would wait to put up any of the barriers until he got a call from Carlyle. The road had to be clear for the men Ganz would send. Then it had to be blocked to keep any late-night citizens well away from the action.

The forest was damp with dew and mostly quiet, except the strong humid breeze was holding steady, coaxing the trees to sigh in chorus. *Wind's aligned within twenty degrees of the strip*, Hardin was automatically thinking, as a mosquito keened on the downwind side of his head, near his ear. The overcast was high but solid, and without their flashlights, the night was going to be hell-hole black.

Carlyle said, "I haven't been able to think how we can do this any better. The scene should work. We'll try it without shooting. I'll challenge. Both of you back me up, and holler out. We'll only fire if they don't give it up right away. If so, we only aim to put them down. Non-lethal, if we can. I'm going to suit up. Let's drink some water so we stay hydrated. Then we'll get positioned."

***

Operated by a sensor buried under the driveway, the outer compound gates opened automatically to let out a new black GMC extended-cab pickup with a bed cap. Cruz was driving, with Waco in the passenger seat. Lupo and his partner Pease, who most often served as part of the security surrounding

Dr. Ganz, rode in the cramped back seat. Lupo had the folded map on his knees and was using a flashlight on it to direct Cruz.

The four men went north on the road that twisted past the compound. They took three turns and made it to the mouth of the graveled forest road in sixteen minutes—forty-two minutes from the time Monroe had awakened them all for a quick briefing in the doctor's study. There had been no other traffic.

Lupo said, "All right, man. Stop here. Then go in real slow and be ready for whatever." Before they'd left the compound, he had removed the bulbs from the interior lights, so he and Pease left the GMC like two shadows, dressed in black and their faces hastily smeared with camo makeup. They drew their handguns, both chunky Glock nine millimeters, with their right hands, and held their switched-off flashlights in their left hands. They had worked together often enough to nearly think alike under stress. They jogged carefully and silently fifty feet behind the slow-moving GMC, one on each shoulder of the gravel road, which just showed as a pale track through the woods in the dim reflected light from the truck ahead of them.

Cruz eased the GMC along, peering ahead. When the gravel road took a wide turn, he could see through the trees. There was a dim light ahead in the blackness. He let the truck slow even more, and both men cracked their doors, ready to duck out fast. He drove now with just his left hand on top of the wheel, ready to wrench it one way or the other, and, from the seat by his thigh, filled his right fist with the familiar comforting weight of his .40-caliber semi-auto.

He braked the truck to a stop, the headlights flooding the scene into stark focus. The road ended in a semi-circular partially-graveled clearing by one end of the grass strip that was cut out of the woods. The high-winged airplane sat slightly canted on the rough grass fifty yards away, sideways to the truck, aimed toward the runway stretching off to the left. The pilot-side door was open, and a figure sat hunched and still at the base of the wing strut. Something dark, probably Brewer, slumped against the passenger-side window. There was a flashlight glowing in the grass by the plane.

They left the truck idling, the front doors open, and they knelt by the front fenders for ten seconds, surveying everything within the sweep of the headlights. Behind them, Lupo and Pease slipped into the woods on either side of the road to approach the clearing unseen through the trees. Cruz and Waco broke away together, moving on into the clearing at a fast walk, crouched, guns held out ahead of them, two-handed, at the ready.

Waco, moving faster than his teammate now, made for the airplane's tail, intending to come around on the passenger side of the plane, and Cruz slowed and went for the near side of the plane, where the figure was sitting hunched and slack up against the wheel fairing and the wing strut. Cruz was thinking, *has to be the pilot, Hardin.*

Carlyle was standing close by thick brush just inside the tree line, the short World War Two semi-automatic .30-caliber carbine socked into his shoulder. He was directly behind the plane, watching the two men from the truck approach, waiting only until the one in front of him moved farther to the side to give him clear shots at both men in quick succession without hitting the plane, or Hardin, or Alden, who was slumped in the plane's passenger seat. Then he would call out a warning for the men to surrender.

But Waco, crossing behind the plane, hesitated, possibly sensing a wrongness to the scene, scanning around in the grass and along the tree line on the dark side of the plane, and then looking at the ground to start picking his footing through a soft, muddy depression. Cruz stopped behind the pilot's-side wing and looked down at Hardin, his gun still held two-handed.

Lupo was moving laterally inside the tree line to the right of the idling truck, which was masking what little noise he made over the damp leaves and through low brush, heading for the nose of the plane. Pease was moving to the left of the truck behind a screen of trees, toward the tail, when he spotted a figure all in black in the woods behind the plane, a rifle up and looking like he was about to fire on Waco and Cruz. Pease leveled the Glock and shot three times fast, the muzzle flashes bright, and the man with the rifle went down like he'd been punched in the back by a huge invisible fist.

The man standing at the trailing edge of the wing near John spun to point his gun behind the plane, and in his peripheral vision, John saw Alden rolling fast and low out the passenger door, firing at the man by the tail, putting him down.

But the shots had not come from either of the two men close to the plane. There had to be at least a third man, maybe more. John raised his head to look toward the road. He was half blinded by the headlights but he saw a figure coming out of the woods to the right of the truck, ahead of the plane.

John was holding the Beretta close to his stomach, behind his curled arm. He had a choice of shooting up at the back of the man close by or at the figure coming out of the woods.

He sat upright and snapped two shots at the figure coming out of the woods, drawing three quick flashes in return, but stopping the figure's advance, making him dive flat. Startled, the man near him twisted around and slammed his forehead into the wing's trailing edge. He stumbled two steps back, stunned.

Using his left hand and his right leg, John uncoiled up from the ground and swung the Beretta at the man's head, missing by inches, but there was another shot from the one out in the grass and the man jerked and grunted, took another faltering step, and went straight back and down, his arms flung out, his gun spinning away.

Carlyle had been hit and was down, but he twisted to locate his attacker in the dim light, and fired the carbine one-handed but accurately, and the man dropped like a stone.

John heard the distinctive crack of Carlyle's carbine back in the woods. He swung around and lifted his gun, looking for the man who had dropped to the grass shooting. There were two more flashes from over near the truck, and John heard the slugs hit the plane close by.

Then the truck was roaring backward, its doors still open. Alden had come around the tail and was running toward the truck. John used a flashlight to check on the man he'd tried to club. He was very still. Obviously out of it. He'd caught one of the shots fired by his comrade in the grass.

John looked up to see the truck slew around sideways. The driver was trying to turn it, but the back end slid into a ditch off the gravel track and the engine raced wildly but it only rocked in place. The driver ducked out, fired four times toward the plane, and ran.

Alden set off after him. John started to follow, but Carlyle called out from the tree line behind the plane, "No. He can handle it. I shot the one back here; he's done. Check the other two who're down."

Alden ran flat out, arms pumping, digging up spurts of gravel. The fleeing man had the head start, but turned to snap off a shot, his eyes wide in the camo grease. The second time he turned to look back, his foot caught in the lip of a pothole and he stumbled, but recovered with two staggering steps and ran on. With his free hand he fumbled for his cell phone and thumbed the speed dial. Brought it to his mouth.

The light from the idling GMC was dimming as Alden and the man he was chasing ran away from it along the gravel track. The escaping man was dressed in black. Next to impossible to spot if he got too far off into the night. Alden stopped. Extended the handgun. Aiming by instinct and long practice. The man in black was not much more than a fleeting shadow already. Alden took a breath and let half of it out. Held it. Squeezed off three shots.

And the man took three more loose-legged steps and collapsed.

Alden ran up, keeping the gun on him. Dug for his flashlight. This one was done. One hit high on each side of his spine. The cell phone lay by his hand. Alden pocketed the gun and picked up the phone in his gloved hand. Put it to his ear. Heard, "Lupo? Report. Lupo?"

He ended the call and slid the phone into the man's back pocket.

They gathered near the truck and John, still enervated from the adrenaline overdose, said, "The two over by the plane are finished."

Breathing hard, Alden said, "Well, that turned into a free-for-all."

Carlyle said, "My fault."

"Nobody's fault," Alden said. "It's done, and now they're four down. The last one tried to call in, but I don't think he could have got off much of a message. I'm still good to go if you both are."

John said, "Yes."

Carlyle shrugged, winced, and said, "Nothing for it now. Let's do it."

The initial shots from Waco had, luckily, caught Carlyle close to the very bottom edge of the vest, under his arm, and had hammered him down. His breathing was shallow and he was favoring his side, moving like an old man.

Carlyle used his cell to call Doyle. Said, "Do the barriers as fast as you can. Yes, we're good here. Go to the pickup point. It'll be me, not Alden."

When Carlyle had hung up, Alden asked him. "You sure you're going to be okay with this?"

"I'm just pretty sore. Possible cracked rib. I've got a roll of duct tape. You can tape me up. Then we'll switch places. I can still do that end of it—mostly just a show, anyway, right?"

After Alden inspected Carlyle's side and taped him up, Alden and John dragged the bodies off into the brush far enough so they would not be found too soon. The GMC was still sitting half off the track at an angle, its engine idling. Alden tried to power it out of the ditch, but it did not have four wheel drive and would not rock free. The frame was solidly on the ground. Carlyle was not in shape to help, so he sat in the plane and rested while John used the GMC's jack handle to start digging the soil away from the frame, making trenches for the rear wheels, and Alden began working with one of the truck's hubcaps to scrape together a pile of gravel they could use to line the wheel trenches for traction.

***

Heading north, Brandon Doyle had reached the deserted fork where he was supposed to set up the first two barriers. He had pulled off onto the shoulder and had stepped down from his idling pickup when he heard a revved engine. There was a dim glow around a curve that curled up the flank of a hill, and then headlights broke over the top, firing white lances through the intervening trees, speeding down toward him around the curve fast. It was hidden behind thick trees and brush now, but within seconds it would blast around the last of the curve out of the forest and he would be flashed into full view.

He bounded back into the truck, slapping off the headlights with the palm of his left hand and turning off the ignition with his right fingers. Felt around under the seat, grabbed a shop rag he knew was red, laid it over the side door sill, and rolled the window up to nip a corner of it, most of it hanging outside. Folded himself over to the side so his face wouldn't show. A citizen would take little notice of a broken-down pickup abandoned beside the road. Even somebody like a county cop might leave it alone, figuring one of the state patrol boys was already on it. A long shot, but better for sure than him having to explain what he was doing out here. If it did turn out to be law, he could say he'd just stopped to take a nap because he'd been about to fall asleep.

He heard the car coming down the last of the hill. Now it was slowing down, lights glaring through the pickup's windshield.

Stopping?

No.

It was turning away along the other fork and accelerating.

He sat up, but only caught a glimpse of the receding tail lights.

Working fast by the glow from his parking lights, he unloaded the barriers and set them up to block both lanes, the DETOUR sign with its arrow pointing to the other branch of the fork. He squealed the pickup around and floored the aged and laboring engine, trying to make up time. He still had to drive past the compound, set up the other two barriers at an intersection to the south, take care of the dogs by heaving the two chunks of beefsteak, which Carlyle had doctored with a potent tranquilizer, over the fence, and return to the pickup point. Thinking, *hell, why didn't they just have me do the whole damned thing myself?*

It took fifteen minutes of hurried work to free the GMC from the ditch. John finally drove it, in three lurches, engine bellowing and rear wheels spraying dirt, up onto the gravel. He got out and

Carlyle put his hand on the door. He looked a little pale, but functional enough. And determined.

Alden said, "Wait a minute. The gate key card." Carlyle stepped aside and Alden looked inside the truck. The between-seat console with its cup holders. The glove compartment. Above the visor. The door pocket. The floor. He said, "Not here. John. Come on."

They ran to where they had left the bodies. Obviously, neither of the black-clad two had been driving. They each took one of the others and searched them thoroughly.

No plastic card.

Aiming their flashlight beams at the ground, they jogged along the tracks where they had dragged the men.

No plastic card.

They searched around the GMC in case it had fallen out onto the ground, both well aware that it might have been churned up into the dirt and hopelessly lost in the process of freeing the truck from the ditch.

Nothing.

In the way a person who has misplaced a ring of keys will check the same empty pockets and all the same likely places several times over, John looked in the cab again. Behind both visors. In both door pockets. Under both floor mats.

Got down low and aimed his light under the driver's seat.

And found it.

It was slid neatly into an alligator-textured vinyl holder that had been taped up under the seat bottom. Accessible to the driver by only a bend and reach, but not likely to be discovered easily by anybody else. Clever. He handed the card to Carlyle, who managed to climb up, grunting, and get himself behind the wheel. Closed the door and gave them a forced grin.

Alden aimed the flashlight at his watch and said, "Burning too much time here."

As Carlyle drove away, John and Alden jogged for the plane.

THIRTY-FIVE

From two thousand feet above the mostly unseen rolling foothills terrain, the night was dark, the ragged overcast not more than two hundred feet above them, wisps of it occasionally whipping past the windshield and momentarily fogging what dim view there was below.

Alden was in the back on his knees, the passenger seat in front of him folded all the way forward. He was hanging onto the safety belt webbing, peering below out the rear side window. John was essentially flying his course by the instruments.

Back in Georgia, using the aged courtesy car from the little Cobb County airport, the three of them had first gone to a Lowe's for the studs, plywood, and paint to make the road barriers. The next stop had been a Walmart, where they had split up in the parking lot so they would not be seen entering the store together. John had only told them, "Smooth and spherical are good. Heavy is good. I'll get the containers."

After a half hour's shopping, they all checked out through separate registers, paying cash. They pushed their loaded carts to the old car and transferred all their purchases into the back seat. They stopped at a combination service station and convenience store and took a slot in a far empty corner. Wearing gloves, they went through the items, cutting off wrappings, removing labels, and dividing the things up into three large rectangular gray plastic storage bins with snap lids. Into each bin they emptied two cartons of golf balls in a variety of psychedelic colors, on sale at $10.97 per carton. Alden had bought baseballs in clear plastic packs of a dozen for $19.96 per pack, and he shook out two packs of them into each bin. Boxes of .68-caliber paint balls—one thousand per $18.94 box, on sale; Carlyle rattled two boxes of them into each bin. Six hundred and eighty large and colorful bubblegum balls in an assortment of "Eight Fruitastic Flavors" next went cascading into the bins.

John had arrived at the produce section in the Walmart at the same time as Alden, but they had not acknowledged each other. John had chosen six five-pound net bags of red delicious apples, fifteen per bag. Alden had rejected lemons, limes, and tangerines as not heavy enough, opting instead for net bags of Florida grapefruit, six orbs in each five-pound bag. Now he emptied three bags into each bin. John had bought eighteen perfectly round seven-inch-diameter miniature seedless watermelons, each one weighing in at five pounds. Four melons for each bin.

Carlyle had spent time in the kitchenware aisles and had bought a dozen shiny foot-diameter heavy aluminum pizza pans on sale for $2.17 each. He also had several five-by-nine-inch nonstick "Professional Weight" loaf pans, some standard nine-inch cake pans at $2.50 each with a three-year limited warranty, and a few heavy-duty fancy Bundt cupcake pans. He had checked each of these items for tonal quality by rapping on them with a quarter. Carlyle had also bought three sets of china dishes, one set per bin. On sale at half off. Each a complete service for four.

Into each bin, Alden poured six containers of inch-and-a-quarter-long oval lead weights he'd chosen from the fishing tackle aisle. These were, most appropriately, called bullet sinkers. A package of five for $4.47.

When they had contributed these and their other purchases, Carlyle dipped both gloved hands into each bin to toss and mix the contents while John got out of the car and bundled all the packaging refuse into a nearby dumpster. Alden eyed the parking lot shoulder, scanned around to make sure nobody was looking, got out and, reaching in though the open side window, hastily sprinkled a heaping double handful of pea gravel into each bin as a topping. John snapped on the bin lids.

When they got back to the airport, each of them carried a heavy bin to the plane. The plywood squares had fit into the big trunk of the old car, but they'd had to leave the two-by-fours sticking out the windows. They managed to fit it all into the plane by removing the rear fuselage access panel behind the folded back seat. On the small deck of the office building, the attendant stood with his hands on his hips and a puzzled frown on his face, watching them. John went over to him, handed over the keys with a smile, and said, "Found a sale on a few things. Thanks for the use of the car. We filled the tank."

The man shook his head and went back inside.

Now the three bins sat together in the back of the airplane. Alden had the front passenger seat reclined all the way so he'd have access to the bins. The Cessna bored through the humid night, bounding slightly in the stealthy feelers of turbulence that reached out ahead of the approaching front. John had the outside navigation and strobe lights off, and the cabin was lit only by the glowing of the instrument array. They were floating through the sky as invisibly as a nighthawk.

When the time to the destination was getting close according to the ghostly hands on his watch, John looked down ahead and spotted the triangle of three area security lights surrounding the compound. He would have liked to be higher, but that would plunge them into the base of the overcast.

He checked the altimeter. They were still at least fifteen hundred feet above the broad low hill. It would have to be good enough. Normally, a light single-engine plane is at best difficult to hear from the ground at any altitude above three thousand feet. Tonight, the wind would serve to muffle their sound more than normal, and he bled off power now to further reduce the noise from the prop and the underbelly exhaust, putting down ten degrees of flaps for increased lift and stability, keeping only enough rpm on to maintain altitude.

Nobody inside the compound should be able to hear them.

As he drew closer, he banked into a wide orbit with the compound at the center. Waiting. Trying to judge the strength of the wind. To keep the orbit circular, he was having to bank steeper in that portion of the circle when the wind was at his tail, and shallower as he headed farther around the circle into the wind. How *much* he had to alter the bank angle had a direct bearing on the wind strength.

It was seven long minutes before he saw the headlights that from this height seemed to crawl along the winding road through the forest. The fan-shaped spread of light slowed, pulled to the road shoulder a mile short of the compound entrance, still well screened from the compound by the surrounding woods, and winked out.

Doyle.

Within another minute a vehicle came in sight from the north. John and Alden both watched as it threaded through the blackness like some bizarre night creature and slid past the compound. Slowed and did a three-point turn in the road, illuminating Doyle's pickup as it did.

Carlyle.

Now the chunky rectangle of the black GMC truck, its high beams spraying boldly ahead and its tail aglow with redness, moved resolutely toward the compound entrance.

John tightened his orbit slightly.

Above him, the misty cloud layer was subtly changing. Billions of miniscule droplets floating on the wind were coalescing into millions of slightly larger drops that were too heavy to float. And so they began falling.

Tiny blisters appeared magically and uniformly all across the windshield, and the ground faded out. The prop blast chased the little blisters into radial runnels that streaked backward. John made a complete orbit on the instruments, and it was as though some giant hand had spray-painted all the Plexiglas gray.

Then the recipe in the mix above altered fractionally again, and the rain quit as instantly as it had begun, the ground emerging out of the veiling grayness into sharp focus.

John took a deep breath and a new grip on the yoke with his left hand, thinking, *hold off on the rain, okay? Just for fifteen minutes.*

A number of years back, he had made several parachute jumps over a mountain strip from a high-wing single-engine Cessna. He'd seen graphs for free-falling objects from great heights through increasingly dense atmosphere, and knew that a jumper falling in the stable, flat, spread-eagled position would initially accelerate, plunging a greater distance each second than the previous second and rapidly gaining speed, but closer and closer to the surface, air friction would increase as well, soon slowing the rate of acceleration, until the two forces equalized. From twelve thousand feet, for example, a jumper would reach what they called terminal velocity in about twelve seconds, and would then fall at a constant speed of about a hundred and twenty miles per hour and no faster. This was true no matter how much higher that jumper might have exited the aircraft. So at any altitude beyond twelve seconds of free fall above the surface, be it five thousand feet or twenty thousand feet, a jumper whose chute failed to deploy would be moving at roughly one hundred and twenty miles per hour on impact.

John was facing a complex problem involving gravity, acceleration, terminal velocity, and other parameters now. Altitude, wind velocity, and wind direction were only three of the variables.

Galileo was reputed to have dropped cannonballs of different weights from the famous badly-constructed tower at Pisa, during his experiments to prove that gravity acts on all objects equally. And when Apollo astronaut Dave Scott dropped a hammer and a falcon feather side-by-side on the Moon, they both hit the primordial dust at the same instant. But on earth, air resistance complicates things.

The variety of items in the bins would have a variety of terminal velocities.

A further variable was the Cessna's speed. Any object dropped from it would initially be going forward at the same speed as the plane, and so would not fall straight down to the ground, but in an arc, at least until it had lost its forward speed and was from then on only responding to gravity. An early parachuting concern of John's had been slamming into the tail right after jumping, until he'd quickly realized that when he and the plane parted, he would be moving just as fast as it was, and by the time he'd slowed appreciably, he would be well below the tail, so it was not a concern at all. The greater danger, in fact, was falling straight down to hit the wheel fairing.

A World War Two dive bomber pilot had only to aim both himself and the bomb pinned to his plane's belly at the target together, punching the release while still just high enough to pull himself out without tearing his wings off at their roots, and the bomb would continue on precisely as it had been manually aimed with the plane.

But in this case, John would have to time the three releases before arriving over the target, to allow for the bleed-off of forward speed and for any drift caused by the wind.

The one variable he could allow for with any reasonable accuracy was the wind direction. He had taken a compass bearing on it while still on the ground at the Forest Service strip, and now he would fly over the compound directly into the wind, both to reduce his ground speed and to minimize any sideways drifting of the items.

He was picturing the problem graphically in his mind like it was chalked on a blackboard, with a tiny stick plane and arrows and dotted arcs, when he saw the GMC turn into the driveway entrance and stop in front of the gates.

***

Doyle was driving the black GMC now and he slowed to swing in and stop at the gates.

Carlyle was hurting, but he had the passenger window down and the carbine clamped upright between his knees. He said, "You did the dogs, right?"

"I heaved the meat over the fence at the far north corner, yeah, and one of them jumped on it like a linebacker on a Whopper, but I never saw the other one. Let's hope it was hungry."

Doyle was wearing his black baseball cap, and kept his head down to shadow his face from the stare of the gate security camera as he reached out the window and placed the key card in the depression on the little box on its post. He had the low beams on, because they wanted whoever was observing to recognize the GMC easily and so, hopefully, to be put at ease. There was a three-second hesitation that seemed much longer, then the gates dutifully swung open, and he took his foot off the brake and drove in.

Carlyle said, "Okay, stop in the middle of that S curve so we're broadside to the wall gates, and flick your high beams twice. We'll wait for John to make the drop, then I'm going to get out and fire over the hood. How about you watch my back when I do, in case that first dog never shared its meal."

"You know what I'm thinkin'?" Doyle said. "I could sure as hell use a cold beer, is what I'm thinkin'." He was steering with his left hand and with his right hand lifting the revolver up from between his legs.

**

John saw the GMC's headlights flash brighter twice and completed a quarter of another orbit before banking into the wind, lining up to pass over the compound.

The timing was, of course, all of it. If he waited until he was directly over the target, the items would overshoot. If he released too soon, the items would fall short. It was one of the reasons to use a series of three bin bombs, to spread out the ground footprint and so to maximize the scoring chances. The individual loads also needed to be something the bombardier could easily and quickly contend with, especially while working within the cramped confines of the Cessna. This had been planned as Carlyle's job, but Alden would have to do it now.

John reached over to unlatch the passenger-side widow and give it a slight push with his fingertips, and the slipstream plucked it upward to float out of the way just under the wing. Over the headset intercom, he said, "Okay, get ready. When I say go, start dumping. Do it one, two, three. Quick as you can."

Alden said, "Got it." He had already removed the bin lids. Now he lifted the first one into position beneath the window where he would be able to quickly tip the contents up and out.

The compound passed out of sight under the nose. The lit GMC was on the drive ahead and down to his left, waiting patiently, well away to the side of his bombing run, and John held off . . . held off . . . until something instinctual whispered to him, *Almost* So he throttled back and rolled right, using opposite rudder to hold course. He did this both to swing the right fixed landing gear—which was directly below the window—downward and under so it would be less vulnerable to the bin bombs, and to help Alden dump the loads.

The instinctual voice judged, and nudged, *Now*.

He told Alden, " DROP. NOW."

Alden tilted the load up to the window and it was gone in a scraping rush. He tossed the empty bin toward the back of the plane and grabbed up the next load. And the next.

That's it, then.

Either John had chosen the correct sequence of seconds or he had been too early or too late. He banked back out into an orbit. He strained to see below. Alden was on his knees, grinning, peering down. But they only caught a few random glimmerings in the darkness.

***

The contents of each bin came out of the Cessna in a thick clump, but gravity and air friction and velocity immediately went to work with apparent whimsy to separate the varied items both vertically and horizontally. The relatively smoother, much more aerodynamic lead-bullet fishing sinkers, especially those that happened to find equilibrium and did not tumble, soon sped—like bullets—past the baseballs and the melons and the golf balls and the paintballs, which were each approaching their particular natural terminal velocities at different altitudes. Some of the dishes came down fairly fast like flowered cold-cut slicer blades, while the capricious cupcake and pizza pans flipped and floated and tumbled prettily this way and that.

By the time the items had fallen some fifteen hundred feet, or roughly the height of the Empire State Building, they had formed three distinct clouds that in all stretched out for perhaps eight hundred feet along the course of the bombing run.

***

A sleepy Wraith named Styles, the number two man on the Gamma team, recently summoned to duty by Monroe out of a warm bed, had been watching the video monitors in the anteroom. He had seen the black GMC return, but wondered why it had stopped halfway up the drive, in the middle of the S curve. And now he was wondering why the driver, who did not resemble any of the men who had left earlier in the vehicle, was looking so intently up at the sky out of the driver's window.

He picked up the intercom to call Dr. Ganz.

***

Fascinated, Doyle was watching the strung-out glittering blizzard of items, lit by the security lights on the property, descend the last few hundred feet toward the compound, and said, "Okay, here it comes."

Carlyle got out of the GMC, took a scan around for the possible dog, and assumed a position with his elbows braced on the warm hood, the carbine aimed. Waiting for a few more seconds.

**

It was utterly unlike anything anybody inside the compound had ever experienced or remotely heard of. Styles, the Wraith on duty in the anteroom, who was staring dumbly at the ceiling now and not at the security cameras, the intercom squawking unheeded in his hand, thought it might be hail. If it was, though, it was hail from hell.

Hail pinged and clattered and crackled, yes, and there was some of all that here, but hail did not thump and splatter. Did not cause a plastic skylight to suddenly split open as though it had been smacked by a rebounding baseball, and then to start bleeding in several colors. Hail did not deliver a series of roof-shaking concussive punches like the fist of God. Nor did hail clang-chatter-ring like dropped restaurant trays.

**

The first half of the first load missed the compound, falling short, but almost all the remaining two and a half bin bombs rained down on the compound in a protracted spattering. As Carlyle saw the initial items dropping out of sight beyond the wall, he gave it two more seconds and fired. One round, neatly aimed and cleanly taking out the main gate security camera. He got back in the GMC and said, "Let's get closer, but don't block the driveway.

We want to leave it open for any deserters to clear out."

A single flowered dish, sailing in out of the darkness like a Frisbee, skidded onto the truck's hood and shattered to shards against the windshield, cracking it and startling both men.

Doyle snorted and got on the gas.

He'd had crockery thrown at him before.

***

Glenda, a painfully thin and pale brunette with long hair and a penchant for gothic makeup and fantasy clothing when she was not on a job with her much older male team mate, was the only female Wraith. Leader of team Beta. She and Styles had embarked on a furtive on-and-off thing about six months ago, based mostly on her liking to hurt and humiliate and Styles liking to be hurt and humiliated. She had been secretly sharing his recently-dampened bed when the whole compound had been awakened by the emergency buzzers and Monroe's voice over the intercom system telling everybody to be ready for anything. Perhaps recognizing a creature disturbingly similar to herself, she hated Monroe, and knew the loathing was mutual. She had gathered her various somewhat unorthodox things and beat it back to her room. She suspected Brain had all the rooms bugged for sound and sight, but she had been keeping up the pretense of discretion with Styles, anyway.

Now, having been summoned to a meeting in the study, she was dressed in a black T-shirt and black jeans, both of which appeared to have been painted on, with her reassuring little Ladysmith nine millimeter compact automatic resting in its nylon shoulder holster. She was padding in her sneakers past the softly lighted, impossibly blue pool, heading for the living area, when the pool erupted and spat a geyser at her, soaking her along one whole side. She stopped dead, stunned. She drew her gun and held it at the ready. Then there were strange noises all around her. Things dancing loudly on the bricks and shredding through a tree, and she backed toward the doors for the living area. Glanced up to see what looked like a cookie pan spinning slantways to clang off of a window.

She turned to run and her foot slid out from under her and she went down hard on her shoulder, numbing that whole arm. She was disoriented and holding her good hand, which was still clutching the gun, on top of her head protectively. Things pelting and splattering her. Stinging. Emitting an involuntary series of mewling sounds in fear and frustration, she tried to see what had tripped her.

Rolling, multicolored balls that looked like bubblegum.

***

John had kept orbiting, waiting for two minutes, then he reached out and killed the ignition, and the prop fluttered to a stop, leaving just the sound of the hurricane slipstream blowing in the vents.

With the mixture set at full lean so the engine would not start, John nudged the starter twice, swinging the prop blades to horizontal, so a tip would not dig in if the landing was hard. He came out of his descending spiral eight hundred feet higher than the compound hillock and far enough out to turn onto a steep final approach while still over the surrounding forest, gliding silently down through the night, guided only by the glow from the security lights and by his memory of the compound layout.

And everything outside went gray again, this time with much larger drops rattling against the suddenly useless windshield like sprayed gravel.

He slapped the mixture to full rich.

Darted his left hand to the ignition switch.

Start it. Full power. Pull up. Get out of here.

But something stayed his hand.

Before he'd lost all visibility, some part of his brain had automatically been counting down the number of seconds to touchdown. *Nine*, it told him now.

So give it five, then start it and pull out if you still can't see.

Gripping the yoke in his right fist, his left fingers on the ignition key, he counted.

One one-thousand. Two one-thousand. Three one-thousand. Four one-thousand. Five . . .

A dim cotton ball ahead and to the left. *Has to be a security light. But which one?* An indistinct mass spread out farther to the left. *The compound.* Murky darkness below giving way to a somewhat lighter expanse. *The field surrounding the compound.*

He let go of the ignition and switched hands on the yoke so he could dump the flaps with his right hand. Gave it some back pressure to bleed off speed.

The rippling grass came up at him fast out of the slashing rain. The STOL kit on the Cessna would slow the landing speed. That, combined with the stiff headwind, would make for a short rollout, but the field was not large enough to allow much margin for overshooting. He had to put it down fast or risk running into the far fence.

He pulled back to flare out, and touched down gently, the grass cushioning the wheels.

But now there was a dark low shape dead ahead—a slick rock ledge jutting up two feet out of the ground at a slant. He had enough forward speed remaining to haul back on the yoke and make the Cessna hop up, and he tensed for a wheels impact that did not come, then she was past the rock and losing the will to fly and they were down again and rolling out, bumping and bounding, the left wingtip just clearing past the security light pole by feet, the black tree line looming at them. He got on the brakes, still hauling back on the yoke to keep the nose wheel from digging in, the plane swerving and skidding on the soaked grass, but the strong headwind was helping now, and they finally stopped, the plane rocking once, eighty feet from the glistening chain link fence.

Over the headset intercom, Alden said, "When I get a few minutes, thinking about that one is going to scare hell out of me." He hung his headset on the dual yoke, grabbed up a backpack, and said, "Let's go. This has to be fast."

Pulling off his headset and unbuckling the seat harness, John nodded.

***

Two men saw the plane materialize from the murk. One was Carlyle, but he only caught a glimpse before the compound wall blocked it out. He looked at his glowing watch and told Doyle to get ready to start their mock attack. The other man was Clint Rader, who had been staring out at the slanted silver strings of rain surrounding the only security light he could see from his window. This night had gone crazy. First the surreal extended cacophony of impossible sounds. Now this impossible airplane floating in soundlessly and landing like a clumsy albatross he'd seen in a documentary once.

Then he stopped breathing and his heart stumbled. He started trembling, sucked in a great gulp of air, and from his raw throat he shouted, "NOLAN."

***

Everything was eerily quiet. They were gathered in the study, Ganz standing behind his polished desk that now had an ugly gouge in it, dug by one of the bullet fishing sinkers that had first neatly holed the skylight above. Monroe stood at his side. The remaining three stood in front of the desk. His fingers were spread out creating bony conical pale cages on the desk top as he stared into their eyes in turn. Styles. Woods.

And Glenda, who was dripping onto the floor. Her hair and shoulders were streaked in paintball smears of bright orange and bloody red. She was staring back at him, shaking her head from side to side just perceptibly.

Ganz said, "This is what you will do—"

Glenda said, "No. I don't think so," and raised the Ladysmith she still clutched.

Monroe began to move but she swung her aim on him and gave him a squint-eyed inviting smile that stopped him. She said, "What just happened can only have been a diversion. I figure we might have some seconds to get the fuck out of here. Styles? You with me?"

Styles looked at Ganz. At the woman. Drew his gun and aimed it at Ganz.

She said, "Woods. How about it? In or out?"

Woods looked at her for three long seconds, shrugged, and said, "Hell, this was too damned nuts to last, anyway. But let's make him open his safe first."

The bony cages on the desktop trembled with suppressed rage. In a guttural basso, he said, "I will have you chased down and exterminated as painfully as possible. I will have your dragons cut off and burned in front of your faces. You will die slowly. Screaming."

***

Looking at his watch, Carlyle said, "Three . . . Two . . . One. Okay, NOW. He pulled the pin on the first flash-bang grenade and lobbed it over the wall, despite the pain he knew would rip at his side when he did. Doyle followed it with a teargas canister, saying, "Let me do this."

"Okay," Carlyle said, but not so close to the main gates. More off to the side there. Like we're trying to come in through the service entrance. And they have to be timed. I'll tell you when to throw each one." The plain double doors of the service entrance were just around the corner from the front gates, and Carlyle had shot out the camera that covered them just after Doyle had slid the vehicle to a stop. The GMC was now parked half on the grass midway between the two entrances. He got busy tamping plastic explosive in a clumpy vertical line down the crack of the heavy service doors.

A lot of plastic.

***

Everybody except Ganz flinched when the first grenade went off somewhere out front. Glenda started backing toward the study doors. She said,

"No time. I think we've got to go now if we're going. Come on." She turned and ran, and the other two watched Ganz and Monroe, backing until they were out the doors, and then they ran after her. Monroe started after them, but Ganz went still and said, "No. Let them go. There is something else you must do. Go get subject eight. Take him outside by the pool. Terminate him. The top of his skull. As though he was hit by one of the falling missiles. Leave him there. Hurry."

There was another stunning detonation, this time more toward the side of the compound, near the service entrance. Monroe nodded and went out the back door of the study.

Ganz quietly said to himself, almost pleasantly, "Let's have a little music." He strode to the low console against the wall and turned the CD player on. A disc bearing excerpts from a number of pieces, which he'd compiled himself, was already loaded. He switched it to play throughout the compound and turned the volume up very loud, until the speakers were overdriven and breaking up, to combat the intrusive detonations that were coming at regular intervals from the front now, and to disorient anyone forcing their way into the compound. The first selection was from Khachaturian's "Masquerade Waltz".

He sat behind the desk and tore open the bottom file drawer. Working quickly, he pulled out the first thick file and began inserting the notes into the heavy-duty shredder that sat on the floor just by the ornate left table leg. It would chew up CDs as well, and he plucked these from their cases and fed them into the gobbling, chattering shredder as he hummed along with a morose and dissonant snatch of "The Human Brain" from *Fantastic Voyage*. He had only included fifteen seconds of it, and it abruptly switched to Bach's "Toccata and Fugue in D Minor," the pipe organ chasing through a chaotic series of phrases.

***

Alden had set the small plastic charge on the back door and they were standing off to the side, pressed against the wall, Alden looking at his watch, rain dripping from his cap brim, counting down, Three . . . Two . . . One . . .

On the other side of the compound, Carlyle had set the detonator in the plastic and he and Doyle were crouched behind the rear of the GMC. Once he had seen the plane descend, he had allowed Alden exactly one minute to get to the rear entrance and begin setting his charge there. He had then lobbed the first flash bang over the wall, and Doyle had followed that with four more, spaced out at fifteen second intervals. Now he tracked the hand on his watch and said, "Three . . . Two . . . One . . . and pressed the button of the little black-box radio trigger.

The back door blew at the same instant as the other, much larger charge bit a gaping hole through the service doorway. The big charge had effectively masked the rear door charge, and Alden, his backpack on and his automatic in a two-handed grip, vaulted over the smoking debris and went in low. John followed fast. Distorted, disorienting music stormed through the deserted hallway they discovered. Both recognized the music but neither could have named it as the "Imperial March" from *The Empire Strikes Back*.

***

The Silver Ford Explorer sat in the open garage at idle, the right front passenger door open. Glenda was behind the wheel and Woods had the whole back seat to himself with the MP5 submachine gun. All the windows were down. They were all stunned from the blast that had just obliterated the service doors. Glenda shook her head to clear it. She nodded and Styles slapped both the large control buttons for the main wall gates and the entrance fence gates and dove back into the Explorer just as Glenda—hunched over the wheel, both hands gripping it tightly but her left also holding her Ladysmith—toed the accelerator to the floor with all the strength in her thin leg, leaving black smoking streaks on the smooth cement. They roared across the wet stones of the entry patio, through a haze of teargas and rain, the gates swinging open just in time, and they charged through, the engine whining high in protest.

Doyle and Carlyle were crouched behind the GMC, which was broadside to the main driveway, each behind a wheel. Carlyle had one eye clear and saw three heads in the car. All three were firing wildly out both sides of the car, a burst from the MP5 taking out all the glass on the GMC. He shouted to Doyle to shoot wide and let them go. He tried to get the plate, but couldn't in the rain as the Explorer swerved and slewed down the drive very fast, heading for the open fence gates. He brought the carbine to his cheek in the prone position and rapped off three shots, pretty sure the last round had gone through the top of the back window, where he'd aimed it, but catching only what he thought must be a distant flash of glitter. Doyle was emptying his revolver loudly but deliberately wide of the Explorer as it careened out the driveway entrance and roared onto the road and away toward the south.

Thoroughly rain-soaked, they crouched behind the wheels and Doyle reloaded.

Waiting for any more deserters.

* * *

Alden and John were both pounding on the locked heavy steel doors along the hallway with their fists.

John stopped and held up his hand. It was hard to hear anything with Leroy Anderson's "Blue Tango" throbbing down the hallway. John thumped that door again and pressed his ear tight to it. Got answering thumps. Three sets of thumps. S-O-S.

John nodded and grinned. Alden swung his backpack down, watching along the hallway. In seconds, he had a plastic lump stuck to the door beside the deadbolt knob. Inserted a detonator. Made the O sign with thumb and forefinger.

John thumped S and B. STAND BACK. Pressed his ear close.

Got the S-O-S again.

Thumped S and B as loudly as he could. "Blue Tango" had given way weirdly to "Danse macabre."

Got two fast sets of thumps. O and K. Then nothing. He looked at Alden.

They stood away to each side of the door and Alden used the black box to blow it.

John was the first in, and Alden was still in the hallway, taking glances both ways, his gun at the ready.

John looked through the dissipating smoke at the figure by the darkened window and said loudly, "You're Clint Rader."

There was a break in the deafening music. The figure rasped out, "Nolan? Where's Nolan?"

"He sent me. Let's go now. We'll get you out of here."

Ravel's "Pavane for a Dead Princess" began playing everywhere.

And Alden ducked into the room as three shots blew down the hall past the doorway. Alden went down on a knee and used his left hand to fire three answering shots blindly around the door jamb. Yanked his hand back in as two more shots came from down the hall.

Alden shouted, "Got us pinned here."

The way Alden had returned fire sparked an idea as John saw the bathroom and stepped into it. There was a metal mirror screwed to the wall. He stood back and fired four shots at the screws. Got his fingers under one edge of it and tore it loose. He took it out and handed it to Alden, who nodded. Kept the gun in his left hand and held the slightly bent mirror by an edge in his right hand, crossed over his left. It took him a moment to get the angles just right, his gun aimed at the corner of the wall where the shooter was hidden. Then he waited.

Monroe ducked out and fired only once before there were three quick flashes from the doorway and his gun was ripped away, his hand stinging like fire. Alden was out the doorway, running, and John followed.

Monroe was backed up against the wall around the bend in the hallway, shaking his right hand, trying to decide what to do, but Alden was there now, training an automatic at his face, its black eye steady. Monroe held up his left palm in surrender. John was watching down the hall for anyone else.

Moving with deliberation, Alden held Monroe's throat clamped, pushed him tightly back against the wall with his left hand, and pressed the muzzle of the automatic into his left eye. He shouted, "How many left?"

Monroe's free eye blinked, saw something in Alden's face, and he mouthed, "One."

The speakers were blaring out "In the Hall of the Mountain King" maddeningly faster and faster. Clint Rader shuffled up and smiled at Monroe. He pointed to the key ring on Monroe's belt. Alden unbuckled the belt and slid the ring off, handing it to Clint, who beckoned them back down the hall. Alden spun Monroe around and took a handful of his shirt at the neck. Pushed him along the hall. Clint unlocked one of the doors and pointed inside. Alden gave Monroe a heavy shove inside and Clint locked the door.

John said loudly, "Okay. Let's get you out of here."

Clint found the key to the leg hobble and bent to unlock it. He seemed dazed. Shook his head and pointed toward the interior of the compound. Started walking.

Alden reached out and grabbed him by the arm, stopping him, shouting, "No. We don't know for sure how many—"

There was a shadow near the set of swinging half-glassed doors at the end of the hall, and both

John and Alden aimed that way. A foot nudged one of the doors open and a man yelled out.

It was Carlyle.

Alden answered.

Doyle was with him, and they met midway along the stretch of hall.

Over the music, Carlyle hollered, "Heard all the shooting back here. Didn't see anybody else on our way."

Clint Rader pointed again and started walking unsteadily. Alden shrugged, took a two-handed grip on his gun, pushed past Rader, and led the way, turning to see which way Rader was pointing. Carlyle took up the rear, covering their backs. The vicious nerve-sawing violin chirpings of the theme from Hitchcock's *Psycho* filled the hallway.

The back door to the study was open. Alden took a quick cautious look inside, then went in fast, gun aimed. John followed him, then the others.

Ganz was seated behind his desk, methodically feeding paper and shiny discs into a shredder, ignoring the men. Alden lowered his aim and shot the shredder. John saw the equipment in the corner, went over and punched off the CD player, and everything went blessedly quiet.

Ganz raised his gaze from the file on his desk and his yellow eyes sought and fixed on John's. They were glowing with a furious maniacal light. He said, "Yes, of course. Mr. Hardin." He sat up straight and Alden said, "Keep your hands on the desk."

They took Ganz back to the cell room and pushed him in with Monroe.

In a roughened voice, Clint told Ganz, "When they put you on death row, you can take notes."

John said, "If you make it there. I figure the Ghosts aren't going to want you talking. Either one of you."

The yellow eyes were still full of hatred, but there was a flicker of something else behind them. The first skitterings of fear?

Clint Rader locked the deadbolt. Thought for a moment, squinting at the ceiling. Said to himself, "Yeah, that's it." Then knocked on the door. Two knuckle raps, a thump, another rap. A hesitation, then two raps and a thump.

F-U.

Alden and Carlyle went through the compound quickly to clear it while John, Doyle, and Clint waited in the study.

When they were gathered again, Clint said, "Where is my brother?"

John said, "Sorry. There's no easy way to tell you this. He's dead. But his last thoughts were about you."

Clint looked stricken. He blinked and said, "What? That can't be."

"I'm sorry. But he sent us. We're here because of him."

"But who are you?"

"John Hardin. These men are . . . friends."

Doyle said, "I got an idea. How about let's get the hell outta here? We can meet someplace later for pizza and beer."

John gave his borrowed handgun and wet vest to Carlyle. Then Carlyle, Alden, and Doyle left quickly out the front way, making for Doyle's pickup on foot.

Clint looked at John. His eyes were brimming. He wiped at them with his fingers and said, quietly and simply, "Thank you. Now you go. I'll stay." Cleared his throat. "I'll give you guys an hour, say, then call in the law, if they're not already on the way. I didn't see any of your faces. Ski masks. Does that sound okay? If they get anything out of Ganz and Monroe, it will be their story against mine. I'll make my story good."

"One thing. Your brother had a disc. Somebody might already have come across it. It can put me in jail for life."

Clint frowned. Said, "Well, not if I can help it, man."

They shook hands and John left the way he had come in.

Clint Rader sat down at the desk, took two deep breaths, pulled out the top drawer, and opened the laptop.

The plane sat rocking gently in the steady wind-whipped rain and John ran for it, but he stopped, skidding on the wet grass, and grabbed the wingtip to keep from falling.

The Rottweiller was sitting on its haunches in the deeper wing shadow close by the pilot-side wheel fairing. Growling steadily.

John backed away, his hands up, glancing over his shoulder to locate the compound door. Reluctant to turn and run because it might spur the dog to charge. The big animal rose and stalked toward him, head down, muscular shoulders bunching with each step.

But there was something wrong with the dog. It seemed uncertain. Unsteady. It took a few more steps, shook its head, and sank down onto its extended forepaws, then its back end flopped over. Groggy, it shook its head again and gave out a whine. John thought, *recovering from the tranquilizer, or it never got a big enough dose in the first place.*

He skirted around the dog, its black eyes tracking him, and made it into the plane.

He started up and back-taxied over the uneven grass. Swung it around close to the fence. Lined up into the wind, with his landing lights cutting a bright cone of needles out of the rain. Ran the engine up to full bellow with the brakes clamped and ten degrees of flaps down for added lift.

He took a fresh grip on the yoke, let off on the brakes, and the Cessna bounded along like a live thing, gaining speed, the wind helping to boost lift.

He pulled her up but kept the nose down to build just a bit more speed in ground effect, then hauled back on the yoke, the prop slapping into the rain smartly, and held his breath as the fence and the tree line passed very close beneath the wheels.

Climbed away on his instruments into the night.

THIRTY-SIX

Two days after the raid on the compound, Pitt Tobin called Sutter Leonard at his New Mexico ranch on the secure line and said, "You caught the news?"

There had been varied accounts of the raid in the media. Light on facts and heavy on speculation. One common theme seemed to lay the responsibility on one or another shadowy covert government agency, and events like Ruby Ridge and Waco were resurrected for comparison. It was known the property belonged to a minimally-published, mysterious doctor of psychology named Kurt Ganz, who was being held in a federal facility without bail, but there had as yet been no mention of the Satan's Ghosts. The whole affair was obviously tightly cloaked, leaving the minions of the media frustrated and irate.

Sutter Leonard said, "Yeah. I'm working on that. Looks like Brain will have to go pretty quick. He's reachable inside. I've been getting other feedback on this. You know where this guy Trey Flores is, for instance?"

"In the wind."

"He's the one we wanted in the first goddamn place. None of this should have happened. And what about this yahoo Hardin?"

Tobin had a brief flash of that hot Indian bitch mouthing off about her gang. The whole damned Cherokee Nation. With a wry grin, he said, "Hey, right now it is what it is. Hardin and his boys only wanted the Rader kid. I say we leave that alone. What's turning a screw in my head is the stuff your man Brain was apparently into. How much do you know about that?"

"I'm as dumb about all that as you are. Big surprise, if it's true at all."

Sure, Tobin thought. He said, "I agree about canceling B's membership quick and final, along with his number one. Monroe, is it? Then let's see what shakes loose and we can talk again."

"Yeah. Later, brother."

So, in maybe a month, Tobin thought, *might turn out ol' Sutter's a lot sicker than anybody knew. Be one hell of a blowout funeral, though.*

***

Three days after the raid, at mid-morning, an immaculate black SUV glided up the mountain to Eaglenest Ridge and parked behind the Wrangler. Two men in suits got out.

John had been expecting something like this. Waiting for it. Unable to do much more than try to catch up his paperwork. This could be the start of a process that would ultimately strip him of his freedom. He took his coffee cup and walked outside to meet them in the yard.

They both showed badges, one saying, "I'm Striker. This is Coyle. Special agents. FBI. May we come in? We have a few questions."

"I'd rather do it out here. An elderly couple lives with me."

Striker nodded. "What do you know about an incident over in Tennessee in which a private residence was attacked?"

"I saw a piece about something like that in the paper."

"And you can, of course, account for your whereabouts during that attack?"

"Absolutely."

"Good. That's out of the way, then. Because we had reason to believe someone took prominent part in that rather bizarre series of events who answers your description remarkably well, even to a similarity in name. But you must have very powerful friends, Mr. Hardin, because our directive is to treat you as an ally of the agency, at least for now. And, after all, the net result of that unusual chain of events can apparently be considered enlightening and beneficial."

"So. I'm a little confused about why you're here."

"We're in the process of tracking down certain individuals who may have been associated with the citizen who owns that residence in Tennessee. Can you help us out in any way with that?"

John thought. Said, "I understand sometimes one elite group or another, one gang or another, will adopt a symbol they can take pride in. That symbol could be a tattoo. Maybe something like a small dragon. The custom with people like this seems to be they all wear it in the same place. Could be on the triceps or the forearm or on the left chest, close to the heart. The symbol might even have some code worked into it. A really elite group might number only about thirteen members in all."

Strayhorn made a wry face and said, "Now, that's certainly coincidental, although we had not considered a code. We've found four such symbols on deceased individuals not far from that unusually damaged residence. We know where two others are. So perhaps there are no more than seven left."

"That could be."

Strayhorn frowned, his features arranged as a question. Nodded slowly. "I see. Well, we have no reason to trouble you further today. But we might well wish to talk at greater length soon. I assume you'll be readily available?"

"Sure. There's one other thing . . . "

Strayhorn said, "Oh?"

"A friend of mine named Nolan Rader died recently in Memorial Hospital in Chattanooga, of gunshot wounds. I met two law enforcement men that day but didn't have much helpful information at the time. Since then I've remembered Mr. Rader told me two names not long before he died. The men he claimed did it. The names were Keller and Engel. Passing themselves off as some kind of mercenaries."

"And you're just recalling this now?"

"Yes. I hope it helps."

"Is there anything else you'd care to share?"

"Nothing I can think of."

They gave him their cards, thanked him politely, and left.

That same day he signed for a Fed-Ex parcel. He looked at the return address and took it out to the shed workbench to open it. There was a cased CD inside with his name printed on it in red felt tip, almost certainly in Nolan Rader's hand. Along with a simple thank-you card signed Clint and Rita.

And a great deal of cash.

There was a note on the card saying, "Here's the CD you were looking for. After you left, I found another disc in Brain's laptop. A friend helped get some usable numbered accounts from it. Share some of this with your guys."

He hid the banded cash in the shed. There was more of it than he wanted to count, but he made a fast estimate. When Hank and Hattie were out walking that afternoon, he would look at the red-marked CD and then he would destroy it.

Later that evening, on the drive to the white farmhouse near Sylva, he began thinking. *Four ways. Including Alden, Carlyle, and Doyle. Then a nice anonymous donation to that new rehab center in Asheville? And why not a really good violin for Hank? Made by some old master two or three centuries ago, with its wood now perfectly aged, and a sweet sound the old man probably never even imagined he could make.* Some high-class place out in the Midwest sold that kind of thing, he knew from Hank. He could fly there and they could help him select one. He could tell Hank he'd bought it for a hundred dollars from some family who'd had it stored in a closet for a couple generations.

He could bolster the boy's college trust fund.

How could he feed some into Kitty's business without her knowing it? Until she got it going well on its own. How about an enthusiastic buyer comes in from the West Coast—an interior decorator maybe—looking for a steady source of Cherokee items?

And there were two duct-taped bullet holes in the Cessna that needed fixing discreetly.

***

Twilight—what serious photographers like to call sweet light—filtered through the trees and floated on the rippled deer pool as shadows materialized among the trees to populate the mountainside for the night. A gusty cool breeze was carrying a change of weather with it.

They had scraped a circle clear of leaves and had laid, but not yet lit, a small fire within a circle of stones. The trickle was making pleasant chuckling noises at it cavorted down the mountain to tumble into the pool. They sat side by side on a patch of cool moss, watching the night come on, John hugging his knees and the boy with his legs out straight because of the bulky cast that encased his left shoulder and arm, a molded-in prop holding it away from his thin body. The treehouse was as they'd left it before John had gone away, so they would spend the night in a borrowed dome tent that John had set up not far from the base of the tree.

In his right hand, the boy held a large turkey wing bone. A gift from Wasituna. The old man had hollowed it out and left the knuckle on one end, drilling an eighth-inch diameter hole in the knuckle at a right angle. He had chamfered the other end. Josh was practicing with it absentmindedly now. He would bring it to his lips at intervals and blow across the chamfered end and the sound would perfectly mimic a turkey gobble. He blew it now softly, and then studied it, rolling it in his fingers. Wondering how it worked.

John said quietly, "Does your shoulder hurt?"

"No. It itches like ants, though. Aren't you going to give me the devil about it?"

"Nope. You've probably done that enough for yourself." As much to himself as to the boy, he said, "I guess I ought to tell you about consequences, though. About how they're built into everything we choose to do. But, down at the core of your mind, you already know that. We all know it."

The boy blew the turkey call again. This time louder. Thought for a moment as the light faded. Said, "I'm glad you're back."

But John had gone rigid and was staring upwind across the fire circle at the crown of a large embedded boulder shadowed by overhanging brush, an icy trickle stealing through his bones.

Yellow eyes.

Glowing in a last hazy ray from the dying sun.

Feral, predatory eyes.

Fixed on him.

Immersed in thought and gazing at the firewood, the boy raised the turkey wing bone to blow it again but John whispered, "Don't move. Look right over there," and lifted his index finger to point.

And the eyes vanished.

The boy whispered, "What? What is it?"

John said, "Bobcat, I think. Gone now. Came looking for a turkey dinner."

***

Kitty was in her shop, helping a woman who was considering Cherokee vases. The double front doors were stopped open to let a warm breeze wander in out of the brilliant morning sunshine. She heard boots on the steps and then on the deck, and turned to see John coming into her shop. She stopped talking in mid-sentence and immediately forgot what she'd been saying.

John looked at her with a raised eyebrow and a shy smile, and went to a display table. Picked up an intricately hand-carved red cedar pencil box. Opened it. Brought it to his nose for a sniff. He'd had a similar one in the first grade, a gift from his adoptive mother, and the rich scent held the magical power to instantly transport him back over all the intervening years. He decided to buy this one for the boy.

Kitty told the woman, "I'm sorry. Don't let me influence you. I'm sure you can find something here your . . . your daughter, is it?—will like."

Kitty went to stand behind the register and ran a dark hand self-consciously down her flank. The woman examined the vases for a few minutes more and went out, leaving the two of them alone.

John walked to the counter and put the pencil box down on it.

He said, "Hattie and Hank have decided to go ahead and renew their vows on their sixtieth. They probably won't do a prenuptial. I'm supposed to be best man. You're maid of honor. Is that going to be okay with you?"

She said, "Of course it is."

"You're not still mad at me?"

"Brandon Doyle came by last night. Told me some things that sort of changed my perspective. Welcome back, John Hardin."

"Can you take Saturday off?"

"Maybe. For something special."

"I thought we might ride the bikes up through the park and over to Gatlinburg. A woman there is holding a cabin reservation open for us. Great view."

She smiled and glanced down at the pencil box, a wing of glossy hair falling over one eye. Said, "Are you sure you want to heat this whole thing up again?" She looked at him, tossed her hair back with a casual flick of slender fingers, and inclined her head. Garnet glints in her amber eyes. "I mean, we don't have all that much in common, do we? I'm an Injun and you're a fork-tongued white man. I ride a sensible Honda and you more or less ride an expensive pile of loose parts they like to call a Harley. I have intelligent, tasteful associates who are fine crafters and artists, and you have crude biker buddies with ape hangers on their choppers and beer for brains, like Brandon Doyle."

"Well, at least I'm a man and from two hundred yards away there's no doubt you're a woman."

"Is that supposed to be a compliment? You can't do any better than that?"

"The closer you get, the more beautiful you are."

"Better. We should go over what else we need to agree on. For instance, am I to trust you're a one-woman man?"

He held up a palm. "Absolutely. I'll have that paragraph put in the treaty."

She suppressed a laugh. "Because as long as you don't even *think* about straying, I believe I can promise not to scalp you. But there are a lot of other questions I've never asked. One, for example, might be particularly relevant this weekend. Which side of the bed do you prefer?"

"The side you're on. I thought I'd made that clear."

"You've never even told me your real name."

"I'll probably tell you in a few years."

"It's that bad? I can't wait."

"Look, if I go ahead and buy this overpriced pencil box, does it come with a kiss?"

Phil Bowie is a lifelong freelance writer with 300 articles and short stories published in national magazines. He writes the John Hardin suspense series and has a collection of his short stories out. He lives on the shore of the wide Neuse River in eastern North Carolina, where he's at work on his next novel.

If you enjoyed *KLLRS*, please take a moment to add a brief review on Amazon, and look for the next John Hardin thriller, *DEATHSMAN*.
All Phil Bowie's books are available in print and e-book forms on Amazon.com.

Visit him at *www.philbowie.com*

Made in the USA
Middletown, DE
21 July 2020